JAMES BABB

Weary Road

Based on a true story.

Amazing! Best book ever! — *Alexander, age 11*

I can't stop talking about it. My new favorite author. This book makes me excited to read! — *Isabella, age 11*

One of the greatest books I've read, and I've read a lot.
— *Hunter, age 11*

This is a great book that's full of history! — *Carlee, age 13*

I can smell the gunpowder and feel the dog's fur! It's amazing! — *Zaylee, age 11*

Being based on a true story only adds to the awesomeness of this book. — *Joshua, age 11*

I loved it! — *Cami, age 12*

The historical people are very interesting! — *Addysun*

Other historical fiction books by

JAMES BABB

THE DEVIL'S BACKBONE

Arkansas Historical Association Susannah De Black Award
Texas Author's Award for Best Juvenile Fiction Series
Independent Publisher Book Award (Bronze IPPY)
Next Generation Indie Book Awards Finalist

THE DEVIL'S TRAP

Texas Author's Award for Best Juvenile Fiction Series
Next Generation Indie Book Awards Finalist

THE DEVIL'S DEN

Arkansas Historical Association Susannah De Black Award
Texas Author's Award for Best Juvenile Fiction Series

Silver Ink Books
Copyright © 2019 James Babb

Book design by Suzanne Babb

First Edition
ISBN-13: 978-0-9914921-4-5

DEDICATION

For my mother. I owe her everything.

Strength is not measured by the weight a man can bear, but by the burdens he endures on life's weary road.

CHAPTER ONE

Salem, Arkansas
May 1, 1862

Most fathers love and care for their children, but fourteen-year-old Travis and his eight-year-old brother, Chet, did not have one of those fathers. Jeb Bailey only loved one thing, and it was not his boys.

Travis watched the sun filter through the branches of the towering old oak that stood between the broken down house and the ramshackle barn he was leaning against. He squinted and tilted his head, trying to imagine what the place must have looked like long ago. It was clear the property had traded hands many times before his father had moved them there, and no one had taken proper care of it in years.

"Travis, you are home!" a voice shouted.

He looked up to see his little brother walking back from the creek. Travis waved and bent down to pick up the burlap bag at his feet, careful not to jostle it too much.

Chet plopped the heavy water bucket on the ground. Small for his age, he had black hair and blue eyes like his father but any other resemblances ended there. He was slender with sharp features like their mother. Pa used to say that Momma had laughing eyes that sparkled, but that was before his love of liquor consumed him.

The purplish bruise across Chet's cheek was a testament to the hardships they had endured and made Travis even more determined to go through with his plan.

"Hey, Chet," he called, "come here for a minute."

"When did you get back?" Chet glanced eagerly at the burlap bag his brother was carrying. "Did you bring food?"

Travis shook his head. "It is hard to find work right now. Everybody is too worried about the war and how they are going to feed their own families."

Chet cast a worried glance toward the house. "No food. Pa will not like that news one bit."

Travis pushed open the barn door and Chet followed him inside. "I want to show you something."

"What have you got in the bag?"

Travis sat and crossed his legs. His brother did the same. Something moved inside the burlap.

Chet's eyes widened. "What is in there?"

"Promise you will be quiet. Pa cannot know."

Chet looked up at his big brother and nodded. His shaggy black hair fell across one eye and covered the bruise on his cheek. He whispered, "I promise to never tell a soul."

"I mean it," Travis warned, "if he finds out, it will be bad."

"Will he get mad?" The bag wiggled and Chet promptly turned his attention back to it.

Reaching over, Travis opened the sack and smiled when two chubby puppies wiggled free, grunting softly. They were mottled in color, one with a white band around its neck and the other without. One of them yawned, its tiny tongue curling inside a pink mouth.

A sudden "Oh!" of delight escaped from Chet, and the puppies immediately waddled his direction, wagging their tails. "Where did you get them?"

"That is not important. One of them is yours, all yours, if you will go away with me."

Chet rubbed a pup gently, and it wriggled and rolled over. "Go where?"

"I am leaving tonight," Travis said. "It is not safe to stay here any longer, and I need you to come with me."

Chet scooped up the smallest one and held it close to his face. He was rewarded with a quick lick to his nose and it made him giggle. In a moment he said, "You always talk about running away, but where would we go?"

The large bruise their father had left on his brother's cheek was fading, but Travis's memory of how it had gotten there was still fresh.

"Anywhere but here. It is too much to bear anymore. Pa is never going to get any better and I do not think I can stop him from…," Travis hesitated.

Chet looked away. "Pa cannot help it. He just gets in a bad way when he has been drinking. He always makes it up to me the next day, and he would be nice to you, too, if you did not talk back so much."

Travis bit off a sharp reply and tried not to lose his patience. He watched his brother stroking the puppy. It's coat was red and brown all mixed together.

He tried another tactic to sway him. "You like that one?"

Chet nodded. "Yes, I never had a dog before."

The pup gave a tiny high-pitched bark, and they laughed.

The other puppy with the white fur around its neck grunted when Travis picked it up. It immediately struggled to reach any fingers within licking distance. "This one is mine then." He looked up. "Do we have a deal?"

Chet seemed to be ignoring the question as he scratched the mottled dog behind its ears.

"If you want to keep that puppy, you have to leave with me," Travis said. "Tonight."

The pup he was holding whimpered and struggled to get down.

"Pa will be mad, really mad. He will find us."

Travis set his puppy back down on the barn floor and gave its soft fur one more stroke. "He will not find us. After he drinks himself to sleep, we will get the pups and slip out. We can be long gone before he wakes up."

The thought made Chet eyes grow wide with fear.

"He beats on us all the time," Travis said. "We do all the work while he drinks whiskey. Why do you want to stay here when we could go find Momma?"

Chet gently set his little pup down. It growled and pounced at his foot, but neither of the boys felt like laughing now.

"Pa said Momma did not want us anymore." Chet avoided looking at his brother.

"We should at least go search for her. Maybe he drove her off. You know how he treated her. It does no good to stay here, working hard just so he can drink. We would not eat at all if not for the jobs I have been doing in town for food."

"No," his little brother said, shaking his head. The pup he had put down now struggled to climb back into his lap. He picked him up. "Pa will find us wherever we go. He will."

Travis breathed deep and sighed. He already regretted what he was about to do to Chet. He did not want to be cruel but there was no other choice.

"I understand," he said as he held his hand out. "Here, give me your dog. It is best you do not get attached since I will have to take them back in the morning."

Chet clutched the puppy close to his chest and his eyes filled with tears. Travis felt like a low-down snake, but he knew this was for his brother's own good.

Chet started to plead, "I want to – ," but was interrupted by the heavy tromp of footsteps.

"Boy!" Jeb's gravelly voice carried across the yard to the barn. "Where are you?"

They froze. Chet looked desperately at his brother. "What do we do with the puppies?" he whispered.

"Hide them! Hurry." Travis opened the bag, placed his in the sack and held it wide while Chet did the same. As he tied the top, muffled whines came from inside.

Travis rushed the puppies to the back of the barn and hid them behind a pile of old hay. He pushed some of the moldy straw on top.

"Shhh. You have to be quiet," he begged softly.

"Chet, get up here! Someone's coming!" Pa yelled. His voice was slurred with alcohol. "Where are you?"

Running to Chet, Travis pulled his brother around so they were face to face and whispered, "Do not tell him about our talk or the puppies."

Chet nodded and hurried with Travis out the door.

Their father was wearing his dirty, ragged overalls and toting two sloshing bottles of whiskey. His blood-shot eyes were worried. "It is a group of soldiers! They are coming."

He noticed Travis, and his brow creased in anger. "What are you doing home already?"

Before Travis could answer, voices came from the hill below the house and Jeb quickly forgot his question. He shoved the bottles into Travis's hands and hissed, "Hurry! Hide these in the barn!"

Jeb stumbled toward the road to meet the visitors, cursing with every step.

Travis took the whiskey into the barn and stopped long enough to listen. He could not hear the puppies and hoped they were fast asleep.

At the east end of the building, far away from the burlap sack, Travis found scattered bits of broken tools and dry-rotted leather straps, but no good place to hide the liquor. He resorted to turning over a dusty feed pail and tucking the bottles underneath.

Chet yanked on his arm, startling him. "Travis, there are soldiers in the yard."

Jeb was in the middle of a heated argument with five Union soldiers by the time the boys got there. His nose and cheeks were red from too much drink and barely suppressed anger. "I am telling you, there is nothing here you men want!"

After his father's outburst, Travis watched the soldiers trade looks. He had never been this close to Union troops before. Three of them were wearing dark blue clothing but the last two had on dingy gray shirts and pants. None of their garments fit properly, with some blouses hanging loose and others about to burst at the buttons. All of the men wore blue caps with black leather brims on the front, and two of the soldiers were carrying muskets.

A tall, imposing fellow with a short beard frowned at Jeb. "Our regiment requires supplies. I will provide you with a signed receipt that you can present at our camp tomorrow for reimbursement. Just ask for me, George Fikes."

Jeb stabbed a finger at his boys, and Chet hid behind Travis. "We are the poorest family you will ever meet. I have spent every cent keeping these motherless boys fed and clothed and now you have the nerve to ask me to feed your men, too?"

A short, wiry soldier shouted "Blarney!" in a strange accent. "George, this man is dodgy as all get out!"

Travis guessed the odd-sounding fellow to be in his mid-twenties. He had wide, black side-whiskers and a fine, sharp face. He noticed Travis looking him over, and smiled. However that smile faded when he saw Chet peeking out from behind his older brother. The man's gaze lingered on Chet's bruised cheek. "The poor lads look like they haven't had a worthwhile bite in days."

"Little Irish," George said. "I believe you could be right. I doubt there is much food here, though I suspect we will find something else."

The little Irishman cocked his head. "What are you goin' on about?"

George cast a knowing look full of judgement at Jeb. "There's liquor here."

Jeb recoiled, throwing both his hands in the air. "Such an accusation is beyond offensive!"

"The alcohol on your breath is offensive and so are the lies coming out of your drunken mouth."

"There is nothing to be found!" Jeb thrust his lower jaw forward making the scraggly hair on his chin jut out defiantly. "Search the house and see if you find any."

George turned to the two soldiers holding muskets and pointed to the house. "John. Arthur." Both men nodded at the mention of their names and headed across the yard toward the front door.

Travis heard the Irishman chuckle and looked to see what amused him. His heart skipped as he saw one of the puppies had just emerged from the cracked barn door. It sat and scratched at the white band of hair around its neck.

"Well, would you look at that," Little Irish said.

George noticed the puppy. "Go check the barn."

"I believe I will." The soldier sauntered toward the building.

Jeb pushed by George and glared at Travis and Chet as he passed. "What have y'all done?" he growled.

He caught up with the Irishman at the barn and tried to block his path. "There is no use looking in there. We are too poor to own any animals, no cows, pigs, or chickens."

"And no dogs for certain?" Little Irish asked sarcastically as he pushed Jeb back, causing the drunken man to stumble over the puppy.

In anger, Jeb snatched up Travis's pup by the scruff of its neck, causing it to squeal. "This mutt is not ours! We can barely feed ourselves!" He marched toward the creek as the crying puppy swung helplessly in his grasp.

"Pa! No!" Chet shouted.

Jeb ignored him. With a few large strides, he was away from the barn and just feet from the wide, fast-moving creek. He threw the puppy, and it tumbled end over end until its pitiful wail was cut short when it hit the water.

A moment of stunned silence fell over everyone but Jeb. His face darkened with rage as he turned toward Travis. "This is your fault!" he snarled, "I know you did this."

Seeing his father headed their direction, Travis took a quick step back and bumped into his brother. George met Jeb's advance with a fierce glare and a raised fist, stopping him from reaching the boys.

The young soldier with long hair that had been at George's side had broken into a run for the creek. Chet started to cry as he and Travis watched the man moving along the water's edge, looking for any sign of the puppy.

"Is he going to drown, Travis?" Chet choked out around his sobs.

Travis curled his hands into fists, anger coursing through him. "I do not know."

"Look what found me!" Little Irish called merrily from the barn doorway. In each hand he held a bottle and at his feet was Chet's red and brown mottled puppy.

Jeb headed straight for him, shouting as he went. "Give me those and get off my property!"

Little Irish promptly set the bottles down and raised both arms, fists at the ready.

The soldier at the creek gave up his search for the lost puppy and ran to get between Jeb and Little Irish. He stretched his arm between them. "You need to calm down," he said in a heavy accent.

Jeb let out a foul curse, but the Irishman just stood his ground. "Let's have us a little donnybrook right here. Emil, just move out of the way."

Emil gave them a bit of space but Jeb hesitated, his cowardly nature getting the best of him. He quickly shifted his anger to the remaining puppy and grabbed it. The pup twisted, whimpering in fright.

Chet launched himself forward, shouting, "Not my puppy!" but Travis caught him by the collar and yanked him back.

Jeb shot a furious look at his boys before heading toward the creek with the dog in his hands.

"No," Chet wailed. "Stop him, Travis."

The puppy flailed as Jeb raised it high in the air, aiming for the rapid water.

CHAPTER TWO

Jeb reared back, but Little Irish grabbed his arm and wrestled the terrified pup from his grip.

Emil retrieved the whiskey bottles and headed toward the struggling men. The Irishman broke free and grinned as he danced a jig around the older man, holding the puppy just out of reach. Emil pushed Jeb with his free hand and they all began a tense shuffle toward the house.

"Get him under control," George snapped.

"Which one?" Emil grumbled as he dodged a wild swing by Jeb.

"You all need to leave," Jeb threatened, although he was pointing at the Irishman.

Across the yard, Arthur banged the front door of the house open, took in the scene in astonishment, and shouted, "Hey, Irish, what's all the ruckus?"

Little Irish ignored him and held the puppy close to his chest with one hand. Chet stepped forward, raising his hands for the puppy, but the man shook his head. "M' boy, it would do no good to leave him here."

The soldier tucked the puppy into his shirt, then took the bottles from Emil, keeping a steady pace as he headed for the road.

John and Arthur met him as they walked across the yard.

"Hey, where are you going?" John asked.

"Back to camp," Irish said, raising one of the bottles in an odd salute.

The pup stuck it's head out of the shirt. It seemed quite content to be out of harm's way. Arthur laughed heartily at the sight. "And you're taking a little mischief-maker with you?"

Instead of replying to Arthur, he whistled a jaunty tune and danced a couple of steps before continuing to the road.

"He took my puppy," Chet whispered to Travis.

"Sir," Travis said to the skinny soldier.

The man turned toward him, the whole whites of his eyes visible around the dark centers. They reminded Travis of the wild eyes of a startled horse. "My name is not sir, it is Arthur."

Travis gestured toward the Irishman as he went over the hill. "Arthur, that was my brother's-"

Jeb bellowed, "I am a southern Unionist from Searcy County and a member of the Arkansas peace corp. I overreacted. I support your cause and beg you to bring back our supplies."

Arthur rolled his eyes. "Liquor? Supplies?"

George laughed. "If you are loyal to the Union, then join us. Fight for your country."

Jeb placed his hand on the small of his back and grimaced. "I am but an old man, barely able to walk at all. I could never march to war." His eyes narrowed as he cut his gaze toward Travis. "But my oldest is strong, both of muscle and will. Take him and leave my whiskey. It helps to dull my pain." He gripped his back with both hands and tried to fake a sorrowful look at losing his son to the cause.

"Take your boy?" George asked with interest.

Jeb and George exchanged words while Travis leaned over and whispered to Chet. "Will you promise to go with me?"

"Where? With them?"

"Not with them," Travis said quietly into Chet's ear. "You see what a monster Pa is. He probably drowned my puppy and he was going to kill yours too."

Chet started to tear up again.

Travis squeezed his brother's arm. "You have to run away with me. I need to get us both away from here."

Chet hesitated.

"Don't be such a baby!"

Travis struggled to hide his desperation. "I am sorry, Chet. I know you are afraid of him, but I can take care of us."

Chet wiped his eyes. "Will they bring my puppy back?"

"I will go get him," Travis said, "if you promise to run away with me tonight."

Chet locked eyes with Travis. He nodded slightly.

Travis leaned down. "You promise?"

Chet nodded firmly. Travis raised his head up and looked at George. "I will go with you!"

Chet's mouth dropped open. "What?"

Travis said loudly. "I'll join the war."

"But you have to leave my whiskey!" Jeb said quickly to George.

George looked at Jeb. "You want to trade your boy's service for two bottles of liquor?"

He did not wait on Jeb's answer. Turning to Travis, George said, "We could always use help, noncombat and otherwise, but you surely do not know what you would be signing up for."

"I am ready," Travis said, glancing over at Chet.

George considered, then shook his head. "You are too young, you have to be eighteen."

Travis quickly studied the two youngest looking soldiers, Emil and the boy with the crooked nose, John. Travis pointed at him. "I'm as old as he is."

"John is sixteen, but joined with his father's permission," George said. "How old are you?"

"Sixteen," Jeb interrupted. "Travis is sixteen."

Chet opened his mouth to speak, but Travis shook his head slightly, hoping his brother would not expose their father's lie. His brother looked upset, but he closed his mouth.

Arthur said, "Pickings are poor, George. All there is in the house is half a bag of corn meal, some dried beans and a bit of salt pork. Not enough to even feed these three for very long. If the boy were with us, that would be more for the youngin' for a while."

George looked intently at Travis and raised an eyebrow. Finally, he nodded. "You are with us then."

"And my bottles?" Jeb quickly asked.

George sighed and stroked his short beard. "I will consider sending them back to you, but I warn you… if that little boy hasn't had a good meal by then, I will make sure your precious whiskey seeps into the ground. All of it."

Jeb licked his lips. "I'll do it, I will get some grub ready right now. Could you have that Irishman rush those bottles back?"

George looked kindly at Travis. "Say your goodbyes and come on."

He motioned for the other men. "To camp, boys."

John ignored Travis, but Arthur dipped his head and winked as they joined George and walked away.

Emil stayed behind, waiting for Travis.

Chet reached up and tugged on his brother's shirt sleeve. "Why are you doing this?" he asked mournfully.

Travis leaned down close to Chet's ear and whispered, "I will be back in no time. Just as soon as I get your puppy. I promise."

Chet's face brightened.

"You made a promise, too." Travis reminded him.

"I know," Chet said quietly.

"I'll see you late tonight or early in the morning." He rubbed his brother's head and cast a worried glance at their father. Jeb was staring at Travis, his face filled with anger. "Just stay out of Pa's way as much as you can until I get back."

Travis stepped toward Emil, being careful to avoid being in reach of Jeb. He imagined his father's glare, sharp as a dagger, stabbing him in the back.

The brown-haired boy reached out and shook hands with Travis. "I'm Emil," he said with a thick accent that sounded much different than the Irishman's. Emil had a round, friendly face. His gray eyes were full of sympathy. "Do you want to go get your things?"

Travis shook his head. "Don't have anything worth taking."

Emil nodded sympathetically. "I'm seventeen. My family came here from Germany."

Travis considered confiding his real age but decided against it. He would not be around long enough to make friends, and he had nothing but worry on his mind.

"I understand," Emil said into the silence. "It was hard for me to leave my brother, too."

Camp was located just outside the small town of Salem in what was once a large hay field. Now it was a bustling tent city with campfires, soldiers, mules and wagons. Travis had never seen this many people all gathered together at once. At one end, troops were drilling in formations. Closer in were men in a motley collection of uniforms milling about, eating, playing cards, talking and laughing. He quickly studied each man, hoping to spot Little Irish. There was no sign of him, but he did see George at a nearby tent that was filled with crates and stacks of bulging burlap sacks.

"Here he is, George," Emil said as they walked up.

"About time you made it. Emil, go make our report about the new recruit." George pulled on his beard and looked at Travis. "And best leave all that business with Irish and this boy's father out of it. No sense asking for trouble."

Emil thumped Travis on the back and grinned. "It's good to have you with us."

George led the way through a section of large walled tents and wagons. Travis followed close behind but his attention was on the faces of the men they passed. None were the Irishman.

Finally, they came to a stop in front of a soldier sitting at a small desk outside one of those tents, but Travis was too distracted to catch his name. The man read something from a piece of paper while Travis continued to look around. He heard little of the man's words.

"I do solemnly swear I have never borne arms against the United States..."

Travis focused on a group of men walking by. Worry gnawed at him and he began to wonder if the Irishman had even made it all the way back to camp.

In front of him, the soldier's voice continued to rattle on. "I will support and defend the Constitution..."

George bumped him with his elbow. "Pay attention."

Travis refocused on the soldier with the piece of paper. "...duties of the office I am about to enter, so help me God."

Travis paused.

"Do you?" The soldier tapped his fingers on the paper impatiently.

Realizing he had been asked to take an oath, Travis hesitated.

The man scowled. "Well?"

Travis nodded and stammered, "Y-yes, sir."

The soldier at the desk handed him a pen and turned the paper around. "Make your mark here."

After dipping the pen tip in ink, Travis wrote his name.

"Now," the man said. "You are a private of the Thirteenth Regiment Illinois Volunteer Infantry, Company H. You will be allotted thirteen dollars per month for the next three years of your enlistment."

"Illinois volunteer?" Travis asked, suddenly understanding what the soldier had said to him. "But I am in Arkansas."

The man ignored him. "George, equip him and find him a spot."

"Yes, sir," George said. "Travis, follow me." He walked into the big tent just behind the man at the table.

George handed him a large black knapsack, and said, "Hold it open." He shoved a waterproofed gum blanket inside. "You will also carry your half of the dog tent in this along with any extra clothes or personal items you may acquire."

Next he handed Travis a canteen and a smaller canvas bag with a shoulder strap.

"You can fill your canteen from the water barrel by the cook tent. This other is your haversack. In the haversack you will put your mess kit of hardtack, match safe, lantern, cup, plate, knife, fork, spoon and pan. We will get that, and your ration of coffee, on the way to your tent."

George pulled the top off of the next crate and brought out a couple of wrinkled dark blue wool coats. He eyed Travis, then selected one and held it up. "You are in luck. We have a couple of the smaller sizes left in Union blue. Sorry, but you will have gray pants until the army sees fit to properly dress our recruits."

He turned to another crate, "Now, let us see what sizes for boots and caps are left."

Later, the sun was starting to set, and campfires dotted the land. Travis anxiously continued to search for any signs of Little Irish as he followed George through camp, carrying his new supplies and uniform.

They came to an area with rows upon rows of small tents. The tents were formed from two pieces of canvas buttoned together and pegged. On most of them, front and back supports were provided by guns with bayonets attached and stuck into the ground, point down.

They stopped in front of one of the little two-man tents. A soldier was sitting on a knapsack cross-legged, taking large bites of food from his plate.

"John," George said.

"Yes?" John answered, looking up at them. Travis recognized him as the stocky young soldier from earlier that day.

"Travis is with you," George said. "He will carry half your dog tent. Show him what is expected."

He turned and shook hands with Travis. "Welcome to Company H. Do not lose your equipment." With that, he turned on his heels and left.

Travis's stomach growled loudly. He remembered passing the cook tent not too far away, so he pulled his plate and cup out of the haversack and retraced his steps.

Quickly, Travis found the big square-fronted tent. The odor of cooked food led him right to it, and a man with a ladle obligingly put about a cupful of hominy on his plate, followed by a chunk of pork and a biscuit. His mouth watered as he hurried back to his assigned spot and sat on the ground by the little fire.

It was the best meal he had eaten in days, and he wished he could save some of it to take back to Chet. He felt guilty, knowing his brother probably had nothing but heartache for supper.

John had joined two young soldiers several tents down from theirs and was deep in conversation. Travis could hear the murmurs of other boys and men around him, and the occasional burst of laughter in the dusk of approaching night. Lanterns were being lit, and soldiers were getting ready for sleep. In the distance a horse neighed and was answered by others.

Amidst all these people, Travis felt very alone. His eyes stung with tears. Chet was with their father, and Travis was not there to take the blows that would surely come.

A while later the sound of drums seemed to be a signal for the soldiers to settle down for the evening, and John returned but said nothing. He crawled into their low shelter, making no effort to leave room for Travis, and pulled his blanket around his body.

That was fine with Travis. The night was clear, and the stars were bright. He put his bedroll on the ground by the fire and stretched out on top of it.

Time passed, and John snored softly. The moonlight was dim, the air cool, and Travis's determination strong. Without a sound, he got out of bed and went to find Little Irish and the puppy.

The rows and rows of pale canvas tents looked ghostly. Some men slept inside, some outside by the glowing embers of the fires. After snooping around for only a few minutes, Travis's foot bumped into a burly man who was fast asleep just outside his shelter. The man snorted and rolled over in his bedding. Travis froze in place.

Holding his breath, he waited until the fellow's breathing settled into a steady rhythm. When his nerves had calmed, Travis continued his uneasy path among the sleeping men.

A whine caught his attention. It was a sad puppy noise, trailing off to nothing more than a quiet whimper. Travis immediately headed in that direction, and in a few minutes he had located Little Irish sleeping just outside his tent. One of Jeb's bottles lay by his head, empty and on its side.

The corner of his blanket shifted and twisted in an odd manner, as if it was attempting to rise and walk on its own accord. Travis gingerly pulled the cover aside, revealing the red and brown mottled puppy. It yipped and pounced at his hand, playfully growling and snapping at his fingers. As Travis reached for it, someone shouted, "Get him!"

CHAPTER THREE

Little Irish startled awake, his eyes wide with alarm. Travis stumbled back, expecting people to rush in and grab him but no such advance was made in his direction. Two lanterns bobbed into the middle of camp and a parade of angry men followed along.

"String him up!" someone shouted.

"Wake the Colonel. They have caught Frederick Hill!"

Travis was engulfed by a closely packed group of men and was jostled and bumped along as they ran toward the center of camp.

When he was finally able to stop he was at the edge of a clearing. Just yards in front of him, a man struggled against the hands of his captives. "Let me go! I am not Frederick!" He looked young, although it was hard to tell in the glow of the lanterns.

"We know you well," someone said. "We camped with you for a year!"

"Then I will rejoin!" Frederick pleaded desperately. "Just let me rejoin and I will be loyal to the Union!"

John appeared next to Travis. "It's too late!" he shouted. "You chose your path."

"No!" Frederick wailed. He yanked free from his captors and bolted straight toward Travis. The soldiers who had been holding him raised their pistols and shot. Frederick fell to the ground just feet from Travis. The men crowded around, their lanterns lighting the figure in the center.

Two wet and dark holes pierced the back of the filthy shirt Frederick was wearing. He tried to push up on his hands, but the effort was in vain. A cough racked his body, and a great shudder followed. Then he was still and breathed no more.

Travis was too shocked to move.

"Deserter." John spat on the body. "He got what was coming to him."

"Deserter?" Travis asked.

Little Irish walked up. "Deserter. Frederick joined with us and after about a year, ran away."

"Yellow dog coward, he got what was coming to him!" John shouted in righteous rage. A chorus of agreeing shouts rang through camp.

A man with badges sewn on the shoulders of his jacket walked up to the bloodied body and examined it. He turned and shouted orders, sending men scattering to find a canvas to wrap Frederick's body in.

"First light is just a few hours away. The body will wait until morning for burial. Get back to your beds."

The men talked excitedly among themselves as they slowly dispersed.

Travis felt numb.

"Well, that's that," Little Irish said as they walked back to his tent.

Irish lifted up a small crate and put the sleepy puppy underneath. It raised its head and yawned. Peter laid down and positioned himself so the puppy was close to his side. "Better take what's left of the night and rest up."

Finally, small steps led Travis back to his bed. There had never been a time in his short life that he felt so lost. He was trapped, confined, and committed. He remembered the words he had been asked to repeat. His oath had been given. They would kill him if he tried to go back for his brother!

The next morning Travis was startled awake by loud musical notes played on a horn. He sat up and rubbed the sleep from his eyes. Images of the shooting the night before flooded through his mind, and the helplessness of his situation filled him. Grimly, he reached for the sack that held his uniform and pulled it open. He had no choice but to dress like a soldier.

John was nowhere to be seen when he crawled out of the tent fully dressed, so he sat and pulled out some flat crackers he found in his mess kit. He put a corner in his mouth and bit down. It did not crunch, crack, or budge. He tried again, biting harder, and a piece finally gave way with a snap.

Travis chewed the hard cracker and fought the urge to spit it out. The brittle dry flakes sucked all the moisture out of his mouth. It was awful but he was hungry. He took the plug out of his canteen and drank.

After wiping his mouth, he glanced around wondering if someone was watching him. Most of the tents were gone, even the largest ones like the cook tent, although a few were being broken down as he watched. It was a hive of activity with crates being packed and loaded onto wagons.

The uncertainty of what he was supposed to be doing made him feel very awkward. His mind kept wandering back to the past night. *I should have never left you, Chet.*

John walked up with a dark look on his face. "Stop eating hardtack and get up! You are going to get us both in trouble."

"Trouble?" Travis pushed the leftover hardtack back down in the haversack, then plugged his canteen. "What trouble?"

"The dog tent should already be down and you don't even have your stuff packed. Hurry, come on." John shook his head as if he had just witnessed the most disgusting thing in his life.

Travis followed John's terse orders as they untied ropes and disassembled the tent quickly. John slung his rifle over his shoulder before kicking the last piece of canvas toward Travis. "Get this packed."

"Why are you in such a mood?" Travis asked.

John walked, yet again refusing to answer his question.

Travis gathered all his supplies and hurried to join a long line of men and wagons lining up. A horseman was riding back and forth, shouting orders. The bugle sounded a melody, and the river of blue moved forward in rows of four men each.

Travis heard hoofbeats, and turned to see the soldier pull his horse up in a sliding stop. "Private, what do you think you are doing?!"

"Sir, no one has told me where to go!" Travis said in a panic.

"Why, I will tell you exactly where you can-"

"I will help him figure it out, sir," hollered one of the marching men. "He's the new fish from yesterday."

Travis felt immense relief to see the skinny wild-eyed man from the day before dropping out of line to come to his rescue.

The soldier on horseback spun his horse around. "You better get him educated. Next time he will be in for it."

Arthur motioned for Travis to join him, and they found a gap in the line and slipped in. "Thank you!"

Arthur grinned. "You need to learn the rules. Rule number one is to not do anything that will draw attention."

Travis nodded. As they marched away from the now empty field where camp had been, he realized they were moving farther away from his home... and Chet. He wondered how he was going to get out of this.

"Arthur, right?"

"That is correct."

"That man last night. John said he was a deserter?"

Arthur nodded. "He disappeared some time ago. One morning he was just gone."

"What happens to men who do that? I mean, if they hadn't shot him, what would have happened to him?"

"Hanged," Arthur said. "They would have probably hanged him."

Travis walked steadily, though his heart was stone heavy.

Arthur glanced sideways at him. "He's not a good guy."

"Who?"

"Your camp buddy, John. He's young and makes up for it by being as brash as he can." Arthur shook his head. "Keep an eye on him. There's a hundred in our company, we will be joining our regiment of a nearly a thousand. Take your pick of friends but don't choose John. Emil would be a much better choice."

"The long-haired fellow from Germany?"

The man gave a quick succession of smiles and frowns making Travis wonder if Arthur was right in the head.

"John has been a little mean to me," Travis said, "but not too bad."

"Give it time," Arthur said brightly.

Marching quickly became something Travis hated. The terrain was rough, the hills steep, and the weather hot. While on the march, Travis's heart gave a leap as he spotted Little Irish several rows back. Travis could just catch glimpses of the wiggling lump inside his shirt. George was next to him, and he towered over the Irishman. Little Irish slipped the dog into George's hands and he hid it in the same manner the Irishman had used.

"Arthur, why are they hiding the puppy?"

Arthur chuckled. "To stay out of trouble with our superiors."

"Superiors?"

"Yes. They would not approve." Arthur cocked an eyebrow. "Do you understand the rank here?"

Travis confessed. "I have no idea."

"Let's see," Arthur said. "How can I make this simple?" He thought for a moment and then laughed. "A private is the lowest of low, especially a green one like you without a gun. What are you, non-combat labor? They will probably give you a shovel or an axe."

"What for?" Travis asked.

"To dig with or cut trees. If there isn't a road, we have to make one, and everybody has to dig when we need rifle pits or embankments. You will probably be digging latrines so we can all relieve ourselves."

Travis wrinkled his nose and frowned. "I see. Well, what rank is above me?"

"All of them," Arthur said. "If a corporal, sergeant, or lieutenant tells you to do something, do it. If a captain or major tells you to do something, do it quickly. If a colonel comes around, you better do what he wants before he even asks you."

Travis got the message. Do exactly what he was told to do or get in trouble. His father had trained him well for this position.

Hours of marching was spent learning everything Arthur had to teach him about life in Company H, such as recognizing officers and how to address them. He also learned the slang often used, with several soldiers around them offering examples, from "shoulder straps" for officers to "gray backs" for Confederate soldiers.

Travis forgot his troubles for awhile, as Arthur mimicked the different melodies of the bugle (which were really orders), and the men joined him, singing words to the music.

Their march took them twelve miles away from Salem where they were ordered to stop for the night at Strawberry Creek.

Travis was tired down to his bones. He was ready to drop where he was and rest but stiffened to attention when an officer approached. He stopped before he got to Travis and ordered several of the men nearby to form a picket line near camp. Arthur had not spoken of what this term meant. He listened to them talk about it long enough to figure out it was a group of guards who would make sure the camp was not ambushed.

Wearily, he wondered how he could get assigned to guard duty. If he did sneak away, it might be easier and give him a greater head start while on a picket line. Of course, that more than likely would not happen, as he did not even have a gun for guard duty.

He was already a day away from Chet, and he could only imagine what Pa must have done to him over the puppies and lost liquor. Travis just had to find a way back to his brother.

He found John sitting on his empty knapsack, the canvas for his half of the tent tossed to the side. Travis did not try to talk to him, and just set up the tent.

After eating a plate of cold beans, he cleaned up his mess kit and crawled onto his bed and listened to a chorus of frogs. As night fell, the camp grew quiet and John joined him in the cramped tent.

"Move over."

Travis shifted until his side was pressed against the canvas sidewall.

John plopped down and immediately sighed. "So boring."

"What?" Travis asked.

"Marching and camping. I'm sick of it. I want excitement like last night. Maybe we can catch another deserter. There was one who slipped away about three months ago."

Travis raised up on an elbow. "You mean to kill him, like the man last night? Why would you want that?"

"He is a deserter," John stated. "That's what they deserve."

"This other man has been gone for months. Why not forget about him?"

John was silent. Just when Travis started to speak again, John's hand gripped his shirt and twisted it tight against his neck. "You are actually defending a deserter? I should punch you right in the mouth."

Travis raised his hand, holding it in front of his face. "Wait. I am not defending him."

"Shut up!" John shook Travis by his shirt before letting go. "Get to sleep and don't talk to me again."

Travis rolled away from John. His heart pounded as he tried to make sense of the unexpected attack. What would happen if John caught him sneaking around camp looking for Chet's puppy? He would surely accuse him of deserting, but that's exactly what Travis needed to do.

While he tried to think up a plan to get back to his brother, Travis fell into an exhausted sleep.

On the next day's march, he fell into line next to Little Irish. Without a word, the Irishman passed Chet's puppy to him. Holding it close to his chest, Travis tried to pet it's head, but ended up with licks and nips as it happily chewed on his fingers. It seemed in good health and it's tight round belly was a clear indication that it was well fed.

A mix of emotions coursed through him as he slipped the pup inside his shirt. He was happy that Little Irish had trusted him but at the same time Travis wanted to run for home as fast as he could, taking the puppy with him.

"It was my brother's," he said to the Irishman.

Little Irish gave him a sharp glance. "What?"

"The pup was my brother's, sir," Travis repeated.

"Knock off with the *sir* stuff. Peter is the name."

They walked in silence for another good while.

It was Peter who next broke the silence. "I wish I could have carried the boy away, too."

"My brother?"

The Irishman nodded. "When this is over, you will be with him again."

"Little Irish…"

"Peter," the Irishman insisted.

Travis bit his bottom lip and whispered. "Peter, I need to get back. I need to take the puppy and get my brother away from my father."

Peter looked around quickly, his voice barely above a whisper, "You should not talk in such a manner. Your loyalty should NEVER be in question."

His voice carried an urgency as if the words that had passed Travis's lips could endanger them both.

The Irishman glanced at Travis before settling his gaze on the back of the man marching several paces in front of him, "It's ill luck. Don't speak of this again."

Travis spent the rest of the day making sure no one doubted his loyalty. He marched like a soldier. He stood like a soldier. He talked like a soldier.

On the third day it started to rain and seemed as if it would never stop. Little Irish found an empty space in one of the wagons for the pup. The men marching around them offered up several names to call it, from Beau to Whiskey, for it was definitely a boy dog, and after several rounds of disagreement, they finally decided on calling him Salem. He would be named after the town where he was found.

Travis was able to walk alongside the wagon and pet the little fellow. He tried feeding him a piece of his hardtack but Salem refused to eat it, preferring the tidbits that Little Irish somehow managed to bribe from the camp cook.

The pup was a constant reminder of his brother. Travis wondered how Chet was managing without him. He shook his head in sorrow, knowing that it was words from his own mouth that had him trapped in his current situation. He should have just kept quiet that day.

The rain worsened and the downpours made everyone short-tempered. His feet burned and ached but he was forced to keep placing one wet foot in front of the other, each step taking him farther from his brother.

CHAPTER FOUR

May 4, 1862

They finally reached Batesville, Arkansas, but exhaustion kept anyone from celebrating their arrival. After the men stopped to make camp at the river, Travis set up the tent with the gummed blanket on top for a rain shield and then slept as if he had been deprived of slumber for months. He dreamed of cornbread and sweet foods he had not enjoyed since his mother had left, back when she used to cook for him and his brother.

"Wake up!" John kicked him in the ribs. "It stopped raining. Go to the river and get us some water!"

Travis blinked hard, trying to clear the fog from his mind.

"Go on," John ordered.

Travis was getting mighty tired of John, but was too wore out to make an issue of it.

On his way down to the river, Travis heard gunshots. They were not chaotic but spaced evenly with a decent stretch between each one. Before he could fill the canteens, he noticed the source of the shots. A pale fellow pointed a pistol toward the rolling river. He fired, causing the water to splash violently, then immediately adjusted his aim to another target. A bloodied fish flopped in the shallow water, and a second man waded in to grab it. This fellow was stocky and walked with a limp. He added the fish to an already full bucket, and headed up the bank toward camp.

JAMES BABB

Travis swallowed hard. His stomach growled at having not eaten all day. "You shot all those fish?" he asked the man with the gun.

The man's eyes were sunken and dark as if he had dug his way out of a cold grave. "Not nearly enough to feed all the Thirteenth. What'ths your name?" He spoke with a lisp.

"I'm Travis."

The man nodded. "Thomasth," he said. "My name is Thomasth." He grew silent and focused on the iron sights on his pistol. The gun kicked and the water exploded. "Get the fiths," Thomas said.

Travis hesitated, not sure he heard correctly.

"Grab it, grab the fiths," Thomas said.

It dawned on Travis what Thomas meant, so he dropped the canteens and rushed to the water's edge. He scooped up the slippery fish before the current carried it away. The second man returned with an empty bucket and Travis plopped the fish inside.

"This is Traviths," Thomas said.

The stocky fellow nodded his direction and placed the bucket on the ground between them. He offered his hand but Travis held up a slimy palm. Before he could wipe it on his pants the man grabbed his hand and shook with him.

"Histh name isth Lawrenthse," Thomas said.

Lawrence released his hand and waded into the water.

"It's good to meet you," Travis said.

Lawrence looked over his shoulder and nodded.

"He'ths a mute," Thomas said while taking aim. "He can hear just fine but can't sthpeak a word." Thomas fired into the water but missed. Seconds later, he fired again and Lawrence waited for the fish to float within reach.

Travis retrieved the two canteens, took the tops off, and began to fill them.

Thomas laughed. "I can't talk right and he can't talk at all."

His observation was humorous and truthful. Travis could not help but smile.

"Have you had anything to eat?" Thomas asked.

Looking up from his task, Travis shook his head. "I ate the last of my hardtack a couple days ago."

"Take the fiths you caught," Thomas said.

A smile spread across Travis's face. "Thank you. I would love some fish."

After arriving back at his tent, Travis gave John one of the canteens and then went to work on the fish. He cut a slit along its belly and spread the ribs.

John watched.

Travis reached inside the fish with his fingers, pulled the guts out, and flung them away from camp. "There was a man at the river shooting fish. Thomas was his name. He's a good shot. Speaks with a lisp. Do you know him?"

John shook his head and drank from his canteen.

Using the knife tip, Travis poked a hole in the tail of the fish near the end, just before the base of the fin. He cut a short twig and pushed it through the hole, allowing it to protrude on both sides of the fish's tail. Using the stick for something to hold on to, he raked the knife's edge against the fish, removing the scales and sending them flying in all directions.

John built a fire.

Travis cut a sapling, stripped its leaves, and whittled one end at an angle to make it sharp. Holding the fish by the lip, he ran the long stick down its gullet until it emerged next to the tail fin. "Here," he said, handing the impaled fish to John. Travis held the sticky knife up and looked at his scale covered hands. "I have to go wash. I'll be right back."

On his way to the river, he met Lawrence, carrying the bucket, now empty. He nodded at Travis and smiled. As Lawrence limped past, Travis saw Thomas talking to Peter. Little Irish held a fish by the gill, letting it hang by his side. As the men spoke, Chet's puppy ran around their feet, stopping momentarily to snap at the fish tail.

Thomas noticed Travis. "I hope you haven't come for another meal. The fiths sthopped coming to the thurface and we gave Peter the lasth one."

"And you can't have mine," Peter said, "My stomach is chewing on my backbone." He looked down at the puppy. "Salem seems to be real hungry too."

"I'm not here for more fish," Travis explained. "I just need to wash the slime and all these scales off."

"You work quick," Thomas said.

Travis smiled and walked past the men, watching Salem as he did. "Thank you. Good to see you, Peter."

"And you," the Irishman said. He patted Thomas on the shoulder. "Many thanks for feeding most of our company today."

The men said their goodbyes and split ways while Travis squatted down and washed his hands in the river. The water quickly removed the scales but the fish slime took a bit of effort. As he scrubbed the knife handle, he felt something tug on his shirttail. Salem let out a tiny growl as he pulled, causing Travis to laugh. "I thought you left with Peter." He looked for the Irishman but he was nowhere to be seen. Travis stood and picked the dog up. In that moment, dangerous thoughts flooded Travis's mind.

He took a quick glance to confirm he was alone at the river. He had his brother's dog and no one was around! The time had come for a decision. His skin crawled with nervous prickles. He faced home, or at least his best guess at the direction of home.

His fellow soldiers would come looking for him.

John would finally get his excitement.

They would follow his tracks.

If they caught him, he would hang.

Travis entertained the idea of desertion, allowing his thoughts to travel down a path that could possibly lead to destruction. Salem licked and bit at his fingers. He played with the dog, grabbing at its nose, but his mind was somewhere else, miles down the road on his way back home.

Gravel crunched behind him.

He jumped and twisted around to see Lawrence. He smiled at the mute, hoping to hide the guilt he was feeling from his thoughts of leaving. Lawrence nodded, motioned to the ground, and then held his hands out with his palms up.

Looking down, Travis saw the knife he had just washed. "You need to borrow this?" He picked it up and offered it to Lawrence.

The man shook his head and started searching near the water's edge.

"Oh, you lost your knife," Travis said.

"There you are," Peter announced as he walked up. "That puppy is slicker than a Confederate spy. I turned around and he was..." The Irishman paused and studied Travis for a moment.

"Um," Travis said, as he quickly offered Salem to Little Irish. "Here."

Peter took the puppy but his gaze remained fixed on Travis's face and it became apparent that he suspected something. Lawrence walked over, showing them his pocket knife.

"You found it," Travis said. He smiled and looked at Peter but Peter was not smiling.

"He is a very busy man," Little Irish said.

"Who?"

"Colonel Wyman. If you can find a moment alone with him, you should tell him your situation. There is nothing so bad that it could not be made worse."

Travis decided to own up to his temptations. Playing innocent would not work with Peter. "I won't," he said. "But I don't know the Colonel."

"I will point him out next time he comes around. If the answer is no, don't become a thorn in his side. He wouldn't like that and neither would you."

Travis started to speak but Peter raised his hand, stopping him.

"Just talk to him, but do so in private. You don't want get the chins wagging amongst the other men. Tell him I can vouch for your story." Peter paused as if he wanted to say something else. With a slight shake of his head he left with the dog in his arms.

Lawrence waited until Peter was gone before nudging Travis with his elbow. His eyebrows were wrinkled in puzzlement.

Travis sighed. "It's a long story." He dried his clean knife blade with his shirt tail.

After shrugging his shoulders, Lawrence raised his eyebrows and mouthed something Travis didn't understand. The two walked side by side until they reached Travis's camp.

He shook hands with Lawrence. "I will see you tomorrow."

Lawrence nodded and weaved his way through the sea of tents.

John was next to the firepit where Travis had left him. He was reclined against a log with his hands behind his head, elbows toward the sky.

"Did you eat?" Travis asked.

John nodded slightly.

Looking next to the smoldering fire, Travis saw fish bones, all of the bones, the whole skeleton. "Where is my half?"

John didn't speak but he locked stares with Travis.

"You ate all the fish?" Taking a firm grip on the knife handle, Travis threw it down, causing it to stick deep in the ground.

John was on his feet in an instant. He raised his fists and came forward. "Are you looking for a fight?"

"I'm looking for some food," Travis answered. "I don't want to fight, I want fish. Why did you eat it all?"

"Was I to guard it for you? Hold it? I'm not your servant." John growled, and then grabbed Travis by the shirt with one hand and swung a fist with his other.

CHAPTER FIVE

Travis ducked, causing John to miss. Although he pulled away hard, John's grip on his clothing remained tighter than a snapping turtle. Travis gave up on separating and wrapped his arms around him, tripping John and sending them to the ground in a twisting, angry tussle. Men in the camp began to run and yell. Travis expected hands to grab and separate John and himself but the excited soldiers ran right past them. More shouts could be heard in the distance.

John stopped struggling and said between heaving breaths, "Where are they going?"

Releasing his grasp around John, Travis fought to get more air. "Truce?"

Someone yelled and there was the distinct sound of clapping.

John struggled to get free. "Alright, truce. Now get off me!"

A thick band of soldiers had formed a large circle around a horse and two men. John pushed and weaved his way through the crowd and Travis followed close behind. In the middle of the gathering stood a fine gray horse with a man in uniform by its side.

"Colonel Wyman," John exclaimed.

Travis shifted to get a better look. *That's the man I should talk to, according to Peter.* He watched as Wyman stood still as a statue while a much taller man berated him with language so foul that the words must have tasted terrible as they flew from his mouth.

The level of calmness in Colonel Wyman's voice was surprising. "You deserved your punishment without a doubt, Henry."

The tall man shouted straight at Wyman. "I deserved no such thing, you coward!"

"Henry Taylor, I have had enough of your sharp words." Colonel Wyman raised one gloved hand, palm out. "We will discuss this at another time."

Henry stepped forward and pushed the Colonel's hand away. "Your shoulder stripes are the only thing keeping me from whipping you like a child!"

The soldiers around them murmured in angry astonishment.

Even in the heat of the moment, Wyman was distinguished. Without an expression upon his face, he slowly removed his jacket, draping the garment across the saddle of his horse. "Henry, now no one can see the difference in our rank. My coat is removed and my rank along with it."

Shouts sounded from the crowd.

Henry snarled something incoherent and came at Wyman.

The Colonel brought his fists up close to his face and circled. Henry picked his moment to charge forward, swinging his arms wildly. Wyman shifted slightly to avoid the attack and punched with a stiff right hand. His fist struck the man on the side of his face, a glancing blow. Henry shook his head and readjusted his attack.

"Coward!" he bellowed.

Wyman easily avoided Henry's second advance by sidestepping. His left hand slammed into the man's ear sending him sprawling on the ground. Henry popped to his feet in a flash but Wyman sent him back to the ground just as quickly.

As he circled with his fists in a boxer's stance, the Colonel said, "Step aside and accept your rank."

Henry struggled to his feet, steadied himself, and then stumbled at Wyman. His feeble attack was met with a quick left jab and an overhead right that sent him down. Blood around his mouth and nose became clotted with dust and dirt. His fighting mood was clearly shattered.

John and Travis cheered along with every man in the crowd.

Wyman retrieved his coat from the horse and draped it across his arm. "Henry, whenever you desire promotion to my rank, I will happily take off my stripes anytime you desire."

As the crowd broke up, the Colonel went back to his horse. Travis stood motionless, watching him mount the big gray. Wyman's battle of fists had thoroughly intimidated Travis, making the Colonel seem very unapproachable as far as he was concerned.

A week after the fight between the Colonel and Henry, the reveille horns sounded about three in the morning, startling everyone. Salem had drifted into Travis and John's camp during the night, and now barked his own alarm. He licked Travis in the face before dashing off.

In less than two hours they were marching to an unknown destination. Knapsack wagons with lanterns followed behind the men, carrying their packs, and someone had put Salem in one. Travis was dead tired and wished he could curl up in a wagon for a nap, too, instead of tramping down the road in the wee hours until he was footsore.

The past few days had been hard on Travis. He missed his brother terribly, and felt the heavy burden of his promise to return. John had stopped talking to him after their scuffle, and his cold attitude gave Travis yet another reason to avoid him when he could.

Desperate for companionship, Travis had spent time with Lawrence, Emil, Arthur, George, and Peter. They helped make the days easier to bear. He had accompanied them on two foraging expeditions and together, they had managed to obtain enough bread and cattle to feed all of the men for one day.

As they marched in the cool morning air, whispered words were passed between marching soldiers until the gossip reached them.

"Did you hear?" Arthur asked.

"What's the news?" Peter chuckled. "Out with it."

"Henry left us a few nights ago."

"Deserted?" George asked.

Arthur nodded.

"Henry who?" Travis asked.

Arthur held his fists up like he was going to fight with someone. "Henry Taylor, the guy who tangled with Wyman."

"That boy has sealed his fate," Peter said.

"Oh, they will find him," Emil added.

George sidestepped a mudhole in the road. "I have some more news. I heard we are headed to Little Rock."

Travis had never been to Little Rock, and even though he wanted to stay involved in the conversation, he faded back in the march until he was behind his comrades. The gossip of another deserter being hunted disturbed him deeply. He felt more trapped than ever.

After they had walked for hours, he began to wonder if they were lost. Just when he had those thoughts, progress was halted for no reason that was immediately apparent, and the men were made to wait for half the day.

Travis sat on the ground and took out a scrap of leather he had found in the wagon. Salem bounced from side to side and barked. Travis tossed the scrap and Salem raced after it. After he found the toy, he grabbed it, flopped on the ground, and began to chew. Travis got up, took the leather away, and tossed it again. After a dozen tries, the young pup began to bring the leather back to Travis for another throw.

"You are pretty smart," Travis said.

Salem's rear end wiggled slightly as he listened to Travis's words. Lawrence walked over and smiled as Travis handed him the leather toy, and they took turns throwing the scrap for Salem. When they heard gunfire in the distance, Salem stopped in his tracks and perked up his ears, staring in the direction of the shots. Travis and Lawrence traded looks, and neither felt like playing anymore.

Rumors floated between groups of soldiers that more than twenty thousand confederates were near Little Rock. A few hours later, they were ordered to turn around and march back. Several men around Travis groaned and cursed, as they reformed to face the way they had just marched.

Word passed down of a skirmish near a town called Searcy, surely the source of the shots they had heard earlier. Regiment soldiers had been forced to retreat from somewhere called Whitney's Lane, although none of which included the men from the Thirteenth.

"Will we ever see any action?" Arthur asked.

"Are ya' daft, Arthur? Never go down the road looking for trouble," Peter said. "I much prefer walking to dying."

He nudged Travis. "How about you?"

Travis said, "If I had to choose, I'd pick walking."

It was at the river in Batesville again that Travis was given his first real task. George shouted his name from the back of a wagon, holding open the top of a large crate.

"Did you need me?" Travis asked when he reached the wagon.

"Sorry, but I was told to pick four," George said, handing down a shovel from the crate. He pointed over to Arthur, Lawrence, and Emil, who were digging in the dirt across a small field. "Go help your buddies."

Emil and Lawrence were wearing cloths that covered their noses and mouths, but Arthur wore none.

As he approached them, Travis could smell the reason for the makeshift bandanas. He tried to keep from gagging in disgust. "Why are we digging in the latrine?"

Emil mumbled and shook his head. The rag around his mouth and nose kept Travis from seeing his full expression, but Emil's eyes were squinted and watery. Travis looked to Lawrence who was digging closest to the piles of human waste. All three men were being extra careful not to splatter anything on them as they worked.

Arthur motioned Travis over and laughed. "Emil won't talk. He wants to keep the smell out of his mouth."

"I don't blame him."

"Orders are to make it bigger," Arthur said. Placing his foot on the back of the shovel, he forced the blade into the dirt. He pulled back on the handle, lifting a large clot of earth, but it slid off, plopped into the trench and sent a chunks of filth flying. Everyone scrambled back in revulsion.

The stench burned Travis's nose and throat. "Are you sure we can't just dig a new one?"

Lawrence shook his head and nudged Emil. "They didn't tell us to dig a new one," Emil said through the rag. "They said to make it longer."

Travis really did not want to join them as the three went back to work digging at the end of the latrine. "Hold on," he said. "We are supposed to make this ditch longer, right?"

Arthur nodded. "Right down through there." He traced a line with his nasty shovel.

Travis walked the direction he had gestured. "All the way to here?"

"That's right," Emil said. "Somewhere around there."

"Then let's dig here first," Travis said. "Let's start here and dig back toward the latrine. Then we only have to deal with that filthy mess one time and not the whole way."

Lawrence playfully jabbed Emil with his shovel handle and snorted, then walked to Travis's side and smiled at him before sinking his shovel into the soil. Arthur and Emil joined them soon after.

"Why didn't we think of this?" Arthur said, then continued in a singsong voice. "Why didn't we think of this? Why didn't we think of this?"

Emil chuckled and rolled his eyes. "What an infernal idiot!"

It had been a long time since Travis had been given anything other than harsh words, punches, and kicks. But in the days after the latrine chore he received something both unusual and unfamiliar to him, respect and friendship.

Unfortunately, his smart work had also gotten him noticed by those higher in rank, and shoveling became something he hated worse than marching. He was taught how to dig rifle pits and somehow acquired the job of burying horse and mule carcasses.

Over the next month, Salem grew and so did his popularity. He became attached to Travis, following in his tracks everywhere he went during the day and begging for a game with his leather toy. In the evenings, Salem would leave him and travel from tent to tent in search of any scraps. Every soldier of the Thirteenth Illinois adopted the reddish mutt and watched after him as if he were their own pet.

Travis had not seen Colonel Wyman since his fight with the soldier. He assumed the Colonel had been away on more important matters. Thoughts of desertion crossed Travis's mind many times but the memory of his fellow soldiers shooting a deserter in the middle of the night was still reminder enough not to take the chance.

CHAPTER SIX

JUNE 18, 1862

Lawrence and Travis had been called for duty in the cookhouse, along with several others privates. There was great celebration among Company H as they had been short on rations for far too long, but now some troops returning from a raid had brought back two fat pigs and slaughtered them for supper.

Much of the meat along with a handful of flour and several quartered potatoes and onions were going into the big stewpots for the men, but under the cook's supervision, Lawrence cut some of the meat into strips while Travis fried it. It was hot work, but much preferred over digging with a shovel.

As the cooked meat, bread and coffee were laid out on a table for the officers, Colonel Wyman emerged from a tent nearby.

Travis's heart jumped to his throat. Wyman came over, picked up a piece of pork and blew upon it before taking a bite. He smiled at Lawrence and nodded his approval. The Colonel's warm grin conflicted with Travis's memory of him punching a soldier to the ground to teach him a lesson.

As the Colonel loaded up his tin plate, a soldier rushed up to him, bumping into the table of food. Travis and Lawrence grabbed the pork to stop it from going over.

"What is it?" Wyman asked.

"Henry Taylor, sir."

The Colonel lowered his plate. "Tell me."

The reporting soldier fought to catch his breath. "I was on an errand to the Sheriff's office in Batesville and two men entered while I was there. One I did not recognize, but clearly the other was Henry." His eyes shifted to the cooked meat on the table. Colonel Wyman cleared his throat, and the soldier hurriedly finished his report. "I followed them outside and confronted Henry. He gave excuses for his desertion."

"There is no excuse," Wyman said, slapping the table with the flat of his hand.

"It was all a diversion," the soldier said. "His friend had unhitched their mounts and when I reached for Henry, they jumped on their horses and skedaddled."

The Colonel's jaw tightened. "You know how they are dressed and the direction they took. Get some horses from the quartermaster and take two teamsters and yourself. Catch him! I don't care if you have to chase him all over Indian Territory." He took a bite of meat, then nodded at the table.

"Get you a meal, soldier, and be on your way. We will shoot him today and hang him tomorrow!"

The men around him cheered. The excitement in the crowd rose but Travis's hope for escape plummeted. Deserting was officially no longer an option for him.

Camp life was as usual for the next three weeks, but on a hot July night reveille sounded at one in the morning. A chorus of groans echoed from the sleepy men.

John sat up and said, "We have not had but a few hours of sleep. Something has happened." It was the first words he had spoken to Travis since their fight.

"Why did it have to happen in the middle of the night?" Travis grumbled, rubbing his eyes in the darkness. He opened the flap on their tent and found Salem standing there in anticipation. The dog jumped up on his hind legs, practically dancing with excitement.

"Everybody up!" A voice shouted. "We are moving out in two hours."

After packing and placing their things in one of the wagons, Travis got in line and marched in the dim moonlight. His feet moved at a steady pace but his mind raced far ahead of the long lines of soldiers. *Where are we going? When will we get there? Will Wyman be there and will I get a chance to talk to him?*

They stopped that evening, exhausted and hungry. There was no food to be had, only coffee. Salem yawned and plopped on the ground near Travis's feet. The dog licked at his paw and whined. Travis guessed Salem's feet were just as sore as his were.

Shouts near camp drew their attention, causing Salem to rise and growl in the direction of the voices. Travis rubbed the dog's head. "Easy, boy. Let's go see."

The source of the disturbance turned out to be four women standing in a nearby graveyard having a heated discussion with some soldiers.

"It is our aunt who is buried here. We have already told you."

"And what killed your dear auntie?" one of the soldiers asked as he examined the dirt atop a fresh grave.

Three of the girls stood defiantly, but one of them advanced, shaking her finger at the man. "Do Confederate women need permission from Yankees to die?"

A tall soldier stopped her with an outstretched arm. "Madam, we cannot help but suspect guns are buried here with the purpose of arming our enemy."

"There is no such thing!"

"We will examine this grave with respect."

The woman glared angrily at the men.

The tall soldier looked to his comrades. "Who has a shovel?"

"I have one with my pack," Travis said.

"Fetch it and dig this up."

Travis started toward his tent at a trot, mentally kicking himself for volunteering to dig up a grave.

Salem ran alongside Travis, the dog yipped and bounced with excitement. "Don't act that way," Travis told him. "What if someone IS buried there?"

As soon as he arrived back at the grave, he did as he was ordered. Travis dug, sending trails of loose dirt flying to the side. He jabbed at the ground, making good progress and reaching a two-foot depth in a matter of minutes. While he might have looked dedicated and determined to the soldiers around him, his mind was screaming for him to stop. He imagined finding a body, partially decomposed, stiff and smelling horrible.

The shovel struck something hard. Travis paused, but the men urged him to continue. Dread filled him as he slowly removed even more dirt, revealing the outline of a trunk's lid. The size of the container was square and not nearly long enough to be a casket. Travis breathed a great sigh of relief.

He noticed the ladies were nowhere to be seen.

"Pry it open," one of the men said.

After jamming the tip of his shovel under the lip of the lid, Travis pulled back. The trunk snapped open just as the wooden handle broke in his hand.

"Apples!" The soldiers laughed and began to gather the fruit, cupping their shirttails into makeshift apron pockets. There were at least six bushels in the trunk but they disappeared in a flash. Travis snatched the last two apples, picked up his broken shovel, and headed back to his tent.

John had already fallen asleep, which was fine with Travis. Salem tried to sniff at the fresh dirt on Travis's boots, but Travis sat and pulled the dog close instead, rubbing his head. They locked stares for a few seconds. Salem's face was a spatter of red and brown, like a painter had wiped his brushes off after only half-way washing them. A good scratch behind the ear caused Salem to groan deep and low.

He leaned in and whispered, "Sometimes I feel like I've lost my brother forever, and sometimes I forget you did lose yours."

Salem yawned with a wide mouth, whining as he finished.

Watching him yawn made Travis do the same. "I've never been so tired."

He ate one of the apples quickly and placed the other next to John. Salem tried to inspect it but Travis distracted him with the core of the fruit he had just eaten. "Here, chew on this."

The dog gnawed on the leftovers, raking his tongue against the roof of his mouth and making a face at the sour juice. Travis chuckled, curled up, and fell asleep with his hand across Salem's back.

The next few days were repeats of the first. Everyone complained of sore feet and being hungry. Men were sent out to obtain supplies but very little were brought back. Most of the soldiers had nothing to eat. Picket lines were set up each night for safety but the guards saw no action or threat.

Finally, the bugle roused them up long before daylight, and sent them marching. By sunrise, any organization among the soldiers had fallen apart. The July heat was already scorching the road and the men along with it.

John walked past Travis and said, "Thanks for the apple." He moved on before Travis could reply.

The road became full of things the overheated men were tired of carrying. Some soldiers were assigned to pick up all the discarded items and load them into the wagons. Even Salem was forced to walk when the wagons got overloaded. Salem panted heavily, his tongue hanging loosely from the side of his mouth.

The soldiers only carried their knapsacks as the road became rougher, and they ended up leaving the wagons far behind. Travis picked Salem up, thinking it would help the half-grown pup, but the extra heat from his furry coat seemed to only make matters worse. He quickly abandoned his good intentions and allowed the dog to make his own track.

Around three in the afternoon the heat became almost unbearable. Men began to fall to the side of the road, seeking shelter in the shade from the trees. Travis wanted to join them but feared what Wyman would think if he found out.

Emil had caught up with him. His cheeks were red as if he had been slapped. "It's good to see you have settled in."

"It does not feel as if I am settled in," Travis said.

Emil pulled a leather thong from his hair and gathered up the loose strands. He re-tied it and wiped sweat from his forehead. His eyes looked odd, and his smile faltered. "Is your brother... I mean, yes, you do have one... a brother...?"

Travis started to answer but stopped. "What?"

Emil stumbled to the side of the road. He hurled a volume of froth into the brush.

"Are you okay? You aren't making any sense." Travis went and stood beside him, not sure what to do next. "Emil?"

CHAPTER SEVEN

July 12, 1862

Emil went to his knees in a crouch, and finally laid over onto his back. "Water." His voice was strained and he coughed after speaking.

"I'm out of water," Travis said. "You need help. Hang on, Emil!" Travis set off down the road as fast as he could.

Salem trotted after him but the bounce was completely gone from his steps. Each soldier they caught up with had the same story, no water. Finally, they reached a group of men standing in the yard of a farmhouse. They were buying water from the well, at one dollar per canteen.

Travis begged pardon of the men he pushed past, saying only that a man was dying. They let him to the front, where he paid the outrageous fee to the landowner, and then rushed back to Emil.

Travis removed the lid. "Here."

He dribbled water into the corner of Emil's mouth. After a few seconds, Emil grabbed the canteen and drank in large gulps. When he paused for air, Travis had a swallow for himself and then poured some into his palm for Salem.

As Emil slowly regained his senses, men continued to seek shade all along the road.

At last, the march was officially halted. Orders came down the line instructing the men to sleep where they were, without a tent. They would be leaving very early while it was still dark.

Propping his head on his pack, Travis fought to keep his eyes open. The location of their destination was completely unknown to him and had he not been so tired, he would have pondered on their reason to travel there.

Peter shuffled past at dusk and gave a weak whistle, prompting Salem to rise. The Irishman bent low and rubbed his head. "Get some rest. Both of you. Tomorrow, we make the last push."

"How far?" Travis asked.

"Thirty-two miles."

Travis sat up. "Thirty-two miles? To where?"

"We are building a fort in Helena. There will be plenty of time for rest there."

"We can't make it." Travis shook his head. "Thirty-two miles in one day?"

"I tend to agree but that's the orders. Get some sleep." Peter started to walk away but stopped and pointed. "You need a new shovel."

Travis rubbed his face hard as if he could wipe away the dread of a thirty-two-mile march. "Yes, I broke it a few days ago."

"Go see the quartermaster when we get to Helena. He will get you another."

Travis nodded.

"Don't forget," Little Irish said. "You will be needing it."

The bugles and long roll of drums pierced the night and the soldiers fell in line. They marched in the dark, and the cool air felt good on Travis's sunburned skin. By daylight, Salem's puppy legs had given out. He limped along, whimpering from his sore paws.

Travis stopped at the edge of the road, allowing both of them a much-needed rest. After a few moments, Emil, Lawrence, and Arthur walked up and decided to have a break with him.

"How are you feeling today?" Travis asked Emil.

"We're young," Emil said. "We should be walking circles around these men, but this march is hurting me."

Arthur pulled his canteen out and turned it up, drinking the last of his water. "It is what it is, boys!"

Lawrence nodded and rubbed sweat from his eyes. He mouthed something a few times before Travis understood what he was saying.

"Hot," Travis said. "Yes, it is almost unbearable."

After ten minutes they were back on the road. Clouds skirted around the sun, teasing them, denying shade they desperately needed.

Not a single soldier had water left in their canteens by noon. Travis carried Salem until his arms cramped. Arthur took his turn with the dog, then Emil, and finally Lawrence. Sweat trailed down both sides of Lawrence's face as he limped down the road but he did not complain. Sometime in the afternoon, men began to stumble into the shade once again.

Arthur shouted with frustration. "I can't stay in this sun any longer. My brains are frying and I can't stand it!"

Travis ignored Arthur and went to Lawrence and held his hands out. "Let me take Salem for a while. You get in the shade. It's my turn to carry him."

Lawrence continued to move forward, not looking left or right, simply staring straight ahead. Travis tried to take the dog from his arms, but Lawrence turned away abruptly, falling into the grass at the edge of the trail.

"Hey," Travis yelled. "Lawrence is down!"

Salem crawled out of the man's grasp and stretched out flat under an oak tree. Travis rolled Lawrence onto his back. "You need some water. Do you have any in your canteen?"

Lawrence didn't acknowledge him. His eyelids became lazy and finally closed.

Travis shook him. "Stay awake!"

Emil and Arthur joined them. "Is he sick?" Emil asked.

"He's bad. Worse than you were yesterday."

"Stay with him," Arthur said. "We will go for water."

Travis nodded and opened his canteen. Turning it up, a few tiny drops splashed across Lawrence's lips. "That's all I have," Travis said, his voice hoarse. He handed the water container to Emil. "My throat is so dry."

"Mine too. We will be back soon," Emil said.

While Travis waited, weary soldiers trudged past. Even though it burned his parched throat to speak, he asked each man if they had any water. No one had any or admitted to such.

Lawrence gagged and held his head with shaking hands.

"They have gone for water," Travis said. "Hang on."

His arms relaxed and fell to either side of his head. Travis grabbed his wrists. Lawrence's skin was clammy and his pulse fast. Jumping to his feet, Travis rushed into the road, trying to stop anyone who would listen.

"Can someone get the doctor? We need water and a doctor!"

Some of the men were barely hanging on and did not seem to hear his pleas, some shook their canteens, proving they were empty, a few soldiers came to the roadside and stood over Lawrence.

"He's pretty far gone," one of them said.

Travis came to his side. "Is he breathing?"

"Hard to tell," the man said.

"He has to be," Travis said.

Most of the soldiers left but a few stayed and rested in the shade.

Travis studied their weary, red faces. "What do I do?"

One of the soldiers coughed. "We are all going to be in his shape if we don't get some water."

Emil and Arthur returned in a rush. "There is none."

"He's worse," Travis said quietly, his voice cracking from the dryness in his throat.

"He's dead?" Emil asked.

"I don't know." Travis felt of Lawrence's neck. "I think he's still alive."

Salem walked over slowly and turned a few circles, before lying down close to Lawrence.

"We saw George on the road," Arthur said. "He's sending the doctor."

"Are we all going to die on this march?" Emil asked.

They waited by his side until a rider arrived on a sweaty horse. After jumping off the horse, he grabbed a leather bag from his saddle horn. "Step aside." The man shook his head and took a deep breath. "Move along but pace yourselves. Find shade if you need it."

"That's the doctor," Emil whispered as they lingered near the edge of the road.

A second man arrived on horseback, forcing Travis, Emil, and Arthur to scramble out of his way. "All of you men keep moving. We don't need any crowds."

The doctor was digging in his bag, but he stopped and looked up. "We need to talk."

"How is this one?"

"Worse than the last one."

Emil and Arthur finally convinced Travis to march on, leaving Lawrence where he lay. Salem reluctantly got to his feet and followed. Travis glanced over his shoulder a few times, still finding it hard to believe that Lawrence would not be joining them.

Two hours later the march was halted and all the men took shelter in the lengthening shadows. Their spirits were dashed when dozens of soldiers suddenly began to turnabout and walk back the direction they had just came from.

One of the soldiers waved at the men under the trees. "We have to double back. We took a wrong turn."

"We are lost?" Emil asked with astonishment.

Every step for the next few hours seemed extra hard since they had already covered this ground once. As they approached the spot they had left Lawrence, Travis noticed a wagon at the side of the road and some men lifting him into the back. One of the men was shouting at the others.

"That's Plummer," Arthur said. "He's another doctor. A good one."

"Which one?" Travis asked.

"The one doing all the yelling." Emil said.

The doctor was middle aged with fair skin and vivid blue eyes. As they walked past, Plummer continued his outburst. "This is madness! I refuse to lose any men. Get me some horses!"

He said much more but his words were lost as they marched further away. A few minutes passed before two riders came through, collecting canteens and hanging them on their saddles. They moved fast and when they had collected at least twenty containers each, the horses were pushed into a trot and disappeared around the corner. An hour later they returned with water, handed the full canteens out, collected empty ones from other soldiers, and then left to repeat the process.

The doctor caught up with Travis, Emil, and Arthur. "Drink it slow," he warned. "Drink it slow!" he shouted so other men around them could hear. "Make it last, boys. They sent some wagons with kegs but we will be lucky if they catch up with us before dark."

Doctor Plummer repeated his message as he went from one group of soldiers to the next. Travis wanted to ask about Lawrence but decided otherwise. The doctor definitely had his hands full.

An hour later, they walked past a dead horse on the side of the road. "That's bad," Arthur said.

Emil tilted his head. "It could be worse."

Travis wiped sweat from his face. "How's that?"

"At least it didn't die in camp. We don't have to bury it."

A mile or so later, they heard a single gunshot ahead. Periodically, additional shots rang out, and soon, the men passed more dead horses and mules along the trail. Each had given up due to the heat and lack of water and some had been finished off with a pistol.

"I'm so glad we don't have to bury all of these," Arthur said.

They caught up with Peter, and the Irishman picked Salem up. "I surely owe you boys an apology."

"About what?" Arthur asked.

Peter put Salem down. "I'm guilty of gossip, pure gossip. I told each of you and others that thirty-two miles would put us in Helena today. I was wrong."

"Wrong?" Arthur's eyes grew fierce.

"I overheard General Curtis and thought I heard we would arrive today."

Travis allowed his shoulders to slump. "Not today? How much farther?"

"Another day, twenty miles."

Emil rubbed a hand through his long hair. "Can we do it? I am not sure I will be able to."

"Sorry, Emil," Peter said. "I need to tell Lawrence. Where is he?"

"You didn't hear?" Travis asked.

"He fell out from the heat," Arthur added.

Peter raised his face toward the sky and shook his head slowly. "I heard we had a few that were very sick. I just never imagined he was one of them. I'm awfully sorry." He walked with them, and no one spoke for a long time.

That evening they traveled through a town called Clarendon, and managed to find water and refill canteens. Plummer had been right when he said the wagons would be late. Men at the back of the line, desperate with thirst, had overtaken the wagons and drank more than their fill.

At the edge of town a few of the men who had found the buried apples came upon a cemetery with a fresh grave. Travis watched them have a heated debate as to what might be hidden under their feet.

"I'm glad my shovel is broken," he said to Emil.

"Why is that?"

Travis motioned for Emil and Arthur to follow him. They took a break from the march and watched the men dig with a shovel they had borrowed from a home nearby. Hunger, fatigue, and a memory of delicious apples drove the soldiers to believe there was bacon, beans and other desired food in the hole.

After digging madly for a while, one of the men jumped into the grave. A few seconds later he scrambled out, coughing and gagging at having found a festering body. The men scattered. The show was over and the march started again.

After it was fully dark and Clarendon far behind them, they stopped at a mud-crusted cypress swamp for the night. The wagons finally arrived with water but no food. The mosquitos were terrible, but nonetheless everyone, Salem included, fell asleep on the ground where they were, in an eerily silent camp.

CHAPTER EIGHT

The last day of the journey was not nearly as hard for Travis. His legs somehow felt lighter for knowing the march would end soon. The skies opened up and dumped water on them for hours but the men did not seem to care.

The irony was not lost to anyone. They had been short on water for days and now that the end of the march was near it was everywhere. Salem ran through the puddles on the road, racing ahead of Travis and seconds later, racing past him again, headed toward the back. The dog's antics caused much needed laughter from the men.

As they neared Helena, the great Mississippi river came into view. The men of the Thirteenth cheered, raising their fists into the air, punching toward the sky in celebration at having reached the end. They were ordered to tighten formation and soon afterwards the band organized at the front, playing proudly as they all proceeded through the middle of town.

Helena was a beautiful place which seemed to buzz with activity. Steamboats churned up and down the river, most of them stopping to load or unload men and goods. The Thirteenth made their camp on a hill overlooking a wonderous sight. Large beech trees grew along the sides of rolling hills that led the eye to the lazy Mississippi and the bustling town.

In the days after arriving, many of the soldiers became very sick with vomiting and diarrhea. Emil was one of the unlucky ones to suffer. All of the men were given a few days to eat and regain their strength. They had been short on food for a long while and now steamers loaded with rations arrived like clockwork. It was an unusual change for the soldiers.

On July the seventeenth, George called for a meeting. Travis, Arthur, Emil, Thomas, and Peter were invited along with another man Travis did not know. He shook hands with the man and Emil did the same.

"This is Alfred," Arthur said, slapping the man on the back.

"It is good to meet you," Emil said.

Travis nodded. "Same here."

Arthur laughed much louder than the occasion called for. "Alfred is a tough man. No doubt about it."

Alfred smiled. "What's this meeting about?" he asked George.

"I'm afraid I have bad news," George said. "All of us were fairly acquainted with Lawrence. Some of us even remember the accident that stole his voice."

"I remember," Thomas said.

"Has he gotten worse?" Alfred asked.

George paused and stared at the ground. "He died this morning."

Travis felt his eyes sting and started to speak. He waited instead, thinking all of the other men probably knew Lawrence better than he did.

"It was a hard march," Emil said. "How many didn't make it?"

"Just him," George said.

Thomas rubbed the stubble on his chin. "He was determined to help me catch fiths for our company in Batethsville."

"Lawrence was a giving soul." Arthur added.

George pursed his lips and turned away. "I just wanted you to know first."

The rest of the day felt strangely empty and quiet for Travis. Everyone in the Thirteenth regiment was reserved, obviously showing respect for Lawrence.

Salem could not comprehend the news, and instead, practiced his running and barking around camp, especially when Travis tossed the leather scrap for him to fetch.

Using leftover food as a reward, he quickly taught the dog to sit and lie down. Salem was still a puppy and didn't get it right every time, but the dog constantly amazed Travis.

One of the most impressive things Salem had picked up was his ability to learn a few names. Travis practiced giving the dog the piece of leather and telling him to take it to Peter. When the dog finally caught on and delivered the toy, he was rewarded with a bit of food from the Irishman. The task was repeated using Travis as the recipient of the scrap leather but when they added George to the mix, Salem seemed to get confused.

After a few days of rest, it was time to go to work. George found Travis playing with Salem. "Go to the quartermaster's tent for a new shovel," he said. "It's time for us to get to work on the fort."

"Yes, sir. Is Colonel Wyman here in Helena?"

"I believe he's away."

Travis groaned. "I needed to talk with him."

"I'm sure he will be busy when he returns. Is there something you need?"

Travis shook his head. "No, sir."

"Go see William. The quartermaster's tent is a big one just over there." He pointed toward the top of the hill they were camped on. "You will see two tents side by side. One is new and the other is a little older." He chuckled as he spoke.

Travis did exactly as he was told. At the top of the hill he found two large canvas tents next to each other, one of them had stains, smudges, and small tears. The other was crisp and clean.

He was not sure which tent was the correct one, and he did not want to just go walking in. "Hello?"

Salem moved past him, stuck his nose inside the flap on the newer tent, and then disappeared inside.

"Get back here," Travis called. "Anybody in there?" He reached for the canvas flap but in that moment something growled. It was a deep, bear-sounding growl. It crashed against the door of the tent and Travis stumbled back. The flap jerked and then another growl.

There was only an instant for Travis to regain his composure before Salem came busting out of the tent with his tail tucked tight against his body. Right behind him was one of the biggest dogs Travis had ever seen. The curly-haired animal did not pay any attention to him, but instead chased Salem about ten paces before stopping. The big dog huffed loudly and promptly positioned himself next to the tent opening.

"Come on in," a voice said from inside.

Travis studied the strange dog. Its wavy hair was pitch black. The length of its coat was not overly long, but it was bushy. While sitting, the dog's head was even with Travis's stomach.

"Come in," the voice repeated. "He won't bite unless I tell him to."

Travis moved through the opening while leaning away from the big animal. The dog ignored him, keeping its attention on the small mutt that had invaded his territory. Salem kept his distance, circling and growling.

Inside the tent, Travis saw tables with supplies arranged neatly upon them. At the back, was a desk with a man behind it. He looked to be in his thirties and was standing with a pencil and paper in his hands.

"Mister William?" Travis asked.

The burly man removed his glasses and tossed the paper on the desk. "Who told... Where are you from?"

"Me? I'm from here." He shook his head. "Not here. Not Helena. I meant, Arkansas. Salem, Arkansas, is where I joined."

The large man heaved a breath and walked around his desk until he was standing in front of Travis. "I could hear it in your voice."

"What could you hear?"

"Arkansas is my least favorite place in the world." The man shook his head with sorrow while looking at him. "I cannot stand it or the people who live here."

"Arkansas?" Travis asked. "But I'm not originally from here."

"Nothing good ever came from this state, but maybe you aren't tainted yet."

Travis waited for a moment. "Are you William? I was told to ask for William."

"Jake," the man said.

Travis nodded. "Good to meet you, Jake. Is William here?"

"I am William." He put his pencil on the desk.

Travis tilted his head. "I'm confused. I thought you were Jake."

"The meanest person I ever knew was Jake Sightsinger. He was the devil without a doubt. Just like everyone from Arkansas."

The dog at the tent opening growled again.

"Are you..." Travis was not sure how to clear up his confusion. "You are William?"

The man nodded and said, "Call me Jake."

"Sir? Yes, sir. I will. Um... Will your dog hurt my dog?"

"That was your little mottled mutt that came in here?"

"Yes."

"He will be fine. Nep is our regiment dog, owned by Captain Henry Noble of Company A, who has entrusted me with his care. Please make sure your pup doesn't hurt him." Jake smirked.

Travis smiled. "He's four times bigger than Salem."

"What brings you to see me?"

"A shovel," Travis said. "I broke my shovel."

Jake retrieved his pencil and paper, rubbed the bristly hair on his chin, and then placed the pencil tip on the paper. "What's your name?"

"Travis Bailey."

Jake's pencil wiggled. "Go behind this tent and look in the third wagon. Get one shovel and go to work."

"Yes, sir," Travis said. As he turned to leave, he noticed a ball on one of the tables. It was old, tattered, and slightly misshapen. He pointed at it. "Is this for sale?"

"That's Nep's old chewed up ball."

"Would you sell it?"

"For your Arkansas mutt dog?"

"Yes, sir. He's smart and our company is attached to him."

"Which company are you with?" Jake placed his pencil on the paper again.

"Company H," Travis said. His eyes shifted up and to the right in thought. "Yes, H, I think."

Jake tilted his head slightly. "You aren't sure? Are you with a tall man named George, and Peter, a short Irishman?"

"Yes, sir."

"H, is correct, then. I heard about Lawrence. Did you know him?"

Travis looked at the ground. "I was with him on the march when he collapsed."

Jake was silent for a moment. "Take it," he said at last, gesturing toward the worn piece of leather.

Travis picked the ball up. "Thanks, Jake." He went to the tent opening and started to squeeze past the newfoundland.

"Nep!" Jake said. "Move."

The dog shifted to the side, allowing Travis to exit. The command and resulting action on the animal's part impressed and inspired Travis to show off something Salem had learned.

"Want to see a trick I taught him?" Travis called back.

Jake came to the opening and held the flap back so he could see.

"Here," Travis said, calling Salem to him.

The dog eased closer, keeping a wary eye on the much larger newfoundland. The big dog growled. Jake nudged him with his foot and the dog flopped down, pawing at one of Jake's boots.

"Here," Travis said to Salem. He offered the leather toy and Salem took it quickly, holding it in his mouth for only a second before dropping it. The pup sniffed, licked, and then picked the ball up again.

"Take it to Peter," Travis said. "Go find, Peter."

Salem clamped onto the toy with his jaws and sped away.

Jake's eyes became wide. "He's taking it to the Irishman?"

"He sure is," Travis said.

"He knows him by name?"

"Yes, sir."

Jake looked thoughtful.

"So the shovels are in the third wagon?" Travis asked.

"Hm? Oh, yes. And you will need to bring your broken shovel back here. And bring your dog with you."

"Yes, sir. I'll do that."

The next two days Travis worked with hundreds of men building the fort. The colored men sang while they toiled, making the job seem a little easier and less boring for all involved.

It provided a wonderful distraction for Travis as he repeated a monotonous task. Dig up dirt, fill a wheelbarrow, watch it be taken away only to be replaced with an empty one.

Salem wandered about looking for bits of food scraps from anyone who was willing to toss some his way. Every hour or so he would come to visit Travis and give him a pitiful look. On his third trip around, Salem sat and raised one of his paws slightly. Travis knew exactly what he was wanting.

"You can have your ball when I am finished."

Salem flicked an ear and cocked his head to one side. His curious mind was working hard to make sense of the words.

Travis tossed a shovel full of dirt and rested for a moment while yet another empty wheelbarrow was parked in front of him. "You will have your toy chewed away to nothing if I let you carry it around all day. You have to wait."

When Travis finished his shift, his palms were blistered and sore. Before eating supper, he grabbed his old broken shovel and returned to the quartermaster's tent. Salem caught up with him just as he arrived, planting himself directly in his path.

"I know what you want."

Salem raised his head, panting with his mouth wide and his lips pulled back into a happy grin. Travis pulled the ball out of his pocket. The dog jumped to his feet and instantly lowered his front half until his elbows were resting on the ground and his rear sticking in the air. Travis threw the ball and Salem sprang away, chasing the bouncing toy as it rolled down the hill.

"You didn't tell him who to take it to," someone said.

Travis looked to see Jake standing outside the supply tent. "No, I didn't. He's so excited right now, I don't know if he would do it anyway." Walking closer, he handed Jake the broken shovel.

"See if he will," Jake said, absently taking the pieces in his large hands.

The dog was busy running around with the ball in his mouth.

Travis whistled. "I'll try. Salem!" Salem stopped and looked at him. "Bring it here." He knelt and motioned for him to come. Without hesitation, the dog sprinted over and dropped the toy. Travis picked it up. "Take it to-"

"Me," Jake said. "See if he will bring it to me."

CHAPTER NINE

Travis said, "But, he doesn't know you."

Jake knelt down with some difficulty. "I'm curious."

After a moment of consideration, Travis held the ball out and Salem took it. "Over there," Travis said as he pointed. "Take it to Jake."

Salem looked the direction Travis was pointing but did not budge.

"Go on. Take it to him." He motioned and made a clicking sound with his mouth to get Salem's attention. "Take it."

Salem started Jake's direction, slowly at first, but then trotted the last few feet. Jake laughed and reached for the ball but Salem turned his head at the last moment. With hardly a pause, he made a small circle and returned to Travis.

"He don't trust that you'll give it back."

Jake stood. "I suppose not. How old is, Salem? Is that right? Salem?"

"That's right." Travis paused to think. "I'm guessing he was about eight weeks old when I found him, so I'd say he's around four months now. Where is your big dog?"

"Nep? He's is in the show tent."

"Show tent?"

Jake pointed to the large canvas structure Travis had noticed on his first trip. It was well used and leaned slightly to one side.

"We've already closed for the day but we could give you and Salem a quick show." He shouted over his shoulder, "Burley!"

"Yes," someone said from inside the old tent.

"Come and show our friend, Travis, the show."

A rather odd man stepped out of the tent. His scraggly, patchy beard was distracting, but his unusual posture rendered Travis helpless to avert his stare. Burley's legs were normal from his feet to his waist, but his torso curved to one side as if he was leaning. To add to his peculiar stature, the man's shoulders, neck, and head were perfectly straight. Burley's waist and chest had simply grown in a manner in which Travis had never witnessed. The man looked to be in his thirties. He wore thick glasses and carried a pleasant smile on his face.

"Take Travis and his dog inside," Jake said.

Burley stepped to the side and held the flap open. "This way."

Travis walked to the tent and Salem followed, chewing on his ball as he went. Travis greeted the man while trying not to stare. Once inside the room, he found the interior had been divided by hanging blankets which formed stalls with three sides and a walkway down the center. The tent smelled like the old barn back home. The scent of stale hay brought back memories of he and his brother laughing and playing with the two puppies, before everything fell to pieces because of their father.

Burley took him to the first stall. "Inside this cage are two squirrels, both came from the north but one is very unusual." He shuffled to the side, allowing Travis a closer look. "Have you ever seen a black squirrel before?"

"No, I haven't."

The squirrels chittered and bounced around the enclosure, scattering acorns, knocking some out of their cage. One of them had coal black fur.

In the next section, Travis saw a pair of miniature donkeys and three goats, surely the reason for the barn smell. He had seen goats like these before but the donkeys had strange striped legs. Salem noticed them and gave a series of muffled barks around the ball in his mouth. The donkeys laid their ears back and the goats bleated loudly at the dog.

"You should like this," Burley said, as he motioned around the next curtain. He pulled the blanket aside.

"Cats and dogs," Travis said. He picked Salem up, not sure how behaved he would be. Two cats were in a cage but the three dogs were tied with ropes to their collars. "Are these special dogs and cats?"

"Smart ones," Burley said. "They can all do tricks. I would have them perform for you but there's no time for that this evening."

Travis pointed. "I've seen this one before. The big black one."

"That's Nep," Burley explained. "He is the regiment dog, The ultimate title for a dog to hold. He belongs to Jake and I. We trained him."

The smallest dog, a terrier, noticed Travis was holding Salem and began barking. His outburst spread to the other canines and Salem decided he would not be outdone. He dropped his ball, barked, and growled deeply, vibrating in Travis's arms. Travis retrieved the toy and Burley led him away from the ruckus, but Salem refused to stop answering the other dogs and continued barking.

Let us move on," Burley said loudly.

The rest of the show was rushed with Burley simply pointing as they walked, having given up on talking above the noise. Before reaching the tent opening, Travis saw some tarantulas, snakes, a racoon, and a opossum.

As they exited the tent, Burley said, "Come tomorrow and you can hear our whistling boy."

"Whistling boy?"

"He joined us in Batesville, a former slave I believe. He's very good."

"I'll try to do that," Travis said.

Burley bumped into him as he turned his bent body around. "Good evening," he said before going back into the tent.

Salem finally stopped growling so Travis put him down, and he immediately begged for the ball.

"Not yet." Travis put it in his pocket.

"What did you think?" Jake asked.

"That was very interesting, until Salem kicked up a row," Travis answered.

"We do what we can to entertain. Consider it a hobby with benefits for the regiment."

Travis took a few steps away. "I need to go eat supper. You have a great collection."

"Could you come by tomorrow?" Jake asked. "I'd like for Burley to work with Salem. He's really good with animals."

"I have to move dirt for the fort," Travis said.

"He could teach Salem some more tricks."

"I'll try to come but it will probably not be tomorrow." Travis smiled and waved as he turned and walked away. "Have a good evening."

The next day, Travis shoveled dirt for hours before needing a break from the heat. He sat under a tree, drinking from his canteen.

John walked past with two other soldiers. Each had their weapons and knapsacks. "Hey, Travis. You want to go with us?"

Travis sat up straight.

"Grab your gun," John said.

"What gun?" Travis asked.

"That one," John said, pointing to his shovel.

Travis took a drink of water. "Very funny."

"Are they ever going to give you a weapon?"

Shrugging, Travis said, "I can do more good with a shovel than a musket anyway."

John and his two companions laughed and went on their way.

"Where are you going?" Travis called after them.

Glancing back, John said, "Joining some other men to search for a deserter."

In the middle of August a steamer arrived with supplies, including new uniforms for each soldier. Travis went to the dock with all of the men and stood in line until he was handed his first complete uniform. He was happy to receive one since his pants were filthy and had small holes in the knees.

After getting back to camp, he crawled into his tent to change pants and heard some men talking somewhere behind it.

"He's on the boat. That's what I heard."

"Are you sure?" The other man asked.

"A soldier on the dock told me he saw Wyman onboard with the supplies."

Travis came out to finish dressing. He checked, but the men who had been talking were gone. In a matter of moments, the spreading news spurred some of the men to rush around camp, cleaning up and getting their things in order.

Travis whistled a few times for Salem but the dog did not show. John was still gone and Travis had his tent and surroundings in good shape so he headed back to the dock. The Colonel had been away on business for weeks and Travis felt he could not wait any longer.

He found the uniform line was down to fifty soldiers or less. Standing tall and holding his head straight, Travis pretended to know exactly what he was doing and walked around the end of the line on the ship side of the wharf. Striding along the edge of the dock, he looked for any excuse he could find to get on the boat. He spotted a coil of rope, picked it up, and continued his path of false confidence.

Two men were handing out uniforms and two others were writing down names. As Travis approached, his thoughts got the best of him. He suddenly wondered how much trouble he could get into for sneaking on a steamboat. He had to get back home and as far as he could tell, Wyman held the keys to his freedom, but asking around for the Colonel had gotten him nowhere.

Travis nodded as he walked. This would be worth the risk.

The men with the uniforms were busy and paid no attention to him. Travis walked right past them, turned, and headed up the wooden planks to go on the ship.

"Where are you going, soldier?"

He stopped dead in his tracks. His mind raced for the correct answer, one that would help him cross paths with Wyman. Travis turned quickly. The man who had questioned him was slim and had one of those faces that always looked mad.

"I'm supposed to check the supplies for some rope," Travis said.

"You are looking for rope? Have you looked in your hands?" The man's laugh was harsh, and his mouth refused to form a smile. "Tell me again. Why are you boarding?"

Travis held the rope out. "For this. The quartermaster sent me to check. He's expecting some I suppose."

"Some rope like that?"

"Yes, sir."

The man spoke to the others, causing them to stop their work with the uniforms. "Did any of you see any rope like this on the ship?"

"Not that small," one of them said. "Not nearly that small."

Travis sighed. "What should I tell him?"

The grumpy-faced man went back to work on the uniforms. "Tell him it should be on the next steamer."

Travis spoke quickly. "He wanted me to give Colonel Wyman a message too."

"You can't do that," the man said.

Feeling defeated, Travis shuffled past them and back onto the dock.

"The Colonel went into town an hour ago," the man said. "You might catch him there."

Those words gave Travis a fresh batch of hope as he rushed toward town.

The streets of Helena were busy with citizens, soldiers, workers, and freed slaves. Travis walked the street and searched for any signs of Wyman. The stores were full of soldiers spending their pay, but he couldn't imagine the Colonel being in those locations, so Travis skipped the stores and continued to look in the windows of other establishments. After an hour of walking back and forth, almost all of the new hope he had found was gone.

Finally, he gave up and decided to go back to camp, but a crowd had gathered at the end of the street, blocking his path.

"I've never seen one," a man said.

A short lady stepped onto a bench, trying to see over the taller people.

"What is it?" Travis asked.

"A camel," she said.

"A camel?"

The woman got down from the bench and looked at him with disgust. "One of *you* was riding it down the street but he is stopped now." Her lip curled. "We don't want y'all. We had yeller fever here a few years back and I almost wish for another outbreak so you Yanks would tuck tail and run."

Two soldiers pushed through, coming from the direction everyone else was looking. "That camel better be careful," one of them said to the other. "Wyman might give it a punch." He raised his fists into a boxer's stance. Both the men laughed.

"Is the Colonel here?" Travis asked.

The soldier lowered his hands. "He's over by the camel."

Travis weaved through the crowd until he could see Wyman talking with Jake, the quartermaster. They were standing in front of a dusty brown camel in the middle of the street. Travis had seen horses of all sizes and had even stood next to a draft horse once, but they all paled in stature when compared to this camel. Never would he have imagined they were so big. On top of the animal, sat a soldier, holding a rope that went down to a ring in it's nostril. He was patiently waiting for the discussion to end.

Travis moved closer so he could hear what they were saying.

"They would be much better," Jake said.

Wyman shook his head. "We both know that isn't true."

"General Curtis has collected quite a few of these," Jake said. "We could at least ask him about them."

"Mules are stubborn," Wyman said. "Camels are impossible."

Jake started to say something else but Wyman cut him off.

"If you are looking for another animal for your sideshow, forget it."

"That's not it at all," Jake said.

Wyman gave him a look out of the corner of a squinted eye. "You mean to tell me that if we tried the camel and if it didn't work out, that you would not try to keep it when it was rejected?"

"Colonel, you wound me," Jake said in mock sorrow.

The Colonel smiled. "No camels."

Jake managed a smile back. They shook hands and parted, allowing the camel rider to continue on his way.

Travis wanted to stay and watch the animal lumber along but he followed Wyman instead. The Colonel was stopped at least six times before he could get to the sidewalk. Each time, Travis waited behind him and listened while he solved regiment problems and answered questions. The urge to tug on his sleeve was strong but Travis remembered the advice Peter had given. Their conversation needed to stay as private as possible.

After a few more delays, Wyman made it to the end of the sidewalk and turned toward the river. There were very few people around and Travis decided it was now or never.

"Sir," he said. "Sir. Colonel, sir!"

CHAPTER TEN

Wyman stopped walking and even though Travis was looking at his back, he could sense the frustration.

The Colonel took a deep breath before turning. "What can I do for you?"

His smile caught Travis off-guard. The warmth of his greeting reminded him of a father he had known when he was little, before liquor had taken over Jeb's life.

"I know you are very busy, sir." Travis shook with raw nerves. "Could I please have a moment of your time?"

Glancing toward the river, Wyman said, "I cannot possibly spare any more time today. I must be on the steamer when it leaves."

Travis nodded and tried to keep his eyes from watering. "Yes, sir."

"I will return soon," the Colonel said. "We can schedule a time then." He began to turn away, but paused. "What is your name, son?"

"Travis Bailey."

Wyman faced him. "Is this a life or death matter?"

"It is a serious matter," Travis said.

The Colonel put his hand in his pocket and pulled out a watch. After a quick glance, he dropped it back inside. "I can't count the number of times I've been told by a young soldier that he is homesick. If you are about to tell me such a story or any variant, save us both the time it will take and return to your camp."

Travis's insides became jittery when he sensed Wyman would not even allow him to explain his situation. His throat tightened as hundreds of thoughts fought to become sentences, until he was afraid to open his mouth, fearing he would vomit words all over the Colonel.

"Do you still wish to tell me something?" Wyman asked.

"It's my brother," Travis finally said. "I'm real worried about him."

"I see," Wyman said. "What regiment is he with?"

"He's not in a regiment. He's eight years old."

The Colonel studied his face. Travis wasn't sure if it would be in his best interest to keep talking or shut up. Wyman must have seen the honest worry in his eyes.

"Let's sit for a moment," The Colonel said. He walked toward the dock and Travis followed. When Wyman came to some wooden crates, he took a seat on one and Travis did the same. The Colonel's genuine smile returned. "Tell me your tale."

With his composure regained, Travis explained how his little brother and himself were treated by their father. He told Wyman about the circumstances under which he joined the war. To sum his story up, Travis said, "I really need to go and get my brother."

"Correct me if I am wrong, but in summation, you joined the war to retrieve your brother's dog so he would agree to run away with you?"

"Yes, sir."

"No," Wyman said.

"You don't believe me?" Travis asked. "Talk to Peter and George from Company H. They were there."

"Oh, I believe you but my short answer is, no. You cannot be discharged at this time."

"But my brother needs my help." Travis could hear the desperation in his own voice. "I'm all he has. Our mother doesn't want us and my father would rather have whiskey than his sons."

Wyman crossed his arms. "A matter like this is indeed serious, but the war and future of our country is most dire at the moment. This fort has to be finished soon and we need all the help we can acquire. If even one soldier finds you were discharged for a family emergency, do you know what would happen?"

"No, sir."

"That news would spread and within a week we would have hundreds of men with emergencies at home. Do you understand?"

"Yes, sir. I don't like it, but I understand."

"I appreciate your honesty. But regardless if you like it or not, that is the way it is." Wyman stood and took a few steps toward the steamboat.

Travis followed. "Is there anything I can do?"

The Colonel turned to face him. "I am responsible for thousands of soldier's lives right here, not a civilian two hundred miles away."

"I understand, sir," Travis said, blinking back the tears. "Chet is my little brother, my responsibility. I just had to try."

Wyman placed a hand on his shoulder. "While I am away, I'll put some thought into a solution for your problem, perhaps a furlough. In the meantime, I will have a telegram sent to your town and request someone check on your brother and let him know where you are."

"Thank you," Travis said. He told the Colonel his father's name and where their house was located.

Wyman said, "You could also send a letter. Perhaps your father would write back?"

Travis shook his head. "I doubt it, but I'll try. Your help means so much. How can I thank you?"

"Just be a good soldier," Wyman said. The bell on the boat clanged, a signal that it would be leaving in moments. "Keep our conversation to yourself. We will talk upon my return."

The Colonel turned and strode to the steamer.

The news had not been what Travis wanted to hear, but he was happy someone would make sure his brother was all right. As he was walking to camp, he met Burley and was astonished to see him carrying Salem!

"Where are you going?" Travis asked.

Burley cleared his throat. "I am taking him to our tent. Jake said I should teach him some more tricks."

Travis frowned and took Salem out of the man's arms. "Jake asked if I could come by sometime and let you work with Salem, but he didn't say anything about you coming to get him."

"But it will be good for the dog," Burley said.

"I will talk to Peter and the others about it," Travis said. "Salem belongs to all of us. I'll ask them what they think."

"That will be fine," Burley said. He continued past Travis and didn't look back.

After arriving at camp, Travis found Peter and Alfred sitting in makeshift chairs, and using an old stump as a card playing table. He talked to Peter in private about his conversation with the Colonel.

"Here's my advice," Peter said. "Be patient and do what Wyman says."

Travis nodded slowly. "There's something else. I had a strange encounter with Burley just now."

"Who?" Peter asked.

"Jake's helper."

Alfred walked over and joined their conversation. "The quartermaster? You mean, William," he said.

"He told me to call him Jake," Travis said.

Peter chuckled. "His name is William, but he will forever be known as Jake by the Thirteenth. Regardless, I didn't know he had a helper."

"I guess that's what he is. I met Burley a while back and again today. He was carrying Salem and said he was taking him to the quartermaster's tent to teach him some tricks."

Peter looked to Alfred and then at Travis. "I don't believe Jake would steal a dog for his sideshow but I've been surprised before. Let's all keep a closer eye on Salem."

"I will," Travis said.

Alfred turned to walk away. "I will tell Arthur and Emil."

"And I'll talk to George," Peter added.

That night, Travis fed Salem some hardtack and bacon. The dog downed the meat in one gulp but played with the crackers, tossing them in the air, pouncing on them, and finally crunching them up. With his stomach full, he stretched out on the ground and fell asleep. Travis rubbed Salem's belly with his foot while writing a letter to his father.

Pa,

Please tell Chet I am in the Thirteenth Illinois Infantry and we have traveled to Helena where thousands have gathered. We are working together to build a fort here. More and more soldiers arrive every day and it is quickly becoming crowded. I will be home for a visit as soon as I'm allowed. Please respond and I will send a portion of my pay for your trouble.

Sincerely, Travis Bailey.

There were only two things that interested Jeb, liquor and money, and money only because it could be used to obtain liquor. Travis was hoping Jeb's love of whiskey would inspire him to reply to the letter.

The next few months were hard. They worked rain and shine to complete the fort. There seemed to be no end to the amount of dirt that was moved and dumped against the walls of the structure. Travis's hands became hard with callouses and his muscles grew strong. He spent his spare time working with Salem, teaching him to keep an eye on the camp. The dog learned who belonged and who didn't. His barks always announced to everyone when there was a strange intruder amongst them.

November brought mild days and chilly nights, and a steamer arrived just in time with thick blue overcoats for every soldier. Travis quietly celebrated his fifteenth birthday while he tried on his new clothes.

Quartermaster Jake and his helper, Burley, bumped into Travis from time to time. Neither one of them seemed to be interested in Salem any longer. Travis could not shake the odd feeling Burley gave him so he avoided the sideshow tent at all cost.

Rumors spread through camp that the Colonel would be back soon. Travis was excited at the news, but John took his shovel and handed him a gun.

"What's this for?" Travis asked.

"Noncombat labor is no fun at all," John said. "You need some excitement. Here's your cartridge box."

Travis took the leather box. He placed the butt of the musket on the ground and held it upright with one hand. "What are you doing? Are you serious?"

John laughed. "I'm just joking with you."

Built up tension left Travis's shoulders.

John laughed harder. "No, I am not. I am just following orders. Your name was on a list and you need to report for training."

"But I will be leaving," Travis said. As the words left his mouth, he wished he could take them back.

John's eyebrows wrinkled together. "Leaving?"

Travis struggled to come up with a good excuse for his statement. He could not let John know about his discussion with Wyman. "I am leaving camp today to do a favor for Peter."

John stared at him for a moment. "Good, you don't have drill until tomorrow."

Worry would not leave Travis alone the rest of the evening. John kept watching him and talking about how he could not wait to see some action and shoot some rebels. Travis finally fell asleep while John talked of the grizzly battlefield wounds he had heard soldiers tell in stories.

The next day, Travis was sent to drill. Most of the men there were young, being about twenty-five years old or less.

The instructor whistled to get everyone's attention. "Most of you are green or have been serving in noncombat positions, but it is time to set aside your shovels and take up arms."

He held a manual up for all to see. "How many of you have read this?"

Over half of the men raised their hands. Travis did not. He had never been given any booklets.

"I suppose we will start with the most important, loading your weapon. Watch me and do it in the manner that I do."

Two young men at the back mumbled something back and forth to each other.

The instructor spoke loudly. "Do we have some hunters among us today?"

A few raised their hands, including one of the men who had been whispering.

"This is nothing like hunting," the instructor stated. "A squirrel or rabbit will never rush toward you with a fixed bayonet, hoping to run it through your guts. You will learn these steps. They will become second nature. When a thousand Secesh pigs are charging down on you, you will reload your weapon without thinking."

Everyone's expression took on a much more serious look. Glances were exchanged between men but there was no more whispering.

"Attach your cartridge box to your belt and let us begin. Hold the musket with your left hand and place the butt between your feet. Keep the barrel about three inches from your body."

He paused to correct a young man who was doing it wrong.

"Now, move your right hand to your cartridge box and open the flap. Take a cartridge out with your thumb and next two fingers."

Travis did exactly as the man said. His father had never taken him hunting and so he had never fired a gun before.

"Place it between your teeth and tear the powder end of the cartridge off. Hold it upright and place it near the muzzle." He stopped again and walked around, showing each person exactly how to hold it.

"Charge your weapon by pouring the powder into the barrel. Remove your bullet from the paper and start it into the barrel, flat end first."

Travis dropped his bullet.

The instructor came and stood in front of him. "Men are shooting at all of you! If this happens on the battlefield, you will get yourself killed."

He walked to the front while Travis fumbled around trying to pick his bullet up.

"Seize the ramrod with your thumb and fore-finger on your right hand. Draw your rammer out half way and hold in position with your left thumb."

Travis got confused and had to sneak a look at what the other men were doing.

"Grasp the ramrod in the middle with your right hand and pull it free of the tube. Place the head of the rammer on the ball and ram the cartridge down the barrel!"

Hesitating, Travis waited until he watched the instructor complete the process with his musket. After he was finished, they were told to line up and face targets.

"Return your rammer in the same manner as you drew it. Now, hold your weapons and observe this last step." He showed them how to hold the musket, half-cock it, and prime the weapon with a percussion cap. After placing his gun on a table, he made his way from soldier to soldier, showing them exactly how to prime their weapons.

He retrieved his gun, showed them the correct stance, and fired. A hole appeared in the target, proving his aim was true.

"Raise your weapons," he said.

Travis put the butt of his gun against his shoulder. The instructor walked from man to man, correcting them as he went. Travis was surprised how heavy the musket became as he waited.

"Fire!"

Travis missed his target.

"Again. Reload and take your time. You will only use two more rounds. We can spare no more ammunition."

They repeated the process twice more and Travis hit the target on his last try. For another hour afterwards, the soldiers had to practice the loading steps, repeating the procedure many times without actually loading the weapons.

"Faster," the man said. "You will be proficient when you can fire three times in sixty seconds."

Travis drilled each day for a week. He became slightly faster at loading and even learned different shooting positions, but could not attain three loading cycles per minute. His competitive spirit made him want to practice more and try harder but the knowledge that Colonel Wyman would possibly allow him to leave made the matter seem less important.

Wyman visited camp often, making sure the troops were being taught as he wanted, but Travis was not called for a meeting with him. The frequency of drills increased, with the focus being on formations and how to work together as a unit. This caused rumors of impending battles to spread. Travis went through the motions of drill, but felt certain he would be gone before the time for battle came.

CHAPTER ELEVEN

December 15, 1862

Travis relaxed in a camp chair and read a manual while Salem slept by the fire. Being in a mischievous mood, John tossed pebbles at them.

Travis moved a few feet away. "Knock it off."

John scooted closer.

"Keep your chair away from mine," Travis said.

"Are you up to three shots a minute yet?" John threw another rock at his feet.

"I'm close. Just a few seconds short."

"I don't want you fighting alongside me until you can do it," John said.

Travis wasn't sure how to take the comment. "Why do you act the way you do? We are two of the youngest here and should be watching each other's backs."

"I don't need you," John said. He threw another pebble, harder this time, striking Salem. The dog yelped, more from being startled awake than from pain.

Travis stood. "Why are you always picking fights with me?"

John snapped to his feet and faced off with Travis. "Get your fists up!"

Salem growled but his attention was not fixed on the argument.

"Travis Bailey?" A voice asked.

Travis noticed a man in his mid-twenties had walked up behind him. The fellow stared at them for a moment, as if he was trying to determine the cause of their argument. "I'm, Corporal Frank Whipple. The Colonel would like to speak with you."

Salem approached and sniffed Frank's pant legs.

"The Colonel sent you?" John asked.

"I'm his orderly." He looked to Travis. "He wishes to speak with you."

John sat in his chair. "What does he want with you?"

Travis lied. "I don't know."

He followed Frank and though he tried, Travis couldn't keep from getting his hopes up at the possibility of getting back to his brother.

After pleasantries and a handshake with Travis, Colonel Wyman motioned for Frank to come over. Leaning close, Frank whispered something to Wyman. The Colonel seemed surprised at the Corporal's hushed words.

Wyman waited for Frank to leave before inviting Travis inside his tent. "I know it has been weeks since we last talked. To say I have been busy would be an understatement but I do have news for you."

Travis felt his heart lighten.

"It is not good news."

Travis tensed. "What is it?"

Wyman removed a piece of paper from his pocket and unfolded it. "This is the response I received from the telegram. *Visited Jeb Bailey's house per your request but found it abandoned.*"

"Abandoned?" Travis rubbed his hands together and swallowed hard. "They are gone?"

"Not necessarily," Wyman said. "Arkansas is a rebel state. We have no guarantee this message is truthful or that they even went to your brother's home."

"I guess that explains why I did not receive a reply from my letter. What about the furlough?"

The Colonel walked behind a small desk at the back of his tent. "We have two problems. If this message is true, you will find an empty house. Where will you look then? How long will it take? The second problem. We are leaving soon."

"Leaving?"

"And you would never make it back in time," Wyman said.

"But..." Travis was at a loss for words. This conversation was not going the way he had imagined, not at all. He fought hard to keep from crying but he could not stop his eyes from watering. He cleared his throat and quickly wiped his eyes to keep tears from falling.

Wyman folded the telegram and placed it back in his pocket. "How old are you, boy?"

Travis wanted to tell the truth but couldn't. He worried if the Colonel found out he lied about his age, he might become upset and stop helping him with his problem. "I'm sixteen," he said.

Wyman nodded. "I was fourteen when I quit school and started work. Life was hard then and I must say, obviously harder now. We must face these hardships together and demonstrate our faith along the way." He pulled his chair away from the desk. "I can see strength in you."

"Yes, sir," Travis said.

The Colonel sat and placed his elbows on the desk. "But you are young." His gaze traveled slowly around the tent, finally settling on the doorway. "Your reinforcement has arrived."

Travis felt something bump his leg and found that Salem had nosed him with his snout.

"This is the dog you told me about?"

"Yes, sir."

"I've heard other men talking about him. He trailed you here?"

"He has a good nose." Travis looked at Salem. "Lie down." The dog obeyed.

Wyman smiled and nodded. "As I was saying, you are young and when young we often make mistakes."

Travis was not sure what the Colonel was trying to say, and he started to think Wyman suspected he had lied about his age.

"Have you told anyone about the conversation we had on the dock?"

Hesitating, Travis considered his answer and decided to tell the truth. "I did, sir. Peter Dugdale had suggested I speak with you and I told him I had done so. I didn't tell anyone else though."

Wyman sat back in his chair. "Peter talked with me today and we discussed you."

"You did?"

"It seems you are a dedicated and trustworthy soldier."

"I try to be."

"Why are you here?" Wyman asked.

"I'm…"

"Are you here simply to find a way back to your brother?" The Colonel stood. "Or, are you here to fight for your country?"

"I'll be honest," Travis said. He pointed to Salem. "I joined to get him. But as the months passed, I grew close to some of the men. They're my friends and I would fight for my country if it helped them survive."

Wyman seemed to weigh Travis's answer and its meaning. "It is obvious you would fight for your brother."

Travis nodded.

"We are all brothers in this war. Our country, our brothers and all of our families need every man available to fight. We leave for battle soon and I can only grant you leave afterwards. There can be no exodus, no matter how small, before then."

"Where are we going?" Travis asked.

"I cannot yet tell you that," Wyman said. "It's not far. We will be joining Sherman and his forces. I know numerous rumors have already started. You have proven yourself trustworthy so do not add to the confusion among the men."

"I can stay quiet," Travis said.

The Colonel walked around the desk and stood in front of him. "It is for the best. They would challenge your knowledge and a few would sentence you with favoritism."

"I understand. You promise I can go back home after this battle?"

"I give you my word. At the very least, you will be furloughed for a length of time."

"Thank you." Travis offered his hand and Wyman shook with him.

The Colonel knelt and rubbed Salem's back. The dog wagged his tail in delight and managed a quick wash of the Colonel's face before Wyman could pull back. The Colonel grabbed Salem's shaggy head in both hands. "Take care of him."

"I will," Travis said.

The Colonel laughed. "I was talking to the dog."

The week before Christmas, all of the troops were ordered to turn in their old cartridge boxes and receive new replacements. The men took this as a sure sign that they would be headed to Vicksburg to take the city.

When a long line of Sherman's steamboats arrived, no doubt was left in anyone's mind. They knew they would be headed to battle soon. Supplies, artillery, and ammunition for the Thirteenth was loaded neatly on a steamer called the John Warner. The Colonel, with upmost efficiency, made sure there was room for everything.

Travis kept his mouth shut as his fellow soldiers told him where they thought they would be going.

Official orders finally arrived, confirming Vicksburg as their destination.

Drills ended and Travis helped load supplies when he was asked, but in his spare time, he played with Salem. The dog made trips throughout the whole camp, visiting tents in the entire regiment. Sometimes, Travis walked behind him, introducing Salem as property of Company H. Everyone welcomed the dog and enjoyed the tricks he had been taught.

Knowing they would be leaving any day, Travis made another attempt to reach his brother.

Father,

I have saved most my pay for months and would like to send you thirty dollars but I haven't received a reply from my last correspondence. Could you write me back to let me know how you and Chet are doing?

Travis Bailey

Travis knew he was holding money out as a reward, but it would be worth it if Jeb took the time to write back. He wished he could have apologized to his brother in the letter, and explain why he had not rushed back to sneak him away from home, but the explanation would have to wait.

With all soldiers aboard the steamers, a signal cannon was fired and one hundred twenty-seven boats left Helena. Most of the troops were excited at the promise of action. The Thirteenth had suffered a hard, but rather boring, stretch of service thus far.

John was giddy with anticipation. Alfred and Arthur were on the boat but Travis had not seen them. Emil swept the hair from his eyes while he talked with George and Peter, and they took turns petting Salem, reassuring him it was safe on the water. The dog paced along the rail, looking back toward Helena. They had camped at the town for six months and Salem was having a hard time saying goodbye.

The steamer churned along in a long line with all the others. That evening, the cannon signaled for everyone to stop for the night. Red and green lanterns were on each steamer, giving a pleasing glow across the water. Some of the men chose to get off the boats and stretch their legs on the bank.

In the distance, cotton fields had been set ablaze. The fire spread to a storehouse with a cotton gin inside and soon became a roaring tempest. Travis wasn't sure if the army had started the fire or if the rebels had done so. Either way, if there had been any supplies inside the building they were gone now.

The following day the fleet headed out and Salem grew happy with his situation once again. Travis and Peter took turns rolling the leather ball, allowing the dog to chase it a short distance which seemed to make him feel even more at home. Salem had developed into a stout, lean animal, but his winter coat made him appear larger than he was.

The John Warner was crowded, which made it hard to get any sleep, and an unusual warm spell in December made it even worse. Troops drew straws to see who would have to go below deck to feed coal into the boilers. The heat coming from the red-hot fires caused the men to be soaked with sweat.

Early Christmas morning, word spread through the boat — the Thirteenth would engage the enemy the next day!

When the steamers stopped, they were at Milliken's Bend in Louisiana. John decided it was time for a party and shouted for everyone to join him.

"Let's celebrate. The Rebels will hear from us tomorrow!"

Men cheered and many of the soldiers followed John, laughing, drinking coffee, and talking. Travis could see worry on a few faces, but for the most part, the soldiers were excited.

Salem must have felt the enthusiasm in the air. He barked and ran circles around the men.

Peter sat cross-legged on top of a large barrel, watching the activity and savoring a steamy cup of coffee. He greeted Travis, with a hearty, "Merry Christmas!"

"Merry Christmas, Peter."

"And there be our other lads." Peter hopped off his perch and called to Emil and Arthur.

They joined Peter and Travis, and were in high spirits, sharing Salem's air of excitement. After a few moments, Peter whispered something in Emil's ear. Emil left right afterwards, but returned minutes later with George, Alfred, and Thomas.

The seven comrades, eight counting Salem, found room near the pilot house on the top deck of the steamboat to sit and stretch out in comfort. They shared stories of past holidays and their families. Travis stayed quiet.

"What about you?" Emil asked.

"Me?" Travis asked.

"Yes. Don't you have family gatherings for Christmas?"

Travis felt uncomfortable. Salem licked his hand and leaned against his knees. Even thinking about the past hurt, but these men had become the only friends he had ever known.

"It has just been me and my brother for several years." He stopped, not really sure how to continue.

Thomas, who had not been present at Travis's home, pressed him. "What about your parenths?"

George shook his head in warning to Thomas.

"Travis, you do not have to talk about that," Peter said.

"It's all right. Most of you know anyway."

"I'm sorry," Emil said. "I should not have started this conversation."

Thomas winced. "I had not thought to pry."

Travis waved away their apologies. "My parents always fought like cats and dogs, mostly about my father's drinking. One morning, my brother and I woke up and our mother was gone. That day, my father loaded up the wagon, and we headed to Salem, Arkansas. His drinking got worse and his fists got harder. So I have no stories to tell of family gatherings."

A somber quiet fell over the friends.

Peter broke the silence. "Until today."

"Yes," said George, "That is correct."

"A story about a band of brothers," Emil said.

There were nods and grins from everyone. Salem sat up and barked once and looked around, causing the whole group to break into laughter.

Travis had not been this happy in a long time.

Alfred's smile dimmed a bit. "One of us *is* missing, though. Lawrence should be here."

"Let us toast to our lost brother," Peter said. He pulled a flask from his jacket. "God with us and a drink, and may we never be poor in friendship."

He opened the container, took a swig, and passed it to George.

The flask made its way around the circle of men until it came to Travis. He took it gingerly, as if he were handling an angry, coiled snake.

He had never tasted whiskey, even though his father's habit had given ample opportunities to do so. As he lifted it close to his nose, the smell brought back countless bad memories.

CHAPTER TWELVE

Travis slowly lowered the bottle. He hated the idea of not toasting with his friends but he could not partake of the very thing that had caused his brother and himself so much pain.

"I can't," he said, still fixated on the container.

Peter reached out his hand, taking the flask. "Everyone has to do their own growing, no matter how long the shadow of their father is."

With his other hand, Peter handed him a cup of coffee. Travis looked gratefully at the tin in his hand and raised it. "To Lawrence and the Thirteenth!"

As the men toasted, Salem stood with pricked ears and his nose pointed at the pilot house. Several figures emerged through the door, Colonel Wyman among them. His presence caused everyone to immediately jump to their feet and snap to attention.

"Take your ease, boys," he said as he walked by. "The infamous Jake Sightsinger has invited everyone to grace his establishment for some Christmas entertainment."

"Well, that sounds like a belly-laugh," Peter said. "What do you think, lads? Shall we?"

The friends walked across the ramp and stepped on Louisiana soil for the first time. Travis threw Salem his ball and the dog followed along, tossing his toy in the air and chasing it as they went.

Once Jake's tent came into view, Travis saw that a crowd had already gathered. Soldiers had separated into groups and each conversation added to the mix of noisy voices.

Near the old tent, the band had joined together and was playing joyfully. A dozen troops were dancing about, laughing at their own silliness.

Tables in front of the tent held a nice spread of salt pork and beans. Jake had temporarily set up his show and had just pulled the flaps open. Burley greeted a line of men who were waiting, and they disappeared inside as he started the tour.

Jake deepened his voice and bellowed, "Come and see what wonders await you inside!"

He slipped on a long overcoat and a tall black hat, smiled and waved at Wyman. "Welcome, welcome! Come in, Colonel. See the show."

Travis's friends headed straight to the food. The men who had arrived with Wyman had paused near the band, but the Colonel stopped to scratch Salem behind the ear, to the dog's obvious pleasure.

"Well, now," he said to Travis. "Let's go see what wonders Jake has put together for us today."

Jake shook hands with the Colonel.

"It is good to see you again, young man," Jake said to Travis. "And Salem, also."

Travis remembered how Salem had acted the last time they visited the show. "Outside," he said to the dog. "Stay."

Salem sat and watched. He dropped his ball and whimpered but stayed put.

"I know you have seen most of this before, Colonel," Jake said. "But we do have a few new additions."

"I did not make any of your shows in Helena," Wyman said. "Is this the same racoon you had at Rolla?"

"Yes, sir, but this calico cat was brought to me before we boarded the steamer. It has a very unusual pattern, don't you think?"

The cat moved back and forth, stropping its face and sides against the cage.

The Colonel stuck his fingers in and rubbed its fur. "It is a friendly soul."

Burley walked past them, leading some men to another part of the tent. Burley smiled. Travis did not. There was still something about the man that bothered him.

Jake, Wyman, and Travis made their way from section to section, admiring the animals.

Jake pointed to a wooden box with a glass front. "This cottonmouth and copperhead were found in Helena."

"I've almost stepped on a few of those," the Colonel said.

Jake tapped on the glass. "They don't move around much in this kind of weather. By the way, I hear there are a number of alligators in this part of the country."

Wyman raised an eyebrow. "Jake…" he warned.

"They would be slow this time of year too."

The Colonel shook his head, but Jake ignored it.

"I don't require a large one, just a foot or so in length."

"Jake, I need you to have all your fingers still attached to your hand."

Someone started whistling a pleasing tune nearby, the notes sliding into one another effortlessly.

Wyman raised a hand to forestall any more argument by Jake. "Who is that?"

"That's our whistling boy," Jake answered. "Come and listen."

The black boy was young, maybe ten years old. He sat on a stool and the purest, clearest of melodies flowed from his pursed lips. He covered complicated tunes with ease and quickly switched to bird calls. It was a talent that Travis had no idea anyone possessed.

When he was finished, the Colonel shook hands with the boy, telling him what a good job he did.

As they left the show tent, Burley was waiting by Salem's side. He stepped into the Colonel's path. "Sir, could I trouble you for but a moment?"

"Yes, Burley?" Wyman asked.

"Tomorrow, while everyone is away for battle, could Salem stay with us and learn some tricks from the regiment dog?"

"From Nep?" The Colonel asked.

"Nep is very smart," Burley said slyly.

"But is he brave?" Wyman asked.

Jake laughed. "Captain Noble won't give him a chance to show his bravery. He wants him removed from service. The Captain is afraid the dog will be killed."

It was apparent this was news to Burley. His eyes widened. "Nep cannot be taken away! I taught him. I trained him. He is the regiment dog, our mascot."

"And he belongs to Noble," Jake said. He gave Burley a stern look. "We will discuss this later."

Wyman looked to Travis. "Where *will* Salem stay tomorrow?"

"I haven't thought about that," he said.

"There will be cannons, gunfire, smoke, and all sorts of things that could scare him away. You wouldn't want to lose him."

"No, I would not."

"The quartermaster will keep him safe and sound," Wyman said with finality, as he headed toward his companions from earlier.

Travis had mixed feeling about Burley, but could not argue with the Colonel's logic.

He looked straight at Jake, making sure to avoid eye contact with Burley. "Can you keep him away from the battle tomorrow?"

"I would be glad to do so," Jake said.

"I am obliged to you," Travis said.

Travis walked over to the big fire ringed by rocks. Long, rough benches had been built to go around it, and he took a seat on one that was unoccupied. Despite his worries, he enjoyed the band playing *Oh Come All Ye Faithful*, and had to smile when he saw a cedar tree decorated with hardtack for ornaments.

He felt something hit his boot and looked to see a ball coated in dog slobber. Salem crouched a foot away, perfectly still, his eyes locked on the ball. "Sorry, boy. I can't throw it right now. I need to think." He kicked it, and Salem snapped it up.

He was not happy about Salem staying with Jake and Burley but there was no better choice. To his surprise, Wyman joined him with two plates of food. He stood and saluted.

"Sit." Travis and Salem both sat, causing the Colonel to chuckle. "Worried about tomorrow?" he asked, as he handed Travis a plate.

Travis answered honestly, "Yes, sir."

"My son is in the Thirteenth."

Travis was surprised and it must have shown.

"Osgood is a good soldier, very dedicated. He's in Company C."

"Is he here?"

"He is visiting on another boat. I will see him tonight." Wyman ate the salt pork and some of the beans, then set the plate down for

Salem. The dog gulped the food, his tail wagging wildly with gratitude.

"I hope they surrender quickly tomorrow," Travis said.

The Colonel smiled his signature wide grin. "Let us pray it is so."

He rose to leave. "I would like for you to stay close to me until this is over. I have not forgotten your furlough or your story. I want to make sure you are fit for travel afterwards."

"Thank you, sir! And I am not afraid to fight, either."

"I'm sure you will have your chance and I am also sure you will change your mind when the time comes. All do, especially the first time." He looked toward the steamers and the slow rolling water. "I will need multiple messengers."

"I can do whatever you need."

"Corporal Frank Whipple will make arrangements," Wyman said. "You do remember him?"

"The man who brought me to your tent, your orderly?"

The Colonel handed Travis his empty plate. "He will come for you. Keep your head down until then."

Travis nodded and watched as Wyman walked away. Travis took a bite of his food, now cold. He did not have the stomach for any more, and Salem was delighted to take care of the rest.

The next day, the boats entered the mouth of the Yazoo river and traveled upstream twelve miles before stopping. Travis took Salem down into the cargo hold to find Jake. He was back in his regular outfit, and looked somehow smaller without the tall black hat and overcoat. He was busy organizing supplies for the coming days.

"I will take good care of him," Jake said when he noticed Travis. He fixed a leather collar around Salem's neck and tied a rope to its metal ring.

"I will be back for him when this is over," Travis said. "Salem will be upset while we are gone. I don't think it would be a good time to try new tricks."

Jake nodded. "You are probably right."

Travis got in line with the Thirteenth and debarked. Everyone stored their muskets in a number of stacks, by leaning them together in a cone shape with the butts on the ground. After the soldiers and supplies were unloaded and assembled, hardtack was placed in their haversacks and then they were ordered to collect their weapons and leave. As the march started, cannons sounded in the distance, echoing along the water, and announcing the attack on Vicksburg.

It was only a short time after leaving when there was a brief fight with a picket line of rebels. Travis was in the back half of the regiment and the skirmish was over by the time his section arrived on scene. They captured some horses and the food the enemy was cooking, which disappeared quickly.

As they continued up the trail through the woods, a Confederate soldier was captured and readily informed them they were within a mile and a half of the rebel's main force. The regiment was ordered to make camp after receiving the news.

The weather had become brisk with cold, and Travis huddled close to one of the fires that dotted the landscape. They ate well but slept very little. Without a tent, Travis shivered. He wished Salem was there to help keep him warm and settle his nerves.

When morning came, they marched early and fought through more guard lines. The forest closed in with undergrowth that slowed their advance to a crawl. Much time was spent cutting briars and vines.

Once again, Travis and those toward the end of the line were lucky. The soldiers in front had cleared a path for them. To make matters worse, it rained as if the heavens had opened up. After a long day, they emerged onto the edges of a narrow field and were immediately fired upon.

Travis ducked behind some brush and fumbled to get his gun to his shoulder, even though he had not seen the enemy that had fired. As he rose up from his cover, men from the Thirteenth returned fire and a few dozen rebels retreated from rifle pits they had dug on the other side of the field. Travis lowered his gun and smiled at how smoothly the battle was going. John had spooked him with all of his campfire war stories.

Travis spotted Emil moving past him. "This isn't so bad."

"Not bad at all, except for the rain," Emil said. "I guess they know we are itching for a fight."

George walked by. "Bivouac here for the night. No dog tents." He repeated his message as he made his way through the ranks of the Thirteenth.

Thomas and Arthur sat on the ground. Travis leaned back against a tree and laid his gun across his lap.

Emil pulled his coat tight around his neck. "This is a terrible place to camp."

"No fire tonight either," Thomas said.

"No fire?" Arthur asked, the whites of his eyes made them seem to bulge. "Are you sure? We need a campfire. It will get cold after this rain moves through."

"We were told to go without," Thomas said.

George walked back through and Arthur stopped him. "George, why no fires tonight?"

"Sorry, Arthur," George said. "Orders. They say we are too close to enemy lines. Rebel sharpshooters have already picked off a few."

"Our regiment?" Travis asked.

"Not ours," George said. "Keep your heads down tomorrow, boys. We are crossing Chickasaw Bayou."

Arthur pointed to George's hat. "You need to be careful then. Your head sticks up so high, it would be an easy target."

George chuckled as he left. Arthur stretched back onto the ground and put an arm over a rotting log. He laid his head in the crook of his arm. "I'm going to sleep. Hey, brothers, get next to me so we can stay warm."

Thomas moved beside him. "That's a good idea. It's going to be a cold night."

"I'm already cold," Emil said as he joined them.

Travis settled against the log, crossing his arms over his chest and tucking his hands in his armpits to keep them warm. He pulled some hardtack out of his haversack, reluctantly snapped off a piece with his teeth, and ate it.

Alfred limped up to them. "Do you have room for one more?"

"Sure," Emil said. "What happened to you?"

"Twisted my ankle," he said as he reclined. "I got tangled in some vines."

"You might go to the doctorths tent," Thomas said.

"I did." He laughed. "Plummer was covered up with sick men."

"Sick?" Travis asked.

"Deadbeats and hospital rats," Alfred said. "Fakers. Cowards."

Thomas shifted against the log. "What waths Plummer doing with them?"

Alfred said, with obvious relish, "He was giving them castor oil and turpentine! They were gagging and coughing. Some of the men in the back of the line decided they weren't sick after all."

Travis joined the laughter that followed, and they all felt lighter of heart.

"That will teach them a lesson," Emil chuckled.

"Let's get some rest," Arthur said. "I had no sleep last night."

Emil held a finger to his lips and smiled. The conversation grew quiet. One by one they nodded off, but Travis was last. Wyman's orderly, Whipple, had not come to get him. He wondered if it had just been something the Colonel said to help comfort his nerves. Wyman had told him to keep his head down, but that had not been an issue at all. The sound of gunfire during the day had put him on edge but he never felt he was in any danger. All he wanted was to get this over and take his leave. It was for Chet he worried most.

CHAPTER THIRTEEN

December 28, 1862

They were woken early, but ordered to hold their positions and wait. George came through the trees followed closely by another soldier, and they headed for Travis. As they approached, he realized it was the corporal, Wyman's orderly.

Emil said, "Are you in trouble?"

Travis shook his head and saluted as the corporal walked up to him. "Are you here for me, sir?"

The corporal returned the salute and said, "The Colonel wants to speak with you."

"Colonel Wyman?" Arthur asked incredulously. "What have you done, Travis?"

"I haven't done anything."

"He just wants to speak with him," Corporal Whipple said. "Follow me."

Alfred shifted his weight off his sore ankle. "Hope we will see you again."

Thomas snickered. "Don't get court marthaled."

Arthur laughed and elbowed Emil. "Should we go and plead for mercy on his behalf?"

Travis caught up with Whipple and followed him through the woods, passing hundreds of men, all waiting for orders.

When they finally reached the Colonel, he was standing by his horse. In his hand was a field glass. The brass on the scope was tarnished in places. His gaze was fixed on a clearing in the woods ahead.

Wyman noticed him and smiled. "I see Corporal Whipple found you alive and well."

"Yes, sir."

"Fall in behind him and do as he says."

"Yes, sir." Travis went and stood by the corporal.

Wyman checked his pocket watch and then motioned a man over. He gave an order to him and the man saluted and rushed away. Moments later a line of ten soldiers marched by with the man in front carrying the color flag of the Thirteenth, and the troop behind him held the state flag. Travis did not recognize the first fellow but he thought he might know the soldier behind him.

Corporal Frank noticed Travis staring. "Do you know the Color Sergeant?"

"I have seen him around camp. He's called Jesse, and he is in our company, right?"

"Yes, but to you he is called Color Sergeant Pierce. Not Jesse," Frank said.

"Why?"

"Both flag bearers have the same given name of Jesse." He chuckled. "Even informally we call them by their last names, Betts and Pierce. Color Corporal Betts is Company I, and Pierce you already know."

While they waited, Travis spotted a tent behind them, mostly hidden by trees. Doctor Plummer stood by the door with some other surgeons and assistants. The sight of medical staff waiting for wounded troops made Travis nervous. He turned away.

They watched the soldiers organize and slowly advance. The men moved forward, and Whipple got behind them, beckoning Travis to follow.

Soon, they were at the edge of the woods. Just beyond them was Chickasaw Bayou, a bare stretch of land with swampy water along its center. Both banks were gently sloped toward the middle but berms and rifle pits had been dug everywhere. The enemy had cut and thrown saplings, thorn trees, and briars into a long heap in an attempt to hinder their crossing.

"Stay with me," the corporal said. "The Colonel will signal if he needs us, so pay attention."

Before any additional orders could be given, rebel sharpshooters cut loose, attempting to pick off those who had stepped too close to the bayou.

Travis could see Wyman on the ground peering over a berm with his field glasses. Out of the corner of his eye, he also saw soldiers backing away from the clearing. They glanced around and continued a nervous, slow motion retreat.

"Hold your ground!" someone shouted.

A concerned voice came from somewhere in the brush. "The rebels are waiting on us. We can't go out there!"

Dread crept over Travis as the reality of crossing the clearing filled his mind. He gasped at a sudden pressure on the back of his leg. Fear propelled him several paces, and then he stumbled and fell. In an instant his face was covered in wetness, and Travis struggled to fend off an excited wiggling, whining, burr-covered dog.

"Salem, sit!"

Salem sat, his tail wagging in happiness. He seemed especially pleased with himself at having won the game of hide and seek.

Travis climbed to his feet. He could hardly believe the dog had trailed him that far, nearly four miles. "What are you doing here?"

Salem cocked his head as dogs do when perplexed. He whined. The leather collar was still around his neck with a short length of chewed rope attached. It wasn't long enough to secure him to anything, and while Travis looked around for another option the rebel guns fired into the clearing again.

Travis grabbed for the dog but it was too late. Salem was off in a heartbeat, searching for the source of the noise. He made a beeline for the bayou, the sharp reports of the guns attracting him like a bug to a glowing lantern.

"Get back here!" Travis yelled and started after him.

"Private Bailey, halt!" Whipple commanded. The corporal grabbed the collar of Travis's coat and yanked him back.

Salem burst from the woods and ran along the sandy ground. He slid to a stop, waited and listened. A mix of excited voices came from the waiting regiment. A hundred yards down the clearing, a bullet struck the ground, tossing dirt into the air. Salem dashed toward it.

As he ran in front of the Thirteenth, a cheer rose among the men. The dog pounced on the spot where the round had disappeared. While he smelled of the hole, another bullet hit the ground a few feet away. Without hesitating, Salem pounced again. Soldiers cheered and laughed.

The dog ran the length of the bayou, barking and snapping at the whizzing sound of bullets. Shouts and calls from Union soldiers followed him like a wave.

A voice rose from the ranks, "Look at that, the dog is not getting hit! He is fearless!"

"That's Dog Salem! Look at him go!!" another shouted. It sounded very much like Peter's voice.

Wyman looked back, smiled at Travis and nodded. He raised his hand and motioned at the Corporal.

"When the cannon fires, we will charge," Whipple said quietly. "The color guard will lead us to victory and, by the looks of it, Salem will too."

Travis swallowed down the hard lump of fear in his throat. "Yes, sir."

A thunderous boom made Travis jump. Wyman lowered his arm and the Thirteenth dashed into the open with the flag bearers leading the way. Drummer boys tapped signals on their drums and followed close behind the color guard.

The Colonel stepped into the bayou while keeping his gaze on the opposite side. Sharpshooters opened up once more, but this time their numbers seemed to have doubled.

The Thirteenth struggled with the obstructions the rebels had laid out. Briars and thorns snagged their clothing and skin, while wet sand sucked at their boots. Salem dashed between soldiers, barking, snapping at the air, and yipping with all his might. Travis stumbled while trying to keep up with the corporal and lost track of Salem in the process.

The air was alive with the angry buzzing of flying lead. Two men near him went down with wounds, one to the arm and the other in the shoulder. The soldier with the shoulder wound rolled across the sand, screaming in pain.

Travis closed the distance between him and Whipple. He tried to keep his focus on Wyman, just as he had been told, but the wounded men they left behind kept drawing his attention. He was not only worried about their condition, but also his safety. The war had just become more real to him than it had ever been before. He remembered the Colonel telling him that he would change his mind about fighting. Wyman's prediction had come to be.

Whipple yanked on his jacket and shouted in his ear, "The Colonel needs us."

Travis tore his gaze away from the squirming soldiers on the ground and turned to follow, but Whipple had outpaced him and was by the colonel's side. Seconds later, he was sprinting past Travis, shouting the Colonel's orders as he went. His shouts reached the drummers and buglers and the signal was given to take cover.

"Down!" Wyman bellowed.

Men scrambled for positions behind earth mounds and in empty rifle pits, anything that would shield them from the sharpshooters. Travis froze with indecision, and suddenly the corporal grabbed him and pulled him down.

After a few tense moments, the shooting stopped. Travis was involuntarily shaking. He barely had the presence of mind to look around.

They were behind a berm that stretched the length of the hill. The corporal had flipped over onto his back and was watching the Colonel several yards away. To the right of Travis was a line of men he did not recognize but on the other side of Whipple was someone he knew well.

"Emil, are you, all right?" Travis had barely managed to get the words out.

Emil's round face was pale, and reflected the fear that Travis knew was on his own face. His friend had lost his hat in the charge and his hair had escaped, making him look like a wildman. "Travis! I'm fine. Yes, yes, I am fine. You?"

"I'm good."

"Hush," Whipple ordered.

The Colonel had not taken cover and was peering through his field glasses at the bluffs across the bayou.

Whipple turned his body and rose to a crouch. "Colonel?"

"I am trying to locate their positions," Wyman answered.

Upon hearing his words, a few troops peaked over the top of the trench, doing their best to help find the sharpshooters.

"They stopped firing," Emil said to Travis. He stood and held his hand above his eyes to shield the sun as he looked for the rebels.

A single shot sounded and Emil collapsed, grabbing a bloody wound in his thigh. "They got me!"

Travis forgot his fear of the enemy and climbed over Whipple to help apply pressure to Emil's leg.

"Stay down!" Wyman shouted to the troops. "They will kill you." He shook his field glasses. "And you can't see them."

"Get down, Colonel," Emil called through gritted teeth.

"It is my duty to stand and see," Wyman said. "It is your duty to follow orders."

A loud pop came from the far bank. The Colonel clutched his chest and looked down at his hand.

CHAPTER FOURTEEN

Wyman wilted to the ground and lay flat on his back.

"Help him!" Emil shouted, pushing Travis in Wyman's direction. "I will be alright. Go help the Colonel."

Corporal Whipple crawled to the Colonel amidst the volley of shots being taken at the invisible enemy. He pushed back several soldiers that were hovering over him, and yanked the colonel's jacket and shirt open. Travis joined him. There was panic in Whipple's eyes, but Wyman showed no alarm at all.

"Leave me," he ordered. "Tend to the boy."

Another soldier low-crawled to Wyman's side. Whipple grabbed the man by the arm. "Captain Dement, what should we do?"

The Captain pulled his arm back, and examined the Colonel's chest. "I believe the bullet has passed through. This may not be a dangerous wound."

Wyman smiled warmly. "Oh, yes. It is all over. One side of me is nearly paralyzed already."

Travis bolted upright. "No, Colonel. Hang on."

The captain tried to grab Travis. "Get down! Are you trying to get shot?!"

Travis shook off his hand, dropped his gun to make himself lighter, and ran at top speed back toward the woods.

Upon seeing a fresh target, the rebel guns opened up, sending bullets into the dirt all around him. An answering salvo helped cover his retreat. Out of nowhere, Salem joined the mad-dash, nearly tripping Travis. When they reached the woods, the firing stopped but

Travis continued running with all his might until he reached the surgeon's tent.

"The Colonel's hurt!" Travis shouted.

Salem barked and bounced straight up in the air over and over.

Doctors were already working on a soldier who had been wounded on another part of the battlefield. An assistant held a face cone and sponge in one hand and chloroform in the other. They all glanced at Travis and then went back to their patient.

"It's Colonel Wyman." Travis said.

Salem continued his bouncing and barking.

One of the doctors pointed with a bloody hand. "Get that dog out of here!"

Travis grabbed Salem's collar and tried to calm him down. While he was doing this, Doctor Plummer entered the doorway of the tent.

"What did you say?"

"Colonel Wyman has been shot."

Plummer disappeared around the corner, and only seconds passed before he appeared again on horseback. "Show me where." He reached down and took Travis by the arm, pulling him into the saddle behind him.

"That way." Travis pointed and then held on tight as Plummer's horse took off.

Someone shouted from inside the tent. "Get back here!"

Salem ran alongside the horse and when they entered the clearing, the sharpshooters did their best to bring them down. Salem peeled off, chasing bullet strikes and yipping as he went. The Thirteenth returned fire, silencing the rebels.

"Which way?" Plummer asked again.

"Over there, behind the mound."

The Doctor turned his horse and slid to a stop next to Wyman. Plummer was on the ground before the horse had come to a halt. Travis was quickly at his side.

"What can we do?" Whipple asked.

"Get the stretcher," he said, and pointed to the horse.

Whipple scrambled to get it loose and lay it next to the Colonel. Plummer quickly examined the ugly wound. When he was finished, they rolled the Colonel onto his side and shoved the stretcher under him. Once they laid him flat and had him centered, Plummer and the corporal grabbed the handles and started away.

The doctor shouted over his shoulder at Travis, "Bring the other wounded soldier." To the captain, he ordered, "Go find the Colonel's son, Osgood."

Travis pulled Emil to his feet and held him upright while they hobbled toward the woods. Occasional shots were heard, but they were a good distance away. That did not stop Travis from feeling like his back was an invitation for the next bullet.

Close to the tree line, an assistant surgeon on horseback stopped Plummer and gave him a message from the ranking doctor at the tent. Plummer and Whipple lowered Wyman to the ground, and the doctor yanked the paper and a pencil from the messenger, read it, and then wrote something in response.

"Go! We will be there shortly."

The assistant surgeon kicked his horse into a sprint back toward camp. The Colonel was lifted once again and they weaved their way around pits and tangles of brush left by the enemy.

Salem passed Emil and Travis at a trot, stopping every now and then to make sure they were still following. The rebels showed surprising restraint and allowed them passage off the bayou before sporadic fire resumed.

Upon reaching the tent, Wyman was placed on a table. Plummer had a short bout of tense words with his superior but they quickly postponed the argument in order to care for the Colonel. Travis and an assistant helped Emil onto his own table and cinched a leather strap on his leg above the wound.

Wyman coughed and asked for his son.

"He is on his way," Plummer said.

Confederate artillery exploded somewhere outside. Shells whistled overhead and worried looks were exchanged between the doctors.

The Colonel growled with anger, voicing his disgust with the Rebel's tactics. In his next breath, he thanked those around him for their efforts and smiled.

Whipple glanced outside. "I hear a running horse. Your son must be here."

"My boy?" The Colonel asked.

"Yes, sir."

Osgood entered in a rush, stopping only when he had reached his father's side. He took Wyman's hand in his own. Both of their faces were streaked with tears.

Osgood's body was racked with silent sobs while listening to the Colonel exclaim his love for God, his son, and country. As enemy shells exploded above the tall timber around them, John Wyman found his peace and passed into the beyond.

The tent was quiet for a few moments. Everyone stood with blank stares, finding it hard to believe that Wyman was gone. Travis wiped his eyes and noticed Emil doing the same. Both of them remained silent while Colonel Wyman's body was covered, and Corporal Whipple and an assistant carried him from the tent. Osgood followed, crying as he walked.

Only when they were far from earshot did Travis finally speak quietly to Emil.

"Are you, all right?"

Emil pulled at the leather strap on his leg. "It hurts."

Plummer walked over. He swallowed hard, then quickly regained his professional exterior. "Here, let us fix this boy's leg."

The surgeons instructed Emil to lay flat. "You and the dog need to leave," one of them said to Travis.

"Will he be okay?" Travis asked.

"He will be fine," the surgeon said.

As Travis stepped out of the tent, Emil called after him. "Was it my fault? Travis, was it my fault?"

"No, Emil," he said. "This war is to blame, no one or nothing more."

After leaving the tent, he stopped and tried to clear his mind of the horror he had just witnessed. The men of the Thirteenth would be crushed at the news. Travis did not want to be the one to tell them but he could not avoid the battlefield. Doing so would result in him being labeled a coward or deserter. He knelt and hugged Salem. The dog licked at his ear. "I can't believe he's gone. It happened so fast." Travis finally stood and rubbed Salem's head. He sighed. "Let's go find my gun and help our friends."

Just before reaching the bayou, Travis met the Thirteenth. They were leaving the battlefield and skirting the edge of the woods. He spotted Thomas and waved him over.

"What about Emil?" Thomas asked.

Travis was surprised. "You heard already?"

Thomas nodded.

"The doctors said he's going to be all right."

"Great newths, then. George and Peter have your gun." Thomas looked to the side. "Here they come. We are being moved to another part of the bayou."

Peter handed Travis his musket and asked about Emil, prompting Travis to repeat what he had just told Thomas.

The frown George was wearing turned into a brief smile at the news. "Good. Will he be out of it for long?"

"I'm not sure."

Peter rubbed Salem's ear. "Alfred found him a bullet too, just before they pulled us off the field. He will be fine though. It just grazed him."

"I'm glad both of them will heal but..." Travis shuffled his feet. "Did you hear about the Colonel?"

"A sergeant told me he wasn't hurt bad," Peter said.

George noticed Travis's expression. "Was that not the truth?"

Travis shook his head slowly. "He didn't make it."

Peter paused, rubbed his face, and turned away.

"Are you sure?" George asked.

"I was there," Travis said. "I wish I had not been, but I was."

Thomas placed a hand on his shoulder for a moment.

George's tall frame seemed to shrink. He motioned for them to follow, and they rejoined the Thirteenth. The terrible news spread quickly and by the time they had marched to the new location on the battlefield, every soldier knew the fate of Colonel Wyman.

The morale of the troops was mixed, some were depressed, others were angered and ready for revenge.

Toward the end of the day, they were ordered to advance into the bayou again. As they neared a creek with tall banks, the attack was called off due to waning daylight. The Thirteenth fell back to the wood line and retired for the night.

George, Thomas, Peter, and Travis laid in a row. Each of them expressed their dismay at how the day had played out. Salem curled up between Travis and Peter and was asleep in a matter of minutes.

"He is tuckered out," Peter said.

Travis ran his hand along the dog's back. "I can't believe he made it here. I guess he didn't like being in the show tent."

"Most dogs run for the hills when they hear gunfire," George said. "But not this one."

Thomas added. "Did you hear how loud everyone waths cheering him on? He ran all the way down the bayou, not only in front of our regiment."

"It lifted the spirit for sure," Peter said. "I only wish the rest of the day could have felt the same."

Travis stopped petting Salem. "Should I chain him in the morning, to keep him off the field?"

"Well, lad," Peter said, "after today, our boys are gonna need all the inspiration they can find."

"I suppose you're right."

Alfred joined them and pointed to a small bandage on his arm. "They got me fixed up. I'm cleared for the battle tomorrow."

"What about Emil?" George asked. "How is he?"

"I didn't hear them say but I do not think he will be cleared for a while."

"We are glad to have you back," Thomas said.

The cold air nipped at Travis's face. He pulled his coat up to cover his head. "Let's all be careful tomorrow."

"Agreed," Alfred said. "I'm beat. Let's get some rest."

Travis curled around Salem and tried to sleep but his mind kept replaying the Colonel's death. It happened so fast. There was nothing he could have done, nobody could have.

The conversation with Wyman about the furlough was still fresh in his mind. The thought of starting that over from scratch was overwhelming. He was not even sure who would replace the Colonel and Travis felt guilt for worrying about a furlough when Wyman would never get to go home. While he milled these thoughts around, he finally drifted off and got a few hours of rest.

CHAPTER FIFTEEN

December 29, 1862

The Thirteenth stood in formation, waiting for the signal to charge. The wide clearing ahead of them had no cover to speak of. A dirty swath of water snaked down the middle of the bayou, and Travis was not sure how they could traverse the steep banks without getting shot. On the far side, a long stretch of breastworks of piled dirt, rocks and logs nearly as high as a man's shoulder had been built by the rebels. In the distance, a tall hill with rocky bluffs overlooked the bayou. It was too far for Travis to see any confederates but he knew they were there, waiting.

Salem weaved his way through the troop's legs, getting pets from nervous soldiers. The dog did not seem to sense any danger at all. He was happy to visit his friends and just as pleased to chase rebel bullets.

Peter nudged Travis. "Have you seen Arthur?"

Travis shook his head.

"The crathzy fool went to the front," Thomas said.

George grunted. "He's mad as all get out about Wyman, just like the rest of us. Today's charge will be like none other."

"What about Alfred?" Peter asked.

"Toward the back," Thomas answered.

Moments later, the signal came and a sea of angry men charged into the open. Travis and those around him came to a tangle of saplings the rebels had laid out. A few troops got their feet wedged in the crisscross of wood limbs and went down. The soldiers behind them had to be careful not to trample their own men.

Up ahead, Travis noticed the two color bearers leading the Thirteenth. Jesse Betts was in front and Jesse Peirce directly behind him. The flags of other regiments were waving nearby, leading their own men on the field, but the Thirteenth hit the steep bank of the bayou first.

Down in the water they plunged to the point that only the flags could be seen sticking above the bank. Peirce was first to begin climbing the other side, digging into the loose dirt with his left hand and gripping the flag with his other.

A loud boom sounded, and seconds later an artillery shell struck far away from the charge, nowhere near the Thirteenth. "They're finding their distance!" George yelled. "Move faster!"

Salem barked and ran by Travis, weaving effortlessly through the piles of thorn trees. The agile dog reached the drop off in a matter of seconds, looked back, and barked over and over as if urging them to hurry.

Beyond Salem, Travis could see Jesse Pierce. He struggled to the top of the opposite bank and reached down to help his comrade. Betts handed him the national color flag to free both of his hands for climbing. Pierce waved both flags and yelled for the Thirteenth to avenge Wyman. A shell blasted into the dirt near his feet and sent him and the flags flying.

George descended into the watery bayou. Peter and Travis followed, slipping and sliding. Thomas was making his own progress twenty yards away.

George crossed, water up to his chest, holding the short Irishman by the collar to keep him from going under. Travis plunged in and lifted his gun high to keep it from being soaked. He sank to his knees in the morass of dead leaves and muck under the water. The thickness of it made progress slow, making his heart race even faster as he churned his legs. Terrible odors were release from the bottom layer, and Travis struggled not to gag. Finally, he made it across.

A cannonball splashed into the mire and its momentum ramped it up the side of the bank. Travis made it to the top in time to look back and see Salem chasing the iron ball as it rolled and bounced. A hundred yards away, mounted officers crossed the bayou, shouting orders.

"Here!" George yelled. He was standing on the other side of the berm of dirt the enemy had built and was helping men over, easily pulling them to his side.

Rebels fired muskets from rifle pits and the Thirteenth reorganized and fired a volley, killing three of their soldiers as they retreated.

At the next order to fire, Travis raised his gun but his view was blocked by his own men.

Peter tried to shoot but his musket misfired. He swore in his native tongue as he replaced the cap quickly and tried again. This time the gun went off, sending a plume of smoke billowing out. All along the bayou, confederates retreated out of their rifle pits and ran for the big hill.

"Get them!" a soldier shouted.

The Thirteenth led the charge, pushing through gunfire of every sort. A soldier running next to Travis fell. Looking back, he saw a hole had been torn in the man's neck. Travis ran harder, as if putting distance between him and the poor soldier would make the tragedy go away.

Peter stopped, shouldered his weapon and tried to find a target. "There's nothing to aim at!"

The rebels had taken cover high on the hill, all around and above the bluffs. They were hidden well and only puffs of smoke hinted at their locations. The boom of cannons from both sides filled the bayou. The ground around the Thirteenth was pounded into an earthy pulp with cannon shot. Shouts and cries from wounded men filled the air. Bugles and drums sounded in the distance and troops continued to yell from one to the other. The press forward became chaotic.

Arthur ran past Travis screaming, "Take the hill!" He looked back with wild animal-like eyes, a feral snarl coming from his lips. "Tell 'em Wyman sent us!"

They fired toward the bluffs and kept moving. Travis fired but kept running. He used one hand to fumble his cartridge box open. When he finally got his load out, he had to stop long enough to finish the process. All around him men were running, firing, stopping and then frantically reloading.

While he was ramming the ball down the barrel, a shell exploded nearby, the concussion knocking Travis down. Two soldiers tumbled opposite directions. One man's body was utterly destroyed. The other soldier rose to his feet, leaving one of his arms on the ground. Before Travis could recover enough to offer aide, the soldier quickly wrapped his tattered jacket around his bloody elbow stump, picked up his gun with his good hand, and continued the charge.

Shaken, and slightly deaf, Travis picked up his gun and finished loading. By the time he caught up with Peter and George, his hearing was almost normal. They neared the bluffs, and the artillery and musket fire from the rebels increased dramatically.

When Travis was younger, he and his brother had accidently disturbed a hornet's nest. The swarm of angry wasps surrounded them and rained down stings from all angles before they could get away. This battlefield was worse, much worse. Soldiers of the Thirteenth were falling all around from a torrent of buzzing bullets.

When they arrived at the base of the hill, everyone saw that the top of the bluff had been fortified with timbers, rocks, and dirt. It became clear there would be no way to take the rebel's position. Officers ordered a retreat.

Arthur screamed. "No! No retreat."

George turned back and grabbed Travis by the coat, pulling him along. "Get your legs under you and get moving!"

Cannonballs screeched down from two different directions and turned the battlefield into a devastating scene of carnage. Travis sprinted back across the opening with several men, his heart racing. The troops scattered in a very unorganized retreat but George kept them on a straight line back toward the safety of the woods.

A hundred yards from the berm of dirt, Travis tripped over a dead soldier and slid through a pool of blood and body parts. George yanked him up and they climbed the dirt breastwork and then tumbled down the steep bank. He flipped head over heels until he landed in the water and came up, spitting and coughing. Looking down the muddy bayou, he saw a flurry of men churning the water as they fought their way across and scrambled up the other side.

After reaching the top, Travis's exhausted legs gave way. He went down to his knees and rested his head on the ground, gasping. Other men who had fallen were crawling on all fours.

His lungs burned but he forced himself to make it across to the cover of the trees. When the Thirteenth reached the woods they were a heaving mess, covered in sweat, blood, and filth. Younger soldiers like Travis fell to the ground and vomited where they lay.

Travis shook all over and felt his legs would never be sturdy again.

Peter reached his side, worry on his face. "Lad, are ye hurt? There's blood all over."

"I'm fine," he said. "I fell... I fell in... It's not mine."

Peter eased himself to the ground, holding his back and wincing.

"Are you hit?" Travis asked.

"Pulled something."

George leaned against a tree and wiped blood from his face. "We made it all the way to the bluffs for nothing. Absolutely for nothing."

John stumbled toward them and collapsed face down on the ground nearby. He turned his head toward the side and stared with vacant eyes. Travis had not seen him in days and he could not help but wonder if the man was happy now. He had gotten the action he had been hoping for.

George spoke to John but he did not look up, and simply waved his hand, as if he were swatting George's words away.

A minute later, Arthur strolled out of the bayou with his shoulders back and chest out. Looking over his shoulder at the battlefield, he shouted, "Shoot me! Shoot me in the back, you cowards. I dare you."

"Arthur," George said. "Did you see where Thomas went?"

Arthur shook his head. "No, but there's a bunch of us still out there." He threw his musket down. "There's a bunch of us gone forever." His eyes narrowed with anger and he turned away. "I think they got our flag, too."

"I did not see any of the color guards carrying it on the retreat," George said.

"I saw one of them go down with it," Travis said. "One of the men, Jesse Pierce, I think. What about, Salem? Did anybody see him?"

George sat next to Peter. "I saw him chasing a cannonball during our charge."

"Me, too," Peter said. "He will show up. Salem is faster than any rebel bullet."

Travis tried not to worry, but there it was, right along with the worry for their missing friends.

"I say, laddies," Peter said. "Did you see the fellow with one arm?"

The memory was vivid for Travis. "I saw that. The one who kept charging, right?"

"That's the one," Peter said.

"I know him," George said. "Captain Richard Smith. I think he's in Company F. He is a tough man, no doubt."

The conversation continued but Travis stopped paying attention. His mind was occupied with worry for Salem.

Clouds moved in and provided a gloomy atmosphere, more than appropriate for a field of slaughter.

Walking wounded formed a line at the surgeon's tent, and it was one of the most pitiful sights Travis had ever witnessed. His brothers in war were battered, bruised, bloody and defeated.

Another tent was set up nearby and quickly nicknamed The Dead House. Those who died on the doctor's table were put there along with the amputated arms and legs. When the flap was pulled back to add another unfortunate soldier, the sight was garish for those who dared to look.

As the sun began to sink behind the trees, it grew quiet except for miserable moans from the doctor's tent. Travis, Peter, and George sat side by side, leaning against a log. They did not speak. Dozens of troops were within sight, all doing the same thing, staring blankly at nothing. Far in the distance, toward the bayou, came a long wail. Travis felt the hair raise up on the back of his neck.

A lonely, pitiful voice called for help.

"Listen," Travis said. "Did you hear that?"

CHAPTER SIXTEEN

George nodded. "I hear it." He leaned into his hands, covering his face. Another cry came from the battlefield and moments later more wounded soldiers were begging for help.

Travis stood and stared in the direction of the voices. "They're calling for us. What if one of them is Thomas?"

"We cannot go," Peter said. "They're too far away and the rebels will be scouring the battlefield by now. We're sure to get captured or shot."

"But we can't leave them," Travis pleaded. "What if that were you!"

George drug his fingers down his face. "The rebels take the wounded who look well enough to live. The others are left to die. Nothing we can do."

The thought of the suffering soldiers weighed heavily in Travis's mind. He imagined Salem lying in the bayou, hurt and whimpering. "Where do they take the wounded men?"

"To a prison camp," Peter said. "But they would be better off dying on the field."

When darkness came, cold rain began to fall. The splattering drops drowned out the faint cries from the battlefield. When orders came to relocate, the Thirteenth reluctantly prepared to leave, but none were more hesitant than Travis. There had still been no sign of

Salem, even though he had asked dozens of soldiers if they had seen him.

He lagged behind, staying out of the glow from the lanterns while trying to decide what to do. He could not leave Salem.

As the Thirteenth moved out, the wounded were being loaded on wagons and there were sharp cries of pain piercing the night.

Shuffling feet squished on the wet ground as soldiers walked by. The rain had slackened to a heavy drizzle but big drops continued to fall from the tall trees.

A wet hand came through the darkness and grabbed him. Travis yelped and jerked free.

"Hush. It's me," Peter said, his accent was unmistakable.

Travis let out a heavy breath. "I thought you were a rebel spy."

"What are you doing back here?" Peter asked.

Travis did not answer.

Peter sighed. "It's Salem you're waitin' on. No one wants to leave him, but we've orders to move away from the bayou."

"Salem is one of us," Travis said defiantly.

"We are not marching out," Peter explained patiently, "we are just relocating. If Salem trailed us from the boat to here, he will have no trouble finding us a few hundred yards into the woods."

"I thought we were going all the way to the river."

"No. Just movin' a bit over."

Travis shook rain off his coat. "But what if he's hurt?"

"We cannot go out there," Peter said. "Wait till tomorrow. There will be a truce flag at some point."

"Can we go then?"

"Not us. The ambulance corps will collect the dead and wounded, but you can tell them to look for Salem. Hopefully they will find Thomas, too."

Travis finally caved in. The heavy clouds blocked any light from the moon, making it nearly pitch black. Some dim lanterns bobbed ahead, signaling the path the Thirteenth was taking. Peter walked toward them.

Travis noticed there were still lamps at the surgeon's tent. "I'll catch up with you," he said. "I'm going ask for an update on Emil."

Peter chuckled wearily. "If he is still in there, tell him to get up and cook me some supper."

As Travis got close to the lanterns, he found assistants pulling stakes and untying ropes.

"Are the wounded all gone?"

One young man with a bandaged head greeted Travis. "Charles Thompson."

Shaking with him, he said, "Travis Bailey."

"I did not catch your question," Charles said, pointing to the bandage covering his forehead and ears. The left side had a large bloody area.

"Where are the wounded?" he repeated.

"They were taken to the hospital tent. It's about a mile and a half from here."

"Thanks," Travis said.

Two men were arguing over by a wagon that was being loaded with crates and canvases. One of them was pointing a finger at the other's chest. In the dimness, Travis thought it was Peter. He edged closer. The man turned out to be Doctor Plummer. Travis did not know the other fellow.

"I saw it," the stranger said.

"I will not give you permission," Plummer stated firmly.

"But that was our flag! I saw it on the retreat."

The doctor shook his head. "If you get shot or captured, it will come back on me."

"I will not be captured," the man said.

"No," Plummer repeated.

"I could bring back any wounded I happen to find. Our lieutenants are missing."

The doctor hesitated, then shook his head. "You cannot carry a man by yourself."

Realization hit Travis. This man wanted to return to the battlefield to look for the flag and lost soldiers. Travis could not pass up what fate had so neatly laid in his lap, no matter the risk.

"I'll help," Travis interrupted. "I will go with him."

Plummer looked startled. "You?"

Travis nodded. "We are less likely to be captured if we are watching out for each other."

The frustrated doctor finally threw up his hands. "If you two get hurt or captured, I will swear I had no part in this cockeyed plan."

The man looked at Travis as if sizing him up. He seemed satisfied. "Let us go find the flag."

"Wait." Plummer turned to the wagon. "Take a stretcher."

They walked quickly, Travis following with the stretcher, and the man leading the way with a small lantern. "My name is Jack Kenyon, Company K."

"Travis Bailey, Company H."

"Hang onto my jacket, Travis. We cannot get separated. It's darker than the devil's eye out here."

When they reached the edge of the woods, Jack stopped and shielded the lantern with his coat. Travis stepped alongside and stared out toward the battlefield. He might as well have had a blanket over his head. The heavy clouds and drizzling rain killed all the moonlight.

After a few moments, Jack leaned over and whispered, "I don't see any lanterns out there, do you?"

"No," Travis said quietly. "It is pitch black."

"I'm going to put this light out, just in case they are watching," Jack said. "We can't walk, or we will trip every other step."

"Then what are we going to do?" Travis asked.

"We have to crawl for now. Watch out for your eyes, a stick or limb can jab them."

Jack got down on all fours and started across. Travis held onto his boot with one hand and pulled the stretcher along with the other. It was awkward and he had to tap Jack on the leg occasionally, signaling for him to slow down.

They had crawled for half an hour when Jack stopped. He twisted around and whispered, "We have to go down field. The water is shallow there."

Another half hour passed before they entered the water. It was not deep but both of them were soaked after wading through it. Travis lost his breath in the frigid bayou and was glad when they made it to the other side. The drizzle stopped and the clouds thinned, allowing a sliver of moonlight to find its way down. Cold mud coated their hands, knees, and feet, draining all the warmth from their extremities.

Their progress slowed to a snail's pace and Travis lost all sense of time. He thought they might have been traveling about two hours but he could not be sure. Jack stopped frequently and each time he did, Travis listened carefully for Salem.

Jack froze. "It's a body," he whispered. "Let's go around."

It was then that Travis wondered if the ground was wet with rainfall or blood. They altered their course a dozen times when the dead blocked their path.

Travis tapped Jack on the leg and whispered, "Can we stand up for a minute? My knees are killing me."

He felt more than saw Jack get to his feet. Travis struggled up, and a small cry escaped his lips at the sharp pain when he straightened his knees.

Jack clamped a muddy hand across his mouth. He placed his lips near Travis's ear. "We are at the base of the bluff. Be quiet." He removed his hand slowly.

Travis leaned close, almost touching the side of Jack's head with his face. "The flag never made it this far."

"I know," was the quiet reply. "Not a word now."

They remained motionless for long minutes, just listening. There was nothing, not a single noise traveling through the air. The moon finally broke through and bathed the battlefield with its soft glow. When their eyes adjusted, dark forms dotted the landscape, hundreds of them. Travis's heart skipped when he realized he was looking at men's bodies.

Jack tugged Travis down and forward.

They got back on all fours and crawled away from the bluff, back toward the bayou. After they had covered a hundred yards, Jack stood up. "I had to make sure the rebels were not watching. I didn't hear any voices or smell any tobacco. Did you?"

"No."

Jack pulled a small rectangle shape from his pocket. As he pried it open, the hollow metallic sound told Travis it was a metal match safe.

"Stand next to me," Jack said.

Travis moved close and watched as Jack struck a match. The bright light blinded them both and it took a moment before Jack could see well enough to set the lantern wick ablaze. He tossed the match and held the light close to his chest.

"Let's keep our backs to the bluffs to block some of the glow."

They moved across the battlefield, walking as if they were attached at the hips. Travis stopped abruptly when he saw a pale face staring back at him. The soldier's eyes and mouth were open with a painful expression that had remained on his face when death came. Shrapnel from a shell had torn through his chest.

It was an appalling sight that made Travis look away. Earlier in the day during the battle, he had witnessed many terrible sights of death but a thousand things were happening all at once. The vastness of the assault had been stretched out before him and each scene begged for his attention, but what he was seeing now was different. The scope of the giant battlefield had been shrunk down to a small circle of lantern light from which he could not escape.

The rebels had taken the man's coat, hat, and shoes but the contents of his jacket and other personal belongings were left behind. The items had not been tossed aside but were arranged neatly, next to his body. A pocket watch was propped against a deck of cards. His folding knife had been laid next to his spectacles. These things did not touch Travis nearly as much as the tintype photo with a woman and child seated on bench. Looking at it hurt him and he could not help but wonder how long it would be before this man's loved ones discovered he would not be coming home.

The scene of dead soldiers stripped of their coats repeated itself as Travis and Jack shuffled along. In each case, the personal items had been left behind.

When they happened upon a dead horse, Jack said, "This is it. I remember this." He changed direction, being careful to block the light with his body. "Stay close. The flag is just ahead."

Travis's senses were becoming numb to the carnage around him, but a man's hand lying on the ground unnerved him the most. There was no body anywhere nearby, and the hand was not bloody or dirty. It was simply there, and the story of how it came to be on the battlefield or who it belonged to would never be answered. He shuddered. He prayed that he would not find the body of Thomas or Salem here.

"That's it!" Jack whispered excitedly.

The corner of a wet and crumpled flag peeked out from under a fallen soldier.

Faint noises drifted across the clearing. Travis looked back and saw the soft glow of lanterns coming from the direction of the bluffs. "They are behind us."

Jack handed him the light. "Put it out."

Travis rolled the wick down, and Jack grabbed the flag, pulled it free, and tucked it and the pole under his arm. The moon illuminated the landscape just enough to allow them to walk carefully around the dead.

They crossed the water quickly, looking back to make sure the rebels were not following. Travis readjusted his grip on the stretcher and nearly dropped it. As he did, he walked straight into Jack.

"Did you hear that?" Jack asked.

"No," Travis said.

But just then they both heard it. Something growled in the darkness.

CHAPTER SEVENTEEN

Jack backed up, bumping into Travis. "What is that?

There was a clattering sound and then the distinct clicking of a musket being cocked. "Do not take another sthep!"

Dark as it may be, there was no mistaking the voice with a lisp.

"Thomas! It's me, Travis."

"Lord help me, I almoths shot you."

A dark form appeared at Travis's feet and nudged his leg. He quickly realized it was Salem and went to his knees, hugging the dog.

Thomas said. "Who have you there?"

"Jack Kenyon."

Thomas greeted him and suggested they get off the battlefield. He had gathered guns from the fallen soldiers and dropped them when he happened upon Travis and Jack.

Jack took the lantern from Travis and lit it. They helped Thomas carry the muskets, and Salem followed them with his head low. The dog limped slightly, favoring one of his back legs.

"Did Salem get hurt?" Travis asked.

"Not bad," Thomas said. "I think he got a thorn."

"What happened to you?"

"Me and a few more made a poor retreat," Thomas said. "We ran right up in the middle of a few rebths. Them around me dropped their weaponths but I ran for the hill. Alfred beat it right behind me." He looked glum. "I think they got him, though."

"They got Alfred?"

Thomas sighed. "Maybe."

"We can check camp for him," Travis said. "What time is it?"

"I have no idea," Thomas answered.

"Jack found our flag," Travis said.

"Great," Thomas said. "Good work, Jack. The Thirteenth will rally."

"Did the rebels chase you?"

"Let me tell you, I would be headed for a prison camp right now if it weren't for that dog."

As if he understood them, Salem trotted past to lead the way. His limp was hardly noticeable.

Thomas continued. "After I put some land between me and them, I ran up a tree like a fox thsquirrel. I made it twenty feet up and got real quiet. With gray-back rebth all underneath me and thsure to look up any minute, that beautiful dog came out of nowhere and barked like mad. They took off after him and I waths able to get away. He mutht have run off and left 'em behind. He trailed me up about half an hour later." Thomas laughed. "I owe that dog a big meal for helping keep my hide on me!"

Hints of daylight had started to peek into the woods when they reached the new camp of the Thirteenth. Salem greeted everyone, waking those still sleeping with licks to their exhausted faces. The troops were all very excited to see the brave dog again. They patted and petted him all over. A few even checked him for wounds and remarked how he must be bullet proof.

As the troops rose to meet the day, Thomas retold his story over and over for anyone who would listen. While everyone talked, Travis tried to forget the things he had seen in the bayou. There had been no sign of Alfred and no other conclusion could be drawn. He had been captured.

In the early dim light, Jack stretched the flag out. Many of the Thirteenth crowded around, only to be greatly disappointed.

What they thought was a thirteen was actually a thirty-one when Jack turned the flag up correctly. It belonged to the Thirty-first Missouri.

No one was as discouraged as Jack. The men quickly got over it and clapped him on the back, proud of the courage both of them had shown even if the flag did not belong to the Thirteenth.

Travis finally found a place to rest and slept most of the morning. After Salem had reacquainted himself with everyone, he joined Travis. The rest of the day was uneventful except for another soldier's quest to find the flag. Two tries had resulted in two flags being recovered, neither belonging to the Thirteenth.

When evening came, orders were given to start some campfires near the bayou to make the rebels think it was camp. When the ruse had been in place for half an hour, the Thirteenth left the woods quietly, without a single word spoken.

They arrived at the landing where the John Warner had been docked and found only the Continental steamer. They boarded, and each soldier claimed a spot on the decks to rest.

"Well, it's the new year's eve," George said.

Travis nodded in agreement. "And not much of a happy one." Christmas and the misplaced excitement of battle seemed a lifetime ago. The last night of the year was crisp and chilly and no one had any blankets or supplies. Everything they needed had been left on the other steamboat.

Travis shivered uncontrollably. Each time he closed his eyes, images of the horrors he had witnessed on the battlefield haunted him. For hours, he tried to clear his thoughts but the memories were too strong, too fresh to be pushed away. Tears streamed from his eyes, leaving cold streaks on his face. Salem whined and burrowed close to his side, sharing his sorrow.

They remained on the steamer all the next day. Travis played with Salem and worked on his tricks. The dog had a scratch on his hip but no other wounds.

No one could believe that Salem had been all over the battlefield chasing cannonballs and bullets without getting shot a single time. Almost every soldier on board made a point to come by and pet him, and give him bits of their meager breakfast. Salem ate up the treats and the extra attention, whacking the people with his tail in happiness.

Orders were received at dark to get off the boat and march a few miles where their old friend, John Warner, was waiting. When they boarded the Warner once again, each man was given his knapsack and a blanket, which they immediately bundled up in against the cold.

The ship that had once been crowded was now eerily spacious. Peter remarked about the difference. "One hundred seventy-three."

"What?" Travis asked.

"I hear that's how many of the Thirteenth who are not on the boat this time. Twenty-seven are singing with the angels or dancing with the devil. The rest are wounded or captured."

"The other regiments lost many too," Travis said. "I bet a thousand were lost. Some of us got lucky, though."

"Blessed," George said. "We are blessed."

"Do you know where Emil is?"

George looked thoughtful. "I heard the wounded were loaded on another steamer. I'm not sure which one."

All the steamers left the following morning and went back to anchor at Milliken's bend. The Thirteenth received news that the dead had been buried before they left, and a few wounded had been rescued in the bayou.

The regiments were allowed to leave their boats and go to a steamer called the City of Memphis to look for the wounded friends. The boys of the Thirteenth reunited with Emil, and found him in good spirits. The visit was soon cut short when a storm with strong winds swept over the boats.

After they returned to the Warner, the little shelter to be found was packed with soldiers, forcing Travis to huddle under his blanket with Salem in the wet weather.

He heard a few industrious soldiers had set up some tents on the top deck to take shelter in, but they were quickly ordered to take them down when the canvas tents acted like wind-sails and threatened to pull the steamboat loose from its mooring.

Travis shivered from the cold rain. There was no escaping the wind and water. He was miserable. Through chattering teeth, he said to Salem, "This is the worst night ever."

A week later, word reached the Thirteenth that Colonel Wyman had been promoted to general but had been killed before he heard news of it. It gave the troops great pride and sadness at the same time.

After Peter told Travis about the promotion, Travis shook his head. "I wish he would have known."

"Me too, lad." Peter winced and rubbed his back. "Did the Colonel come up with any solutions about your brother?"

"He did," Travis answered. "He was going to give me a furlough."

Peter raised a hand and fluttered his fingers. "Guess that flew out the window."

"Do we have a new colonel?" Travis asked.

"I'm sure we will be passed around until someone is promoted or transferred. What are you going to do?"

"The Colonel received word that our house had been abandoned. I sent a few letters but had no reply. At this point, what can I do?" Travis pondered on it. "Peter, I've been with the Thirteenth for nine months. At first, I felt trapped, but that has changed. Why is that? At first, I was dead-set on getting back to my brother, no matter the cost. Before Chickasaw, I certainly would have taken whatever leave I could, but now I am not sure I could leave you and the others."

Tears filled his eyes. "Does that make me a bad brother? Have I abandoned Chet to be whipped and beaten by a man not fit to be a father?"

Peter sat quietly before answering, choosing his words carefully. "A happy man is one who remembers his blessings and forgets his troubles. Having trustworthy soldiers at your side is a blessing many regiments cannot say."

Peter eased down to sit by Travis. "You feel you are truly your brother's keeper, and a noble attitude indeed, but this country is being torn apart. Your da' and brother cannot escape this war no matter where they go. There is only one way to end this."

"Win the war," Travis said.

"Yes," Peter nodded. "We just had our arses whipped, and yet we are headed to another battle. There will be no furloughs anytime soon."

"I guess everyone here is fighting for someone back home."

"Travis, you have not abandoned your brother," Peter said. "You are still fighting for him."

The boats traveled up a few different waterways, finally reaching the Arkansas river. The Warner stopped and allowed the Thirteenth to get off several miles from a rebel fort called Arkansas Post.

While waiting for orders, several soldiers wrote letters home and played cards. Travis whittled the shape of a dog out of a chunk of wood while Salem napped at his feet.

Without warning, the gunboats in the river started the assault against the enemy. Salem leaped up and tried to run toward the fort, but Travis grabbed his collar, almost stabbing himself with his knife. The bombardments continued off and on for hours, and Travis had his hands full keeping Salem from speeding off. He hoped this was one battle they would not have to fight.

CHAPTER EIGHTEEN

January 11, 1863

After noon, they were ordered to advance on the fort and add musket fire to the artillery striking the target. When the cannisters and cannonballs struck the fort, dirt and timbers flew in all directions. Confederates shouted and cried out before finally raising a white flag. When the Union entered, thousands of rebels surrendered.

George, Peter, Thomas, and Travis walked together as the Thirteenth surveyed the damage to the fortification. Salem ran all amongst the captured men, smelling their legs, feet, and hands. A few rebel soldiers tried to pet him but Salem dodged their hands.

"Look at this," George said.

They found a thick-walled section at one edge of the fort. It formed a square and the timber walls had been reinforced with dirt piled against the sides, all to protect a cannon. A shell from one of the gun boats had found its way through an opening and exploded inside the enclosure, killing six men. Parts of them were strewn everywhere.

"This is awful," Travis said, trying not to retch. "They never knew what hit them."

Peter laid an arm across Travis's shoulders. "Poor lads. They were somebody's darlin's."

Arthur heard them talking and came over. "What is in there?"

"Take a look," George said.

Arthur went in, stayed for a moment, and came out. "That is the biggest cannon I have ever seen."

Peter shook his head. "Is that all you saw in there?"

Arthur shrugged. "It was the only thing I saw worth caring about."

"Careful, Arthur. Death demands respect, and it matters not one bit to him the color clothes you wear."

The Confederates had built log cabins at the back of the fort and they made fine lodging for the men. Travis slept on the floor in one of the houses. It was the best night's rest he had experienced in a month.

The next morning, they were ordered to burn everything and leave. It was sad to see the cabins go up in flames. Travis wished they could have stayed in them a few more days.

As the Warner traveled along the river the next week, the weather became frigid and it snowed. Travis and Salem squeezed into the boiler room with many others to find warmth. He looked up saw John coming toward him.

"I saw what you did."

Travis got ready for an argument. It had been a while, and he guessed a fresh confrontation with John was long overdue. "What are you talking about?"

"I was close enough to see you when Wyman and Emil were shot."

Travis was not sure at what point John would turn the conversation into a fight, so he just kept quiet.

"You left cover and went for help," John said. "You are either stupid or brave."

Travis thought, *Here it comes.*

John moved past him and toward the stairs. "You remember when I said I did not want to fight next to you until you could load three bullets per minute?"

Travis nodded.

"Well, I changed my mind." John climbed the stairs and stopped at the door. He looked down at Travis. "And what Salem did was also either stupid or brave. With Nep gone now, Salem should be our regiment dog."

Travis's eyes grew wide with surprise. "Thanks."

Later that evening, Travis joined Peter against the wall of the second deck. "I spoke to John earlier, and he actually said something nice to me."

"Are you sure?" Peter chuckled. "Well, maybe he learned that a good word never broke a tooth."

"Pretty certain. He also said Nep is gone."

"I heard that too," Peter said. "Heard he was put on another ship headed north to keep him safe."

"Jake mentioned something about it."

"I bet Jake and Burley are fit to be tied," Peter said. "Especially Burley. He doted on that dog."

"It is more amazing that John was nice to me."

The last day of January, Travis and the Thirteenth had arrived at Young's Point near Vicksburg. They worked many days on a canal being constructed to disrupt supplies into the city. Once again, a shovel was in Travis's hands and new callouses on his palms.

"Peter," he said. "This stump must have roots all the way to the other side of the world."

"I have worked about as long as I can stand," Peter groaned. He threw his shovel down. "My back is hurting like the devil stepped on it himself."

George rolled a large wheelbarrow over, set it down and picked up Peter's shovel. "This stump is six feet through. The last one was half this size and I thought it would kill us."

"Can't we burn it?" Travis asked.

"It would burn for a week," Peter said.

The sound of musket fire came from the direction of Vicksburg.

"Should we get our guns?" Travis asked.

George shook his head. "Our pickets have it under control. Shall we keep digging?"

Peter growled with frustration and the noise woke Salem who had been sleeping nearby. The dog jumped to his feet and barked.

Travis chuckled. "Easy boy, it's nothing to worry over."

A few minutes later, it was Salem who growled.

"What is it?" Travis asked.

Burley walked along the freshly dug earth. "The quartermaster wants Salem at the camp for a while."

"Now why would he be asking for Salem?" Peter leaned back against the stump.

Burley stood next to the wheelbarrow. "Just doing what I am told. You should do the same."

"We are doing what we were told," Travis said. "Digging out this stump."

"I am to bring the dog," Burley said.

Peter put his hands on his hips. "Not until you tell us why."

"What is this about?" George asked. "Are you trying to replace a vacant spot in your sideshow?"

"Oh, that's right," Peter said, winking at Travis. "Ol' Nep got shipped out, didn't he?"

Burley's face turned beet red with anger. George clapped his hands together. "We need a new regiment dog and I've heard Salem is being nominated by the men of the Thirteenth."

"There is only one regiment dog!" Burley said in a temper. "Nep is our mascot. I trained him."

An incoming shell whistled overhead, giving short warning. Travis ran and shouted for Salem. Peter and George dove behind a pile of dirt and Burley took cover next to the wheelbarrow.

The artillery shell blasted into the ground at the base of the stump. The force of the explosion ripped it out of the ground and split the wood into a multiple pieces.

Salem ran over to the debris, barking excitedly. Travis, George, and Peter checked each other for wounds and discovered they had escaped without a scratch. Muffled shouts directed their attention to the wheelbarrow that had been overturned. It had landed perfectly on top of Burley, trapping him underneath with only his arms and legs sticking out.

"He looks like a dad gum turtle," George chortled, as they all erupted in laughter.

When George pulled the wheelbarrow off the twisted man, Burley got to his feet and stormed away.

"He didna' think that was funny," Peter said.

"Looks like we can take a break." George pointed at the splintered stump. "The rebels did our work for us."

After two months of hard work the rains set in and the land was drenched for days. The canal flooded and the project was abandoned. Camp was moved to avoid the rising water.

Salem was with the men each step of the way. His actions on the Chickasaw battlefield had grown to epic proportions. Some of the troops joked that the dog had taken down a squad of Confederates all by himself.

Thomas continued to share his story around the evening campfires, and it was not long before the men of the Thirteenth called for a meeting.

John stood upon a log and addressed the regiment that had gathered. "All of us witnessed Salem's actions at Chickasaw. He is probably the most loyal member of the Thirteenth."

The men whistled and clapped.

Salem trotted into the center of the gathering, trying to see what the disturbance was all about.

Arthur looked at Travis. "Is this a different John? One I have not met?"

Travis shrugged.

John glanced at Peter and Travis. "We know Salem has his favorites, but he claims each one of us as family and I believe he should be our regiment dog. The mascot of the Thirteenth."

A cheer spread through the crowd. Salem barked, causing some troops to laugh.

George slapped Travis on the back. "This is a different John, indeed. Good behavior must be rewarded."

"What do you mean?" Travis asked.

George stepped on the log with John. "This young man gets smarter every day. He has grown wise beyond his years and I think we should put this matter to a vote. What do you say, Father John?"

John smiled and nodded.

George raised his hand high. "If you wish to have Salem as your regiment dog, let it be known."

A flurry of hands went into the air.

"Any opposed?" George asked.

There were none opposed and the Thirteenth roared with approval. Salem turned circles, yipping and barking.

That night, Travis crawled into the tent. John joined him a few minutes later. His quiet, moody exterior had melted away.

"Where's Salem?" he asked.

"He is out making his rounds begging for supper scraps," Travis said. "John, can I ask you a question?"

"Surely."

"What changed? You hardly had two words for me in the past."

The conversation stalled and Travis began to regret asking the question.

"There was death all around us at Chickasaw," John said. "It made some of us value life less and some of us cherish it. That is all I can tell you."

Travis accepted his answer. The carnage on the battlefield had definitely changed all of them.

CHAPTER NINETEEN

April 2, 1863

They received orders and marched toward Greenville, Mississippi. After two days of travel, they arrived and were instructed to destroy a massive granary to disrupt enemy supplies.

Travis had never seen a storehouse so large. It was filled with corn. Some of the troops of the Thirteenth had been lifelong farmers and estimated the amount to be at least one and a half million bushels. After the warehouse was set ablaze, they moved onward and burned the mills and gin houses.

Salem barked and stuck his nose to the ground, going back and forth searching for a scent. After a moment, he zeroed in on the trail and took off, barking every few seconds as he went.

"Salem is on the trail of something," Travis said to Peter.

"Rabbit or rebel?"

"He will find it, either way."

The dog went around the corner of a building with his nose in the air. His barking escalated. He suddenly backed up, putting distance between him and whatever he had found. Travis could only see half of the dog's body sticking out from behind the building. Salem barked so hard that he shook with each effort.

George came up to Travis. "Is he mad or scared?"

"Let's go see what our mascot treed," Peter said.

"It might be a snake," George shuddered. "There's some woods behind that building."

When they rounded the corner, the sight shocked them all.

A black man was hanging from a rope in a tree. He had swung his feet over to a wood-rail fence about three feet away. The angle kept him from standing up but it had allowed him to take some of the weight off of the rope around his neck.

The man had gotten four of his fingers under the noose and was pulling outward, trying to keep his air and blood flowing. His other hand was above him, gripping the rope, straining to hold himself in a way to keep the noose from retightening.

George exclaimed, "Sakes alive!" and ran to the struggling man. He bear-hugged him around the hips and lifted a few inches. The small amount of slack was not enough to free the man but it did give him some relief.

"Cut the rope!" George ordered Peter.

"It is out of reach," Peter said, stretching as high as he could. "They must have had him on a horse."

Travis found an old crate along the building's back wall. With Peter's help, they shoved it across the ground until it was close enough.

George grunted. "He's slipping! Hurry."

More troops came around the corner.

Travis jumped on the crate and Peter handed him the knife. He cut the rope and George and other soldiers lowered the man to the ground. After the noose was removed, he heaved and coughed, and rubbed his neck while he cried in relief. A short piece of smaller rope was still attached to one of his wrists. Peter took the knife from Travis, knelt, and cut the knot.

"You boys saved my life. I'm most grateful." The man was racked with emotion. His voice was so hoarse the words were hard to understand. He cleared his throat over and over.

"What happened?" Travis asked.

"Some rebs caught me. I heard you soldiers were coming through town but they caught me before I could get to ya."

"When?" George asked. "How long were you hanging there?"

"They just left." The man pointed the direction they had gone.

Several of the soldiers started off at a trot. George was eager to join them. "I'll be back. Those rebs need to come to judgement, and not only for trying to kill this poor man." Without a look back, he headed after them.

"Why did they do this to you?" Travis asked.

"For trying to get to you soldiers. I ran away from the farm. Almost made it." He held his hand out and Peter and Travis helped him up. "They were watching me swing when that dog came barking around the corner. Guess they knew it would make you guys come. One of 'em jumped on his horse and the others ran."

"Well," Peter said. "You made it by the skin of your teeth."

"I sure did. Hey, if I tell you fellers something, could I join in walking with y'all?"

"Depends on what you tell us," Peter said.

"Has to do with some wagons full of food."

"Wagons of food?" Peter grinned and glanced at Travis. "Tell away."

According to the grateful man, while he was fleeing through the woods, he happened across a train of wagons that had been hidden. Each one was filled with supplies.

George and the others returned, having found no sign of the rebels. The man's story was relayed to them and everyone followed him into the woods. After a short walk, they found exactly what he had described.

The Thirteenth was overly excited when wagons of supplies, meant to feed the Confederates, were brought into camp. The inventory was vast. They had eggs, chickens, sweet potatoes, and everyone's favorite, honey.

While they ate and celebrated, Francis Manter rode into camp. Soldiers put their food down and stood. Manter was the latest Colonel to take command of them. He always looked serious and this visit was no exception.

He pulled back on the reins, stopping his horse. Salem went closer and tried to sniff one of its front legs but the animal stomped the ground. The dog backed up, growled, and barked. Colonel Manter watched Salem's reaction.

"Is this the regiment dog I have heard about?"

"Yes. That's Salem," one of the soldiers answered.

The Colonel observed the dog a few more seconds. "While I believe every regiment should have a mascot, I must order this dog to be removed."

Mumbling broke out among the men. Peter pushed between some soldiers to get closer. "And what would cause you to order such a thing, Colonel, *sir*?"

George went to Peter's side. "Because he growled at your horse?"

To keep Salem from acting out again, Travis walked over and put a hand on him.

"I do not have to explain myself to a private," Manter said, a frown furrowing his brows.

Several troops began to speak up, voicing their concern. Other men joined them. Word was spreading among the Thirteenth.

Manter shifted in his saddle. "This dog will either be put down, or left in the next town we pass."

"Put down?!" Peter shouted. Salem started barking, and Travis had a hard time holding him back.

The crowd began to grow agitated, and a man yelled, "He is one of us!"

"We deserve an explanation," George said.

Dozens of troops loudly agreed.

Manter scowled. "I received complaints about the dog. He has bitten two people in camp, drawing blood from one of them."

"Who?" Peter asked. "Who has claimed this malarky?"

The Colonel held his hand up to stop Peter's questions. "This is not up for discussion. I have also been told the dog is a distraction on the battlefield."

The men of the Thirteenth erupted with bold words, pushing forward, suddenly closing the circle around Manter. Salem whined and yipped, straining against Travis's grip.

The Colonel stood in his stirrups. "This behavior is unacceptable! I will not be intimidated! Turn in your weapons, you are all under arrest!"

"All of us?" Peter asked.

"The whole regiment?" George asked. "There's nearly a thousand of us."

"Turn in your weapons," Manter repeated. "The Thirteenth is under arrest."

The Colonel yanked the reins, pulling his horse around in a wide circle and sending the men scrambling away from the heavy hooves. Manter cast one last angry look at Salem, then loped away.

Travis went to George and Peter. "I can't believe that just happened. Who was it that Salem could have bitten?"

"That's what I want to know," Peter said. "He has been with us the whole time."

Thirty minutes later, officers received orders to collect weapons from all the privates and turn them in. A sergeant in his mid-twenties pushed a wheelbarrow up to Travis, George, and Peter.

"Sergeant Eli Bailey. I've been instructed to take your guns."

George looked down at the sergeant. "This is ridiculous."

"I agree. I'm in the Thirteenth too, Company K." He pointed to the weapons in the wheelbarrow. "I had to turn mine in also."

"Your last name is Bailey?" Peter asked.

"It is."

"Would you be any kin to Travis? He's a Bailey too."

"Is that right?" Eli said. "Who is your father?"

"You don't want to know," Travis said. He sighed. "Jeb Bailey."

"I haven't heard of him," Eli said. He pointed to Peter. "Aren't you the one who brought Salem to the regiment?"

"I did," Peter said. "Travis had him on a farm in Arkansas. They both joined the Thirteenth that day."

"It is a real shame," Eli said. "That dog was anything but a distraction at Chickasaw. He sure inspired Company K. Who did he bite?"

Travis shook his head. "The Colonel said he bit two people but he didn't. Salem went with us to Greenville and was beside us the whole time. Is there something you can do?"

"I'm just a sergeant."

"Could you at least find out some details?" Peter asked. "Maybe as you make trips to turn the guns in?"

Eli pursed his lips in thought. "I can try."

An hour later, he sought them out. "I managed to discover a few things."

"What is it?" Peter asked.

"It was the black boy that joined us in Batesville, Arkansas."

"The whistling boy?" George asked.

"Yes. He claimed that Salem growled at him and bit his leg."

"What?" Travis glanced from Peter to George. "When did this happen?"

"I think he said on the boat at Chickasaw, but I'm not sure. The other guy said he was attacked before you left for Greenville."

"Who?" Peter asked.

"I don't remember his name but I'm sure you have seen him helping with Jake's show tent."

"Burley?" Comprehension made Peter angry. "Burley!"

"That's him. He has a wound on his hand from the dog."

"Impossible," Travis said. "Why would the boy wait so long to tell anyone? And how could Salem bite Burley when he has not been around him since... When was the last time we saw him, Peter?"

"The stump," George interrupted. "That's the last time they were around each other that I know of, when the rebs blasted that stump for us."

Travis held his hand out. "Wait a minute. When that wheelbarrow flipped over on him, could that be when he hurt his hand?"

Peter spat on the ground. "That dirty scoundrel. He needs both his eyes blacked!"

Eli looked from one to the other. "How do we find out?"

George shook his head. "I know the quartermaster pretty well. Jake is a good man. If he knows the truth, he will not hesitate to tell it."

"Jake has been gone since yesterday for supplies," Eli said. "He should be back anytime."

"Find him," Peter said. "See what he knows."

Since the soldiers were confined to camp while under arrest, they took the opportunity to spend time with Salem. Arthur and others tossed the ball and played chase with him. Some of the troops seemed to enjoy being arrested because it excused them from their drill duties.

Peter limped past Travis and sat. "My back is getting worse."

"You should see the doctor," Travis said.

"I will after Manter releases us."

"What is going to happen, Peter? I have never been arrested before."

"It will be interesting to see how this plays out. I do know we are in the middle of a war, and it would be a silly thing to pull a whole regiment out of service for insubordination."

"I guess there will be no furloughs anytime soon for the Thirteenth," Travis said.

Peter laughed. "I suppose not."

Colonel Manter rode back into their part of camp with an orderly, two aides and several troops behind him, and called for attention. Salem barked at his horse again, but Travis pulled him back by his collar. "Easy boy."

"Private," Manter said to him. "Tie a rope to the dog and bring it here."

Arthur stepped out of the crowd. "Where are you taking him?"

Manter said, "I have heard whispers of you men attempting to hide this animal."

"Why he is right here, and we would never do that," Arthur said. He walked over to Travis and whispered, "I'll hide Salem."

Travis gave the Colonel a nervous glance to see if he had heard.

Arthur held his hand behind his back, turning it slightly, revealing Salem's leather ball. He shook it. The motion got the dog's attention. He locked onto the toy with his eyes. "There is some rope in the tent over here. I will be right back." When Arthur pushed through the flap, Salem followed.

George, Peter, and a dozen others started throwing questions at Manter from all directions. The Thirteenth truly cared for Salem and they were letting it be known, but the Colonel ignored them.

"Get back out here, private!" he shouted at the tent. Manter waited a few more moments before pointing to a young soldier. "Stick your head in there and tell him to hurry along."

The soldier did as he was told, but quickly stepped back. "There's no one in there."

Manter's eyes narrowed. He looked at Travis. "You boys are digging a deep hole for yourselves. You planned this, did you not? Come here!"

Travis felt his heart drop.

CHAPTER TWENTY

"Colonel! I have some news you need to hear." Sergeant Eli emerged from the crowd. Arthur followed close behind Eli, and Salem behind him.

Manter yelled at Arthur. "Soldier! You disobeyed my orders." He looked to Eli. "Good work, Sergeant. I'm glad you caught him."

Quartermaster Jake and the whistling boy came out of the crowd.

Eli gestured toward the quartermaster. "That wasn't the news. This is, sir."

"May we have a word, Colonel?" Jake asked.

"In private?" Manter asked.

"No, sir," Jake answered. "I believe the men will want to hear what I have to say."

"Speak your mind."

"After arriving back to camp today, I was informed of the claims against the Thirteenth's mascot. I am here to inform you that those allegations are untrue."

"Be specific, man. Explain yourself," the Colonel snapped. "It was two of your own helpers who made these claims."

"That's what I have been told." Jake put his hand on the black boy's shoulder. "But I know Burley is telling a lie."

The whistling boy spoke up. "Burley made me say the dog grabbed my leg. Threatened me if I didn't."

Manter looked put upon. "Is this another play on saving this animal?"

"No, sir," Jake said. "I know the boy is telling the truth."

"And how do you know this?"

"Before I left for my trip, I noticed Burley had a wound on his hand. I inquired and he told me it was from some sort of accident with a wheelbarrow."

Peter stepped forward. "The rebs sent a shell into the canal and it flipped a wheelbarrow on top of him. Looked just like a turtle, he did." A laugh went through the crowd.

The Colonel looked anything but amused. "Bring Burley to me."

"I cannot," Jake said. "I just confronted him about his claim and he promptly left camp."

"A good thing," Peter said. "I would have punched his bloody eyes out."

The men around Peter struggled to hide their mirth.

A soldier on horseback galloped into camp and up to the Colonel's side. Manter turned to him, and the man quickly saluted and handed over a note.

The Colonel read it, his face losing all expression. He looked around at the crowd. "Get your weapons, men of the Thirteenth. The enemy is coming."

All traces of humor vanished as the men ran to prepare for battle.

Travis lingered briefly with Peter and Arthur. "We're not arrested anymore?"

"You are released," Manter said. He looked to Arthur. "You walked a fine line though."

"Salem stays?" Peter asked.

The Colonel nodded slightly, turned his horse and kicked it into a gallop, followed closely by his men and messenger.

This time the threat was repelled with no casualties to the Thirteenth. When they arrived back at camp, Jake was waiting for Travis.

"I need to speak with you. Apologies are in order for Burley's actions. He spent a lot of time with Nep and liked to claim him as his own. He took great pride that he had trained the regiment dog."

"I could tell," Travis said.

"When Nep was shipped home Burley moped like he had lost his best friend, until he started talking about what a great addition Salem would be for the show."

"He came and asked for him," Travis said. "He claimed you told him to bring Salem back, but we wouldn't let him go, of course."

Jake nodded. "Of course you would not. You have a very special dog there. There aren't many dogs that can inspire men like Salem can."

"Thank you, sir."

Jake said his goodbyes and left. By the time the sun was setting, everything seemed back to a regular routine, as if the strange day had never happened.

Three weeks of boring camp life passed. The days revolved around the drum schedule, drills and waiting. Some of the men played horse shoes and cards to pass the time. Others wrote letters daily to loved ones. Travis spent it with Salem and his friends.

Travis, George, and Arthur were eating when Peter walked up to them. Salem was stretched out in a spot of sunshine several yards away, deep asleep.

"Hi, Little Irish! Where have you been? We were certain you had gone and found some new friends," George teased.

Peter had no answering grin. He looked downcast.

"What's going on?" Travis asked.

"The doctors had me discharged today. A steamer is leaving in an hour and I'm to be on it."

They were shocked into silence and disbelief. All of them got up and peppered him with questions.

"Why are you leaving?"

"Is it because of your back?"

"How can you leave us now?"

"You cannot go," Arthur stated with finality. "We need the luck of the Irish here with us."

Peter placed a hand on his hip. "I hurt something at Chickasaw and it just won't heal. My three years are nigh up anyway. I hate to leave you lads, but I guess my fighting days are over."

"I do not know what we will do," George said sadly.

Arthur shook Peter's hand warmly. "I will defiantly miss your sage wisdom, Little Irish."

Peter chuckled. "Know when to keep your tongue under your belt, my friend."

Peter turned to Travis.

Travis felt his eyes water with unshed tears. "Peter, I am going to miss you something fierce." His throat thickened with emotion and he could not go on.

Peter put a hand on his shoulder. "There, my lad, you'll do. You have brothers here, you have heart, and you have Salem."

Travis embraced him, and quickly stepped back. "It will not be the same without you."

"Take care of our dog Salem."

"I will. I'll make sure we both get home."

Peter cleared his throat. "All of you never be forgettin' the fightin' Irishman that was your friend."

He walked over and knelt next to Salem. He gently brushed his fingers against the side of the dog's face. Salem's eyes fluttered for a moment. The corner of his mouth pulled back slightly, almost forming a smile, and his feet began to kick.

Peter looked up at his friends. "He's chasing rebels or rabbits." He took a deep breath and whispered, "I hope he catches all of them he wants."

Little Irish walked out of camp, and waved once before he disappeared over the hill. The day Wyman died had left Travis feeling empty and lost. This day felt no different.

By the time May rolled around, the Thirteenth had traveled many miles south and fought small groups of Confederates along the way. The trip had been rough with lots of rain and dense thickets to walk through. When they were near New Carthage, Louisiana, they came to a fine plantation.

"That is the biggest house I have ever seen," Travis said.

Ever impatient, Arthur stepped onto the long porch with white columns. "Come on."

Travis hesitated.

Arthur swung the ornate double doors open. Salem trotted past Arthur and went inside like he owned the place. Travis followed, fully expecting to find it full of people, but nobody was inside.

"It's abandoned," Arthur said.

Travis looked at the fancy furniture and cabinets filled with glassware. "They left everything."

Travis saw some letters written on fine stationary on an entry table. They were addressed to a Mister Bowie.

Arthur flopped down onto a stuffed chair. "They must have heard we were coming."

Other soldiers began to wander into the house. A few officers were with them, and the order was quickly given to make camp. Men started rushing upstairs and into all of the rooms, fighting for the empty beds.

"You better make your claim," Arthur said.

Salem came around the corner and went up the stairs. Travis whistled and the dog doubled back to join him. "Let's go find a place to sleep."

In the front part of the mansion, near a big set of windows, was a pair of sofas. One was finely upholstered and had no wrinkles at all. The other had divots were people had sat. He chose the newer sofa and when George entered the room, Travis pointed. "You better get that one before someone else does."

Salem found a thick rug between the sofas and claimed it for his resting spot. Travis ate hardtack, sharing some with Salem. Someone started playing a piano in another part of the house. The music echoed across the hardwood floors and lulled the lucky few who had found refuge inside into the best night's rest they had experienced in the war.

The next morning, they left just before daylight.

Travis stopped in the yard and looked up. "No stars, George. Think it will rain today?"

"Probably not, but I have been wrong before."

The double doors on the mansion burst open, slapping against the walls. Arthur and two other soldiers shoved the big piano through the doorway and across the porch. It bounced down the stairs, playing a terrible tune along the way.

When it landed, miraculously still upright, one of the soldiers tapped on the keys and sang "Home! Sweet Home!" while Arthur poured kerosene on the top and back of the piano. After the fire was lit, the player continued with his song.

The Thirteenth marched onward while being serenaded in the strangest fashion Travis had witnessed yet. When they were a mile away, the sky behind them glowed from a massive fire. The mansion was engulfed and Travis wondered if the flames had spread from the piano or if someone had flung a torch inside.

They went on many long marches over the next month, built bridges, and had a number of skirmishes, but their orders finally took them back to a hilltop overlooking Vicksburg and a place they never thought they would see again. Chickasaw Bayou.

The Fourth Ohio Battery arrived and put their big guns in place. While the Ohio men prepared for the Vicksburg assault, the Thirteenth quietly paid homage to their friends who had gallantly given their lives in the valley below.

"George," Travis said. "It has been nearly five months, but it feels like yesterday."

George crossed his arms. "It still hurts to think about it."

"Guess who is back!" The words were spoken with a thick German accent.

They turned in anticipation. Emil smiled and held his hand out to shake. Travis bypassed his extended arm and hugged him tight.

"I cannot believe you are back with us," he said.

Travis moved aside and George hugged Emil, too. "I did not think we would ever see you again."

Emil slapped his leg. "Good as new. How is everybody?"

"Alfred is still missing," Travis said. "Thomas and John are fine. They are around here somewhere."

"Did you hear about Peter?" George asked.

Emil's eyes widened. "He didn't get shot, did he?"

"No. He had to leave because of a bad back."

"I am very sad to hear that he is gone, but very glad he left alive."

"It's been strange without either of you around," Travis said. "Where's Salem?"

"He's visiting with the Ohio boys," George said.

"Salem is our regiment dog now," Travis added.

Emil's eyebrows rose. "He's our mascot?"

Travis nodded and smiled happily. It was good to have his friend back.

Chapter Twenty-One

May 22, 1863

They had been sent to a camp up the Yazoo River, close to Vicksburg, where the Confederates had constructed a series of trenches and forts in a ring around the city. Soon after they arrived, they were ordered to participate in a grand assault against the enemy's fortifications. The Thirteenth looked like someone had kicked an ant hill.

George picked his way through all the activity until he got to his friends. "Travis, we are not going."

"Not going?"

"You and I are on cook duty."

Thomas grinned. "Well then, how about you bring food to me today?"

Emil smiled and chuckled. "Yes, I am already hungry. I would even eat those 'desecrated' vegetables right out of the sack!"

Men laughed at the absurdity of George braving the battlefield to deliver something for their bellies. Shouts sounded off as soldiers turned in their imaginary orders.

Salem was stretched out enjoying a nap while Travis and George worked. Travis was dumping the dried potato cakes into a big kettle of water when the battle started. On hearing the noise, Salem leaped to his feet and took off.

Travis dropped a tin full of cakes and shouted "Get back here!" but the dog was gone in a flash.

George mounded the hot coals up in the center of the fire pit. "I cannot decide if Salem is brave or stupid."

"Both, I think." Travis picked up the tin he had dropped. "He is going to get shot one of these days."

"We all have the same chance of that," George said.

Doctor Plummer walked by the tent.

"Doc," George said. "Any wounded yet?"

"Not yet," he said, "but I expect them anytime now."

A stray shell whistled to the ground, exploding about a twenty yards from the cook tent, shaking everything inside. When they looked out, Travis saw a smoking hole in the ground. Doctor Plummer struggled to his feet, holding his ears.

George ran to help him up. "Are you hurt?"

Plummer looked at him and turned his head slightly. "Huh?"

"Are you hurt," George repeated, louder this time.

He winced and rubbed the side of his head. "I'm fine, except for this eardrum."

"Is there anything we can do?" George asked.

Plummer walked away. "I know a good doctor."

A few hours later, George brought two wooden poles into the cook tent. "There is a lull in the battle. Want to go out on a limb, a very dangerous limb?"

"What are you going on about?"

George held the poles out. "Let's take our company some soup and coffee. Are you with me?"

Travis listened, and George was right, there was a blessed quiet in the distance. "Might as well. Let us hope they will return the favor next time we are out there."

They put one pole through the handles of two large kettles of coffee and the other through two kettles of soup. With the end of a pole in each hand, Travis and George carried the food like a stretcher.

When they reached the edge of the battlefield, the charge had been halted and thousands of men had taken cover behind banks of dirt and in rifle pits. The Thirteenth's flag led them to right area, and shortly they could pick out the soldiers of Company H.

Emil was among them, using a shovel to make his part of the trench deeper.

Upon seeing the food, the men yelled their approval. Travis's heart raced as they left cover and made a crouching run for the trench, doing their best to keep the liquid in the pots. Eager hands reached up to help them in and to get the food and coffee.

Travis sat and kept his head down, doing his best to catch his breath. Emil squatted beside him, using his shovel to keep steady. "You brought dinner! My belly will be eternally grateful and in your debt," he joked.

The enemy's forts were still hundreds of yards away. A couple of shots rang out, and bullets started striking the field. While the food was being passed along, Travis heard cheers from another company and saw Salem darting across a road. There was a boom, and dirt and debris flew into the air to the far left of him. The excited dog jumped a ditch and raced after the still rolling ball to more cheers.

Emil leaned on his shovel and slurped down a bowl of soup. "The sharpshooters are making a sport of trying to pick him off."

"He's going to get killed," Travis said anxiously. He tried whistling and calling, but Salem was oblivious.

George put the lid back on the pot. "The next group of hungry men awaits."

The men thanked them as they picked up the poles. The thunder of cannon fire and explosions, along with the pop and buzzing musket shots, picked up in cadence.

"Hurry!" a soldier shouted through the melee. "I'm starving to death!" A nervous laughter spread through the company.

Travis looked back at Emil. "Did you get some coffee?"

Emil was kneeling as he jabbed his shovel into the ground and tossed dirt out of the pit. "I did." He looked past Travis. "George! Stay low." Emil raised his shovel and motioned with it. "They can see your head and shoulders."

"I cannot help being tall." George carefully went from a crouch to down on his knees and smiled. "Is this better?"

Emil laughed. The blade on his shovel twanged with an awful sound. A bright streak of shiny metal from a ricocheted bullet strike appeared near its middle. Emil dropped the shovel and looked from it to Travis. His grin disappeared, his mouth opened slowly, and the color left his face.

Travis shouted, "Emil! Are you hit?"

Emil grabbed his side and fell.

George dropped the poles and jumped to his feet. He shoved Travis out of his path and ran to Emil. He picked him up in one swoop and took off through the trenches, pushing soldiers aside, clearing a path.

Travis was on his heels. "Hang on Emil. You will be okay, just hang on."

Before they reached the surgeon's tent, George was exhausted and Travis helped by carrying Emil's legs. They hefted him onto the table and the doctors went to work.

His shirt was bloody on the right side under his ribs. He was still breathing, but his body was limp, and he had not spoken a word. Doctor Plummer and his superior opened Emil's shirt and examined the wound.

Travis backed away from the table and squeezed his hands into tight fists. George placed his hand on Travis's shoulder, but he shook it off. "George, why did this happen to him again? Why?!"

George walked to the entrance of the tent. "Only our maker knows."

Travis followed, but stopped next to a barrel. White hot anger filled him, and he slammed his fists down on the barrel top with all his might. Pain shot through him, but he hardly cared.

"Private, control yourself," one of the doctors exclaimed with a frown.

"Give me a minute with him, Doctor Morrison," Plummer said. He stepped outside. "Listen to me well. I know he is your friend, but both of you need to let us do our work. Distractions will do no good for him."

Travis took a deep breath. "Is it bad?"

Plummer leaned close and turned his head to one side. "What did you say?"

"Is it bad?"

"I have seen worse," Plummer said. "But it is not good. If you are a praying man... well, it would not hurt."

"Please, will you keep us updated?" George asked.

"I will." Plummer went back inside.

Travis and George left with reluctant steps, not sure if they would ever see Emil again.

That evening, soldiers were ordered off the field. The charge had failed. Travis checked Salem and found he had once again avoided any serious injury.

"You can't keep doing this." Travis rubbed the dog's chin. "I don't know what I would do if you got shot too."

The next day, new tactics were put in place – digging more trenches. Lots of trenches. Deeper trenches. The goal of their work was to get close to the enemy fortifications without getting slaughtered.

Salem stayed with Travis but he was constantly complaining with yips and whines. He kept trying to dart away. Stern commands were the only thing keeping him nearby.

While Travis and George dug, artillery filled the sky overhead, crashing into Vicksburg. Mortars whistled through the air and musket balls thumped in the dirt. "How far away are we?" he asked George.

"About eight hundred yards, more or less. Here is what I want to know. How close do they need us to get?"

A cannon ball came hurtling out of Vicksburg and slammed into the ground. Salem barked and started climbing out of the trench but Travis grabbed him. "We have to keep him off the field while we're digging. I am desperate for ideas, George?"

"There is something, but you will not like it," George said.

"What?"

"Let Jake keep him. You can bet he has his precious cargo well away from any action."

George was right. He did not like the idea but there was no other way he could think of to keep Salem safe through the day. He asked permission from the officer in charge to take Salem to the quartermaster. His request was granted, and he found Sightsinger at his desk, coughing into a handkerchief.

"Are you sick?" Travis asked.

"I've been under the weather for a while."

Salem rose on his hind legs, placed his paws on a table, and sniffed at a row of leather shoes.

Travis pulled him back. "Salem, stay down."

"He is looking for another ball," Jake said. "Do you still have the one I gave you?"

"I do. Salem has just about worn it out. He loves it."

"Well, then, are you here to ask for another ball?"

"No, sir. The shelling is really thick today, and he is trying to chase cannonballs again and just will not stay in the trenches."

Jake laughed. "And you want to keep him safe."

"I hoped you might help, sir," Travis said. "Could you keep him in a cage while George and I are digging trenches?"

Jake coughed and wheezed into the rag. "I will not do that. It would be a sin to cage a dog like him."

"He will get shot, or become a distraction like the Colonel said, if you cannot help."

"A rope will not do," Jake said. "We already know he can chew right through one. Hmm, I do have some small chain. I will give you twenty feet. Let the men who have camp duty keep him."

"That will work," Travis said with relief.

Jake opened a crate and reached inside. "Here, take this." He tossed a new ball to Salem. He caught it and ran outside as if he were afraid he would have to give it back.

"Maybe that one will last him until the war is over," Travis said. "Have you heard anything about Burley?"

"Not hide nor hair."

Travis smiled. "Good. Is your show tent packed? I didn't see it outside."

Jake looked solemn. "I've been too sick. The animals are residing with a friend at the moment."

"Salem and I will come and see it when you start feeling better."

Jake got the piece of chain and gave it to him. "I will see you soon, then."

After Travis hooked Salem to a stump at camp, he yanked and pulled, nearly strangling himself. It took him a few days to accept that he couldn't run free on the battlefield. Travis gave him his old toy and held the new one back until the evenings, when he tossed it only for brief periods. The work in the ditches left him without any extra energy.

Travis asked about Emil everyday, but he had not improved. One day he was told his friend was taken to a hospital in a nearby town, and no other word about his condition was forthcoming.

Every day Travis had a shovel in his hands. The trenches were deep and slowly they snaked their way closer to the walls of

Vicksburg. Most days, the sun beat down on him, scorching his skin. The rare times it rained, the water flooded into the ditches. Regardless of the weather, work continued. There were no pleasant days in the trenches at Vicksburg.

CHAPTER TWENTY-TWO

June 12, 1863

Doctor Plummer walked into their camp. "I have no choice but to bring you all a bit of devasting news."

"What is it?" Travis asked in concern.

"There is no easy way to say it," the doctor said. "Emil has succumbed to his wounds. I am sorry." He turned without another word and left.

George sat on a nearby log and Travis collapsed onto a homemade chair. They both sat in shocked silence for a long time.

That night, Travis took his blanket as far away from camp as he could get without passing the guard line. Salem seemed to sense his mood, and followed quietly.

With the blanket spread and Salem curled next to him, he stared at the stars. He was amazed at the countless sparkles in the sky and wondered if Emil was up there among them. Grief seized him in the depths of his soul. He had lost another brother.

Though he tried to fight it, the tears came and he cried silently until he passed into a dreamless slumber.

The following days, the barrage from the Union into Vicksburg was nearly continuous and Travis could hardly believe the city had not surrendered. Sharpshooters peeked over the walls and flung lead at them until the Thirteenth returned fire, then the shooting would stop for a while.

The number of Union forces continued to grow until the countryside was covered with tents. Closer to Vicksburg, the land was dotted with batteries of large guns that pelted the city day and night.

On the fourth of July, after five weeks of digging, the Thirteenth had come within one hundred and fifty yards of their target. The ground rumbled under their feet from the Union shelling, causing rumors to spread that Vicksburg would fall soon.

A few hours later, loud cheers spread throughout the battlefield. Men shouted and whistled. Looking toward town, Travis saw a white flag fluttering above the fortification. The cannon fire slowed until it finally petered out. The battle was over.

Even though the siege was done, there was no rest for Travis and his fellow troops. They left the next day in pursuit of other Confederate forces. Salem was glad to be off his chain. He weaved between soldier's legs with an extra bounce.

Each march and skirmish with the fleeing rebels kept Travis's mind busy, but he thought about Emil often. If they lost the war, Emil would have given his life for nothing, and Travis was determined not to let that happen.

The following months were full of long marches back and forth across the country and into other states. They built bridges and destroyed others. Sometimes they would be ordered to pile timbers on railroad tracks and burn them so the heat would warp the rails. The destruction was meant to hinder the Confederate forces but on occasion the Thirteenth would be required to travel the same route again, so they then had to repair the damage.

Travis stood near a cave called Nickajack, outside Chattanooga, Tennessee. Cool November winds nipped at his face. They had fought in numerous skirmishes to get there. It had been constant travels by steamer, train, and marches, and he yearned for rest.

"Are you tired?" he asked Salem.

The dog whined and sat.

"Good idea." Travis took a seat next to the dog and they both watched the bustle around them. There were thousands upon thousands of men making camp.

George joined him. "It's getting chilly."

"It's November," Travis said.

"I had lost count of the days," George said slowly.

"It happens to be my birthday." Travis laughed. "We were so busy, I nearly forgot."

George chuckled. "Why even count them."

Travis studied his face for a moment. "Can I tell you a secret?"

"You know you can."

"I just turned sixteen."

"Let me tell you a secret," George said. "You are not the only young one in this war. I see lots of youthful faces that are nowhere near sixteen."

He looked through the thinned timber at the outline of the mountain peaks, lost in thought for a moment. "In your sixteen years, have you ever seen Lookout Mountain?"

"I have never even seen Tennessee," Travis said.

"We are only a day or two away."

"Have you been there?" Travis asked.

George shook his head.

Salem put his paw on Travis's knee. "Hang on, boy," Travis said. "We will eat in a few minutes. George, do you think this will be the last battle we have to fight?"

"I hope so." He made a face. "What is that?" He pulled his shirt up close to his nose and sniffed it. "I can still smell those dead mules in Chattanooga. The odor is still in my clothes."

"Mine too," Travis said. "I thought we could hurry past, but there were thousands of them."

"So many buzzards. I never knew that many existed."

"Neither did I. It gave me the willies, the way they were staring at us as we walked by."

"I think they were too fat to fly." George snickered. "You know how Arthur acts so tough?"

"Yes."

"He gagged the whole way."

Travis chuckled. "He wasn't the only one."

George said, "His eyes were watering so bad, it looked like he was..." George burst with laughter. "It looked like... like he was crying - crying and gagging!" He slapped his knee and Travis joined him, laughing until his sides hurt.

Finally, they settled down. George perked up. "Hey, I want to take a look at the big cave in the rock face over there. Want to come?"

"It's too crowded," Travis said. "I'll wait a while."

Salem laid down, stretched out on his belly, and placed his chin on his paws. He let out a heavy sigh. Travis reached into his haversack and removed the tin box holding his year and half's worth of pay. He had spent a bit of money along the way for essentials, but managed to save eighty-nine greenbacks. If he could get back and find Chet, he could take him far away from Jeb. He would have enough money for them to live on until he could find a place and a job. After shoving the money back in the tin, he sat back and watched the bustle around him.

Soldiers from a mix of regiments walked around. Salem kept his head still but his eyes shifted constantly, watching the men as they passed. Travis dug some hardtack from his haversack, divided it, and gave the dog half. He dunked his in coffee, although it did little to soften it. They were both crunching on it when George came striding back.

"There is a lieutenant from another regiment that wants to talk to you. He is in the big cave."

"To me? What for?"

"He wants to ask you about Salem."

Travis followed George through large groups of men until they reached Nickajack cave. The opening was massive, at least a hundred feet wide, and a stream flowed through the mouth of it. The top was nearly forty feet high with an incredibly large flat rock that stretched the width of the it. A line of soldiers with smoking torches were coming out as George and Travis entered. Salem's nose twitched at the strange musty scents in the air.

"Here he is," George said.

The lieutenant walked over. His uniform was covered in dirt and his hat had a smear of mud across one side. He eyed Salem. "Does he have a good nose?"

"Yes, sir. A real good one," Travis said. "What's going on?"

"How much do you weigh? The man asked.

"I am not sure," Travis answered.

"You look fairly lean. Skinnier than me, for sure."

Travis looked to George. "Why are we here?"

"I heard him say he wished he had a dog."

"Deep in the cave," the man said, "three soldiers got lost not too long ago. I went in earlier and could hear someone calling for help. The passage eventually splits three ways and becomes very narrow.

My body is too big to fit. I am not sure which direction the calls were coming from. There are too many echoes and noises from other soldiers helping. If your dog has a good nose, we can find the missing men."

"You want me to go in?" Travis asked.

"You will fit and he is your dog."

"Sir?" George asked. "Can I come?"

"Certainly not, you are much too big. Stay with my men if you like, but I have already ordered everybody out." He took several candles out of a small box and dropped them in a haversack, checked his match safe, and seemed satisfied.

Lastly, the lieutenant checked his pistol load and put it back in the holster. "If we hear something, I want to be sure it's our missing soldiers and not somebody else." He looked at Travis. "Are you ready?"

"How far back is it?"

"Quite a ways."

Travis, worried that Salem might get separated and lost if allowed to range free, requested a rope. After tying it to his collar, Travis was ready.

"On my orders, do not let anybody else in here," the lieutenant told the soldiers waiting at the entrance.

A set of iron tracks ran along the smooth bank of the stream and into the dark beyond. An overturned cart, blackened by fire, was lying next to the water's edge. On it, a tin lantern containing less than half a candle sat on the side of the cart. The lieutenant picked it up, opened the glass door, struck a lucifer and lit the nub inside.

Salem pulled against the rope, first one way, and then another. He was eager to take in all the smells the cave had to offer. Travis had to use both hands to keep a grip on him.

"Which way?" Travis asked.

"We follow this stream about half a mile, and then we will have to cross. After that, we need to listen carefully."

"Half a mile? How deep is this cave?"

"A long way," the man said. "Some people have told me it is at least ten miles. Stay close."

Travis walked right behind the lieutenant, but had a terrible time keeping his footing. He tripped on the uneven path, got tangled in Salem's rope, and fell to his knees more than once. The lieutenant relentlessly pressed on.

When they reached a crossing, there was an old boat resting in the water. The lieutenant climbed in. Travis was confused. "Lieutenant, if we are going in a boat, how did the men cross."

The lieutenant looked impatiently back at him. "This boat was on the other side when we arrived. We had to swim across to retrieve it."

Travis nodded, and stepped in. Salem jumped past him without hesitation, rocking the boat. Travis sat quickly to keep from overturning it.

They paddled across the gently flowing water. It took on a bright green hue in the light of the lantern.

Once they were on the other side, the passage closed in. They had to stoop down as they continued, until the cave opened up into a large cavern. The walls and ceiling sparkled in the light.

"The rebels were mining saltpeter out of here," the lieutenant said, his voice echoing against the stone walls.

The corridor undulated like a snake, twisting and curving in the light of the lantern. The ceiling height changed dramatically without warning, and several times Travis knocked his head on the rock when he was not paying attention.

When they came to the first split, he saw chalk marking a passage. The lieutenant took it without pausing. They came to many junctions with multiple passages as they walked. Travis quickly understood how easy it would be to get lost, with just a flickering candle to light the way.

Several times they had to crawl, and Salem took this as a time to play, licking Travis in the face and tugging at the lieutenants boots.

They came to a jagged walkway where the ground opened up, leaving a dark gorge. Old timbers had been laid down to span the gap. The light failed miserably at revealing its depths. Travis carried Salem across, moving in careful steps. Once past the void, the walls became smooth again and made their clothing wet each time they brushed against them.

"Hold up," the lieutenant said. "Listen."

There was the sound of dripping water but nothing else.

Travis whispered, "Were you here when you heard them the first time?"

"A mile or so farther."

"What did they say?"

"The words were too faint to make out. It was like a high-pitched yell for help. There was too much noise from the other men and the dripping water to be sure."

He held the lantern up. "The candle is getting low." He removed a new one from his pocket and used the burning one to light it. After replacing the candle, they kept going deeper.

They walked through more caverns and then crawled down some oblong passages about four feet tall and nearly twice as wide. Travis's knees began to hurt from the rocky ground, and he thought his forehead might be bleeding from an earlier encounter with a rocky outcrop.

The ceiling angled down until they were scooting on their bellies. The tin and glass panels on the lantern rattled, and their clothing rustled each time they moved. Salem's claws scratched on the rocks.

The Lieutenant stopped. "Listen. Did you hear something."

"No, sir."

They waited for a few seconds in silence.

"Crawl up here beside me."

Travis made his way next to the Lieutenant. Salem obediently followed close behind.

"See where this tunnel splits?" He held the light forward so Travis could get a better look.

On the left was an opening, nothing more than a slit in the rock wall, and it was not much greater than a foot wide. Next to it, another passage continued, possibly two feet square. On the right, a tunnel turned a different direction at a sharp angle. Its ceiling was very low.

"You think they are down here?" Travis asked.

"I heard them down this way, but it is too small for me to even look down those other tunnels. We lost their trail a ways back, but with so many passages doubling back and reconnecting, we could still meet up with them. I called out to see if I could get an answer, but other soldiers in the cave thought I was yelling for them and it became a confusing mess."

"I think we should try again, sir," Travis said.

The Lieutenant nodded and they shouted a few times and waited in the silence, but received no response.

"Let your dog check it out. If someone is down one of those passages, he should smell them."

Travis crawled past and squeezed through a narrow spot. His body blocked most of the light behind him, casting long dark shadows across the rocks in front. "Hand me the lantern," he said. "I'll look down the tunnels."

"Here," the Lieutenant said. "Take it, but let the dog check it out first. Do not mix your scent in there too."

Travis called Salem to the front. He was not sure how to direct the dog to search. He had taught him to find a few men in the Thirteenth but not complete strangers. "Find 'em," he said. "Come on, Salem, find 'em."

Salem tensed and started scenting the air.

"Watch him," the Lieutenant said.

The junction roof was just high enough for the dog to stand. He went to the right first and showed no interest. Salem's nose made little snorting noises as he worked his way to the middle tunnel. He stuck his head in, wagged his tail, and crawled inside. Travis let the rope slide through his hand as the dog disappeared. He struggled with the decision whether to let go or not.

"I bet they are down there," the Lieutenant said. "Let him go."

"I'm afraid he will get stuck," Travis said.

A cry sounded from deep in the tunnel, muffled by all the noise. Salem barked and yanked the rope free of Travis's hand.

"That was them! Get down there."

Travis hesitated. Salem barked again. "It looks small, and I am not sure I can fit," he said.

"Private, I urge you to try. Those men's lives are depending on you!"

Travis plucked up his courage and began to work his way inside, holding the lantern in front and squirming like a worm to move through the cramped space. While he crept along, he wondered why the lost soldiers would have ventured into the tiny corridor.

The walls closed in and tugged at him with each effort to move forward. Panic threatened to overwhelm him, and he had to calm himself and focus on breathing.

Salem growled somewhere in the dark ahead and Travis froze in fear. "Salem?" he whispered. It was deadly quiet.

He inched forward and saw where the tunnel turned a sharp corner. With no sign of Salem, he had no choice but to continue.

At last he squeezed up to an opening that overlooked a room-sized cavern. A light brighter than his lantern lit a circle in the middle of the floor, but only pushed the gloom back a few feet. At one of the top corners was a ledge with a small passage, filled with sunshine. Looking down, he estimated he was still ten feet from the cavern floor. He could see in the dim light that the wall below him was on a slant and wet with moisture. Slide marks showed him where Salem had gone but he could not see the dog. "Salem?" he again called softly.

One of the shadows moved.

CHAPTER TWENTY-THREE

Salem growled loudly and it was amplified by the hard walls of the cavern. Something made a high-pitched yowl in answer. A dark shape dashed across the high ledge and went out through the lighted opening. It was agile, quick, and definitely a mountain lion.

Salem continued to growl and bark after it was gone. Travis suspected the Lieutenant had heard the big cat and not the lost soldiers, so he called for Salem to come back to him. The dog tried coming up the hard slope but his paws could not get enough traction. He struggled for a few steps but slid to the bottom, his legs splaying out.

"Come on, boy. Try again. Come on."

Salem got a running start but became tangled in his rope and only made it half way.

"You will not be left down here."

Travis whistled and clapped his free hand against the rock wall. The dog raced up the incline. Travis grabbed for him but his fingers only brushed Salem's fur. The dog twisted to slide down face-first, instead of backwards. The movement flipped the rope up and Travis grabbed it, but the lead was too short and Salem's momentum yanked it out of his hand.

"Wait, boy. Even if I grab you, I cannot crawl backwards while I'm holding you and the lantern. Let me back up and make some room and you can try again."

His hope was that Salem would be able to get into the tunnel if he got a good run. After a few minutes of trying to move, Travis found that retreating into the passage without anything to push against with his hands was nearly impossible. He wiggled, shifted, and flexed his feet, even pulled with the tips of his shoes. Each time he moved back, his jacket bunched up around his waist, stopping him from making any progress. His arms, shoulders, and top of his head were still in the cavern so he kept trying and only stopped when he realized he was wedged tight.

Not able to move at all, Travis panicked. His jacket and shirt were crumpled and packed around his stomach and chest, putting pressure on his lungs. Sweat beaded on his skin, and he shouted for help.

He flailed his arms and pushed against the cavern wall, nearly losing his grip on the lantern. The light swung wildly as he tried to pry himself free. In his desperation, Travis pushed too hard and fell out of the tunnel, tumbling and sliding to the cave floor.

When he hit the bottom, the lantern struck a large rock. The candle dislodged, dousing the flame. The shadows expanded, covering him in gloom. The small shaft of sunlight gave him some small comfort.

He brushed himself off and picked up the lantern. It was not broken but he had no way to relight it. He tried climbing, jumping, and running up to the shaft he had come through but it was too steep and slick. Salem bounced in the air and ran around yipping with excitement.

"Salem, hush!" Travis commanded. Salem sat down contritely.

"Lieutenant, help!" Travis shouted at the opening he had fallen from. "Can you hear me? HELP!"

After a moment, the Lieutenant yelled back, but the distance kept Travis from understanding his words.

He cupped his hands around his mouth. "I fell down a cavern and I am trapped!"

Travis heard a faint reply but could not make out a single word. He bent and picked up Salem's rope. "If I cannot understand him, he cannot understand me. We are on our own, boy."

After working his way around the cave, he found there was no way up to the ledge where the big cat had gone, twenty feet above his head. The spot of light on the floor did not reveal signs that the animal had found a way down either. There were no bones, scat, or pawprints.

Travis looked up. "That is not a way out for us."

He sat while Salem explored the room, and tried not to let the fear keep him from thinking clearly. It would take the lieutenant a long time to get back out of the cave, find another skinny soldier, and return with him.

"They will need rope. What if they forget to bring some?"

Salem's lead was not long enough. If they forgot rope, the men would have to make another trip. What if the battle moved toward camp, and everyone had to fight? What if the lieutenant went to help and got killed? No one else knew where they were. Would they give up and leave him trapped?

The sound of Salem's claws, scratching on rock, came from a dark corner. Travis got his useless lantern and went to see what he was doing. After his eyes adjusted, he could see the dog had jumped onto a bolder and was attempting to climb another one. He had his nose in the air and paid no attention to Travis.

"What is it?"

He pushed Salem up on the next boulder and followed him. Salem hopped to a small ledge and disappeared into a crack. Travis felt the dog's rope dragging across his hand. He grabbed it and scrambled up to the opening. When he stuck his head inside, he experienced the darkest black he had ever known. He paused and wondered if he should stay in the dimly lit cavern or let his dog lead him into the unknown.

While he thought, the rope became tight as Salem continued deeper. He whined impatiently.

"Salem, you better be right."

The opening was big enough to squeeze through, so he followed Salem slowly, using his free his hand to feel the top of the passage. A ways in, it slanted up until he could stand. A few steps farther, and he could not reach the top at all.

With one hand tight around the rope, he used his fingertips to brush the side wall. The other hand holding the useless lantern was used to sweep in front of his face for any outcroppings. Salem tugged him forward in the pitch black.

"Are you leading me out? I hope that nose of yours knows where we are going," he nervously joked.

Salem stopped pulling on the rope and growled.

Travis held his breath and opened his eyes as wide as he could, but it did no good. Something was in the tunnel with them and he was totally blind!

He grew more alarmed as thoughts of panthers and cave monsters flashed through his mind. The rope slackened for just a second then tightened again. Travis held the lantern like a weapon, ready to bash it at some unseen creature.

Salem's growl faded into a whine, followed by sounds of licking. Travis had no inkling of what was happening just feet in front of him. "Salem, come here boy," he whispered.

The dog whined, and Travis felt the line go slack. Just as he started to pull, it became taut once more. He could hear Salem licking something again.

The corridor grew silent and then there was a tug on the rope. He took a step forward to give some slack, and waited to see if the growling would start again.

Another pull.

Another step.

A giant yank on the rope jerked Travis off his feet, sending him sprawling over something. His body hit solid ground but Salem's lead pulled his arm over the edge of a drop-off.

The dog flailed as he hung by his neck, making horrible gagging noises. The weight of Salem started to drag Travis over the ledge.

There was no way to know how deep this crevice was, but in his mind, it was hundreds of feet to the bottom. He desperately grabbed for anything with his free hand. When his searching fingers felt a board fixed to the floor, he gripped it for leverage and worked his way back, hoisting the dog up a few inches at a time. After he was away from the edge, Travis pulled the rope hand over hand, raising Salem to the top and into his arms. He hugged the dog while Salem wheezed. They sat there, both of them huffing to catch their breath.

"Please be okay, Salem!" Travis said, his throat tight with panic, feeling him all over. The quick lick on his face was reassuring.

A few moments passed before Travis could bring himself to let Salem out of his grasp. He made sure the rope was tight in his hand before he felt he could move again. He shifted the dog around behind him, keeping him away from the gap. Feeling of the cave floor, he found the board he had grabbed. Following its length toward the ledge, he felt where the timber had rotted, leaving jagged splinters sticking out. How Salem had come over that without getting stabbed was a miracle.

Moving the other direction, behind him, his fingers slid through some sticky goo. He brought his damp fingers to his nose and sniffed, and immediately recognized that coppery smell from the battlefield.

Blood!

Gingerly he reached further and touched something soft. At first, he thought it was Salem's fur, but no, on second thought, this felt altogether different.

He jerked his hand back. "Aah!"

The hairy thing did not attack, and all was silent except for Travis's heavy breathing. He felt Salem bump him and move to snuffle at the floor right in front of them. When his nerves settled, he gingerly extended his hand until he reached the mysterious thing again. Light touches led to bolder pokes.

Travis felt skin, and his brain caught up to his senses. This was someone's head, and a face. The flesh was cold and clammy.

Stubble. A man.

The fellow was on his back, on top of the board.

Travis could not stop his morbid inspection. Delicately, he ran his hand from the man's shoulder on down to reveal an image in his mind of an arm bent unnaturally. He moved his hand back to the man's chest. There was no movement. The feel of the material under his hands, the spacing of the buttons, all felt familiar to Travis.

The pieces were coming together.

Travis whispered. "You're one of the missing soldiers."

Hoping to find matches, Travis carefully searched the man but his haversack and kit was not there. He must have left it at camp when he went exploring. Just like Travis had done.

Rolling the body, he felt the old timber move underneath. He worked the board free. Travis wondered if it would span the gap that Salem had fallen into just minutes before.

"Back, Salem," he ordered. Travis scooted forward until the hand holding Salem's rope found the edge of the opening. He drug the board and swung it out into the dark, and was rewarded with a 'thunk' when it hit the opposite wall.

Suddenly, it slipped from his hands and fell at least three seconds before slamming into the bottom of the crevasse below.

Travis felt his heart drop. The despair was overwhelming. The blackness was almost like a physical weight pressing in.

He crawled backwards, avoiding the body, but bumped into Salem. He put his arms around the dog and buried his face in the dog's fur. He had to find a way out!

To try and think it through, he pretended he was back at camp sitting with his eyes closed on his bedroll. He thought back over the moments before. So his best guess put the piece of timber at four feet long and he figured his arms might have added another two feet.

"At least six feet across, boy." Salem whined in answer.

Travis opened his eyes in the inky black, and felt around until he found some pebbles. He tossed them to the other side and listened as they rattled into another tunnel across the way.

Hope flared, quickly followed by dread. Jumping six feet would be simple outside, but in total darkness? He played through different scenarios in his head. With three or four quick steps he could make it, but could he do it with Salem in his arms? What if the opening was small, or narrow and they simply jumped into the wall and fell onto the rocks below?

Travis started to shake. What other choice did he have? If they did not try, they would still end up like that soldier.

Dead.

In desperation, Travis tried one more time to call for help. He yelled at the top of his lungs, "Lieutenant! Can you hear me?"

Salem whined. He tried again. "Lieutenant!" Salem barked and Travis felt paws on his leg. Then he shushed the dog, and listened for an answer. None was forthcoming.

He stood up and called over and over, accompanied by the anxious barks of Salem. In between he waited in vain for an answer. Travis's voice was a scratchy whisper by the time he finally gave up.

After a rest and he came to a decision. He stroked Salem's shaggy head before he picked him up, trying to gauge if he could make the leap. He realized it would be extremely hard to know where to jump from – too soon and he would fall to his death, too late and he would simply run over the edge, again, to his death.

A miniscule light appeared across the void. He was certain it was his imagination playing tricks, but it moved. "Lieutenant?" It came out in barely a whisper. Salem whined.

He cleared his throat and tried again, louder this time. "Lieutenant?"

"Private?" a loud voice answered.

"Thank all my lucky stars," Travis said, fighting back tears. "I thought we were done in."

"I am nearly there. I have to move slow or this candle will go out."

The candlelight glowing against the walls across the way was the most beautiful thing in the world to Travis at that moment. "Be careful," Travis cautioned. "There is a gap between us."

As the Lieutenant moved closer, Travis could see him holding his hand in front of the flame to protect it from the air he stirred up.

Travis used the growing light to retrieve the lantern. "We are so glad to see you, sir!" he said. Salem barked in agreement, his tail wagging.

"I am pleased you are whole and sound," said the lieutenant.

Travis gestured to the body. "Those sounds you heard earlier, they were not what you thought. But I did find one of the missing men."

"Where?" The Lieutenant's ask sharply. His steps quickened. "Is he alive?"

"He is behind me," Travis said. "But he is dead."

The candle flame moved about wildly. "Is he... How old is he?"

Travis stole a glance at the body, his first sight of the poor soul. "He's thirty, maybe forty. I see a dark shaft in the ceiling here, so he must have fallen from somewhere above us."

"There's nobody else there? There were three of them."

"I only see one."

"Are you sure?"

"Yes, sir."

He waited a long time for the Lieutenant to leave, find a couple of timbers that were not rotten, and return. Travis felt like a nervous cat as he carried Salem across the gap.

When he reached the other side, the candle was placed in the lantern and they made their way out of the cave. The Lieutenant explained they were in an area he had not discovered before and if it had not been for Travis calling his name at the right moment, he might have never found it.

"I will get some help to look for the others and get the body out," he said. "Get some water and food. You and your dog found the area we should be looking in. Thank you for that."

"You are going back in right away?" Travis asked.

"I have to," he said. "My son is one of the missing soldiers."

Travis felt at a loss for the right words and could say nothing.

As they left the heavy blackness of the cave, the night surrounded him like a friend. The stars were bright in the sky and he looked fondly at the warm, flickering campfires dotting the land. He would never think of the dark the same way again.

The lieutenant thanked him once more and turned to leave.

Travis said, "I hope you find your boy soon, sir. I truly do."

Chapter Twenty-Four

November 24, 1863

Travis stood in a beautiful valley with Thomas, George, and John while Salem chewed on a stick, holding it down with his paw and cracking it with his teeth.

The Thirteenth had moved through some rough country over the past few days to arrive near the base of Lookout Mountain. The scenery was spectacular with a grand mountain rising up a few thousand feet. Its sides were heavily forested but a stone crest jutted above the trees at its peak. God's handiwork was almost beyond description and would have been utterly enjoyable to look at, if it were not for the Confederates hiding on its steep slopes and a sea of Union forces gathering in the valley below it.

Travis waited quietly with the other soldiers. A creek burbled nearby and morning birds chirped. Behind them, dozens of big guns were pointed at the mountain.

Suddenly trumpets sounded, and drums beat rhythmically. Seconds later, cannons belched loudly and the battle of Lookout Mountain started. The explosions blasted the trees, splintering the evergreens and shaking brown leaves out of the oaks.

The Thirteenth advanced toward the creek and received fire from some hidden Confederates. Travis shouldered his gun and aimed toward the far side of the stream, but could not find the enemy. Concealed cannons on the mountain fired down the side, resulting in a crisscross of deadly artillery. Salem barked and streaked across the open, snapping at whizzing bullets. There was no calling him back, he was fighting the battle in his own way.

A cannonball blasted across the battlefield, bouncing and spinning as it went. The projectile zipped past Travis and clipped one of the Thirteenth's musicians in the head. The boy was knocked unconscious and when Travis ran to him, he found that part of his ear had been torn off. Thomas stopped to help but when they picked him up, the boy regained his senses. He smiled, blinked hard, and grabbed his drum.

"Are you hurt bad?" Thomas asked.

The drummer shook his head, gathered his drumsticks and continued his cadence as he moved forward with blood dripping down the side of his face.

A large group of rebels emerged from the brush, waving a white cloth. The prisoners were taken to the back, and then orders were given to take the mountain. Travis crossed the creek with his fellow soldiers, where they found a wagon trail that led up the side.

Their eager legs were soon burning from the incline. The charge continued but the terrain dictated the speed. Salem caught up with them, passed Travis, and yipped as he ran up the mountain.

Travis struggled to breathe. "Slow down."

John came up next to him. "He doesn't get tired, does he?"

Up ahead, they saw Thomas waving for them to stop. "General Garey told uths they have taken the ridge above, near the top. The Thirteenth and the Fourth Iowa are to head up and join them."

"So," John said. "You're saying we won't get shot at for a little while."

"Yep."

It took hours to reach the top of the ridge, where Travis saw dead troops from both sides and abandoned Confederate cannons. A Union soldier was down on one knee next to one of the carriage wheels. He was positioned as if he was about to fire but his gun barrel rested on the ground.

"How many did you get?" John asked.

When the soldier did not answer, Travis studied him closer. "He's dead."

The poor man had been shot in the head and died instantly without even falling over.

George walked by. Sweat beaded on his forehead. "Leave him. He will get a proper burial tomorrow."

When they stopped for the evening, dense mist covered the top of the mountain above them and spread out across the valley. The clouds and fog brought dusk sooner than normal. The temperature dropped and every soldier shook uncontrollably. Their rushed effort to get up the ridge had left their clothes soaked with sweat.

Travis found Salem and pulled him close. When that failed to provide enough warmth, he walked in large circles. Other soldiers did the same until there was a sizable parade of men, pacing, and staying active. Salem found this very interesting and followed along even though his fur was more than adequate to keep him comfortable.

There was very little light remaining when Travis walked past a large boulder and noticed a musket that had been dropped by a fleeing rebel. He picked it up and was headed to turn it in when John stopped him.

"Can I see that?" he asked.

"Sure." Travis handed him the weapon.

"I need a new rammer. I cracked mine down by the creek."

John pointed the barrel up and pulled the ramrod out of the musket. When he lowered the gun, it slipped from his hand and he grabbed for it. A sharp concussion with flames and sparks shot from the muzzle. Travis jumped back. John dropped the weapon, and Salem darted one direction and then another, looking for something to chase.

Every soldier in camp froze, eyes darting as they looked for the enemy.

"I did not check it, and it was cocked!" Travis was shaken. "That's my fault, John. I am sorry."

A soldier came storming over, shaking his finger at John.

"You nearly shot me!"

"But I did not," John said. "It was an accident. No big affair."

An officer arrived. "What is going on here?"

"Lieutenant Gifford," the angry man said. "This soldier fired his weapon in camp and split a sapling I was standing by."

The Lieutenant stepped closer to John. "You discharged your musket in camp?"

Travis held his hands out. "Wait. This is all my-"

"I did," John said. "I found this rebel gun and didn't realize it was cocked."

"Private," Gifford said. "You will hand me that gun and come with me."

John got a look in his eye that Travis had seen many times. "Yes, sir," he said sarcastically. "And might I inquire as to where we are going?"

"Off the mountain, Private," the lieutenant said. "We cannot have soldiers risking the lives of our own men."

Travis opened his mouth to speak but John shook his head.

"Get those rebs, Travis," he said as he walked past. He disappeared into the gloom with the lieutenant.

After they had gone, Travis stood alone in the dark, trying to come to terms with the consequences of his mistake. He wondered if John would be back soon and if he would be subject to some sort of punishment.

He had seen how soldiers were disciplined, and none of it was pleasant. Minor infractions were usually addressed by many extra hours of guard or latrine duties. Crimes of insubordination and thievery could mean standing on a barrel for hours wearing a large card stating your crime, or being bucked and gagged with limbs bound and a rag stuffed in the mouth. Spying or desertion would see you hanged or shot, as he well remembered from his first days with the Thirteenth.

He wanted to ask John why he had taken full blame for the incident, but that would have to wait.

Glowing fires caught his attention. Out of desperation to escape the cold, some troops had started campfires on the lee side of the ridge.

Travis went to warm up and found George visiting with other men huddled around the flames. Salem trotted up behind George and nosed him on the leg. He looked back. "Where have you two been?"

"Did you hear the shot a while ago?"

"I did, but it was only one."

Travis stepped over and quietly explained what happened. They held their hands over the flames while he talked.

George leaned close to his ear. "John was right to take this alone, he knew he should have checked the gun, too."

He hesitated, then added apologetically, "And we can't risk losing you. If you were gone, Salem might not be the same dog on the battlefield."

The soldiers around the fire talked about the different things they had witnessed during the battle. Not a single one of them had seen any of the Thirteenth killed. It had been a lucky day for the regiment.

A shot came from the top of the mountain and one of the men at the fire cried out and grabbed his shoulder. George kicked dirt on the flames and told everyone to take cover. Over the next few minutes, other shots followed and the rest of the campfires slowly disappeared one by one. But down in the valley, long lines of bonfires, hundreds of them, gave hints of the picket lines and sheer number of forces still gathering.

When morning came, the Thirteenth had to march down the mountain to eat breakfast in the valley. The trees that had covered its slopes were now nothing but bare trunks and shattered stumps. After eating, they went back up, and were ordered to press on to the crest of Lookout Mountain. There was no resistance. During the night, the Confederates had snuck away. For the next few days, the Union was in sharp pursuit. Most times the trail was easy to follow, with abandoned wagons, crates, and guns littering the path.

Salem kept his nose on the ground. His tracking ability was not needed but no one dared to tell him. The soldiers were impressed that he was as determined to find the enemy as they were.

A few days later they came to a town called Ringgold and flanked some of the enemy by crossing a covered bridge. A small group of Confederates ran, and the Thirteenth chased them through town. Travis jogged shoulder to shoulder with his fellow soldiers while Salem ran in front. The rebels disappeared into a stretch of woods on the far side of Ringgold, and the Thirteenth charged toward the last place they had been spotted.

As they approached a ridge covered with a thick stand of saplings, some hidden Confederate cannons blasted them with canisters of grapeshot. A soldier next to Travis was hit in the mouth with one of the lead balls. Blood trailed down his chin and onto his chest as he was taken to the back of the line. Another man crumpled to the ground with a shattered leg.

Officers shouted commands to advance and find cover. The flag bearer led the way, waving the colors for the men to see, but a musket ball pierced his chest and sent him twisting to the ground. He rolled twice and the flag wrapped around his body. Another determined soldier yanked the flag free and pushed forward to an apple tree, where he stuck the flag in its branches, before jumping behind a pile of railroad ties.

Men scattered in all directions, taking cover behind anything available. The sudden ambush scared Salem. Normally he seemed unphased by war, but this time he cowed and headed for a log cabin nearby. Soldiers sought refuge behind the cabin, barn, pig pen, and a bank formed by some train tracks. The Confederate guns belched deadly missiles again and again, cutting down more troops.

Travis ran for the cabin.

"Keep firing at those heavy guns!" Arthur shouted when he broke from his position. "Don't let them reload!"

A cannister roared into the tree trunk he was headed for and Arthur tumbled into the dirt with a wound in his arm. "Run!"

Other troops fell on their way to the barn and cabin. A soldier in front of Travis, near the log house, flopped to the ground, his knee blown out by a musket ball. The man tried to stand but his leg failed him.

"Stay down, Walter!" another soldier yelled.

Travis raced to the corner of the structure and fired at the ridge. While reloading he noticed a member of the Thirteenth leaning against the house. The top of his skull had been blown away, exposing the gray color of his brain.

"Charles Peck," the man said, his eyes wide in shock. "Charles Peck. Charles Peck."

George kicked the back door of the cabin open and motioned for Travis. "Get in here!"

The owners of the house rushed into the cellar while shouting for the soldiers to get out of their home. George grabbed Travis by the arm and pulled him up the stairs to the second floor.

"Get down!"

The cabin was pelted with musket balls but the Thirteenth returned fire, doing their best to keep the Confederate cannons silent. All of the companies became mixed in battle. George helped a man named Howe of Company E, by wrapping a pillow cases around his wounds. He had lost four fingers on one hand and three on the other.

Lieutenant Eli Bailey rushed past him and opened a bedroom door. Travis recognized him as the lieutenant who had helped defend Salem from Colonel Manter. Bailey used his gun to knock the glass out of the upstairs window.

Two other soldiers carried a an officer with shoulder straps on his uniform into the room and placed him on the bed. It was the poor fellow with a terrible wound to his knee. Although his leg hung loosely, the man's face was stern. He swept his gray hair back in place.

"Stay here, Captain Blanchard," one of the men said.

A short soldier entered the bedroom, yelling for muskets. His accent reminded Travis of Peter. The man fired out of the broken window, grabbed a fresh gun, and fired again.

"Reload!" he shouted.

Travis handed him his gun and began to reload the empty one. The Irishman fired and Bailey took the empty musket and shoved another weapon into his hands. The barrels on the guns became hot as they raced to keep up with the man's pace.

"Slow down, Ed," Bailey said.

The Irishman tossed the empty gun to him, laughed and slapped his thighs. "Ha! Be off with you then, Lieutenant. Get a body that can load 'em faster!"

As the fight wore on, Ed shouted, sang, and cursed while he fired shot after shot through the window.

Loud demands for more ammunition came from the battlefield.

"How many do you have left?" Bailey asked Travis.

"Three," Travis said.

"I have six."

The soldier tending to the wounded Captain came over. "I have about twenty left in my cartridge box."

"Can you reload for Ed?" Bailey asked.

"Yes, sir."

The lieutenant looked at Travis. "I hear calls for ammunition. We have to do something fast, or the rebels will crank those cannons up again."

"What can we do?" Travis asked.

"There are plenty of dropped cartridge boxes laying out on the ground or on those dead men, but there is a good chance we'll be shot while gathering them," Bailey warned.

"I am with you."

"Are you sure?"

Travis knew if the Thirteenth ran out of bullets, they would be cut to shreds. "If we do not go, we will be shot for sure."

CHAPTER TWENTY-FIVE

Travis followed Bailey down the stairs and outside. He glanced around for Salem but did not see him. The lieutenant ran to a dead soldier and took his ammo box. Going to his hands and knees, Travis low-crawled to another body where he found a handful of unfired rounds.

The Confederate bullets zipped into the ground, tearing up the dirt around their feet. Bailey ran toward the pig pen, while Travis made for the railroad tracks. After he topped the rise, he saw three bodies near the wood line, two Confederates and a member of the Thirteenth. An open cartridge box was at the waist of the Union soldier, nearly full. Travis ducked low, dashed to the fallen men, and grabbed the ammunition. When he looked up, a rebel was standing over him.

The butt of the Confederate's gun smashed into Travis's chin.

A flash of sky filled his view.

Someone had his feet.

Brush scraping against his face.

While Travis was flat on his back in the woods, a soldier in gray shouted questions down, spit flying from his mouth with each word. When Travis did not comprehend, a fist sent him into darkness.

Fluttering eyelids gave him glances of towering oaks with brown leaves. His head pounded with a painful rhythmic throbbing in time with his heartbeat. His body was jolted. Something rattled.

As the fog lifted from his mind, Travis looked around to find he was in the back of a wagon traveling down a bumpy road. Next to him were six other prisoners, none of which he knew. The ammunition he had gathered was gone, along with his haversack and gun. That meant his money was gone, too.

Two Confederates were on the wagon bench, one facing forward with the reins in his hand, the other holding a gun on the Union soldiers. "Stay down," he warned.

The bouncing and rattling had gone on for half an hour, or so, when the guard shouted to the driver. "Hold up!"

The wagon came to a halt. "What is it?"

"We are being followed."

While they were distracted, Travis glanced at the other men stretched flat in the wagon bed. Three of the other prisoners were unconscious, one looked to have bled to death, and the last two were staring right back at him.

"You boys raise up, and I'll put a bullet through your head."

Travis rubbed his sore jaw. It hurt when he moved it.

"I don't see anybody following us," the driver said.

"Right there," the guard said.

"That's nothing but a dog."

Travis sat up and instantly felt a gun barrel pressed against his temple. He raised his hands and laid back slowly but not before he saw Salem. The dog was standing behind the wagon, watching and waiting.

"Should I shoot him?" the guard asked.

"No!" Travis begged. He chopped his words to keep from moving his bruised mouth. "Please. He is just trying to find me."

The guard raised the gun to his shoulder and aimed.

"He won't hurt anyone," Travis pleaded.

"A Yankee dog," the man said. "Good for nothing."

He pulled the hammer back until it clicked and then eased his finger onto the trigger. Travis tried to get up but the guard put a boot across his neck. "Hold still, boy. You wouldn't want me to make a bad shot. No need for the mutt to suffer." His finger tightened on the trigger.

The driver reached back and pulled on the guard's shoulder. "We don't need the attention a shot would bring."

After a moment, the gun dropped. "I suppose not."

"He'll get tired of following us," the driver said. "Let's go."

The wagon continued bouncing down the trail and even though Travis wanted to look, the guard's careful watch kept him still.

That evening, they were held in a thick patch of woods while the guards took turns watching them. Any attempts by the captives to speak were met with threats.

Sometime during the night, two of the knocked-out Union soldiers came around with much moaning and head holding. At some point, Salem jumped into the wagon and curled next to Travis. The guard on duty said nothing. When morning came, both the Confederates laughed at the sight.

"We started with seven and now have eight. I do have to say, he is a determined cuss."

"That man at the back is dead," the driver said.

"I think this man is too," Travis said quietly, indicating the prone body next to where he sat.

One of the rebels walked around, pulled the first body out, and tossed it into the brush. "Push the other one down here," he ordered.

Under the careful watch of the guard, Travis helped the others push and pull the unlucky dead man to the back.

The guard nodded toward the dog. "Well, at least we still have six live ones."

"For now," his companion laughed.

Travis expected them to remove Salem, but the rebels did not speak another word about him until arriving at a train station. They joked with the other soldiers there about their canine captive.

A train whistle shrieked in the distance and the prisoners were forced out of the wagon at gunpoint. A little shack served as the depot, and a few worn buildings huddled a short distance away. Confederate soldiers and a few regular folk had gathered to whisper and stare at the prisoners. Most faces were twisted with bitterness, some smiled mockingly, and a very few just looked sad.

"Where are you taking us?" asked the Union soldier next to Travis.

A guard smirked, "You will find out soon enough, blue-belly."

A dozen Confederates talked amongst themselves. Travis could not hear all of the words but he got the gist of their conversation. They spoke of prisons that were full and the outcome of recent battles.

Salem growled low as an old man walked past and spit at the prisoners, but Travis tapped the dog's head to silence him, afraid he would provoke the rebels. Since the ambush at Ringgold, Salem had stuck close to his side, and Travis wondered if he had been shell-shocked by one of the explosions.

The train engine chugged by slowly, steam blowing and breaks screeching, until it came to a full stop. Several of the waiting soldiers shouldered guns, while two soldiers walked to the first boxcar and slid the door back to reveal twenty other Union prisoners. A rank smell spilled out of the enclosure, causing the guards to step back. A women dressed in homespun clothing raised a hand to cover her nose, mumbling, "Disgusting pigs."

Two Confederates on top of the train looked down and shouted, "Why do you think we are up here and not inside with them!"

A gun poked Travis between the shoulder blades. "Y'all get in."

They obeyed and climbed in the car. The bulk of the men were pressed more to one side, most of them lying on the floor. There were a couple of buckets at the other end, the source of the stench.

Travis looked back and motioned for Salem. The dog jumped, barely making the distance. His hind legs scratched at the lip until Travis pulled him inside.

"The animal isn't going," one of the Confederates said.

Travis's heart quickened. Pretending not to hear, he stepped over and around the men, until he reached the back wall. Salem followed and they both sat, facing away from the door.

The soldier who had spoken said "Hey, bring that dog back!" and started to jump in. He hesitated. "That smell is horrible," he said, and jumped back to the ground. "Shut the door and get them out of here!"

As the train pulled away and picked up speed, light spilled through small gaps in the walls, exposing a vast array of expressions. Some soldiers had tired faces and were whispering to others, but a few men were wild-eyed with fear. Many troops held a bewildered look at their predicament. This was the group in which Travis belonged.

A man in his thirties leaned in and tapped him on the shoulder. "Your dog?" he asked loudly over the clatter and clang of the rocking boxcar.

"Yes," Travis answered.

"Where did he come from?"

"Near my house in Arkansas."

The man held his fingers out, and Salem cautiously sniffed them. A slow wag of his tail encouraged the man to gently rub his head.

"He's a good dog, I can tell." The man dropped his hand, and studied Travis.

"Listen, our best hope is to get swapped in a prisoner exchange, but more than likely we'll end up at a prisoner camp. Either way, when we get to wherever they are taking us, don't tell them you hail from a southern state."

"Surely."

"Hear what I say, boy," the man warned. "What regiment do you hold to?"

"Illinois Thirteenth."

"That's good. Tell 'em you are from Illinois. If you don't, they will call you a traitor and treat you accordingly. Understand?"

Travis nodded.

The man stood, struggling to keep his balance in the rocking boxcar. "Ya' got a nice bruise on your jaw."

Travis rubbed it gently. "It's getting better."

The man clutched his stomach. "I would choose a messed up jaw over what I have any day. What was the town we just left called?"

"I never heard it. They caught me in Tennessee but I do not think we are anywhere close to there now."

"We're headed south." The man doubled over with a belly cramp. "I'd guess Mississippi." With those words he made a dash for one of the buckets.

They traveled for an unknown number of miles and, after dark, were unloaded and marched a few hours to another train. One bucket of tepid water was shoved in the boxcar with them. Each of the men used his hands to scoop up a few swallows. Although his throat was parched, Travis shared his handful with Salem.

The train crept along at a snail's pace all night on railroad tracks barely fit for use. Several times the whole car shifted violently, and tilted at horrifying angles.

The next day around noon they arrived at a town the soldiers called Selma, and were transferred to a steamboat. More prisoners were already held there. Travis kept Salem close to him, trying to avoid attention, but the guards taking down his name and rank stopped him before he could move on. The Confederate was young, maybe seventeen years of age.

"Your dog?" he asked.

"Yes."

The young man lowered his voice. "Don't take him with you."

Travis bit his lip and the knot in his gut tightened. "He tracks me everywhere, and I cannot stop him. He always follows me no matter what I do."

"It's just I would hate to see him shot."

An older guard with hard eyes walked over. "Turn around, Yankee."

Travis quickly did as he was told, using his foot to push Salem. "Stay back," he whispered anxiously.

The man grabbed Travis's coat at the collar and peeled it down. His own gray jacket was just as quickly doffed and tossed at Travis's feet. He walked away while shoving his arms into his new garment, oblivious to the fact it barely fit his larger frame.

Travis picked up the old jacket. It was dirty and had holes in both elbows. The kind-hearted guard whispered, "Put it on before somebody takes your shirt too."

"Thanks," Travis said quietly. While he was buttoning the jacket, he asked, "Can you tell me where we are?"

The rebel's eyes were full of pity. "You are in Alabama. Your next stop is Cahaba prison."

Chilly December winds stung Travis's face as the steamer chugged along for most of the day. It finally stopped at a river bank with a steep incline leading up to a thick timber wall. The guards attached bayonets to their muskets and stood ready.

A stern Confederate officer ordered the men to form up. "We are stopping at the commander's office first and then on to prison. If you do not do exactly as you are told or give us the slightest reason, we will shoot or run you through with a bayonet."

Salem followed as the men marched in line up the hill. They were ordered to halt just outside a small building that was by the stockade. It had recently rained, and the ground was a churned up mess.

Travis studied the wooden structure around the prison. It was made with thick planks standing on end, forming a fence. He guessed the height to be twelve feet, maybe more. Cross pieces had been attached to hold the timbers in a straight line. A set of heavy wooden gates looked to be the only access inside. The roof of the prison rose above wall but nothing else of the building could be seen.

Travis heard his name and rank called, and walked into the building under the watchful eyes of the guard. Salem shadowed him, but the soldier at the door kicked Salem. With a snarl and flash of teeth, the dog lunged. Travis yelled "No!" and held him back. There were shouts and the sound of guns being lifted. He crouched and curled his body around Salem to shield him from the bullets.

"HOLD YOUR FIRE!" a voice thundered.

In the quiet that followed, Travis slowly raised his head, still keeping a tight grip on the struggling dog. They were surrounded by angry soldiers, guns pointed at his head. One of them said loudly, "But, Commander, that son of a – !"

"Private! I advise you to keep a civil tongue in your head. Now you will explain to me why there is a dog in here?"

"Yes, sir. This savage brute charged in here and the prisoner –."

"Begging your pardon, Commander Henderson," interrupted another guard, "but that dog did not show one tooth until he was kicked. He has been with the prisoner since he was loaded on the steamboat. We all kind of took to him, as he was quiet and seemed devoted to his master. Many of us miss having a good dog around."

Travis stood up, and was grateful to see the young soldier from the steamboat. The fur on Salem's back was raised, but he obeyed when told to sit and stay.

"Now, young man, let us have a word. My name is Henderson," the commander said to Travis. "You will address me as Commander."

"Yes, sir."

Henderson was a short man with a heavy mustache adorning his upper lip. Though lacking in stature, he made up for it in his calm air of authority. His attention was drawn to Salem, now sitting quietly. "So once more I ask how this dog come to be in this prison under my command?"

Travis stiffened. "He's my dog, sir. Please don't kill him."

Henderson walked to Salem. Travis clenched his jaw, hoping with all his might that the dog would not growl. Salem sniffed the commander's pants from cuff to knee, then wagged his tail slightly, apparently not holding the previous incident against this particular man. The officer smiled and nodded.

"Where did you find him?" Henderson asked.

"In Arkansas, where I..." Travis choked off what he was about to say.

"Arkansas, where you what?"

"Where I was marching with the Thirteenth Illinois." He silently apologized to Salem as he played him off as a confederate dog. The fact that he was a regiment mascot for the Union was something he was definitely not going to share.

"We tried to scare him off, with him being a southern dog and all, but he fell in behind us and followed along. I even tied him up once but he chewed through the rope and trailed me for miles."

"He must have a good nose," Henderson said, and Travis felt the first stirring of hope that neither he nor Salem would be shot.

"He does, sir. I've grown fond of him and would not want anything to happen to him."

The commander stood and motioned for the guard to come over. "This animal seems to have a great amount of practice scenting Yankees." They both laughed. "Take him to the dog pen."

"Sir," Travis said. "If you don't mind, might I say goodbye?"

"Make it quick."

While the other soldier went to retrieve rope, Travis knelt, took Salem in his arms, and fought back tears. Salem was his last link to freedom and his friends of war. He wanted to believe that the dog would somehow track down the remaining members of the Thirteenth but the distance was much too far and dangerous.

"Will he be hurt?"

"He will not," Henderson said. "You have my word as a man of God."

"And when the war is over, can I get him back?"

"That would require me to foretell many events in the future, and over which I have no control. I cannot make such a promise. Now, be done and get back in line."

The commander turned away, giving orders to continue processing the prisoners, and the room began filling up with captives once more.

The soldier was back. Travis reached for the rope hanging in his hand. "Let me do it. He will go easier that way."

He made a loop through Salem's collar and tied it, whispering words of comfort to him while doing so.

"Be good, boy. I'll find you when this is over, I promise. Be good and do not cause trouble for yourself. It would please me greatly if you do not get shot."

Salem licked his face, and Travis hugged him one more time. The soldier took the rope and pulled. Salem took several steps, then stopped and pulled back toward Travis.

"Go, Salem." Travis ordered firmly, struggling not to cry. "Go."

The captives were removed of any valuables and knives, and were given a small box with eating utensils. Travis and the other new prisoners were led past two cannons. The barrels were pointed toward the prison, their muzzles disappearing through a set of holes in the wooden wall.

Around the corner were the stockade gates. A small door was located in one of these gates. After a metal bar was raised, the narrow door was opened and they walked through, single file. The wooden wall formed a rectangle that enclosed the brick prison. The stockade was within fifteen feet of the bricks along the sides but in the front was a bigger yard area.

In this space, men were cooking food in large cast iron pans over small fires. They stopped what they were doing and watched as the newcomers were led into the prison.

"Fresh fish! Fresh fish!" a couple of the men yelled toward the inner prison.

The prison was large. Once inside, Travis saw the walls were tall, maybe a little higher than the stockade outside. The floors were comprised of sandy dirt, and on the river side of the building was a small room with a closed door. Toward the back, on the same side, was an opening in the wall with a guard standing nearby. Travis supposed this to be the outhouse.

Very little of the brick building was covered by a roof and even then, he could see daylight in many areas. A few hundred men gathered around the new prisoners and pelted them with questions. Each man was asked for updates on the war, which battles they were in, how they were captured, their names, and what regiments they belonged to. Travis answered each inquiry many times over and, remembering the advice of the man on the train, lied each time he was asked where he was from.

Some of the men had rough blankets and walked around with them draped over their shoulders. Others had coats or jackets, and still others had nothing but thin shirts to cover them. Armed guards were spaced out along the outer walls, and a few were conversing with prisoners.

Travis had not slept well in days. He wanted nothing more than to sit and lean against something while he rested. He walked toward the western brick wall but just before he reached it, a hand grabbed his jacket and jerked him back.

"Are you trying to get killed?"

CHAPTER TWENTY-SIX

Travis recovered his balance and turned to face the man who had pulled him. The prisoner was an older gentleman with one arm. His beard was speckled gray, as was the hair sticking out from under his hat.

"You trying to get killed?" The man asked again.

"No. I just want to sit down.

"That's the dead zone, boy."

"Dead zone?"

"Did you not wonder why none of us were in the space around the outer wall? Stay five feet away, unless you want to get your head shot off."

Travis looked at the ground. "Five feet? There is no line."

"That's right. It's best to keep your distance. Do not even stumble across the dead line. Do not reach across it. Heck, I would not allow my breath to cross it. Same thing in the cook-yard. Subtract the dead line and the guard room and all of us are left with one hundred ten feet by one hundred sixty-four feet of space to live in. I've stepped it off. Do it yourself if you don't believe me."

"No, I believe you and thank you for your help. What do you go by?"

He wiggled his scarred stump. "Everybody here calls me Lefty."

"Should not the guard have given us warning about the deadline?"

Lefty glanced around at the Confederate sentries. "It depends on which guards brought you in here. Most of them are decent men but there are always three or four who are just looking for an excuse." The man tipped his hat and walked away.

Travis explored the prison, searching as he did for any familiar face, possibly another member of the Thirteenth. There were none.

The water supply of the prison entered through the middle section of the west wall, by means of a covered trough, diagonally to the center of the yard. Midway, a ditch held two open barrels buried a couple of feet in the ground. On the other side of the containers, the water in the ditch entered another buried pipe that went to the outhouse. It flowed under the wooden toilet seats and carried most of the waste outside.

Travis had not had a drink since the tepid water on the train. He suddenly craved the taste of cool water. When he had a turn, he dipped his tin cup in and brought it to his lips. An overwhelming stench of rotten eggs assailed his senses, causing him to gag.

One of the nearby men laughed and said, "You will soon be thirsty enough not to care what is in that water."

At five 'o clock, they were called forward for counting. When the guards were finished, the men were allowed to go back to their spots. As the sun fell, the temperature dropped with it. A fire was started a few hours after dark just outside the prison doorway. Two guards stood by the flames, but they did not share it with the prisoners.

Some of the men began to lie down in large numbers, quietly talking amongst themselves. They formed rows, side by side and scooting close together, apparently for warmth. None of these had blankets or any other covering. Those with coats and blankets, on the other hand, curled up in depressions in the sand, many in small groups of two or three.

Travis used his heel to dig a spot for himself. He had not eaten since the day before and his growling stomach did its best to keep him awake, but finally failed.

During the night, strong hands grabbed Travis, flipping him onto his stomach. He tried to shout but someone pushed his face into the sand. His jacket was pulled and yanked until it was over his head and both his arms slipped through the sleeves. Within seconds, the attackers were gone. With sand in his eyes, he tried raise up and see the men, but it was too dark.

He spit out gritty dirt. No one around him had made any move to help, nor had anyone called out.

Travis blinked and tried to clear the sand from his eyes. He got up and stumbled to the barrels of water. With cupped hands he splashed his face with the freezing liquid and rinsed his mouth. He spat the sulfur-tasting water out.

He went back to his spot and shivered. The cold mixed with fear had removed all thoughts of sleep. Behind him, he could hear rats squeaking and gnawing, an accompaniment to the snores and coughing of the captives. There was a quiet murmur from the guards by the fire.

War is a simple three letter word until you live it. This was his new life, and he had never hated anything so much.

The next morning, they were ordered forward for roll call. As soon as this was finished, Travis tried to spot the men who had taken his jacket but it was impossible. The old Confederate coat was filthy and had holes worn in it. In front of Travis were at least a hundred men wearing dirty gray jackets with holes. He found out he was not the only one to be targeted. Other soldiers he had arrived with were missing various hats and garments too.

Out of necessity, he visited the privy. Its floor was higher than the prison's and was made of wood. There were six toilet holes positioned so the water would wash the waste toward the river. Privacy was nonexistent with no doors or dividers. The smell was awful and caused Travis to take care of his business quickly.

Even though he fought it, thirst became too great and he finally gave in and held his breath while he drank the terrible smelling water.

Rations were doled out, and he received a little over a pint of raw cornmeal with a small piece of rancid bacon. This was to be his food for the day. The prisoners had divided themselves into squads of ten men. Each squad chose a man to cook their food on small fires outside. There were ten fires with skillets and kettles that the men took turns with. When the food was done, it was carefully divided, but some of the squads argued over the portion sizes.

A guard brought a newspaper inside and read articles about the war. It was easy to hear the slant of the media. While he listened,

Travis walked toward the doorway to receive his serving of cooked food. He saw a familiar face on his way. "Lefty!"

"Mornin' boy. I heard you and several other fish were baptized into Castle Morgan right proper," Lefty said, nodding at his thin shirt.

Travis frowned. "It was not right what they did. We are all in the same mess, how can they prey on each other?"

Lefty snorted. "You better get some friends real quick if you want to keep your skin on. There is those that will take that, too, if you are weak enough."

Travis shook his head in dismay as Lefty kept talking.

"And you better stay clear of the entrance. Wait here for your meal."

"Why?"

"You can go out to cook and back through, but never stand in the opening."

"Another dead line?" Travis asked.

"Pretty much," Lefty said.

Travis added water to his corn meal to make it softer. The corn patty was coarse and crunchy with big pieces of husk and cob. The bacon had shriveled up until it was no more than two inches long. While he ate, Travis spit the bits of husk and cob out. He knew he should save half his meal for later in the day but his stomach was empty and he could not wait.

That night, a cold drizzle fell into the prison. Men tried to huddle under the portion of the building that had a roof but it did no good. The wind blew the tiny drops into every corner. The water collected above and dripped through dozens of holes in the roof. Lefty took mercy on Travis and shared a blanket with him and two others. It was a miserable night in Cahaba.

Christmas of 1863 was not celebrated with singing carols or gift giving. Instead, three men in the prison turned sick with terrible coughs that worsened with each passing day. One of the men by the name of Douglas, shivered in his sandy hole. The muggers of Cahaba showed him no mercy, stealing his blanket during the night. A combination of cold air and pneumonia was too much for the poor man and he became the first death in the prison. Just days later, the other two sick soldiers followed the same path to their graves.

Travis had taken up with Lefty and a few of the other veteran "pickled sardines" for protection against the muggers. Each night he curled into a tight ball with them, trying to stay warm enough to fall asleep. His thoughts wandered back to Chickasaw and the terrible things he had witnessed there. Memories of Colonel Wyman and Emil haunted him. He wished with all his might that he could talk to Peter, just for a while, but Travis would never want the Irishman to step foot in Cahaba.

While he struggled for sleep, a dog in the distance began to bark. He held his breath and listened as hard as he could. He alternated between conviction and doubt that it was Salem's voice. The faint yips finally faded away, leaving Travis, once again, alone in the dark with his thoughts.

CHAPTER TWENTY-SEVEN

March 1864

It started with a cramp in his gut but soon doubled him over in pain. A few hours later, it moved down into his bowels and sent him rushing to the toilets.

After a few days of sickness, Travis began to feel better. The men in his squad voted him cook for the day and he followed the other cooks, learning the steps as he went. They left the prison, under guard and threat of being shot, and searched for any deadwood that had fallen from the trees. Outside the back corner of Cahaba was the largest oak Travis had ever seen. Long strands of Spanish moss hung from its limbs. While he was gathering wood underneath the behemoth, a bright colored bird landed above him. He was not sure if it was a parakeet or a parrot but he had never seen a bird so vividly green. It tweeted, chirped, and then fluttered away. So easy was its path in freedom.

Travis looked for any signs of Salem. He longed for a visit from his furry friend, his last connection to his brother. One of the guards noticed him glancing around and mistook his intentions.

"If you are thinking 'bout running, go ahead." He raised his gun. "I need some practice."

"I am not," Travis said. "I had a dog with me when I came. I was just hoping he would be out here."

The man lowered his musket. "If he is smart, your dog skedaddled."

On his way back to the prison, Travis saw a young girl standing with her mother. They were positioned close to the barricade and watched as the cooks walked by. Behind the women was a two-story house, only a few yards from the prison fence.

"Who is that?" Travis asked another cook.

"Amanda Gardner, and she is a kind soul indeed."

The bitter nights finally passed and allowed Travis some much needed rest. The peace was short lived. Tiny bugs crept along his skin, especially at night, and mosquitos left whelps on his arms and face. The cold had been hard to deal with, but the insects where just as bad.

His stomach problems returned and kept him from cook duty for days. If it had not been for the men in his squad, he would not have eaten. New soldiers arrived, bringing their numbers close to seven hundred.

"Some rebels are coming in," Lefty said.

Travis raised up on his elbow. His head pounded with pain. "Who is it?"

A guard escorted a well dressed man around Cahaba, answering questions as they walked.

"This is where it comes in," the guard said. He pointed at the water ditch.

The stranger sighed. "It's open to the world until it reaches the prison wall." The man went from one sick soldier to another, checking them for fever. He came to Travis and felt his head. "I am Doctor Whitfield. How are you feeling?"

"My stomach is messed up," Travis said.

The doctor pressed on his gut, asking if the action caused him any discomfort. Whitfield pinched his skin, pulled Travis's eyelids down, and looked closely. "This water is not fit to drink."

"It smells awful," Travis said.

"It's from an artesian well. Small doses of sulfate in the water by itself is good for you, but this one runs along the streets where things I will would rather not mention get mixed in. Avoid drinking any more of it."

"What can I drink?"

"I'll have some guards bring some well water. I strongly suspect the contamination is the source of your sickness." The doctor produced a bottle and gave him a swig. The liquid was strong and burned his throat.

"What was that?"

"Whiskey and dogwood bark. It should help you get some rest." The doctor left and soon enough the medicine worked as prescribed.

When Travis woke, he found Lefty by his side, stricken with the same sickness. They both labored with stomach pain. The clean well water never arrived and after a full day, both men could not resist the ditch any longer. The liquid sulfur offended their noses, cured their thirst, but prolonged the suffrage.

A vast improvement was made to Cahaba in the form of massive bunk beds. The tiers were long and wide, allowing many men to sleep close together, like sardines in a tin. There were five levels in each bunk. Six of these had been built and provided nearly enough room for all the men to avoid sleeping on the ground. Prisoners quickly nicknamed the beds, calling them roosts. Some even squawked like chickens when they retired for the night.

Days later, rumors spread that Cahaba was being closed. At first, the news was ignored, but toward the end of the month, the transfers started. Every able-bodied man was moved out, but those who were sick and weak were left behind. Travis rushed to the toilets at least a dozen times a day. His bowels churned and caused him great burning pain when relieving himself. The sick men did not speak. They sat and endured their trials in silence, praying to live through it, and hoping to fool the guards enough to get transferred out.

The prison closure was over before it started. Captured men began to arrive at a steady pace. The doctor visited Cahaba and assured them the open ditch bringing the water inside had been replaced with a pipe the whole way. Travis and the other sick men were given more medicine and dry crackers to eat.

The bugs that had annoyed him multiplied. He could see the grayish-brown lice on his clothing and skin. Lefty had so many that his hat seemed to be moving when he was sitting still. The itching, rubbing, and scratching was constant.

As his strength returned, Travis resumed his rotation as squad cook. While he was outside gathering wood, the young girl he had seen a month before approached him.

"Here," she said. Her arm was extended with something in her hand.

"Back!" the guard shouted.

"Private," an older woman said as she approached. "Belle simply wishes to bless this young man's life. Will you deny her?"

"These prisoners are dangerous, Ms. Gardner. You and your daughter know that."

"This one is just a boy," she said. "I can tell he is sick and doesn't have enough strength to harm anyone."

In the girl's hand was a sweet potato. Belle looked to be a few years younger than Travis, and she had warm and friendly eyes. He smiled at her and she smiled back.

Just then something tickled the side of his face and Travis realized some lice must be moving about. He rubbed the spot and dropped his head in shame.

"Here," the girl said again, "take it."

"Make it quick," the guard said.

Travis held his hand out for the potato. "Thank you. Thank you both, so much."

He cooked the food and split the sweet potato ten ways with his squad, and all of the men thanked him greatly. Lefty encouraged him to volunteer for cook duty more often with the hope that Amanda Gardner and Belle would gift him with more food.

When the men could not stand the lice and fleas any longer they cut each other's hair with a jackknife someone had smuggled in. Travis sat still while Lefty sawed his locks away. The dull blade pulled and tugged his hair as it cut, making it a very painful process.

"It's the only way to get some relief from these graybacks," Lefty said.

"Yes, it is awful," Travis agreed heartily.

Lefty piled the hair, saving it to toss in the fire. "I have scratched sore spots on my head and the green flies have warted me to death."

"They are buzzing me, too."

"Don't let them lay eggs on you. I saw a man with maggots in his skin. He was crying and I can't say I blamed him. Best thing to do is dip water out of the ditch, downstream of the drinking barrels. Rub your skin with it every morning. It helps, but they will be back eating on you before bedtime."

Travis stared miserably at the sand. "I can see them moving. Between them, the flies and the fleas, we will scratch ourselves to death by morning."

The number of guards increased. One called Hankins held a special hatred for the prisoners. Travis walked close to the cook-yard deadline and Hankins hit him in the gut with his butt of his gun.

"You are one step from death," he growled.

Several of the prisoners helped Travis back to his feet. "He wasn't even close," a fellow prisoner said.

Hankins narrowed his eyes to slits. "There will be no more warnings."

Travis studied him before turning away. He was young, maybe seventeen. Hankins kept his mouth tight, causing his jaw muscles to bulge. A sparse mustache was the only facial hair he had. Most of the guards had shown hints of kindness or at least indifference, but not this one.

Someone tapped Travis on the arm. "Hankins is an alright fellow if you stay out of his way."

The short, thin man had pants on that were too long and he was only covered above the waist by a tattered gray jacket. His shirt and shoes were missing, and the socks on his feet allowed most of his toes to poke through.

"Hankins is not that bad," he said again.

Travis shrugged and rubbed his sore belly. "I'm not so sure." He offered his hand. "I'm, Travis."

"Name is Eddy, but everyone calls me Teddy." He shook with Travis. "I have bought some good food from Hankins."

"You bought food from him?"

"He has come through with it every time."

"How did you manage to get money in here? Mine was taken."

"Some of us are better at hiding things than others," Teddy said mysteriously. "See you around."

The next morning after the prisoners were counted, the guards gathered in a line with their bayonets pointing forward. They waved their guns with shouts of "Where are they?" and "Everybody line up!"

Cahaba was searched and a secret hole was found. Twelve men had escaped under the brick wall and then climbed the stockade during the night, all without being noticed. That afternoon the prison buzzed with laughter, joyful shouts, and spontaneous bursts of popular northern choruses. Men made bets, gambling rations and clothing on how many of the escapees would be caught and when they would be returned.

Travis saw Teddy at the water barrels and joined him. "The guards are furious."

Teddy did not appear as overjoyed as the others. "The plans were kept so close it was not even on the grapevine. There will be a comeuppance for this from our keepers."

Travis was concerned now. "But the rest of us are not to blame."

Teddy remained silent, looking worried.

After roll call the following day, Travis started cooking breakfast for his squad. While he was tending his fire, Teddy walked past. He stood patiently until Hankins motioned him to the gate. They exchanged money for several sweet potatoes and Teddy held them out for Travis to see as he walked back toward the prison.

"Wait," Hankins said, holding a greenback in the air.

Teddy stopped in the doorway of Cahaba. "That's what we agreed on," he said over his shoulder.

With no warning, Hankins shouldered his rifle and fired into Teddy's back.

Guards rushed from several directions. "What happened?" one of them asked.

"He was blocking the door," Hankins said.

"Everybody inside!" the guards ordered.

As the cooks entered the prison, Travis and two others dragged Teddy inside. He was barely breathing. A cough racked his body, and he whispered, "Never forget this day."

Bloody potatoes slipped from his hand and starving prisoners snatched them up in the blink of an eye. Someone shouted, "Murderer! Hankins, you're a murderer!"

An hour later, Teddy was taken to the hospital where he died.

As darkness fell upon the prison, the gates were opened and twelve men filed inside. The escapees were wet, covered with cuts from briars, and slumped at the shoulders with defeat. They told of their harrowing adventure and capture. Two of them had bandages on their legs where tracking dogs had mauled them.

"The dogs reached us long before the men did. They had their way with us until the handlers arrived."

"Then they pulled them off?" someone asked.

"Not right away. One of those men is a devil in disguise. He beat those dogs into a fury, laughing when they took their anger out on us."

"There's no escaping those dogs," the other man said. "We ran for miles and they tracked us the whole way."

The bets on the prisoner's capture was forgotten. Teddys death had brought a great depression upon Cahaba.

CHAPTER TWENTY-EIGHT

June 1864

Travis lost count of the days. Each morning when he lined up for rations, he hoped for something different than corn meal, but disappointment was the way of life in Cahaba.

Working in the cook-yard was almost unbearable. He held a hand to shield his face from the firepit heat, but the hot weather mixed with a dozen piles of embers made it like working in a furnace.

One of the guards walked purposefully toward Travis. When he was close he said, "You there. What is your name?"

"Travis Bailey, sir."

The guard pointed to a hole in the stockade. "The Gardeners wish to speak to you."

Travis walked toward the wall but stopped. "It's across the deadline."

"I will stand by you," the guard said. "Nobody will shoot."

Travis remembered what had happened to Teddy. The man understood his hesitation. "I'm Lieutenant Crutcher. Hankins is gone until this evening."

Travis continued cautiously to the small opening in the wall. When he reached it, he bent close to the hole and said, "I am here."

"I am Amanda Gardner," a women's voice said.

"Travis Bailey is my name, ma'am," he answered.

"Yes, we spoke outside a while back. I have a bit of food for you today."

His mouth watered. "We would appreciate anything you can spare."

A squash, two potatoes, and a piece of pie wrapped in paper were passed through the hole. Travis used his shirt to hold the items and could hardly contain his excitement.

"Thank you!" He said a little louder than he intended to. He cleared his throat. "All of us are very grateful for your kindnesses."

A second piece of wrapped pie appeared in the hole. A sweet voice said, "It is Belle. Will you give this to Mr. Crutcher."

"Yes, ma'am." Travis looked up at Crutcher and handed the pie over, and then put his mouth close to the hole again. "Can I ask you a question?"

Belle's voice sounded as if it she smiled when she replied, "You may."

"Have you seen a dog out there? He has a shaggy head, knee-high in size, and has fur that is shades of reddish browns and black mixed together."

Belle shook her head. "The town has many hounds wandering around but I have not seen one the likes of this."

"He is my dog and he is very smart. Salem is his name. If you see him, would you consider keeping him for me?"

"I will be on the watch for him," Belle said.

"That's long enough." Lieutenant Crutcher said as he brushed crumbs from his uniform. "Get back to your cooking before other squads start complaining."

Travis thanked them again and returned to his cook fire. After the food was done and divided among his squad, some of the men cried when he produced the pie and split it between them. Travis ate his bite of dessert and fought back his own set of emotions at the sweet taste of sugar, one he had not experienced for a long while.

Lefty refused his portion. "You got this for us, you eat it. I don't believe I can stomach it."

"Are you sick?" Travis asked.

He eyes filled with unshed tears. "I can't take this anymore. Our government has abandoned us to this hellhole."

No one disagreed, and an awkward silence fell over them. Travis struggled to lift his friend's spirit, but he had no words to do so.

Lefty rose and climbed awkwardly into the roost, paying extra attention to not bump the end of his shortened limb.

"He has gangrene in his stump," said a private from the 102nd Ohio Infantry. "He refuses to ask the guards for a doctor, and the infection is spreading."

Later in the evening, Lefty came to the men in his squad and said calmly, "They stole my blanket."

"Who?" Travis asked.

"Some of the muggers. Thompson, Jack, and Tom."

"We will get it back," Travis said angrily.

Lefty simply nodded and smiled. "I want to thank all of you for being such a fine group of sharing souls."

He patted Travis on the shoulder. His eyes glistened as he turned away and went toward the front of the prison, weaving through the crowd on his way.

"Where is he going?" Travis asked.

Lefty continued walking straight toward the doorway.

"Oh, no," the man next to Travis muttered, "I think he is going for a parole."

Travis watched in stunned disbelief.

Lefty thrust out his boney chest and marched until he reached the prison doorway leading to the cook-yard. There he stopped.

"Back inside!" a guard shouted.

"No, sir, I do not have a mind to do so."

A crack of gunfire rang out, and a musket ball sent Lefty to the ground.

Travis and other prisoners rushed forward with shouts but stopped short of the dead line. All the guards had rifles at the ready, and more were gathering. Hankins reloaded his gun.

Lefty's body was carried into the cook-yard and through the wooden stockade doors. Hankins followed behind them while keeping his musket ready.

The air was filled with angry shouts. A prisoner hollered out, "Hankins, God will judge you!" and several others joined in with similar sentiments.

The guards ordered everyone back from the deadline with threats of death. The crowd eventually broke up, more from lack of energy and will, than anything else.

Travis stood still and stared above the brick wall at the giant oak tree. Its massive branches waved in the evening breeze. A few of the green parrots he had seen while gathering wood were scattered among the limbs, chirping and cleaning themselves. How could such beauty and peace exist just yards away from this horrible place?

That night, the rats were out in force, crawling over Travis as he tried to sleep. He kicked and slapped at them in the darkness but the rodents were too fast. Lice wiggled their way into his ears and mosquitos sucked blood from his arms. The prison was full of moans and cursing as the vermin stealthily attacked the men.

The heat in the roost was sweltering, the stench of sweat filtering up through the boards. Travis had positioned himself on a bottom bunk, near the end. Someone above him grunted and began to scramble. The man gagged and hurled, sending a shower of warm liquid down through the stacked rows, splashing Travis and the others.

"Ah, forgive me, gentlemen," the man moaned weakly. "I could not get out in time."

"God help us, man, just sleep on the ground!" came an angry reply.

Travis and the others who had been splattered with vomit, went to the ditch to clean themselves.

Travis had come to understand Lefty's final decision. All of them were dying in small measures each day from poor food, and little of it, dysentery, and disease - but the worst offender of all was the lack of hope.

More bunks were built bringing the total roosts to nine, and giving those who had been sleeping on the ground a little relief from the fleas. The population of Cahaba fluctuated on a daily basis. Men were constantly being transferred to Andersonville each time the numbers swelled.

Sixty newcomers walked into the prison.

"Fresh fish! Fresh fish!"

Thompson, Jack and Tom – the three men known to be the worst of the muggers – were waiting to size up the potential targets. All three of them had the best clothing in Cahaba, no holes, few stains. At least fifty other prisoners surrounded them, ready to do whatever the trio commanded. The prison gang had become more brazen with their growing numbers, sometimes stealing what they wanted in broad daylight.

They circled the newcomers, asking questions while taking inventory of what each man was wearing and carrying.

Two men walked past speculating on which regiments the new men were from. "One of the guards told me yesterday they were getting new fish from an Illinois regiment. They surely have the most recent news about the war."

Travis jumped to his feet and elbowed his way through the crowd calling out to the newcomers. His heart raced as he recognized some of them. One man was a head taller than all the rest. He moved closer and shouted for joy.

"George!"

Travis ran toward him but George caught him by the shoulders, holding him at arm's length. His face slowly lit up in recognition. "Travis? Travis!" He hugged him and they slapped each other on the back over and over. "You have lost weight and your hair... you look...older."

They both talked over each other while Travis led George to an unoccupied spot on the ground.

"Is Thomas or Arthur here?" Travis asked.

"No. The rebels got about seventy of the Thirteenth at Madison Station but only eight in our company."

A man with red hair sat next to George and acknowledged Travis with a nod. "John Nichols, from Company F. George and I were captured together."

"Travis Bailey. Good to meet you."

"You were in the Thirteenth?"

Travis looked at George and smiled happily. "Yes."

"I remember seeing you during a battle. Dog Salem followed you around."

"Any idea what happened to our dog?" George asked Travis.

"He is here. At least, he should be."

George's eyebrows rose. "You are kidding me."

"He followed me," Travis said. "Stayed with me the whole time."

"That dog is unbelievable," John said.

"The prison commander..." Travis tried to remember his name.

"Henderson," George said.

"Yes. He said he would take care of Salem for me."

"I think he was the kindest rebel I have ever met," John said.

Travis told them the rules of Cahaba, warned them about the muggers, and suggested they form their own squad. While he talked, John watched him closely.

"I hate to offend," he said, "but you have some tiny bugs on your collar."

"Lice," Travis said. "They are thick in here. That's why most of us have cut our hair."

"You think we will get them too?" George looked horrified.

"You already have," Travis said. "Look at your pants."

George and John swatted at the lice on their clothes, and Travis laughed.

"It's pretty terrible here," Travis said, though he was feeling true hope for the first time since arriving. "With us together, though, I think we can see the end of this war in one piece."

A month later, new food arrived. "Beef!" A prisoner shouted as he ran through Cahaba. "We are getting beef today!"

His excitement spread to everyone. They had eaten bacon every day for months. The thought of something different made Travis's mouth water and he quickly volunteered to cook for his new squad.

"I like my steak medium-rare," George joked.

As the rations were being delivered, men began to shout. "Cowpeas instead of cornmeal! Hurrah!"

In the middle of the celebration, Thompson, the mugger, knocked a sickly prisoner down and took his food. Other men tried to stand up for the victim, but Thompson had numbers on his side and they quickly backed down.

"Keep your eye on our beef," George warned.

"I will," Travis replied grimly.

He took the rations for his squad into the cook-yard and quickly noticed a rank smell coming from the meat.

"This beef is bad," he said to another of the cooks.

"Worms in the peas, too," the man answered.

Travis held the kettle close and examined the cowpeas. Tiny larva wiggled in and out of holes they had made.

"What should we do?"

"Cook them," another man said. "I'm not starving because of a few bugs."

Travis held a piece of the meat up and sniffed it. "What about this?"

"Roll it in the charcoal from yesterday. That's all I know to try."

After taking the man's suggestion, the beef turned black but it stopped smelling so offensive.

While the meal cooked, Crutcher came over. "You are next."

Travis looked at the guard. "Sir?"

"At the fence. Ms. Gardner and Belle are there."

Travis set his fry pan aside and went to the hole in the stockade, passing another prisoner with a piece of bread in his hands. Belle was peering through the space between the planks.

"Are you Travis? I remember you asked about a dog."

"Yes. Did you see him?"

"I'm sorry. We did not."

Travis was amazed at how beautiful the girl was. He was ashamed she was seeing him with patchy hair, a dirty face, and covered in lice.

Amanda Gardner gently shifted Belle aside. "Have you sent any letters home? Do you need a pencil or paper?"

"No, ma'am. I wrote some letters to my father a while back but he never answered."

"What about your mother?"

"She left us. I do not know where she is. My father brought us to Arkansas. There is no one else to write to."

Amanda sighed. "I am sorry. Here, take this." She passed some bread through the hole. "Travis, I would love to talk more but a new man is in charge of the prison while Henderson is away working on transfers."

"A new man?"

"Jones is his name. He is very strict and does not approve of my visits, but, nevertheless, I shall be back." She smiled and Travis waved as she and Belle disappeared from the crack.

"Go finish your cooking," Crutcher said.

"Yes, sir." Travis pinched a piece of bread off and handed it to him. The guard grinned and popped it into his mouth.

The thick smoke from all the fires choked Travis while he tended to the rancid meat and wormy peas. Heated voices came from outside the stockade. He recognized Ms. Gardner as one of them.

"My actions have hurt no one."

A gruff male voice said, "That was the last time! We have rules here."

"Henderson never had a problem with our gifts."

"He is a hundred miles from here. I am in charge. There will be no more passing items through the fence. Understand?"

They was no further conversation, and Travis was disappointed he would not see Belle again.

In August, the increased number of prisoners required more fires, turning the cook-yard into a furnace. The sun blasted the men, scorching their skin both outside and inside the prison. They crowded under the small sections of roof and the shade that was cast from the brick wall. The stench of hundreds of sweaty men burned Travis's nose, making him want to bury his head in the sand.

Dead wood became very scarce and some cooks were not able to find enough tinder before being ordered back inside. Travis had found just enough for himself and was preparing his food as fast as he could while the sun blistered the skin on the back of his neck.

"Excuse me," a voice said. "Do you have any coals to spare?"

Travis looked up, squinting in the bright light.

"Frederick," the man said, holding his hand out.

"I'm sorry, Frederick. Mine are about to die out and I am not even finished."

The man glanced around. "It's my first time cooking. What do we do if we do not have enough wood?"

"Check the other fires. Maybe someone has more than I do."

"There is a small limb," Frederick said. "Somebody must have dropped it."

Before Travis comprehended what the man meant, Frederick stepped across the dead line to pick up a branch. He was shot without warning, the bullet ripping through him. Cooks scrambled, kicking up sand as they ran for cover in the prison. Travis looked back to see a pool of blood forming around the poor man. His stay at Cahaba was over.

A week later, John came to George and Travis. "Those devils raided me this evening. Took my coat."

"Do you know which ones?" George asked. "Maybe we can get it back."

"There's too many of them, George. It's hot as blue blazes anyway. Maybe I can get another one before winter. It sure did make a good pillow though." He stepped closer and whispered, "I'm not too keen on being here when winter comes."

"What are you saying?" Travis asked.

John wiped sweat of his forehead. "A plan is being made. It still lacks some pieces, but I will soon figure it out."

Travis glanced at George. While the thought of escaping scared him to death, it certainly was not without appeal. He wanted out of Cahaba.

CHAPTER TWENTY-NINE

September 1864

The hardest rains the men had seen while in prison came, overflowing the water ditch. Some prisoners gave it the nickname Cahaba Creek. It bubbled out of the dirt around the barrels and ran above ground and under the toilets. The downpour drenched everyone and provided them a short-lived relief from the lice and mosquitos.

After a full day of heavy rain, Travis heard, "Fresh fish! Fresh fish!"

Nearly two hundred men filtered into the prison. Most of them were from Tennessee and the thieves went to work right away, some so brash as to strip the smaller prisoners before they were too far past the deadline. Scuffles broke out with yells and threats.

The whole population of Cahaba paused, though, when a towering figure entered the wooden gates. Some tall men are bean-poles but not this fellow. His broad shoulders and stocky arms made him imposing, but his height made him intimidating. Travis had never seen anyone like him. George was a little over six foot but this man could easily rest his chin on George's head.

"Do you see that man?" Travis asked.

George chuckled. "How can you not see him."

"How tall do you think he is?"

"He has got to be seven foot, or near to it."

Travis stared at the giant man. A group of young men, some not much more than boys, stayed close to the tall fellow. Not one soul touched them as they moved through the prison.

In answer to the barrage of questions, Travis learned that the large man was named Richard, but called Big Tennessee.

After the crowd finally broke up, he had a chance to talk to one of the younger boys and his tall friend.

"My name is Stephen," the boy said. "This is Richard, but we call him Big Tennessee."

"I can see why. My name is Travis."

"Can we ask you a question?"

"Surely," Travis said.

"Where do we sleep?"

Travis quickly explained the rules of Cahaba, how the roosts had been built to get the men off the ground, and that they were now overflowing with prisoners, forcing newcomers to sleep in the sand.

"And be careful of the muggers," Travis added. "They will come in the night and take your things, coats, shoes, anything they can use or trade."

Big Tennessee looked down at him. "I don't care for thieves."

"Me either." Travis glanced from one to the other. "I'm guessing you are both from Tennessee?"

"We are in a regiment from there," Big Tennessee said, "but I'm from Kentucky."

"I'm in an Illinois regiment, but I am from Arkansas." Travis instantly regretted his words and looked around to make sure there was no nearby guards, or anyone known to be too friendly with their captors. Stephen and Big Tennessee did not give his comment a second thought, though, and Travis sighed in relief.

Shortly after roll call the next morning, a ruckus broke out in Cahaba. Travis, George, and John went to see what all the noise was about.

They found Big Tennessee standing in the middle of a group of thieves. "Give him his stuff back."

One of the muggers pointed a finger up at the man's face. "Are you accusing us of stealing? You should not meddle in what is none of your business."

As quick as a cat, the thief balled his fist and struck Tennessee in the side of the neck. Another man stepped forward and punched him in the ribs.

George started through the crowd intending to aid Tennessee, but it quickly became clear the situation was under control.

The gentle giant suddenly transformed into a man with the rage of a bear. He swung his left arm, smashing one of his attackers in the face, sending him flying through the air and knocking two additional muggers to the ground. The thief who had punched Tennessee in the ribs took another swing but missed. A massive right fist crushed the man's nose, rendering him unconscious with one blow. A third mugger decided to give it a try and rushed Tennessee, but the giant of justice caught him by the throat and lifted him from the ground with one arm. The man's feet kicked as he struggled to free himself.

"It will be very unhealthy for any of you to continue with your tricks." After speaking, Tennessee dropped the choking thief to the sandy soil.

Every soldier not part of the gang cheered and clapped when they realized the reign of the Cahaba muggers had just been ended by one man.

John caught the attention of Travis and George, and signaled them to follow him away from the crowd.

"I figured it out," he said excitedly.

"What?" George asked.

"We are getting out of here."

Travis looked around and lowered his voice. "How?"

"Did you see all that water running under the privy?"

"Yes."

"Look at it now."

The rain had washed some of the dirt away from the doorway leading into the toilets. The wooden floor of the room now had a small gulley opened underneath it.

"Are you sure?" George asked.

"Yes. Give me a couple days to plan it out."

"A couple days?" Travis asked. "That soon?"

"Waiting is not possible," John said. "If they fix that hole, we will be stuck."

"But a guard is there all the time," George said.

"Let me work on it."

"All right, John," George said. "Let us know what you come up with."

That night, Travis had trouble sleeping, but it was not the lice and rats keeping him awake. His insides were all jittery with the thought of escaping Cahaba. One of his biggest worries was centered around Salem. He had mulled over a dozen different ideas but none of them reunited him and the dog. He did not know where Salem was nor would there be time to find him, and this caused a great struggle with Travis's emotions. The dog had always been there for him and he was not sure if could bring himself to leave Salem behind.

A few days later, on the first cool morning in September, John outlined his plan.

"We leave tonight," he whispered.

"What about the guards?" George asked.

"Curley is a friend of mine, he is going to keep the privy guard busy. Another man will distract the guards at the front. When the time is right, we will slide through that hole and crawl under the toilets."

"I am fine with staying in the water," George said. "At least it has washed most of the filth away."

Travis looked from George to John. "What happens after we go under the privy? How do we get past the stockade?"

"There are gaps between the planks big enough for our fingers. We will scale up and over the top as quiet as we can."

"Where do we go from there?" George asked.

"North. The Union lines are north. We might have to sneak all the way to Vicksburg, but if we all stick together, we can do it."

"How many are going with us?"

"About twenty."

Travis frowned. "Twenty people cannot sneak through that hole without getting caught."

"It is okay," John promised. "I have it all planned out."

When the sun faded, the conspirators talked with the guards, showing them items for barter or cash. Thunder rolled in the distance, echoing along the river outside.

John motioned for his accomplices and, after glancing across the prison, he went into the hole. A few men Travis did not know went next. George looked around and took his turn. He grunted and wiggled.

"I'm stuck," he whispered.

"They are going to see you!"

"Pull me out," George said.

Travis looked to the nearest guard just as the prisoner who was talking to him shifted slightly. The guard's line of sight was unblocked. If he looked to his left, he would see George's waist and legs sticking out from under the floor of the latrine.

The guard's head turned. "What are you doing?" he asked.

Travis tried to speak but his tongue refused to cooperate.

"Waiting for our turn," George said. "The toilets are full."

Travis jolted around to see his friend standing calmly behind him.

The guard gave a brief nod and went back to his conversation.

George and Travis turned away. "Get in there," George whispered.

"What about you?"

"I do not fit."

"You cannot stay here," Travis said.

"Go," George ordered. "Get to our lines and tell them how bad the conditions are here. See if you can make a plea to the big bugs." He gestured toward the gully. "Hurry."

Travis crawled into the dark hole, through the cold water, and under the privy wall. When he stood up, John pulled him toward the stockade.

"Where's George," he said in his ear.

"He could not fit," Travis whispered.

They climbed the wall, taking their time, trying not to make a sound. Clouds had moved in, blocking most of the moonlight. Lightning streaked across the sky, flashing bright light on the escaping men. When their feet hit the ground outside, Travis collapsed. The fear of being caught had drained all his strength from his legs. John yanked him up, and he and the others moved down the river bank. Rain spattered them and another bright bolt of lightning revealed more men crawling over the stockade wall.

"How many are coming?" one of the men whispered.

"Prisoners saw us going through. Anybody brave enough will give it a go."

The raindrops multiplied until the noise made it impossible to speak to each other without raised voices. Lightening flashes revealed two canoes on the river bank. John and a second man claimed the first boat, and another escapee quickly joined Travis in the last one. They shoved off before any of the other men could reach them.

The downpour continued as they quietly paddled across the fast-flowing Alabama river. Just after they reached the other side, the storm stopped.

"Get in the woods," John ordered. "The ground is soaked and we will leave tracks everywhere if we keep walking."

They spent the rest of the night in the cold, huddled against tree trunks. The two men with Travis and John were nicknamed Shell and Booze.

The next morning, they walked an hour before coming to a road. Booze pulled back and quickly whispered, "There's some men waiting down there."

The escapees ducked into the brush and watched. The men were walking up and down the road, looking for tracks.

"Let's double back," John said. "They are going to see where we crossed, so we shall parallel the road and then head back to the river."

They ran hard and fast, putting as much distance between them and the searchers as they could. Shell finally stumbled and went to his knees gasping for air. The rest were not in much better shape, their bodies weakened by time in captivity.

Above the sound of heavy breathing came the sharp wail of a tracking dog.

Shell's mouth dropped open. "They found our trail!"

They got to the river's edge, a far cry from where they left the boats. John pulled his shirt off. "We have to cross, boys. Can all of you swim?"

Everyone nodded.

"Swim with one hand and hold your clothes out of the water with the other."

Travis stripped and rolled his shoes inside his shirt. When he stepped into the water he lost his breath again. Several dogs barked in the woods behind them. Travis bailed in and struggled against the current. As he finally emerged with the others further down on the opposite bank, he fought to get air into his lungs.

"Get dressed!" John commanded. "Hurry."

Moments after they were clothed again, three dogs burst out of the wood line and sighted them. Travis stopped in his tracks.

One of the dogs was Salem!

A big red bloodhound ran to the water, throwing up it's head as it bayed. The second dog, a white and black bulldog cross, joined the bloodhound, barking and growling. Salem was the third, and moved silently back and forth, smelling the ground while the other two continued to make a racket.

"We must go!" John yelled. He hesitated. "Wait, is that…?"

Travis could not pry his feet from the ground.

Two men emerged from the thicket behind the dogs. "You boys better give up!" one of them shouted.

"Come on across," John hollered back

"Get 'em," the man said to the dogs.

At his command, the bulldog mix lunged toward the water, his feet splashing in the shallows. His lips were pulled back, exposing sharp teeth when he barked. He swam a few feet, then lost his nerve in the current and swam back.

"Go on! Get across!" The second tracker shouted. He kicked the dog and then grabbed a beaver stick from the bank. He raised the limb and all three dogs cowed. Salem gave a high-pitched whine.

"Hey!" Travis yelled.

John took hold of his arm. "Let's put some miles between us. They will have to boat those dogs across." The dogs squealed as the stick descended. The other tracker raised his gun and aimed at the escapees. Shell and Bush vanished into the brush.

The tracker shot, and dirt flew into the air just feet from Travis and John. They both scrambled into the thicket.

At the last second, Travis looked back and saw one of the men attaching leads to the dogs.

He followed close behind John, Shell, and Booze, and they covered a few miles before their burning legs finally forced them to stop for a rest. Within moments of stopping, they heard the bloodhound bay.

"They are coming. We need to cross again."

"I don't know if I can face that cold water and current another time," Shell said.

"Would you rather go back to Cahaba?" Booze asked.

They shucked their clothes and swam the frigid river for the second time. Once on the other side, they redressed and debated on which direction would be the best choice. Travis heard some more dogs.

"It's a different set," he said.

"Set of what?" John asked.

"Now they have dogs on both sides of the river."

Four dogs ran out of the woods about fifty yards away. Sand kicked up behind them as they closed the distance quickly, yipping in excitement.

Travis dove in the river a third time, clothes and all. The other three followed and were too tired to do more than tread water and let the current carry them where it willed.

His wet pants and shirt pulled at his limbs. Exhaustion took over and his head slipped under. Water rushed into his ears and nose, and he fought to hold his breath while still kicking. Three strokes later, his shoes struck the bottom, pushing him above water again.

With shaking arms, he crawled out of the river and lay flat in the dirt. "I cannot do that again. I just cannot."

Next to him, John groaned, "But we have to keep moving."

Once back on their feet, they stumbled into the woods and moved as fast as their legs would allow. Ten minutes turned into thirty and then an hour. As daylight faded, John led them up the steep side of a tall hill. Travis held onto trees to keep from falling. He had never been so almighty tired. They reached the top and flopped to the ground.

"Not another step," Travis mumbled.

John coughed. "We did all we could. If they find us here, so be it."

Before Travis fell asleep, he wondered if he would wake up to a set of sharp dog's teeth digging into his neck. The memory of Salem cowed and whimpering stabbed him like a knife. What had they done to him?

CHAPTER THIRTY

"Wake up," Booze said. "There's a cornfield over there." The morning air chilled Travis to the bone, but walking to the field got his blood flowing properly again. The corn was green but their stomachs demanded something, so they shucked it and ate it anyway.

"Look at that," John said. "Milkweed is growing here."

"Can we eat it?" Shell asked.

"We rub it on our feet," John explained. "It will throw the dogs off our trail."

He broke the stalks and spread the milky sap on his shoes and legs. When they all had done the same, John pulled some of the plants to take with them. Travis took an ear of corn and sank his teeth into it while they walked.

A few hours later they heard dogs in the distance.

"They are still on us?" Booze asked. "I thought this weed would keep them from finding us."

John broke open the rest of the milkweed and began to rub it on his feet. "It should have. Let's use the rest of it and keep going."

He offered the handful of plants to Travis but he did not take it. "He's not going to stop." Travis looked behind them. "Those dogs will find us."

"But I don't hear them anymore," Shell said.

"They will find us," Travis said. "I know they will."

"You think Salem will find you?" John asked.

Travis nodded. "He will, without a doubt."

"Who will?" Booze asked.

"Our regiment dog," John said. "He is a captive just like us."

"And he has trailed me for miles before," Travis said. "Milkweed will do little to fool him."

Shell threw his hands up. "Then what do we do?"

John dropped the weeds. "We have two choices. We give up, or we keep trying."

"No," Travis said. "We do have a third choice. We split up."

"Travis, I am not going to leave you."

"Salem is going to follow my scent above all others. If I go a different direction, maybe he will lead all the dogs after me."

"Then you will get caught," John said.

"Salem is fast. Hopefully he will reach me first." Travis grunted with frustration. "If I can get him, we all might have a chance."

"I do not like leaving you," John said.

"Just get to our lines. George said to tell them about the prison. Let them know how few the rebels are at Cahaba. Maybe our boys can come and bust everybody out."

A dog barked, this time closer. The tone was excited, indicating he had found a hot trail.

Shell stiffened and Booze edged away. "Let's go!"

"Go." Travis pushed John.

With a last look at Travis, John sprinted after the others.

For the next hour, Travis pushed his body to the limits. He went up and down hills, crossed creeks and fields. Each time he paused, the sound of a barking dog was behind him. When he felt he could not muster another step, he stopped and leaned against a rail fence.

This was it, he could run no more.

The barking grew closer and closer, until it was within a hundred yards. The brush shifted and Salem trotted out, his tongue hanging.

Travis leaned down. "Salem! Here, boy."

Salem came forward but stopped short. His ears folded back, then pricked again.

The sound of other barking dogs was clear now, and with each passing second, Travis's heartbeat quickened. He stepped toward Salem.

The dog's ears flattened and he growled low.

"Easy. It's me, boy." Travis extended his hand toward his dog's head.

The bloodhound and bulldog pushed through the brush just a few yards away.

Salem snapped at Travis.

Shocked, he backed into the wooden fence. The bulldog had froth around its mouth and its short hair was spotted with mud. It moved toward him with hackles raised.

Salem advanced on Travis as well. His growling intensified as he bared his teeth into a snarl.

Salem had turned on him! Travis's spirit was crushed.

The spotted bulldog lowered its wide head and charged. Travis reached back, trying to grab the fence but there was no time to climb. Salem rushed in with his teeth flashing.

Travis threw his arms up to ward off the attacks.

Salem's mouth closed around the bulldog's ear and yanked. In a flash, the dog twisted its head, taking ahold of the flesh on Salem's neck. The two dogs growled, pulled, and twisted on each other's skin while they turned in a circle. The bloodhound arrived but kept his distance, sounding off with his deep bellow.

The two men Travis had seen at the river, stepped out of the woods. One of them pointed a pistol at him. He said something but his words could not be heard above the fighting dogs and barking bloodhound.

The bulldog pulled free from Salem's grip and clamped tighter on his neck. Salem squalled in pain as the bigger dog pinned him on the ground. Travis started toward them but was knocked flat on his back by the man with the gun.

"I said, get down!"

The other tracker kicked the brawling dogs.

"Stop!" Travis cried out.

The man's foot connected with both of the animals over and over.

"You are hurting him!" Travis shouted. "He's going home with me when the war is over. Henderson said so."

"Roll over right now, nice and easy." The tracker had the gun close to his head. Travis did as he was told.

"That's it, boy. What are you spouting off about?"

"That's my dog. He followed me here and I'll take him back to Arkansas when…"

A knee pressed hard into the small of his back. "You an Arkansas boy, huh?"

Travis stayed quiet, biting his lip.

The man on him roughly pulled his arms back. Travis winced as a rope was pulled tight around his wrists. He twisted his head around and saw the bulldog being pulled off Salem. Salem's neck was bloody and he was not moving, his heaving chest the only sign of life.

"Is Salem all right?" Travis strained against his restraints.

The man on Travis's back ground his knee into his spine. "Keep your mouth shut, traitor."

"Please, sir, I just found him in Arkansas," Travis said. "I'm from Illinois."

"The best thing for you right now is to tell us the direction your buddies went, and we'll do our very best to get you back to Cahaba in one piece."

Travis decided to stop talking. While the men took turns threatening him, Salem struggled to his feet. Blood dripped from the matted fur around his neck and one of his eyes was bloodshot. His legs shook. Travis wanted to comfort him, but he was helpless.

The trackers gave up trying to force him to talk. He was pulled up to his feet non too gently and a length of rope was tied to his bound hands. He was led, just like the dogs, back to the prison.

Henderson was away from Cahaba, leaving Jones in charge, the man Amanda Gardner had warned him about. Henderson had been a kind commander, but Jones was not. He slammed Travis against the wall and pushed his forearm into his throat.

"Who planned this escape?" The anger in his voice was thick. His thin lips formed a deep frown.

Travis swallowed hard. "I do not know who planned it."

"You stinkin' Yank. I don't believe your lies for a second. Write your name on that list."

He released him and pointed to a piece of paper on a desk. With a shaking hand, Travis added his name under a long list of others.

"There's only three left," Jones said. "Nobody gets away from here and every one of you are gonna pay for trying."

George greeted Travis inside Cahaba, his disappointment apparent. They talked about the escape and Travis found out that over forty men had made it out, but most were caught the next day.

"What about John?" George asked.

"His name was not on the list, so I believe he is still out there," Travis said, "with two other guys, Shell and Booze. I think they are the only ones who have not been caught."

"How good are their odds, do you think?"

"Well, if they have not collared them by now, I think they are pretty good." Travis shook his head slowly. "I have to get out of here, George. They hurt Salem pretty bad."

"That dog is a survivor," George said. "Our boys are winning this war. We'll all be out of here before you know it."

Travis appreciated George's words but he did not believe them. The past days left Travis spent of all energy. He slept graveyard-hard, not stirring until the next roll call.

The following day, a guard came into the prison with a piece of paper. "I need Owens and Bailey, front and center." A lanky man that must have been Owens walked across the yard to the waiting guard, but Travis looked to George.

George squeezed his shoulder. "They will ask more questions about the escape. No one will blame you for talking."

"Travis Bailey," the guard said. "I need you here, now."

"I'll not squeal," Travis said to George.

Travis and Owens were taken outside the stockade where Jones was waiting.

"It's time you two traitors learned a lesson."

A ladder had been leaned against the side of the wooden wall. Jones pushed Travis that direction.

"Take Owens to the blacksmith," he said to the guard. "I'll take care of this Arkansas boy."

Chills ran along Travis's skin. He was about to pay for his loose lips.

"Get under the ladder. Reach up and hang by your hands."

Travis did as he was told, but he could not understand how this action could be considered punishment. He and his brother had swung from tree limbs for fun when they were younger.

"Do not let go until I tell you," Jones warned.

Travis hung for several minutes before his arms started to burn. His fingers strained to hold his grip so he extended his feet, barely touching the ground and supporting hardly any of his weight. Jones began a countdown but Travis could not hold on and released the rung.

Jones snorted. "Figured you wouldn't last. Kick your shoes off."

"Sir?"

"Kick your shoes off, now."

Once he was barefooted, Jones pointed to a limb about the thickness of his wrist.

"Stand on it," he said.

Travis obeyed and immediately felt pain in the arches of his feet.

"Raise your right leg," Jones commanded. "Balance until I say stop."

Raising one leg placed even more weight on the other, doubling the pain. Each time he shifted to keep from falling, the stick dug into the bottom of his foot. Within moments, sweat beaded on his forehead.

"I'm sorry for what I did."

"Sorry?" Jones laughed. "You are not half sorry yet. We are just getting started."

After standing on the stick until he fell off of it, Jones ordered him back to the ladder. Back and forth he went many times until his arms ached, large blisters formed on his fingers, and his left foot was bruised to the bone. Travis limped to the ladder but could not raise his arms high enough to hold the rung.

"I can't reach it," he said. Tears ran from his eyes.

"Jump up and grab that ladder," Jones ordered.

"I will not escape again, I swear it!"

"Do it!" Jones shouted, aiming his gun at Travis's head.

Travis bent at the knees, placing as much of his weight on his good foot as possible, and jumped. His sore hands slapped around the rung, and he cried out. The muscles in his forearms shook from the effort to maintain his grip. Blisters on his fingers burst and the fluid oozed down his wrist.

The pain became too much for him to bear.

Travis yelled so hard his throat burned and he fell into a heap.

Jones kicked Travis hard in the ribs. "Get up, you filthy traitor. Stand on the stick!"

"Stop this," a woman's voice pleaded.

Travis groaned in agony and struggled to his knees. Ms. Gardner was facing off with Jones.

"Go back to your home," he ordered.

She did not budge. "I have given you and your officers use of my house for your comfort and convenience. Grant me this request."

Jones crossed his arms. "This is none of your business."

She stepped between him and Travis. "I beg you. Take this boy back inside and remove the location of this punishment."

Anger spread across Jones's face. "Your sympathy for the Yankees is odious to me."

"We are all God's people," she said. "For the sake of my children, do not continue this where we must be unwilling spectators." She stepped closer to Jones. "It is brutalizing in its influence."

Jones stared at her, unblinking for many seconds, a dark scowl across his face. Finally, he pointed to Travis. "Go."

While Travis struggled to his feet, the conversation continued.

"Amanda, only my forbearance saves you from being sent away from your invalid husband, your children, and your home. Now, bear yourself with the utmost care in the future or you will be in exile."

Travis wobbled and fell many times on the way to the prison gates. He wiped his eyes with his sleeve, trying to dry his face before going back in. Owens and a guard were waiting. Owens had ball and chain shackled to his ankles. The skin was already bloody from his walk back to the prison. The doors opened like a monster's mouth and Cahaba swallowed them once more.

CHAPTER THIRTY-ONE

October 1864

Travis was lame for days after his punishment. While he rested, the Confederates built an elevated walkway attached to the outside of the stockade wall. It would allow them to patrol the entire prison from above, and Travis felt sure there would be no future escape attempts by anyone.

John, Shell, and Booze were captured but Henderson had returned and their punishment was not too severe. Owens pulled his ball and chain around the prison until the cuffs cut deep into his ankles. His pain was a constant reminder of the consequences of trying to escape, but Owens swore he would try again.

The bugs tortured Travis but he had become calloused to the rats. They sniffed and nibbled at his clothes each night. Flailing and slapping would only scare them for a few moments, so over time, Travis learned to ignore the rodents.

Jones had put a stop to Amanda's gifts through the hole in the stockade, but he could not stop her kindness. As the weather grew colder, she sent blankets, and when she ran out of those, she cut up rugs and drapes from her house. Many prisoners in Cahaba included Amanda Gardner in their prayers each night.

November brought chilly nights that dampened the spirts of everyone. Travis stared out through the open roof of the prison at the giant oak tree. Its massive limbs swayed in the breeze, the force of the wind sending burnt-orange leaves tumbling through the air. The last few weeks had been hard. The rain, cold weather, and bad food sent a steady stream of deathly sick men to the hospital. Many died but Amanda's gifts saved many more.

Most days, Travis shivered with a rug pulled around his shoulders. George had managed to keep his coat, though it had fist sized holes. Big Tennessee had a jacket and a blanket that he shared with Stephen. All of them had cursed the fiery summer sun and now they longed for its warmth again.

Travis sat quietly, embracing his misery while he thought about his brother. Chet had the kindest heart of any person he had ever met. This trait had been passed from their mother, definitely not their father. Travis listened to his parents fight every night until the day she left. Shortly after, they moved to Arkansas and never did they hear from her again. Not a day had passed that he did not think of her and the love she shared with him and Chet.

Jeb fed them a constant diet of lies that their mother did not want them any longer, but Travis knew the truth. She had left Jeb, not them, and there was no blame attached to her actions. Travis wanted the same thing, to get Chet far away from Jeb.

While he was deep in thought, a boy using crude crutches sat next to him. He shifted his bandaged leg and covered it with a blanket.

"Would you like some company?"

"That is probably what I need," Travis said. "Something to bring my spirits up."

"Mine could use a boost too. I'm Perry Summerville."

"Travis Bailey." Travis looked over his shoulder. "This is George, Stephen, and Big Tennessee sitting on the roost there."

They all exchanged greetings.

"Did you just get here?" Travis asked.

"I have been a guest in the hospital," Perry said. "They wanted to keep me longer but I could not stand it."

"How can it be worse than here?"

"Four died just today," Perry said. "That makes twelve this week. I would rather be here."

Big Tennessee grinned. "You picked wrong."

Stephen elbowed him in the arm. "If you can stand the lice, you'll be fine."

George scratched at his chest. "I would rather have poison ivy."

Stephen chuckled. "I would rather smear poison ivy on my face."

"Heck," Tennessee said. "If those be my choices, I would rather rub my butt crack with it."

They all busted out with laughter. The ridiculous conversation was exactly what Travis needed to push back his sad thoughts.

Perry, Stephen, and Travis formed a tight friendship. They were younger, similar in attitude, and shared the desire to live through the war between the states. Travis showed Perry how the cook-yard worked and even helped him on occasion. The boy's crutches slowed him down, but did nothing to keep him from trying, even when the cold rains made the yard a muddy mire.

The rain had momentarily passed, but Travis was having no luck getting the tender lit for his cook fire. "I cannot get my wood to catch." He looked over at Perry in frustration. "You having any luck?"

Perry shook his head. "Everything is soaked. All I'm getting is smoke."

"Our bellies will growl today, then. Maybe they will bring us some hardtack."

Perry waved for Crutcher to come over. When the guard arrived, he said, "Could I borrow that fine pocket knife you have?"

Crutcher dug the blade out and handed it over. Perry whittled on one of his wooden crutches. When he had a few dozen slivers, he gave the knife back along with a heartfelt thanks.

The dry wood caught almost immediately. The flames got bigger, and Perry added the least damp tinder he had on top of the flames. Slowly, the number of coals grew, and other cooks took some of the embers to get their fires going.

Travis used a tin cup to transfer part of Perry's fire to his pit. "You are pretty smart."

"I am not smart, just very, very hungry."

It rained nearly every day and Perry usually got his fire started by whittling more bits of his crutch away. The day soon came that it was completely gone, and all he had now was one crutch with which to get around.

Travis wiped the moisture off the boards and laid down on one of the bottom bunks for the night. Perry hobbled over, using his crutch to keep his balance. He settled into his spot and spread his damp blanket across Travis and himself.

"Perry," Travis said. "Do not cut your last crutch up, you have to have it."

Stephen looked down from the tier above them. "Yeah, you need that one, 'cause you are much too heavy for us to carry around all the time."

They all had a good laugh as they bid each other good night.

"It's gone!" Perry shouted.

Travis sat up and rubbed his eyes. "What's gone?"

"My crutch. Someone took it."

"Tennessee," Stephen said. He shook the sleeping man. "Tennessee! Wake up. Somebody took Perry's crutch."

He rose immediately and jumped from the roost. His gentle demeanor disappeared. "Let's go find this rascal. I'll choke him till his eyes bug out."

Tennessee and Stephen stormed away, but Travis stayed to help Perry. He pulled his arm across the back of his neck and supported as much of his weight as he could. The lack of calories had weakened them both. They wobbled and shuffled their way to the front of the prison, arriving in time to meet Tennessee and Stephen.

Stephen held up a small, charred piece of wood. "This is all we found."

"The tip of my crutch," Perry said. "They used it to cook with."

"Do you know who?" Travis asked.

"There was not a soul at the pit where we found it," Tennessee said. He walked to the middle of the prison and cupped his hands around his mouth. "Listen up! When I find out who took Perry's crutch, you are going to pay for it!"

Though his threats surely frightened the muggers of Cahaba, they kept their lips tight, protecting whoever had stolen from a crippled man.

The dark clouds thickened and spread across the land, dropping a steady rain on Cahaba that soaked every man to the bone. The drizzle continued for a week, with no break, causing the skin on Travis's feet and hands to become pale, wrinkled, and sore. Walking was necessary to keep him warm but each step tormented him with pain.

No sooner had the rain stopped, when the gates opened and Confederates entered. One of the officers stood on a box and promised warm clothes, blankets, food, and fair treatment to each man who would swear an oath to the Southern army and join them.

George laughed at the idea, but his humor left when a group of men stepped forward. "Bunch of traitors," he said.

Travis nudged him. "Look at that. They all belong to the group of muggers."

"I guess their milk cow dried up. Tennessee saw to that."

"Hey, Tennessee!" someone shouted. "Look what you did! You drove the raiders right into the bosom of the Confederacy."

Instead of cursing and shouting at them for joining the rebels, the population of Cahaba cheered when the band of thieves left the prison.

In December, more captured men were brought into Cahaba. Some had supposedly been transferred for exchange, but now they were back. There was always talk of prisoner trades but Travis had lost all belief that any actually happened.

The increased numbers meant even more men had to sleep on the ground. Cold rain turned the sandy dirt in the prison to gritty mud, a freezing thick paste that clung to their clothes. Out of desperation for a dry place to sleep, the men scraped the mud into piles but their efforts did little to keep them warm.

Travis's shirt was ripped up the back from where it had worn so thin, and the knees of his pants were completely gone but he considered himself to be one of the lucky ones. Some of the prisoners were without shirts or shoes. Perry only had one shoe. His bad leg was getting better and he was able to move around on his own, until his toes would go numb from the cold.

According to the grapevine, a few men had developed another escape plan. Each night, some of them would keep the guards busy while a short skinny prisoner squeezed through a hole under the guard-house floor. The grand idea was to tunnel a way out but the process of disposing of the dirt was slow, with prisoners having to sneak it into the privy and toss it in the outhouse holes. Travis steered clear of this plan. He had learned his lesson.

"A steamboat is here," one of the cooks shouted. "I can see it through the cracks. They are unloading blankets!"

Excitement spread like the most pleasant disease ever.

"I hope they are for us. They have to be for us, right?"

"I'm thankful for the darlin' Missus Gardner and her curtains," someone said, "but I'd truly love to have a blanket."

Guards kept the men under control while the new supplies were handed out. Perry, Stephen, and Travis waited their turn.

"What vision is this," Stephen said. "Tell me, am I seeing hats?"

"Hats and blankets," Perry said.

"There are coats too," the guard said. He looked at Perry. "You already have a coat. I'll swap some food for your new one."

"Keep your new coat," Travis whispered.

"How about his old one," Stephen suggested.

The man shook his head. "Lice."

"Are there any shoes in there?" Perry asked.

"Socks," the guard said.

"I need some shoes." Perry glanced at his feet. "I've only got one."

"I have another pair at home," the man said. "Those for the coat?"

"The shoes," Perry said, "and three sweet potatoes for me and my friends."

They shook hands and the deal was made.

The feeling of clean cloth and the smell of new garments overwhelmed some of the prisoners. Grown men wept while changing. They petted the warm wool as if it were the most precious thing to ever grace their lives, but in the following weeks many of them would trade it all in order to fill their bellies.

Travis collected his new blanket, hat, coat, underwear, pants, and socks and revelled in the luxury of how they felt on his skin. That night he curled up on the roost and pulled the new blanket up to his chin, grateful for the dark that hid his tears.

CHAPTER THIRTY-TWO

January 1865

B itter, frigid winds blew through Cahaba. It snowed for days and the desperate men who had traded their clothes and blankets for food paid a hefty price. The icy flakes fell through the open parts of the roof and stiff breezes spread it throughout the whole prison. Over a thousand men walked on the snow and packed it into a sheet of dirty ice. Those without a squad and those who were not tough enough to fight for a spot in the roost slept on the frozen ground.

In the middle of the night, George shook Travis awake. "I have to move around, there is no feeling left in my feet."

Travis shivered and tried to wiggle his toes. "Blast this cold! My feet are numb, too."

He reached on his other side and shook Perry. "Wake up! We need to get on our feet."

"Chicken," Perry mumbled. "Fried."

Travis poked him. "Come on, eat your dadgum chicken and get up."

"What?" Perry sat up. "Oh, I was dreaming about food."

"How are your feet?" Travis asked.

"Freezing. My hands are too."

Uncontrollable shakes spread through Travis, causing his chin to quiver. "We have to walk."

Prisoners continued to wake each other until most of the population was up, walking in circles. They shuffled along, holding the blankets around their shoulders.

"We are going to die in here," George stated. His breath puffed moist fog with each word.

Travis pulled his blanket tighter. "If we die, the war is over for us. They win."

"They have already killed us, Travis. We might as well be dead."

"George...."

George coughed. "How much can a man lose and still be who he is?"

A few moments later he spoke again. "If we live through this, will we ever be the same?"

"We will be alive," Travis said. "Some of our friends lost that chance."

George fell silent.

Travis sighed. "Bitter talk will just give us all a bellyache. We need Peter here to give us some of his bejabber blabber."

"I would love to hear that scoundrel share some of his Irish sayings."

They walked several minutes before George spoke again.

"I will not give up."

"Neither will I," Travis said.

From behind them, Perry spoke in a strong voice. "Nor I."

"I'm not giving up!" Stephen shouted.

Tennessee bellowed, "Not giving up!"

The human will to overcome was present in Cahaba that night, as more than a thousand voices took up the defiant chant while circling in the frozen cage.

The prisoners who were without shoes suffered horrible frostbite. A few of them refused amputation and the black flesh on their toes fell off, leaving the bones hanging by ligaments.

Travis and his friends avoided injury from the cold, but the urge to escape the awful place would not leave George. He talked of it often. Travis listened carefully but offered no encouragement. The previous torture Jones doled out would seem like child's play if he caught Travis on the run again.

"It is going to take them too long to dig that tunnel," George said. "And I would not fit anyway. Neither would Tennessee. We have to think of something else."

"Do not ask me for ideas," Travis said. "If I crawled through the tunnel and ran off, Salem would just track me down again."

"That's the problem," George said. "How do we get away from the dogs."

Travis shrugged. "George, do you think Salem is all right? Those guys treated him horribly."

"I think he will be fine. Those were just the trackers using him, I am sure there are others assigned to feeding and taking care of the dogs on a daily basis. Most folks love dogs. It is like how some of the rebels would rather spit on us than look at us, and others care for us like family."

"There is good and bad in every group," Travis said. "Look at us in here, living with thieves that should have been our brothers."

"Boatload coming in!" someone shouted.

"Supplies?"

"Prisoners. Lots of prisoners."

Hundreds of men entered. They were from a closed prison in Meridian. Days later, more captured soldiers arrived and were packed into Cahaba. The population soon reached three thousand, and tensions were high.

Travis was frustrated and angry. The usual spots he liked to sit and rest were now filled. There was always a crowd, bumping, and pushing. A constant queue stretched out from the privy. Six holes for three thousand made the wait too long for some and they did their business on the ground, kicking sand over it before walking away.

A man among the newcomers stood out. He seemed to possess great intelligence and spoke with authority. He looked to be perhaps forty years old, with dark thinning hair. His clean appearance and healthy stature told Travis that he had not been a captive for very long. The man introduced himself as Captain Hanchette, and he took time to speak with nearly every captive in Cahaba.

George sat down with Travis. "Hear me out before you say anything. Hanchette has the key to getting out of here."

He lowered his voice. "He is an officer in the Sixteenth Illinois and he has a better plan than the tunnel. There is going to be a meeting this evening. All I want you to do is to listen."

Travis looked down at his hands. "I will listen but I will not do much else. Jones just needs a reason, and not even a good one, to kill me."

"I think Henderson is in charge again," George said. "He came back with the blankets and supplies."

"That was weeks ago," Travis said. "He could be gone by now."

"Just listen to Hanchette," George begged.

When the time for the meeting came, the group gathered in the middle of the prison. Their actions and conversation went unknown to the guards. There were thousands of prisoners crowded close together, talking, singing, bickering and sometimes fighting – plenty of distraction.

Hanchette spoke to the twenty chosen men and laid out his plan for escape. "Many of us who have been recently captured are of good health. There are hundreds of us in such shape, and three thousand in total being held here. There are but nine guards inside each night. If we take these men, we have control of Cahaba."

Owens, the man who had been punished the same day as Travis, said, "They shackled me with a ball and chain. They bucked and gagged me. I'm not taking a chance on your plan. We already have a tunnel started. Let's stick with that."

"And while we wait," Hanchette said, "we all get weaker. We freeze. We starve."

"If we overtake the guards, that would only give us nine guns," George said. "How can we win against the fifty rebels and two cannons outside?"

"We capture the nine inside," Hanchette said, "but we do it just before the shift change. When the nine fresh guards enter, we will be waiting. We will have eighteen weapons and an open door. We can step outside, turn the cannons, and take the city in a matter of minutes."

His words were filled with passion and stirred hope in the hearts of many of those listening, and it spread to all but a few holdouts for the tunnel plan.

Taking the prison by force made more sense to Travis. At least they would avoid being tracked by the dogs. It would also give him an opportunity to find Salem.

"What I can do, I will," he said to George. "Though I am only as strong as a weak kitten."

"Me, too, but we will not give up, remember?"

The plan was attempted on three different nights before enough men could find the courage to position themselves in the way Hanchette instructed. Each time, George and Travis got up and went to the privy, pausing to speak to the guard. Finally, enough prisoners felt confident that they were ready.

The guards called out, announcing all was well to their replacements outside the stockade, signaling to them it was safe to enter. When the last guard finished his declaration, the prisoners attacked.

George rushed the privy guard, grabbing his rifle and pinning him against the wall. Travis slapped both of his hands across the man's mouth. More prisoners joined them, until there was no chance the guard could get free. Eight other guards were soon in the same predicament.

Mumbling spread between men who had been sleeping and were unaware of the escape attempt.

"Hush," Hanchette said as he weaved through the waking prisoners. They started calling out questions as they become aware that something out of the ordinary was happening. "Quiet. The new shift is coming through the gate now."

The metal bar on the wooden stockade door rattled.

The hinges squeaked.

One of the captured guards near the gate jerked his head back from the hands covering his mouth and blurted a muffled warning.

The door slammed and the metal bar snapped back in place.

Hanchette cursed. "Our timing was off, but we cannot give up now."

"Get ready," a prisoner said. "They are going to kill us all."

"Not me," someone said. "None told me this was going to happen, and I will have nothing to do with it." A murmur ran through the prisoners as word spread.

The captured guards were taken to the back when Hanchette stepped to the gates and yelled to his fellow captives. "We have nine muskets. Over the wall, boys, and we will take the town!"

The response was less than enthusiastic.

"We can do this," he shouted. He raised a musket above his head. "Join together and fight."

George and Travis traded worried looks. Perry sidled over to them. "With my leg, I will never make it over the stockade."

"I'll go," Tennessee said. The towering man had not lost height, but his shoulders, arms, and chest had shrunk from lack of food. Even so, his courage remained.

"Who else?" Hanchette asked.

The wooden gates burst open and soldiers pushed the stockade cannons into the prison opening. "These Napoleons are double loaded with grapeshot. Surrender now!"

Hanchette cursed, but dropped his captured musket and motioned for others to do the same.

Jones appeared behind the cannons. Guards joined him on both sides with their weapons pointed toward the cowering mass of prisoners.

"Have you killed my men?" Jones bellowed.

Emphatic denials came from many men as the crowd pressed toward the back, away from the intimidating cannon barrels. "They are here! We have not harmed them."

"Send them out now!" Jones commanded.

"We will release them when you let us out of here!" Tennessee shouted.

Stephen yanked on his friend's coat. "He's going to shoot you."

"He cannot see me. It's too dark in here."

"Bring more guards up here, with extra lamps," Jones said over his shoulder. He turned back to face the prisoners. "This is your last warning. Let my men go."

Ten more soldiers joined Jones.

"Fire on my command," he ordered.

"Both cannons?"

"They have killed our men. Why should we spare them?"

A mass of thousands surged back, nearly crushing the men at the rear of Cahaba.

George tried to turn around but he was pinned by bodies. Travis struggled to breathe.

"Five!" Jones announced. Men shouted and cursed, pushing each other as they tried to get out of the path of the cannons.

"Bring the guards!" Hanchette yelled. "Quick, before he shoots us all."

"We are trying," someone hollered above the noise. "It's too crowded to get them through. Move forward and make some room."

Jones raised his hand. "Four!"

Tennessee and Hanchette began to pull prisoners out of the way, as if they were digging through a human wall.

"Three!"

Some of the men dropped to the ground, hoping the blast would pass over them.

"Two!" Jones cried out. Those prisoners near the front of the crowd began to climb and leap over the ones blocking the way.

"George," Travis managed to say over the noise around them, "do they have the guards yet?"

George looked over the top of the crowd. "They will never make it in time."

"One!"

The bodies around him became even more frenzied in their efforts to escape the bullets.

"Fire!"

"NO!" a voice yelled.

The tumbling balls of hot lead did not tear through their flesh.

Travis pulled his body up by using the shoulders of the men around him as leverage. He saw Lieutenant Crutcher standing in front of the cannons, holding both his hands out as if he were willing the guns not to go off.

"If you fire, you will kill me," he said.

"Crutcher!" Jones walked between the Napoleons. "Get behind me. That's an order."

"I do not believe they have killed our men," Crutcher said.

"Here they are!" Hanchette shouted.

"Is it true?" Crutcher asked. "Are you men back there?"

"We are coming out," one of the captured guards yelled back. "Working our way through the crowd now."

"Are you all accounted for?" Jones asked.

The guards broke free and walked to the front. "We are all here. None of us are hurt." They picked up their weapons.

Jones stood in silence for a moment. "Who are the men that did this?"

"It was too dark, sir. There is no way to tell for certain."

"I may have wounded one of them," one of the guards said.

Jones pointed. "Listen up, Yanks. Expose the conspirators now or you will all suffer punishment together." He waited for a few seconds. "So be it. You will starve until I am told the names of those involved."

Rations stopped coming into Cahaba and since there was nothing to cook, the men were banned from the yard, confined in the prison. Much of the time, Travis stood and listened to his stomach growl.

There was not enough room for everyone to lie down at the same time, so they slept in shifts and the men who were sleeping were invariably tread upon by accident. After many days without food, no one had come forward.

Travis was by the west wall when he saw Jones enter the cook-yard with the guards that they had captured the night of the attempted overthrow. Jones formed two lines of men facing each other, five on one side, four and himself on the other.

"Strip your clothes," he ordered the prisoners nearest the gate. "Roll them up. Hold them above your head. Form a line and walk between us. Pass the word back to the others."

Men started to undress. A wild-eyed prisoner ran past Travis. Curious, he followed the man straight to Hanchette.

"They must have found my blood on the bayonet after the struggle. They are going figure out it was me."

"They will not, Mart. Keep your palm against your rolled-up clothing. The cut will be hidden.

Mart pulled something out of his shirt and handed it to Hanchette. It was a folded piece of cloth with a pattern, a regiment flag.

Travis drop his jaw in amazement. "How did you sneak that in here?"

Mart cut his eyes at Travis. "I'd consider it a great favor if you kept this to yourself. This is one flag the rebels won't capture."

When Travis removed his shirt, pants, underwear, and socks, the frigid air stung his skin. He rolled his clothes up, held them above his head, and got in line. Completely naked, they walked between the guards, pausing for inspection. Travis watched Mart holding his hand tight against his clothing, concealing the cut on his palm. The guards looked him over and sent him through. Jones had failed again at finding those responsible.

As the days passed, the hunger became unbearable and the men became weaker. The day came when Hanchette, Owens, and a few others were removed from the prison. Shortly thereafter and to the great relief of the weakened and malnourished prisoners, rations resumed once again.

CHAPTER THIRTY-THREE

March 1865

"I can't take this anymore," Perry said. "It's been pouring for days."

A gust of wind blasted them with cold rain. Travis pulled his blanket over his head.

"My entire body shakes." George said.

Travis peeked out from under his blanket. "The war has to be over soon. It has to."

"The government left us," Perry said. "That's what they did. They abandoned us."

George raised a wet, wrinkled finger. "Don't fret. Our boys will come through for us."

"Well, tell them to hurry up," Perry said.

When the clouds allowed the sun to finally shine through, the prisoners walked in circles, warming themselves and drying their clothing and blankets. Having had no real sleep for days, that night was unusually quiet. A solid mass of bodies covered the floor, heads and arms draped across legs, as over two thousand slept on the ground and the rest in the bunks.

Shortly after noon the next day, a few inches of brown water from the Alabama river crept its way into the fire pits, carrying bits of charcoal and debris with it. Travis pointed at the cook-yard. "Water is coming through the stockade. Hey! The river is rising."

"What does it look like?" George asked one of the guards who was standing on the stockade walkway.

The man looked out across the river and then down into the prison. "It's coming up fast, but I don't believe we will get our boots wet."

Tennessee gave a nervous laugh. "You talking about us, or you?"

"That's right," George said. "Your brogans are ten feet up on the walkway."

The overflow rose like a brown plague, pushing the men deeper into Cahaba as they desperately tried to avoid its touch. It came up through the privy floor and poured inside. Hundreds of prisoners climbed the roosts, shoving and pushing each other.

Water soaked Travis's shoes while he looked for an empty spot on the bunks. "They are all full. What now?"

George was not paying attention, but watching two figures struggle in the water. "We have to help those men. They are in a bad way."

The prisoners were very thin. One of them was trying to stand but the other was too weak to even raise his head.

"I have this one," Travis said. "Get that one. His face is nearly in the water."

Between them, they managed to half walk, half drag the poor souls to the roost, and willing prisoners crowded close to make enough room. After they were safe, there was nothing else Travis could do but stand and watch the water rise.

That night it was dark, except for the dim light of the lanterns at the top of the stockade. Before long the river was up to their knees.

With no way to lie down, there was no sleep. Travis stood in the freezing water, praying that the flood would be over before morning. In the darkness, twigs, sticks, and leaves brushed against him as they bobbed by.

"They are crawling on me!" Perry shouted. "Get off!"

"I think it is just stuff floating in the water," Travis said.

"There are rats!" Stephen shouted. "The water has flushed them out of their holes."

Moments later, the splashing and cursing started in earnest as men slapped and swatted the vermin that crawled up their clothes. A big

one latched on the back of Travis's shirt and clawed its way up. He
tried hitting the animal but it was just beyond his reach. Another rat
churned the water around his knees, trying to get ahold of his pants.
Travis kicked and twisted, managing to fling off one and scare the
other. The swimming rodents moved away and attempted to climb
another squirming prisoner. Some of the soldiers were screaming
with fear.

"Talk to the guards," someone begged. "See if they will let us
out."

"No guards came into the prison tonight."

"Maybe they are gone. Go to the cook-yard and see."

"They will shoot us!" another prisoner shouted.

George volunteered. "I will go to the doorway and call out."

Travis followed him, sloshing through the murk. As they went, the
water got deeper, nearing mid-thigh. When they reached the opening,
George put his hand out to stop Travis.

"Guards! Are you there?" George eased forward. "Do not shoot,
we just want a word with you."

"We are here," a voice said. "Step into the yard."

Travis and George waded into the dim light from a set of lanterns.

"No funny ideas," one of the guards said. "Jones has stationed us
around the walkway."

"Show us some mercy," George pleaded. "We are chilled to the
bone and drowning rats are trying to climb to the top of our heads."

"What can we do about this?" a voice behind one of the lanterns
asked sarcastically.

A third and fourth lantern bobbed along the top of the stockade
wall.

"What is going on here?"

"Please," Travis said. "The water is getting deeper. There is no
way to sleep without drowning, and many of the men are sick."

"What do you expect to happen?" The man repeated.

"Talk to Jones," George said.

"No sense in us even trying. You boys are marked, 'cause Jones is
madder than all git out over your escape attempt. Now, best you find
your way back inside."

Travis huddled with thousands of other shivering men as the
morning sun sent its rays streaming through the big oak tree limbs
and into the prison. The warmth on their faces did very little for their

legs. The river was now up to Travis's waist, thigh-high on Tennessee and slightly higher for George. Ripples in the water spread outward from each man, vibrations from their uncontrolled shaking.

"No one came for the count this morning," someone said.

A prisoner waded toward the cook-yard. "Why count us? We are trapped here, and I am about to do something that may get me shot. Wish me luck, boys."

"Go get 'em, Jesse!"

"What is he doing?" Travis asked George.

"Who knows."

Most of the prisoners followed. Perry forgot where the water ditch was located, stepped in it, and sank up to his chin.

Tennessee grabbed his coat and hauled him up. "You all right?"

The shock of cold water had stolen Perry's breath and he fought to get control of his breathing again. "Yes, I will make it," he finally said.

The prisoner leading the way continued into the yard. "Don't shoot. It's me, Jesse Hawes."

From the doorway, Travis could see Crutcher and a few other guards on the walkway. They were leaning on the top of the wall. Their faces were unshaven, and their eyes tired from lack of sleep.

"What do you want?"

"I need... no, I demand to speak with Jones," Jesse said.

"Well, you are in luck. He's in a rowboat and headed this way."

After a few moments, there was the sound of oars splashing and the thump of a wooden hull against the stockade. Boots thudded up the steps and Jones appeared on the walkway.

"Jesse has asked to speak with you, sir," Crutcher said.

Jones looked through the doorway of the prison at the mass of pitiful souls. His gaze slowly shifted to the lone man standing in the cook-yard. "There is no time to talk. This flood is causing us great problems."

"We can help," Jesse said. "We can carry and move supplies to dry ground. Not a one of us will try to escape. You have our word."

Jones placed his hands on the top of the wall. "All of you have demonstrated your desire to take leave of this prison. It would be foolish to provide you with another opportunity."

"Then help us find a way out of this water. We have been standing in it for twenty-four hours and some of the weak have nearly drowned. As if that were not terrible enough, many are also ill."

Jones turned to leave.

"Please," Jesse said. "I would guess that even the livestock of this town have been moved to higher ground. Do we not at least deserve the same treatment as your hogs?"

Jones stiffened and slowly turned around. "Not so long as there is a filthy Yankee's head above water, can you come out of that stockade."

The stark faces of the men around Travis said everything. There would be no mercy. Even the guards were speechless.

The gates opened slowly, pushing water as they moved. Guards rowed a boat into the prison, handing out rations.

"How are we supposed to cook this cornmeal and bacon?"

"It's all we have," Crutcher said.

"We will have the scours if we eat this meat raw."

"Then soak the corn until it softens," said the other guard.

"In this water?" George said. "Sick men in the bunks are spewing from both ends."

Crutcher sighed as he handed a pint of meal to George and Travis. "We are here only to deliver food." He lowered his voice and said, "Your suffering is pretty clear. A petition has been started by the guards."

Travis took his bacon and cornmeal. "For what is the petition?"

"Requesting Jones to change his mind."

Upon hearing the news, the prisoners around them quietly spread the word.

"I hope he does reconsider," George said.

Travis grabbed the boat to stop it from moving away. "Mr. Crutcher, would you please do something for me? The dog that came here with me, could you check on him? Do you know the one I'm talking about?"

"The dog you were asking Ms. Gardner and Miss Belle about? I remember."

"Could you?"

"I will try," Crutcher said.

Travis put the cornmeal in his mouth, using his spit to make a gummy paste. Most of the men did this and some even choked down the raw meat.

"My stomach feels like its boiling," he said to Perry.

"I'm feeling awful." Perry's eyes were sunken and hollow looking. "I have the trots. I did not want to go in the water, but I had no choice."

The water splashed as a prisoner behind them vomited his cornmeal and greasy bacon. The gagging nearly caused Perry to lose his meal too.

Travis fought the urge to throw up his cornmeal. "I think most of us are sick."

Stephen waded up to them, Tennessee behind him. "We are standing in a slurry of filth."

The big man groaned. "It's getting worse by the minute and I'm already dying of thirst."

"Me too," Travis said.

Perry stared down at the soupy, brown water. "Some of the men are drinking it, but I cannot bring myself to do such a thing."

A loud crack echoed off the water, followed by multiple screams. One of the bunks gave way from the weight, dropping hundreds of men into the murk. They struggled to their feet, coughing and spitting. Some of them were bleeding.

"Will Jones let us all die in here?" Tennessee asked. "Is that what he wants?"

Late on the third evening, Travis took his turn on one of the remaining roosts. He removed his boots to give his aching feet a short rest. Rubbing them made the pain worse. The tops were puckered and wrinkled. Travis turned his foot over to look at the bottom.

What he saw did not even resemble a body part any longer. The soles of his feet were puffy and pasty white, as if they had been drained of blood. The skin was bubbled up in several places, as if air had formed pockets underneath. The pain was intense.

He stared at the water, and at the men standing in it. They were all in sorry shape and leaning on each other, intertwining arms to keep the sick and weak from slipping under. Some were praying, some were cursing, and others were talking quietly to stay awake.

Travis wondered how any of them, himself included, were still willing to live. His bowels burned, he had sores in his mouth and his skin was scarred and stretched taut over his ribs. Yet he refused to quit. If he did, who would find his brother? If he quit, what would happen to Salem? They needed him, and he had to find them. He laid back and closed his eyes. Within moments, he was asleep.

"Get out of the bunk. Let someone else have a turn."

Travis raised up on an elbow. "I just laid down."

"No," the prisoner said, "it is morning."

"Morning?" Travis rubbed his eyes and noticed dawn's first light spilling into the prison."

"Hurry up," the weary man said.

He pulled his boots on and cried out in pain. His body had the shakes and his heart raced. He slipped back into the waist deep water, knowing there was fever in his body. Travis lost his breath and struggled to find a board he could hang on to at the corner of the roost. Coughs racked his body, leaving his throat sore.

The guards rowed the boats in and brought hardtack to the men. They devoured the dry, crunchy, crackers. Unfortunately, it also sucked the moisture from their mouths.

"My head is pounding," Travis said.

"You need water, and I do also." George held up a tin cup.

Travis quickly shook his head. "This is just a filthy soup."

"We have to drink," George said. "Let us ask to enter the cook-yard. It must be cleaner out there."

Travis waded after him, refusing to look too closely at the things that floated past.

George called up to the men on the stockade walkway. "Guards, may the two of us come out?"

Several of the soldiers quickly shouldered their weapons. "Yes, but you will be under the gun at all times."

George lifted his cup. "We are desperate for cleaner water. Could we cross the dead line and drink from where the overflow is coming through the stockade?"

The guards looked at each other. Finally one of them lowered his weapon, shrugged and said, "Go ahead."

On the way to the wall, George said, "We were told there was a petition. Is there any news about that?"

"Nearly all of us signed it," the guard said, "but Jones would not reconsider."

"We appreciate your effort." George dipped a cup of brown water and handed it to Travis.

He drank in big gulps and his teeth crunched sand, dirt, and other debris, but he could not stop. When he had filled the cup twice more, he passed it back to George.

"Might we send the others out two at a time?"

The guard nodded.

The next day the gates opened and a Confederate rider came inside. The horse's legs churned the muddy water.

"I need two hundred men."

He rode down the middle of the prison, using his horse to push through the crowd.

"Hey, be careful, that brute came near stepping on my foot!" Stephen exclaimed.

The man frowned. "I will ride wherever I please. I need two hundred of you outside to bring in some boards." Eager to escape the prison, even if only for a few hours, groups of prisoners splashed forward.

This action frightened the horse, and the animal shied back right into the submerged water barrels. It sank up to the saddle, throwing the rider into the filth. The man went completely under, leaving only his hat floating. He came up, spitting and cursing, and quickly remounted his horse.

When he regained his composure, the guard quickly counted off the least broken-down or ill prisoners, and led two hundred of them outside. When they returned the first time, a few of the guards helped stack the wood, and on the last trip inside one of them said, "Don't whisper a word of this to Jones."

Crude wooden platforms were constructed inside Cahaba, allowing two hundred more men at a time to find some much-needed rest. Travis took his next turn out of the water on the fifth day. Struggling through the pain of removing his boots, he sat them to the side and let the sun warm his feet.

On the eighth day, the water dropped, only coming up to Travis's knees. By that evening, it was just below his calves.

Stephen leaned against one of the bunks, waiting his turn. "Did you see the men with the rats?"

Travis walked in place, trying to warm his feet. "No, what are they doing?"

"Skinning them."

"But how will they cook the meat."

"How, indeed," Stephen said.

A loud cracking sound came from outside. Travis looked up in time to see the thick limbs on the giant tree fall from sight. A deep thud shook the ground and water splashed high enough to be seen above the wall. The towering oak was gone.

Chapter Thirty-Four

The next morning, the river receded, leaving just enough water to cover the shoes of the prisoners. Word was whispered that a steamboat had arrived, possibly with supplies. Hope lifted the weary spirits of those within Cahaba's damp walls.

A few hundred prisoners were abruptly called to the front, and quickly removed. The soldiers were not answering any of the inquiring shouts asking what was going on. Rumors immediately spread through Cahaba. Some believed they were being transferred to another prison, others thought the prisoner exchanges were finally happening.

After the excitement had died down, Travis noticed other men besides him were suffering with sore feet as they limped painfully, looking for an open spot. There was no place to sit if you were not taking a turn on the roost, except in the sludge left behind by the flood. The odor from it was foul and revolting.

Some of the prisoners came up with the bright idea of using scraps of lumber to scrape the mud into piles. As soon as enough drier, less offensive dirt was cleared, men collapsed on the ground.

When Travis removed his boots, they made a wet sucking sound. Tears filled his eyes as sharp pains ran up his legs. He slowly pulled his sock down and gritted his teeth. The skin on the bottom of his feet had sluffed off and was embedded in the fabric. As he peeled his socks off, the skin came with them. The swollen, raw, puffy flesh left behind pulsated with searing pain. He laid back on the damp ground and cried.

All around the prison, men removed their clothing and shoes in an attempt to dry the garments and themselves. The water may have left the prison but its effects were far from gone.

As the days passed, names were called in groups and when it was Travis's and George's turn, Travis took a deep breath and pushed his feet into his boots. He could not hold back and yelled in anguish.

"George, I cannot walk."

"Can you make it, if I help you?"

"I will crawl if I have to," Travis said. "Any place has to be better than staying here."

Each step rubbed his raw skin against the soles of his shoes. Before they reached the gates, he was already shaking from the painful effort.

"Keep me upright, George, whatever it takes."

The prisoners were told to take an oath not take up arms against the south. Everyone eagerly accepted the terms. They would have agreed to anything to escape Cahaba. When they were finished, they were ordered down to a waiting steamboat.

Crutcher waved for Travis to step out of line. "Belle has something for you."

George steered Travis around to face Crutcher. Belle and Amanda were at his side. They were grinning widely.

Lying at their feet was a muddy brown dog. He was visibly shaking and twitching at every loud noise.

"Is that... George, is that Salem?"

"If that is Salem, he is not the dog he once was – but then we are not the same men, either."

Travis pulled away from George and stumbled forward. "Salem?"

He fell to his knees and reached out, but the dog cowered back. Travis dropped his hands and felt his heart break.

Belle spoke softly. "I am sorry, Travis. He came to our hands in terrible shape." She handed him the leather lead attached to Salem's collar.

Ms. Gardner took Travis by the hand and helped him to his feet. "It was my son William that found him."

Crutcher nodded. "William had been captured by the Union but he was brought back here. It seems that news of Ms. Gardner's good deeds and influence has spread far and wide."

"We asked if he would search for your dog, and William looked for days," she said. "He found him tied on a line with two others, both dead." She bent and tried to brush some clots of dirt from Salem's fur. "How he survived, we will never know."

Travis pleaded to Crutcher. "Can I take him with me?"

"If you can get him on the boat before Jones comes out."

Travis cleared his throat and wiped his eyes. "How can I thank you."

"Hurry," Belle said.

Travis looked at her in gratitude. "You and your mother…" He glanced at Crutcher. "All of you. You saved our lives."

He pulled on Salem's leash but the dog refused to move.

George picked their broken mascot up, knocking off dried mud in the process. "Hold onto my arm, Travis. We better move before Jones returns."

As they boarded the steamboat, Travis looked back and waved. He wanted the memories of Cahaba to be pulled from his mind, but those of Belle he would treasure forever.

Travis traveled with his feet exposed to the air. The breeze helped dry his raw skin but did little to relieve the pain. Hardtack was poured on the deck and starving prisoners fed much like pigs.

George, Perry, Stephen, and Tennessee ate and talked. Travis was not much interested in food or conversation. He sat and watched Salem.

The dog was curled in a corner, six feet away. The old Salem would be exploring the steamer, greeting the soldiers and begging for scraps, but this Salem was much different. His anxious eyes were always looking, and he was easily startled. His tail remined still. There was not one thing that told Travis that Salem was happy to see him. His behavior and his muddy coat made him seem like a complete stranger, instead of an old friend.

"What did you live through, buddy?"

Travis gave a quiet whistle but Salem's tail did not thump, and he did not even raise his head. Travis had to look away for a moment to keep himself together. George came over and knelt next to him.

"How is he doing?"

"George, you said something a while back. Something like, how much can a man loose and still be who he is. I'm wondering if Salem will ever be the same."

George sat and handed him a piece of hardtack. "We are going to need time, all of us."

From the boat, they were transferred to a train, and then a second train, and finally they arrived at Jackson, Mississippi. They were being ordered to an open field where other prisoners waited. George helped Travis up and waited to see if he could stand on his own. Travis's feet were still raw and swollen, but slightly better since he had managed to rest them for several hours.

"I heard some men talking," George said. "The Union lines are thirty-five miles from here."

"Thirty-five miles?"

"We have to walk it. There's no other way."

"I can barely move," Travis said. "Salem will have to be carried, and you will not be able to walk very far with him."

"We can try." George went to one knee and reached for the dog, but Salem growled and snapped. George spoke soothingly and tried again, but got the same result. "I think he is worse, Travis. He is not even going to let me pick him up."

"What do we do?" Travis asked.

"We have to think of something." George looked around. "Everyone is leaving."

A guard walked over. "You two need to fall in with the rest."

"His feet are in terrible shape," George said.

The guard motioned at Travis with his hand. "Show me."

Travis eased one of his boots off and let the man examine him.

"You can travel with the sick." He looked to George. "You need to catch up with the others."

"But he needs help."

"The wounded and sick can take their time but all others will stay together, no exceptions."

"But…"

"No exceptions," the guard said. His attention turned to Salem. "That's a pitiful looking dog."

Travis tightened his grip on the leather leash. "He is going to make it. We both are."

The man's eyebrows rose. He nodded his head at George. "You need to move along."

George tried to pick Salem up once more but the dog nipped his hand causing him to take a step back. He looked sadly at Travis and shook his head.

The guard frowned. "He will catch up with you."

"I will be there as soon as I can, George. We will make it, so do not worry."

"You know I will, Travis."

Travis forced a smile. "Not giving up."

With great reluctance, George went with the guard.

Travis lowered his body carefully next to Salem, reached over and pulled the dog close. He was greatly relieved that Salem did not growl, he only stiffened somewhat.

They were in the middle of at least a hundred sick prisoners. Some coughed and vomited, while others struggled with their bowels throughout the night. Men were suffering from all sorts of devastating illnesses, and many had feet as bad or worse than his.

The next morning, the group woke for the day's march, but a few did not rise from the cold, hard ground. Their last day had come.

The wounded and ill soldiers made very little progress and were forced to stop again after only covering a mile. Travis paused repeatedly to give his sore feet a rest. Salem would drop to ground, anxiously eyeing the prisoners shuffling past. This process was repeated until the sickest of the men could move no more.

The next morning, Travis worked for several minutes to get upright. He tentatively took a few painful steps. Salem whined and dug his feet in, only moving forward when he felt his leash being pulled hard.

In a short time, Travis was at the rear. His feet burned and ached with each movement. He would take two painfully slow steps and then pull Salem's lead. Sometimes the dog would crawl, sometimes he would let Travis drag him. After an hour of this, Salem began to whine with each tug of the leash.

"Please walk," Travis begged.

He tried to squat next to Salem but his feet hurt so badly, he teetered and fell to his knees.

A guard walked up behind him. "We can't have that. This dog is slowing you down. You'll have to leave him here."

"I cannot," Travis said. "I will not."

"The rest of the men have left you behind. You are at the rear and I will not stay back just to watch one prisoner."

"He is my little brother's dog. It was a promise I made to him — that I would bring him back."

The southerner looked to be in his thirties. His hands and face were tanned and weathered. "Where is your brother?"

Travis felt tears sliding down his face. "I do not know."

He pushed his arms under Salem's belly. "Please do not growl," he whispered.

"Stop." the man said.

With all his strength, Travis stood with the dog. Struggling to keep his balance, he took a hard step back and cried out in pain.

"Stop!"

Travis started forward, each step sending shooting pains up his legs. "This is a promise I have to keep. I will not leave him."

The man stepped in front of him, holding his gun across his body and blocking his path.

"I will do this," Travis said, looking the guard straight in the eyes.

After several tense seconds, the man sighed and stepped out of the way. "We have to catch up with the group before dark. If the sun sets and we have not reached camp, you will leave the dog."

"Yes, sir."

The first half-mile carrying Salem was very painful, but the next stretch was agony. His feet felt as if they were on fire and his biceps burned nearly as much.

When he could take no more, Travis heaved Salem up and over his head to rest across the back of his neck. He held the dog's legs with his hands and was relieved to have the weight out of his arms.

"You need to hurry," the man said. "The day is getting long."

"I am doing my best."

Travis tried to take his mind off the pain. "Are you from Mississippi?"

"Why all the questions?"

"I'm just trying-" Travis stepped on a rock. The sharp sting was almost too much to bear. He fought to catch his breath. "I'm just trying to get through this and make it back home."

He felt a wetness squish under his foot.

"You should stop and take care of that," the guard said. "Blood is seeping out of your shoe."

"I will not make it if I stop, and I do not believe I could get back on my feet." Travis started moving down the road again.

His shoe continued to fill with blood. It made his toes slick. He cleared his throat and gritted his teeth. "Just give me something else to think on. Do you live in Mississippi?"

The guard walked grimly next to him, not sparing a single word.

The sun rested at the tops of trees on the horizon and the shadows stretched across the beaten road. Travis's weary steps had been reduced to nothing more than a shuffle.

Salem's head hung near Travis's ear and the dog's breath was ragged and raspy. They both needed water and rest but Travis could not bear the consequences of doing so.

He pushed forward, fighting through the agony while watching the sun sink with each passing minute. When it became clear they would not make it in time, the dread turned to misery. The pain was too much, and sorrow overwhelmed him. Slowly, dusk folded in around them.

He closed his eyes and felt darkness take his mind and heart.

"Salem...," Travis whispered hoarsely as his legs gave way.

CHAPTER THIRTY-FIVE

The guard caught him under the armpits from behind as Travis started to collapse.

He swallowed hard and slumped forward with his hands on his knees while the man removed Salem from his shoulders. With his hands now free, Travis wiped his eyes and looked back, expecting to see Salem on the ground.

But the guard had the dog in his arms. "Let's get moving."

Travis rubbed his face, wiping away what were now tears of gratitude. "Yes, sir. Thank you."

Upon reaching the camp, Travis fell to the ground and groaned. The man placed Salem next to him and turned away.

"Wait, I want to thank you." His voice trailed away. The guard was gone.

Salem roused enough to licked the mud off his paws. After some water and crumbled hardtack, he seemed to be feeling better. His eyes were brighter.

As the darkness pushed in against the little islands of light in camp, Travis rolled until he could reach one of Salem's ears. He rubbed it, and felt the dog slowly relax. He fell asleep with his fingers tangled in matted fur.

Something wet touched his face. A soft hand caressed his forehead. For a moment, he was young in his dream and his mother was checking him for fever, but when he opened his eyes, it was a stranger hovering over him. Light from a lantern illuminated a pleasant older woman with a sweet smile. In her hand was a damp cloth, with which she swiped across his cheeks and under his chin.

"We need to get those shoes off."

"Who are you?" Travis asked with a weak voice.

His guard's face appeared in the dim light. "This is my mother. Give her no trouble and do what she says."

"Yes sir, and thank you for what you did on the road. I will never forget it."

The woman raised her eyebrows in question and turned toward her son. He looked uncomfortable but gave no reply.

Travis heard a dog lapping. Salem was eating some kind of broth from a bowl on the ground.

"Is he, all right?"

"Let us just worry about you for now," the woman said.

The guard patted the woman on the shoulder. "I'll be back after daylight."

"Be careful, son."

"I will."

She rose and kissed him on the cheek, and then focused her attention back to Travis's feet. "This is going to hurt."

She pulled his boots off, and Travis gritted his teeth to keep from screaming. When the pain had passed somewhat, he propped up on his elbows to ask, "Why are you helping me?"

The lady uncorked a blue bottle and sprinkled something white into her palm. "You reminded my son of his boy. Now, this is going to be painful, but there's no other way to apply it."

"What are you going to do?"

"I have to rub it in."

"What is it?"

"Sage powder mixed with flour."

Travis gasped when she touched his foot. She applied it to his feet as quick and gently as she could. He bit his lip hard and did his best to keep from kicking her. He groaned and covered his face with shaking hands, and when it was finished he was slick with sweat. "I hope you will not have to do that again. It is more than I can take."

She pulled a roll of bandages from her apron. "I'm going to wrap your feet and that will be the last time I have to touch them."

"Will I be able to walk tomorrow?"

"You're not going anywhere for a couple days. My son has gone for a wagon to carry you and a few others the rest of the way." She started to bandage his feet. "Does this hurt?"

He winced, and lied, "Not bad."

She glanced at his face. "You know, my boy was right. You really do look like my grandson."

"How old is he?"

The woman paused and her eyes glistened in the lamplight. "He was seventeen. They were trapped in Vicksburg during the siege."

"They?"

"My son's wife and his boy, my grandson." After securing the wrappings, the woman stood. "I have to tend to a few other men. Get some rest. Some ladies from the church are bringing food in the morning."

Travis wanted to ask more questions about their family and Vicksburg, but it was a different kind of pain that filled her face. He knew her story would be too recent and painful to recount.

When the sun had warmed his bones the next day, Travis ate biscuits and bacon. Cooked bacon. His mouth watered with each delicious bite. Salem sat up and stared at him while he chewed. A pinch of bread sent the dog's tail into a frantic wag. It was the first sign of the old Salem Travis knew so well. After eating, they slept most of the day.

He dreamed of playing with his brother. They were both young and his mother was drinking tea and watching them. Chet threw a walnut and hit Travis in the head. Everyone laughed, but then the peaceful scene changed.

The walnut became a speeding piece of lead that Travis narrowly ducked. Explosions shook the ground and his family was gone, disappeared from his memory. A cannonball blasted into the earth at his feet and sent him spinning into the air. Looking down, he could see Emil, Wyman, Lawrence, and all the other friends he had left behind. They were bleeding, dying, and calling for him.

Gravity yanked him back, splashing his rag-doll body into the flooded prison of Cahaba. Thousands of prisoners were drowning in the filthy water and pulling at him as if he were an island of refuge. A hand closed around his face and the dirty, brown liquid crept across his cheeks as he sank into blackness.

Travis jerked upright, gasping for air. It was dark and mostly quiet, except for a few noises from the sick prisoners, and his heaving breathing. Salem licked his hand and the dog's concern brought him back to the real world, crashing down with the weight of reality not far behind.

He pulled Salem close. "It has been hard, boy." Travis wiped his face. "We made it, though. Together."

The healthiest of the sick left the next morning, and the next day a wagon arrived for the remainder. The guard with the kind heart helped Salem and Travis into the back. Travis held onto the man's hand.

"I wish this war had never been. I am sorry about your son."

The man squeezed Travis's hand hard and closed his eyes tight. "Go home, boy. Go home."

"I am doing the best I can," Travis said.

As the wagon pulled away, the guard said, "Let us find peace in this fray."

After bouncing over a rutted road for miles, the wagon slowed and finally came to a halt.

"We're stuck tight," said the driver. "Y'all have to walk the last few miles to camp Fisk."

Travis had been drowsing with several others, but now they all sat up to find they were surrounded by water. "Why is the road under water?"

"The Mississippi is flooded from all the rain. Sorry, boys, but y'all have to make the rest of the way on your own feet."

The stronger of the sick were helping others out of the back of the wagon. When Travis got to the edge, he looked down in distaste. Several hands steadied him as he eased his feet into the liquid.

He was back in his nightmare – faces swirling in the brown nasty soup. Water splashed on his legs and brought him to his senses. It was Salem, and he was enjoying pets from the wounded men standing there.

The group sloshed slowly along the road until they emerged from the water and reached a vast, green field. The camp was nearly empty. Tents were scattered, supplies in some, sick soldiers in others. A doctor stopped them and quickly examined everyone. Finally, he motioned for them to continue.

"Go to the Vicksburg train. It will take you to the river. The last steamboat will be leaving soon, the Sultana I think."

And just like that, Travis was back at Vicksburg where Emil had been killed, a memory he wished would go away.

He walked slowly. His feet were soaked and hurting, but it was a small thing compared to the torment he had experienced days before. Salem stayed on his heels, limping, but keeping up.

They approached the train, and a Union soldier asked for his name and regiment. Travis complied. The man shuffled through some papers.

"Your enlistment is up. The Sultana will take you back to Illinois."

Travis was not sure he heard correctly. "You mean the war is over?"

"It's over for you unless you reenlist."

Travis was dumbfounded. Realization set in, quickly followed by excitement. "I need to go to Salem! Salem, Arkansas."

"Arkansas? Where is Salem?"

"North, close to Missouri."

The man thought for a moment. "Your best bet is to get off at Memphis."

"Yes, sir."

The railroad car he was directed to was packed, and there was barely room to stand. Travis managed to carry Salem to a corner and squeeze in. He sat and hugged his dog with something close to happiness. Salem seemed to catch his mood and took a moment to wash Travis's face.

The war was over for them.

The railroad cars stopped at the Mississippi river where a steamship was docked. Travis gawked at it in amazement. Every deck, from bow to stern, was seething with soldiers, and a long line of men were waiting to board. He looked down the river's edge on both sides for another boat, but there was not any to be seen.

Travis sighed. "Well, Salem, I guess we should be used to crowds by now."

The press of men was overwhelming. It was useless to try and keep Salem on his lead. Travis rolled it up and put it in his pocket, trusting Salem to stay close. Some of the soldiers noticed a dog was on the ship and tried to call or pet him, but he dodged in between all the legs and deftly kept up with Travis.

The steamer had many levels but each was packed. Travis moved slowly, being careful to keep all the feet from stepping on his. When he found an empty space next to a handrail, he sat and leaned against it. Salem tucked in close.

He rubbed the dog's head. "We made it, boy. We made it."

"Travis? Is that you?"

"Perry!"

His friend plopped down and gave him an unexpected hug. "We wondered what happened to you. Is this the dog you talked about?"

"Yes, this is, Salem."

"Can I pet him?"

"Maybe," Travis said. "He's been acting a little strange."

Perry bugged his eyes to make a funny face. "We all are a little strange now to some degree."

"Where is George?" Travis asked.

"His name was called a few days ago. He is on a different boat. Stephen and Tennessee are with us though, somewhere in this crowd."

They watched a steady stream of men moving slowly, each one exploring the ship, looking for a place to call his own. Travis frowned as he realized he would probably never see George again. They had split ways without even a simple farewell.

"Goodbye, George," Travis whispered.

A colored soldier approached them. "Do you fellas need anythin'?"

Perry elbowed Travis. "We sure would like some steak and potatoes."

The black man smiled. "If I could make that happen, I would. They should be handing out some crackers soon."

"Whatever we get is good enough at this point," Travis said.

The man adjusted his uniform. "Well, sir, we sure appreciate everythin'." He studied Travis and Perry. "There's about twenty of us on board and I wish we could do more for you boys."

"Were you captured?" Perry asked.

"No, sir. We volunteered to help get you fellas home."

"And we appreciate that," Travis said. "We sure do."

The man shook hands with them and went to the next group.

The Sultana left Vicksburg. A set of large paddles churned the water, propelling the boat up the muddy river. Colored lanterns hung from iron rods, casting light upon sleeping men.

"You missed some excitement," Perry said.

Travis shook his head. "I think I have had plenty of excitement."

"Did you hear about Lincoln?"

"No."

"They announced that all prisoners were to be paroled. There were parades, parties, and singing until this boat arrived."

"This boat?"

"It brought the news that Lincoln had been killed." Perry rubbed his face. "That sure brought an end to the fun."

Travis sat quietly and Perry gave him a moment, having gone through the vast swing of emotions himself a few hours earlier. An empty feeling crept over Travis, like being adrift at sea or wandering in the wilderness, hopelessly lost. Part of America had been stolen and it would never be the same.

"Did we win the war?" Travis asked sadly. "Because it does not feel like it."

Perry got up. "I plan to look around. Do you want to come?"

"I'm exhausted." He patted Salem on the back. A cloud of dirt puffed into the air. "We are both worn out. Neither of us got much rest the past few days."

"I'll be back in a little while, then. Get some sleep."

Travis watched as men climbed out on the paddle-wheel covering and claimed a precious bit of uncrowded space. The ship had a big housing, at least ten feet wide on each side to cover the turning wheels. A few men laid on top with their hands behind their heads, making Travis nervous. He could not imagine sleeping out there, where it would be so easy to fall off into the cold water.

"Move aside," a voice said. Members of the crew pushed their way through, carrying a timber. One of them measured while the other cut the board, and then it was wedged under the lip of the deck above.

"Hurry," one of them said. "The starboard side is sagging even more."

The men rushed away. The supporting timber bowed and creaked from the weight of hundreds of soldiers above. Salem cocked his head from side to side at the noise. The crew returned, slapped a second board in place and headed off with another thick timber on their shoulders.

A wake spread across the river as the overloaded boat pushed its way through the water. The Mississippi was much wider than Travis remembered. The flood waters had pushed the river over its banks and far out into the farmland. While he watched the soggy landscape pass, his eyelids grew heavy.

"Travis!" Perry shouted. "Come here. You have to see this."

Travis reluctantly climbed to his feet and limped after Perry and up a set of stairs, past four massive boiler smokestacks.

At the back was a sight he was not prepared to see. Lines of cots had been arranged in rows across the deck. The makeshift beds held men in different degrees of horror. Some had open wounds from the war that had become infected. There were a few dozen who were curled into tight balls, holding their stomachs with one hand and a vomit bucket in the other. Missing legs, arms, men with diarrhea, and other sickness was not the worst by far.

The remainder of the cots held the poorest souls Travis had ever witnessed. Men with hardly an ounce of muscle left on their bodies, looked through sunken, hollow eyes. Their heads turned, their mouths moved, all of which Travis found hard to believe. These men looked more like skin covered skeletons than real people.

"How are they even alive?" Travis whispered.

"They are from Andersonville," Perry said quietly.

Travis turned to face the river. "The thin sticks we became at Cahaba are nothing compared to these poor, poor souls."

They went back to the other side of the boilers. "Stephen is here somewhere," Perry said, "do you want to join me in a hunt?"

"My feet are hurting," Travis said. "I believe I will sit here and take my shoes off. The warm air coming up from the boilers is just what I need."

Travis removed his shoes and bandages and gingerly brushed the caked mixture the woman had applied. It flaked off and exposed a thicker layer of wrinkled skin forming over the wounds. The milky color was gone and he was left with a nice pink tone, tender and slightly raw, but Travis felt better. He was on the mend.

The warm air wafted up from the boilers and sent him to sleep quickly, but he jerked awake when Salem licked his hand.

"How can you not be tired?"

He scratched the dog's ear and Salem's tail thumped against the wooden deck. Travis smiled. "It's been a long time since you acted so friendly."

He wondered what Salem had been through at Cahaba and if he would ever fully recover.

A woman knelt next to Travis. "Your feet look like they could use some tending to." Her dress pooled around her on the deck. She wore a thin jacket with a single button and there was a stain just below her collar. "I'm with the Christian Commission."

"It's a pleasure to meet you," Travis said.

She wiped her forehead. "With just twelve of us on board, we are sadly outnumbered." She rubbed salve on his feet and picked up the bandages he had removed.

"Are they dry?" Travis asked.

"They are. Would you like for me to put them back on?"

"Yes, please."

When she was finished, the woman recited a short prayer and stood. "I am sorry to hurry away, but like I said, we are of short supply."

"I understand. Thank you."

The excitement of going home spread from man to man, until the equivalent of a party broke out in the middle of the night. Dozens of lanterns on each deck illuminated men dancing, laughing, and singing. A beautiful chorus of voices rose above the rest, prompting everyone to join in.

Sweet hour of prayer, sweet hour of prayer.
That calls me from a world of care.
And bids me at my Father's throne.
Make all my wants and wishes known.

"Who started that song?" Travis asked.

"Me. Could you not tell?" Perry belted out a sour tune. Salem howled and Perry laughed. "I heard some sort of opera group is on board, from Chicago, I think."

"Well, they are much better than you," Travis said. "Salem and I both think so.

Hours passed and Travis tossed and turned, getting very little sleep on the noisy ship of men who shouted and celebrated until the wee morning hours.

CHAPTER THIRTY-SIX

April 25, 1865

Neighing horses woke Travis early. A cacophony of animal squalls made an unearthly noise.

"Why does this boat have to be so noisy?" he complained.

Perry grabbed his arm and shook it. "Come see this."

He sat up, and discovered Salem was gone. His heart sped up. "What has happened to Salem?"

Perry pulled him to his feet. "He is being entertained watching the crew feed the livestock. You need to get up and see what I found."

Travis followed him until they got bogged down in a thick line of men.

"What are we in line for?" Travis asked. "Breakfast, I hope?"

"Wait and see."

When they reached the front, Travis saw a huge alligator inside a large cage. "Good night! I have never seen one so close."

"Or so big," Perry said. "You better hide your fingers."

"Fingers? I bet he could swallow me whole." He walked to the front of the enclosure to get a closer look at the gator's head. "Why do they have an alligator?"

Perry shrugged. "A mascot, I guess."

The gator let out a deep hiss, and Travis stumbled back. "Why would one want a mascot that could eat a person."

They took their leave of the gator, and Perry took Travis to meet up with Stephen and Tennessee. The big man shook with him, his giant hand engulfing Travis's.

Stephen smiled and slapped his shoulder. "It's good to see you again."

Travis spent the rest of the day laughing, eating crackers, and listening to his friend's plans for the future. Darkness brought a steady rain and forced men to try and crowd under the decks and any other structure to keep them dry.

"There is not nearly enough room for everybody," Stephen said. "It is a good thing we got under here early."

Travis did not feel so lucky, packed in shoulder to shoulder, an impossible position to get any sleep. Salem chose to brave the elements, lying in the rain as if it were sunshine. The deck around him became a dirty puddle as the last of the caked mud was washed from his fur.

"Your dog does not have the sense to come in out of the rain." Tennessee observed.

The men around them laughed.

The rain stopped just before daylight the next morning, and Travis managed to grab a couple hours of rest while leaned back against the wall. Mosquitos woke him and made any more sleep impossible. Salem was also awake early and was up to his old tricks, wandering around begging for scraps. It warmed Travis's heart to see the old Salem back.

A member of the crew passed by. "Quick stop at Helena, Arkansas. Stay on board." He repeated his announcement as he kept walking.

Travis scrambled up and made his way to the railing to see the town he had spent months in. It was much the way he remembered, but less crowded. Salem came and sat at his feet. He raised his nose high and whined.

"You remember this place, don't you, boy?"

"You been here before?" a woman asked. She was a middle-aged, tough looking lady with high cheekbones. Next to her was a young girl about seven years old.

"Yes," Travis said. "We built a fort here."

"Your dog, too?"

"Well, he thought he was helping."

The woman laughed. "We love our dogs."

"You are not from here, are you?" Travis asked.

She smiled. "My accent gave me away? My name is Anne Annis. This is my daughter, Isabella."

"Where are you from?" Travis asked.

"She was born here but I am from England. Moved to Wisconsin fifteen years ago."

"Are you visiting family in the South?"

She looked to her daughter. "We had to come and help her father, did we not?"

The girl nodded. "He was sick."

"My husband is a Lieutenant. Harvey is doing better, and so we are headed home."

"Picture!" someone shouted. "Come on, let's get in the picture."

A rush of bodies pushed toward the railing. A photographer was on the dock and had set up his camera. He waved and the men waved back. The lopsided weight on the boat caused it to list. When the ship tilted, Travis held onto the rail. Salem's legs sprawled as he tried to dig his claws in.

Crew members shouted frantically. "Back! Get Back!"

Once the weight was spread evenly again, the Sultana leveled out.

Anne's hands were clamped around the rail. Her knuckles were white and she was shaking.

"It is all right now," Travis said. "You can let go."

Slowly, she released her grip. "Forgive me. I am not fond of boats." She leaned close and lowered her voice. "I lost my first two husbands in shipwrecks. Being on a crowded steamer sets my teeth on edge."

"I am sorry for your misfortune," Travis said.

"Ah, well, I will be glad when we are back on land and not tempting fate." She chuckled, turning back to her daughter. "Isabella, we should go check on Papa."

"Where is he?" The girl asked.

"Let's go find him." The woman smiled at Travis and left.

One of the crew walked by and Travis motioned him over.

"Yes?" The man asked.

"I was told to get off at Memphis. Can you tell me how far away that is?"

"It's our next stop. We are due in Memphis this evening, just after dark."

"Thanks."

Travis searched the decks until he found Stephen and Tennessee on the top one.

"Where's Perry?"

Stephen laughed. "He's probably poking at that alligator again."

Salem laid down and Tennessee rubbed his belly with his foot. "Does he follow you everywhere?"

Travis nodded. "He has been with me for nearly three years." Travis sat and leaned against the pilothouse wall. "This day has worn me to a frazzle. Can you wake me when we get to Memphis?"

"Sure," Tennessee said.

Stephen nodded.

With his collar pulled up tight around his neck, sleep came quickly.

Shouting.

Cursing.

Rumbling.

A dog barking.

Travis sat up and rubbed his eyes. It was after dark and the lanterns on the boat were glowing. A light drizzle tickled his face and, in the distance, lightening flashed. Thunder rolled. More shouts and cursing came from somewhere on the ship. Salem growled and woofed. Travis patted his back to calm him.

Perry came and sat next to him. "You will never guess who's making all the noise below."

Travis blinked hard to clear his blurry eyes. "What is going on?"

"Tennessee is wall-papered," Perry said. "He went into town at the last minute and drank some whiskey. He made it back to the boat but he has been yelling like that for a couple hours."

"Where's Stephen?"

"He is down there, trying to keep Tennessee under control."

"Wait," Travis said. "We were told to stay on the boat at Helena. How did he get off?"

"He got off at Memphis."

"Memphis?"

"Yes."

"Memphis! Where are we?"

"We left Memphis an hour ago," Perry said.

"Someone should have woken me. I was supposed to get off!"

"You did not tell me," Perry said. "You were in the Illinois regiment, so I thought you were going all the way."

Stephen picked his way through the men and joined Travis and Perry. A bolt of light streaked from one cloud to another, and thunder rumbled.

"Why did you not wake me?" Travis asked.

"Oh, my gosh," Stephen said. "I apologize, Travis. They asked for volunteers to unload some cargo. Tennessee and I went, and he used his money to get drunk on some pop skull. What a mess. We forgot."

Travis took a deep breath, and released it slowly. "It is all right. I'll get off at the next stop."

"Do you know where that will be?" Perry asked.

Travis stood and stretched his tight muscles. "I shall find a crew member somewhere in this horde and ask."

"Travis I am truly sorry," Stephen said.

"Forget about it. Salem and I will be back in a few minutes."

"You better hurry back," Stephen said with a grin, "if you want some sugar. Seems like I owe you for causing you to miss your stop."

"Sugar?"

"Found some in the cargo." He held up a bag. "Probably two pounds in here!"

"Hush down," someone said. "I'm trying to sleep."

Perry jabbed Stephen in the side. "Shhhh."

"You better save me some," Travis whispered.

"You bet I will."

Travis walked across the deck slowly, dodging around those that slept with their heads propped on knees, rails, and crates. Salem paused and his ears perked.

Travis watched him curiously. "What is it?"

A concussion like a dozen cannons blasted him in the chest, throwing his body. He crashed against the railing, losing the air from his lungs, and then he fell to the deck. As he staggered to his feet, he heard a scream. The cry quickly grew louder, suddenly ending when a body fell from the sky, hitting the floor next to him. Another thumped the deck, and then another splintered the wooden floor. Heavy splashes came from the river as more victims landed in the water. A severed arm came tumbling across the deck to a rest at his feet.

Travis sucked in a deep breath against the pain in his body. He frantically looked for Salem but the dog was gone. More screams filled the air, desperate, blood curdling shrieks that sent chills up his back. A massive hole had been blown open in the middle of the boat. Wounded men fell into the void, landing in the burning coals where the boilers had ruptured. Dozens walked aimlessly, feeling their way with blistered hands and useless eyes from the hot steam.

"Perry! Stephen!" There was no sign of his friends.

"It's coming down!" someone yelled.

One of the towering smokestacks groaned as it fell, crushing at least a hundred people under the hot metal. Moments later, a second stack went over and a shower of glowing embers shot into the air. People shouted from all over the boat, wailing for help. Thousands of voices screamed and yelled so loudly that Travis covered his ears.

The whole structure of the steamboat had changed. The decks had collapsed on top of each other, the smokestacks were gone, and rubble and bodies were strewn everywhere. Most of the men were disoriented and confused as to what had happened. One of the colored troops ran back and forth yelling for a fire bucket.

"The rebels got us," someone shouted.

A thick crowd of bodies pushed Travis to the edge, overlooking the water, where he saw a few hundred men who had been blown overboard during the blast. He squirmed his way back toward the center of the ship. Across the smoking hole Tennessee was bent low, pulling on part of the structure where a man had been pinned down.

Splintered deck boards that had fallen into the gaping hole were ignited by the burning coal. It ate up the dry wood in blue, curling flames that climbed upward and quickly spread.

Travis ran helplessly, looking for anything that might hold water.

Burning heat radiated out and forced Tennessee to leave the man he was trying to rescue. Seconds later, the fire raged up the boards and finally silenced his cries.

More trapped victims yelled for help as the flames swept over them. Out of the smoldering hole, came the form of a man fully engulfed. Not a sound escaped his mouth, and once on the deck, he fell face first and did not move again. It was too much for most of the survivors to witness and they began to abandon the ship, stripping off loose clothing and jumping into the water by the hundreds.

Travis tried to spot Tennessee again but there were too many running people. "Perry, Stephen! Where are you!"

A sprinting figure knocked Travis off his feet, and he was trampled before he could rise. His back and legs were stepped on, and a volley of discarded shoes and clothing rained over him. He rolled to the railing and held one of the post tight. Desperate souls dove in, some landing on top of others, many going down and not coming back up.

The shrieks and groans of drowning men filled the air and echoed off the side of the boat. Hundreds of pale faces, filled with fear, stared up at Travis. Lightening flashed, creating ghostly specters on the water. The fire on the boat intensified, exposing the struggle in the river even more. Pulling himself up, he heard people begging for help.

"Throw us something down. We are drowning!"

Travis tossed a broken board over. Other men who were still on the ship did the same. Soon the river was littered with bales of hay, cotton, and parts of the boat. While he was throwing another timber, Travis saw horses and mules in the river. Some were alive, some dead. Drowning men swarmed beast and man alike, pulling them down. The panic spread and soon the river was a writhing mass.

Travis turned away from the sight.

"Travis!"

Turning back, he saw Perry out in the water, holding onto a board and floating away from the crowd. He had but one second to wave before the current took him beyond the firelight.

The sound of breaking wood drew Travis's attention. Men were pulling boards, doors, and shutters off the boat. Most jumped in right away, but a few waited.

"Stay here for the moment," one of them said. "They will pull you under."

Pigs squealed and mules brayed as the flames reached them.

"My Lord!" A voice yelled. "Look at that. Oh, my Lord!"

Chapter Thirty-Seven

From the end of the boat came a terribly fearsome sight. Comparable to a Biblical revelation, death produced a white horse, running with its head held high, desperate for an avenue of escape from its torment. With flames streaming from its mane and back, it screamed as it passed the heat coming from the hole in the deck. The poor animal headed for a break in the barrier and jumped from the ship, smoke and steam trailing from its body as it went over the edge.

Near the spot where the horse made its exit were a dozen people waiting for their turn on a rope that had been let down. Travis saw Anne Annis in this line and limped over quickly, but she made no notice of Travis. She took her grip and started down, but her eyes were fixated on the river.

"Please, keep her head above water!" she shouted. "Stay up!"

A man was in the water, trying to swim with her daughter on his back. Travis watched in horror as the man and Isabella went under.

"No!" Anne wailed.

She stopped moving on the rope. A waft of heat from the fire hit Travis in the back. The man who was next in line had scalded skin from the exploding boiler steam. The hot air blew across his peeling back and neck and caused him to scream out in pain. He jumped over the railing and knocked Anne off as he fell.

The fire forced Travis away and effectively blocked any path to the back of the steamer. Retreating to the bow of the ship, he saw a lifeboat in the water. It flipped over and over as dozens of men clamored to get inside. After a few more turns, the rowboat went down and took all of the men with it.

Numerous voices shouted in unison, "Jump! Jump!"

The Christian Commission lady that had helped Travis was trapped by the flames. She shouted down to the struggling men who were treading water. "I am afraid I could not control my fear and would drown some of you."

"Jump. Save yourself!"

The woman refused and the fire closed around her. She was gone.

A steady breeze seemed to cooperate with the current and pushed the steamer backwards, keeping the smoke off the bow. The men at the rear were not so lucky, where the choking soot forced them into the cold river.

With each passing moment, Travis's gaze darted from one moving form to another on the water, hoping one of them would be Salem. He whistled, but could not be heard above the dreadful cries of animals and men.

A faster moving river current caught the floating sea of bodies and began to pull them away. The storm had skirted to the north, but one last bolt of lightning illuminated the stark faces of struggling victims. Within moments, the last ghastly figure disappeared from the firelight.

"You, Cahaba boy!"

Travis looked across the deck and saw a man he recognized from the prison, waving frantically.

"Come and help us," he cried.

"What can I do?"

"The heat is nearly unbearable. We have to work fast."

Three men were holding a wounded victim with crooked, broken arms. The man nodded and he was dropped into the water.

"Smith!" One of them shouted and pointed. "I see a few more."

Smith surged ahead of them until he was less than fifteen steps from the fire.

There they found a man with a bloody gash across his side and stomach. The scalding temperature was hard to face, so Travis turned his back to the flames and tried to shield his face with his hands.

"I cannot stand up," the wounded man said. "Drag me to the edge."

Smith took one arm, Travis the other, and they pulled him to the side, where he tumbled into the dark water below.

Smith shouted to the others. "Billy, Walter, are there more?"

"One here!"

Travis arrived in time to hear a soldier say, "In case I die, tell my family of my fate. I am Daniel McLoyd, Eighteenth Illinois."

"Can you walk? We can take you to the front."

"Both my ankles are broken with bones coming through the skin. Throw me in the river is all I ask. I shall burn to death if I remain here."

As careful as possible, they picked the poor fellow up and sent him into the Mississippi. Travis quickly turned away, not willing to witness the man's fate.

On the way back to the bow, Travis ran his fingers through his hair. He had seen and been part of the most terrible things man had to offer on the battlefield and in Cahaba, but this was beyond the sum of it all.

On the front of the steamer, he and a hundred men waited for the fire to come. It would eat away the deck until they would have to make the same decision so many others had, burn alive or brave the flooded river.

"Attach it here," a man said. "Samuel, here, on this ring."

Two fellows secured a chain and threw the slack over, the links rattling against the boat as they went.

"Bring me another," Samuel said.

When a second one was found nearby, it was added to the same ring. Ropes were tied to the links in a way that would allow the knots to hang over the edge, away from the fire.

A crash came from the side of the steamer as one of the massive paddle wheels fell away. With the ships drag uneven, the steamer began to turn slowly.

"Get ready, boys!" a voice yelled.

When the boat had fully rotated, the wind covered them with thick smoke, strong with the odors of burnt wood, singed hair, and cooked flesh. The fire jumped forward like a hungry, starving animal. With no other choice, all of the men bailed into the water.

Exertion and flames had heated Travis to the point of sweating and upon plunging into the chilly river, there was no stopping an involuntary breath. He was back to the surface in seconds, coughing water, spraying it out with each effort.

The sound of gagging and gurgling was all around him.

A hand on his shoulder, pulling downward.

Someone choking in his ear.

He kicked and fought, scratched and punched, until he managed to swim back to the boat. Men held death grips on the chains but he found one of the ropes and wrapped it around his hand. Most of those who had jumped, swam for pieces of floating boards and other debris. Many of the fellows went under and never resurfaced.

Sparks and embers fell into the water, spitting and sizzling as they were extinguished. Dancing flames caused the amount of light under the bow to change over and over, dark to light.

"Samuel," one of the men said. "Did you see what became of the gator?"

"It surely burned," Samuel said.

"I hope so."

A few other fellows swam over and took ahold of the ropes. "We are freezing to death."

"It's better than roasting. If'n I don't make it outter here alive, I'm Samuel, Sixth Kentucky."

A man on another chain said, "Joshua, One Hundred-Fourth Ohio."

On the other side of him, came a third voice. "Thomas, Third Tennessee."

Travis's teeth were chattering too hard for him to talk. The water had quickly sucked the heat from his body and the feeling in his legs with it.

"What about you?" Thomas asked.

"Travis," he managed to stutter. "Thirteenth Illinois."

A large creature came around the corner, churning the water. The cold was suddenly forgotten.

Joshua shouted, "The gator!"

Samuel scrambled up the chain until his feet were above the river, stark terror on his face.

"It's a horse," Thomas yelled above the panicky shouts. "Just a horse."

The animal snorted and wheezed as it swam into the darkness.

Samuel was staring at the deck that was now eye-level. "Hey! There's a huge pile of clothes and blankets up there."

"I will not climb up there," Joshua said. "The heat will cook us."

"No," Samuel said. "If we splash as much water on the deck as we can, I think the wet clothes will stop the fire from burning the bow."

Desperately, they drug their free hands across the top of the water, sending sheets of it onto the deck. Travis kept it up until his shoulder muscles burned. He swapped arms and continued splashing.

One of the men swam back a few feet so he could see the deck. "Were done, boys. The flames are spreading to the clothes now."

There was a chorus groans and curses.

"At least it warmed us up," Samuel said.

Over the next few hours, the bow of the steamer continued to burn. The intense heat and falling coals forced Travis to duck under the water. He held his breath, came up for air, and went back down over and over, until the flames reached the waterlogged hull and died a few inches above the water-line. There was barely enough wood left to keep them afloat.

Near daylight, the heat had lessened, and some of the stronger men climbed over the edge careful not to burn themselves on the smoldering wood. They helped the others, and when Travis was pulled up, he found the boat unrecognizable. It was nothing but a black shell filled with warped metal and pockets of burning wood.

Miraculously, their efforts hours earlier had paid off. A small portion of the deck remained, and on this section was a pile of blackened fabric. They pulled the scorched clothing off and found dry undamaged garments and blankets several layers down. The freezing men quickly changed.

Travis donned a wooly shirt and jacket. Next, he found a pair of pants and boots. The last item he grabbed was a blue hat that he socked on his head. Nothing fit correctly but he did not mind at all. The warmth made him feel like a new man.

"We are not safe yet, the fire is still burning under us," Samuel stated.

Travis picked up the wet clothes they had taken off. "We can use these to help put out the flames."

They all worked together and dipped the blankets and other pieces of clothing into the river. They wrung the water onto the fire and slapped it with wet garments which produced a massive amount of steam and smoke.

"Look," Travis said excitedly. "A boat just passed us."

"Yell! They do not see us through all this smoke," one of the men said quickly.

They hollered and whistled shrilly, but the boat disappeared into the billowing clouds that floated near the surface of the river.

An eddy caught the Sultana's hull and slowly spun it in a circle. Travis choked and gagged on thick smoke each time the boat turned.

When the first light of morning came, a gentle current of air blew the smoke back and it exposed a gruesome, nightmarish scene. The flooded river was filled with snags and treetops sticking up, and the dead were caught in every section of brush as far as they could see.

The men stood in silent horror at the vision before them.

A shout broke the stillness, and a man let go of a snag and struck out toward them.

More survivors swam to the boat and were pulled inside. Owens, the escapee from Cahaba, was among them. Travis help pull him up, and the grateful man embraced him. Another of the new arrivals was scalded all over with large blisters on his face and hands. He sat unmoving, overcome with shock.

It was Samuel that broke the stillness. "This fire is gaining on us."

The need to survive gave them strength, and each man redoubled their previous efforts, slapping the flames with wet blankets.

Thomas pointed to the bottom of the steamer. "See that big bed of coals? There's a lot of steam coming from there. I think water is leaking in."

"We are going to sink," Joshua said.

Samuel shook his head in denial. "I cannot swim."

"Nor I," Thomas said.

The scalded man roused and shouted, "If I go back in, it is to my death. I cannot last another moment in the water."

"Hello, on the boat," a voice called.

Thirty yards from the hull was a large crude raft made of long, thick logs. An older man held up a paddle and waved with it.

The survivors crowded to the edge of the deck, exclaiming with hopes of rescue.

Samuel shouted. "Here, sir!"

"What guarantee have I," the man called, "that you be reasonable? If y'all every one come on, we'll be swamped for sure, and I can't swim."

"What is your name, sir?" Samuel asked.

"Fogleman."

"Mr. Folgeman, we give our word. How many can you take per trip?"

"Six, but only if you keep yourselves calm."

After the most wounded half-dozen left, the wait was horrible. The flames quickly spread, and at the same time the hull began to sink. Fogleman returned four more times before returning for the last of the survivors. The water on deck was lapping at Travis's ankles when he finally stepped off the bow.

"Don't rock us," the old man warned.

Travis and several others picked up some boards on the raft, and used them to help paddle away from the wreck.

The remains of the Sultana slipped under the water, sending up a huge spray of steam.

Mr. Fogleman guided them a half-mile up the river and to an open area where the brush had been beaten down. Just up the hill was a white house. In the middle of the yard was a big fire with survivors huddled around it.

"Go warm up," he told them. "I have to go back. I left some men hanging in the trees."

"We are in your debt," Travis said. "Nor do I have anything to pay you. These are not even my clothes."

Fogleman shook his head and pushed his raft back from the land with the paddle. "T'would not be right to profit off the suffering of my fellow man."

"Mr. Fogleman, have you seen a dog?"

"Horses, mules, pigs, men," he struck his paddle deep in the water, and the words seemed to tear him apart, "women and children. Nothing else."

Dozens of survivors were scattered around the yard. A wagonload of women had arrived and were handing out blankets and spooning soup into tin cups and bowls. Some were caring for the many scalded and horribly burned unfortunates. Travis limped through them, looking for anyone he might know.

A familiar face looked up.

Anne Annis's cheeks were streaked with tears and soot. Travis could tell she recognized him but the woman went back to a conversation she was having with a man next to her.

"You are wrong, friend Albert," she said. "I would not have made it, but for you." Anne removed a gold ring from her finger. "All I have is lost, except this. It is all I can offer."

The man raised his hand and pushed the ring away. "This is not right, Anne."

"Albert, do not take away my power to show gratitude. I insist." She placed the ring in his hand and closed his fingers around it.

She spoke so unemotionally. Travis had experienced this before when he lost Emil. It was hard to come to terms with losing someone that just hours or sometimes moments before had been laughing and talking to you.

Travis backed away. Her blank gaze locked with his.

"Are you looking for your dog?"

He suddenly felt shameful. Anne Annis had lost her daughter and three husbands in shipwrecks. What dog, even Salem, could compare to the grief of that?

"A dog?" Albert asked. "I saw a dog running on the boat. I think he went into the hole."

Travis stepped forward. "Into the fire?"

Albert nodded slowly as he stared at the flames in front of him. He swallowed hard, surely hearing the haunting cries of burning victims in his mind.

CHAPTER THIRTY-EIGHT

The news took the strength from his legs. Travis limped out of the yard and slumped against the trunk of a large cottonwood. He balled up his right fist and brought it back, aiming for the tree, but hesitated as memories overwhelmed him. He finally lowered his arm. No outburst could bring Salem back.

None of this would have happened to him if his father had not traded him to the Union army for two bottles of whiskey. Instead, he would have stolen away with his brother and both puppies. He could have traveled until he found his mother. He would never have suffered these horrors, and Salem would still be alive.

His jaw tightened. He would lock his anger away until he could stand face to face with his father.

"You put me here, and I will find you again someday."

"I did what?" a man asked.

Travis looked up to see a fellow in his twenties getting off another homemade raft. Two soaked and shivering men followed, thanking him over and over for rescuing them. He sent them off to warm up by the fire.

"I am sorry," Travis said. "I was talking to myself."

"It is quite understandable after this dreadful night," he said sympathetically. "Have you seen my Pa, Frank Folgleman?"

"Yes, he saved us. He is back out there looking for more survivors."

The man said, "Go stay warm by the fire and eat some soup. I heard from our neighbor up the river there is a steamer coming to take all of you to the hospital in Memphis."

Travis stared at the ground. "I'm not going to Memphis. I'm going to Salem, Arkansas."

"Surely you will find a wagon out of Memphis when all this excitement dies down."

"I am not going there." Emotions swelled his voice, "I do not want to see any more bodies in the water, or people burned and broken in hospitals. I am headed to find my brother."

The man studied him. "If you are up to it, there's an old pig trail behind the house. It is the only road out of here that has not flooded."

Travis nodded.

"Wait here," the man said. He walked up the hill and disappeared into the house. A few minutes later, he returned with a haversack. "Two biscuits and some matches. That's all we can spare."

Travis shook his hand and took the bag. "My brother needs me and I'm ready to put this war behind me."

"Believe me, I'm ready for it to be over, too," the man said.

The rough trail led Travis through old timber stands with trees six feet thick. Hills and gorges made his progress painfully slow. His feet ached and hurt but nothing like they did on the long road to Vicksburg. He walked until dark, made a fire, and laid awake for hours.

Each time he closed his eyes, he saw the horrors of war, the battles, the marches, prison, and the Sultana. He had survived the journey, now he had to survive the memories. Salem had been with him each step of the way and Travis felt the nightmare of losing him would last the longest.

The next morning, he ate half of a biscuit and then made it to the end of the trail where it joined a narrow rough wagon track. Sprigs of spring grass had sprouted down the middle and the rest was covered in dead leaves.

After a few miles, Travis sat on a log to give his feet a rest. He removed his shoes and watched a black cricket crawling in and out of the brown leaves. Memories of the previous day seemed as if they had happened ten minutes before. He wondered if Perry, Stephen, and Tennessee had survived. Part of him felt that he had abandoned them, but there was nothing he could do to help. The thought of seeing even one more wound or burn on a person was almost too much to handle, especially if he knew them as a friend.

He bent down to put his shoes back on. The hoarse caw of a crow came from somewhere back down the road. Travis got up and walked a few feet, when a squirrel started barking. Another closer to him took up the warning. Something was behind him on the road, and getting closer.

Travis listened. The dry leaves rustled faintly as someone or something came through them. The hairs on his arms raised up. He had no gun, not even a knife. He quickly picked up a thick limb from the ground next to his feet.

A hundred yards away, an animal with a mottled coat of reddish-brown came around the bend. Its nose was on the ground and its tail high in the air. There could be no mistake. Only one dog in the world looked like Salem.

The limb fell from his lifeless fingers, and Travis dropped to his knees. He choked out a whistle.

The dog immediately looked up and sprinted straight to him. With open arms, he caught Salem and tried to hug him, but Salem was a writhing ball of excitement. Travis laughed and cried, and petted him all over. Salem struggled to lick every inch of exposed skin, and his butt wiggled so hard he nearly lost his balance.

"I thought you were dead. How did you make it?" He gasped, pushing Salem's face back from his. He tried to gain control of the squirming dog. "Let me look at you."

It took several moments before Salem calmed down enough for Travis to examine him.

He smelled like smoke and had singed fur on his haunches. The hair had been burned to the skin in two spots, but judging by his actions, the dog seemed fine.

"I wish you could talk, because I bet you have some wild story to tell."

The dog licked his ear and cheek. Travis laughed and pulled the other half of the biscuit from the haversack. Salem immediately sat and waited expectantly for it to be tossed to him. He jumped and snatched it right out of the air.

Travis could not stop grinning. "Hey, boy, let's go find Chet."

As they walked, there was a bit of true joy in Travis's heart, something he had not felt in a very long time. After the old road joined with a main one, a family in a wagon came along.

They eyed the blue cap on his head. "Stinkin' Yank!"

As they passed, an apple core hit Travis in the side of the head. He wiped his ear with his sleeve and wished with all his heart for them to know everything he had been through.

When they disappeared over a hill, he threw his cap in the brush and picked up the core. He washed it off in a trickling creek and ate it seeds and all. It had been many months since he had tasted an apple, way back when Anna Gardner had passed him pie through the fence.

Thirty minutes later, an old man in a rattletrap buggy gave him and Salem a ride. He was kind enough to feed them leftover cornbread and beans, and allowed them to sleep in his barn that night.

The next few days were filled with walking and wagon rides from strangers. The closer they got to the town of Salem, the more nervous Travis became. He kept playing scenes in his head of what he would do when he saw his father and brother. He was worried about his brother, and scared to face them both. But most of all, he feared the house would be empty and he would never find out where they were.

On the first day of May, Travis and Salem walked into the yard and stopped. It had been three years to the day since he had seen the house and barn, and Salem had only been a small pup when he was here last.

Everything on the property looked much the same, except there was a horse tied out front. He took a deep breath and walked to the front door. He reached for the handle but stopped, raised his hand to knock but paused. Finally, he rapped his knuckles on the door frame.

The door opened a few inches. A girl, maybe ten years old, stared cautiously at him through the opening. She saw Salem and opened the door wider with a smile. "You have a dog!"

He looked past her and saw nice furniture sitting in the middle of the room, things his father had never owned. "I am... I am looking for my father."

"We just moved in today." The girl turned her head. "Mama! Someone's here!"

She squatted down and scratched Salem behind the ears. "I like your dog."

A woman came out of the bedroom, and frowned when she saw Travis. "Katie Jean, get back in the house." The girl reluctantly gave Salem one last pet before going back inside.

The woman stepped out and pulled the door closed behind her. She looked Travis up and down. "You were in the war, I take it."

Travis nodded. He supposed he did look like a vagabond, covered in soot and scars, wearing ill-fitting clothes and shoes that were obviously several sizes too big. He could only imagine what his singed and patchy hair looked like.

"Well, I care not to know what cause you fought for, nor do I have any work for you. I can offer you bread with a slice of cheese, and water, but then you and your dog best be moving on."

Katie Jean pushed up the window by the door and stuck her head out. "He is looking for his pa, Mama."

The woman looked at her daughter crossly. "Katie!"

Katie grinned mischievously.

The mother turned back to Travis, but this time she spoke more kindly to him. "No one has lived here for a while. My husband paid the owner this morning and we started moving in."

"Was the owner a man by the name of Jeb?"

"No. He told me it was a lady." She looked to her daughter. "Right?"

The girl nodded. "I went with Pop. It was not a man we met, but a lady."

Travis's shoulders dropped. His next nightmare had started. "It has been a while since I left."

The woman tapped her chin. "Hmmm. Now that I think of it, the lady probably bought this house from your father. Maybe she will know where he is."

Katie Jean leaned further out the window. "I heard her say she was going to eat at that little restaurant in town."

"You might catch her there," the woman said.

Travis felt a glimmer of hope. "What was her name? Who do I ask for?"

The woman looked to her daughter. "Honey, what was her name?"

The girl squinted as she thought. "I don't recollect."

"My husband will know," the mother said. "He will be back soon."

"She had black hair," the little girl said, "and she was wearing a blue dress with flowers."

He thanked them and jogged down the road with his furry companion right beside him. When Travis reached town, he left Salem outside of the only restaurant, and pushed open the door. It was empty except for two grizzled old men, drinking coffee.

"Was there a lady in a blue dress here?"

One of the men said, "You look like you been through it. Were you on that boat that burnt?"

"Yes, sir. But right now it is most important that I find a lady in a blue dress with white flowers. Have you seen her?"

"Humph. We ain't seen a woman in a blue dress."

Travis stepped outside. He saw Salem several buildings down on a storefront porch sharing lunch with a couple of young boys.

Across the street, on the courthouse lawn, he saw a woman and an older boy walking away. She had black hair done up in a bun, and was wearing a blue dress with white flowers.

"That's her!" Travis walked quickly to catch up with them.

"Ma'am? Could I bother you a moment? I'm looking for a man you might have bought a house from."

The lady and the boy turned around. The blood drained from her face. Her eyes widened and she covered her mouth with both hands.

Travis struggled to speak. "M-Momma? Chet?"

His brother had grown a foot. He screamed "TRAVIS!" and rushed his brother, wrapping him in a tight hug and nearly knocking him over. Their mother added her arms to the embrace and they all broke down and sobbed. A passing stranger would have thought there was great sorrow in their hearts but it was quite the opposite. Every boy needs to be held by a loving mother at certain points in his life and Travis had needed these moments hundreds of times over the past years.

"Boys," she finally said, "my legs are so weak, I am about to fall."

They moved to a nearby bench but kept hanging on to each other as if life itself depended on it.

"Travis, you are skinny as a rail." Huge tears ran from the corners of her eyes. "You look like a grown man. We thought you died in the war. Oh, my, your hair. Are you hurt anywhere?"

"I'm going to be fine. Mama, what happened?"

"Oh, Travis, I would never have left you," she said.

"That is not what I meant."

Chet nodded. "You want to know about Pa."

"Wait." His mother dabbed tears from her cheeks. "Let me finish. I did not leave you, Travis. Your father sent me on a long errand and then left with you and Chet and all our money, while I was gone. I had no idea where he had taken you boys. Son, I would have never left either of you. I have never stopped looking all these years."

Those words healed a broken part of him he had held deep inside. He wiped his nose on his shirt-tail and cleared his throat. "There would have been no blame if you had left. Where is he now?"

"The whiskey finally got him," Chet said. "The doctor sent him to the hospital in Batesville, but there was nothing they could do. After he died, they asked me lots of questions."

His mother said, "The sheriff managed to track me down and get Chet back to me. The house sat empty for a long time while the courthouse got the papers straightened out."

Travis hugged her again and shook his head in disbelief. "I do not know how it is that I arrived on this day, when you happened to be here."

"Sweetheart, I have prayed to find you one way or another since the day you boys disappeared. It's not our place to ask why or how."

Travis looked at Chet. His little brother had gained some height, and though still a lanky boy, the dark hollows under his eyes were gone. "Brother, I broke my promise to you when I said I would be back soon. It took me three years, but I did keep my word about one thing."

"What?" Chet asked.

Travis smiled. "I brought your dog back."

Travis whistled and Salem trotted across the street. He sat and looked at them.

"He stayed with you through the war? This is my dog?"

"He's more than a dog, Chet, much more. Salem has been a true friend and soldier on a long and weary road. I want you to meet the mascot of the Thirteenth Illinois Infantry."

Chet stared at Travis, and then at Salem.

"I'm telling the truth," Travis said. "Your dog is a war hero."

Chet reached out and gently touched Salem's head. He looked up at Travis. "I think my brother is a hero too."

Salem's tail swept back and forth in agreement.

THE END

HISTORICAL NOTES

› Rank from lowest to the highest: Private, Corporal, Sergeant, Second Lieutenant, First Lieutenant, Captain, Major, Lieutenant Colonel, Colonel, Brigadier General, Major General, Lieutenant General, General

› Soldiers of the Thirteenth stood with Chickasaw Bayou before them, their first real battle. Cannons and musket fire were ripping the ground to shreds, ground they had been ordered to cross. How frightened would you be? Most dogs will scatter at the sound of gunfire but even the concussion of cannons did not scare Salem away. To their surprise, he charged ahead of them, chasing spent artillery and snapping at the sound of bullets in the air. What caused Salem to act this way? Irrational behavior? The simplicity of a dog's mind? A chase instinct he could not subdue? No matter the real reason, scared soldiers saw a brave dog, dashing across the battlefield without a scratch, giving hope to each man that if Salem could do it, they could too.

Dogs are said to be man's best friend. Throughout time, they have been there for us, providing companionship, protection, and sometimes inspiring us. Give your dog an extra pet, for his ancestors may well have led men into battle.

› **Travis Bailey**. Though fictional, Travis is the glue that binds this story together. Through his eyes we are able to learn the true story of Salem and the soldiers he encountered during the war.

› **Salem**. This Arkansas dog meant the world to the Thirteenth Illinois. He traveled with them to many battles and was eventually separated from his regiment. It is not known exactly where Salem was lost or what became of this special and cherished mascot.

› **Peter Dugdale/Dougdale - Private, 13th Illinois Company H.** Were it not for Peter Dugdale, there would be no story for Dog Salem. His love for animals spurred him to leave Salem, Arkansas, with a puppy hidden in his shirt. Also known as "Peter the irrepressible little Irishman." He was from Aurora, Illinois, and was discharged from service on April 22, 1863, due to a disability. He rejoined the war in December with the Fifty-eighth Illinois Infantry and served until the end of the war. Peter lived to be eighty-five years old.

- **George W. Fikes - Private, 13th Illinois Company H.** George was born in 1837. He was a brave soldier who never avoided his assignments, whether it was the battlefield or Company Cook duty. At Vicksburg on May 22nd, 1863, George braved the battle to bring hot food to his fellow soldiers in Company H. He was captured at Madison Station, Alabama, on May 17th, 1864, and taken to Cahaba prison. He was a major part of the escape attempt during the flood. After the war, George moved to Hoopstown, Illinois.

- **Thomas Bexon - Private, 13th Illinois Company H.** Thomas was a small, sickly man but a wonderful soldier. He shot fish in the White River at Batesville, Arkansas for hours to help feed the men. His speech suffered from a lisp. Thomas fought in all the hard battles and hid in a tree top at Madison Station to avoid capture. The date of this event was moved in this book in order to completely tell his story. After the war, Thomas was killed in an accident at Aurora, Illinois.

- **Emil Kothe/Kotha - Recruit, 13th Illinois, Company H.** Emil was born in Germany. He was seventeen years old when he joined. Emil was shot in the leg at Chickasaw after being ordered to stay down by Colonel Wyman. He recovered from his injury and returned to service, but he was shot again at Vicksburg in 1863, suffering with his wound until he finally passed away on June 12th 1863.

- **John W. Williams - Private, 13th Illinois, Company H.** He was one of the youngest of the Thirteenth. John was dishonorably discharged and sentenced by general court-martial for firing his gun carelessly in camp and nearly hitting a soldier in another company. His nickname was Father John.

- **Arthur B. West - Private, 13th Illinois, Company H.** Arthur was born in New York in 1839. He was wounded at Ringgold on March 28, 1863. Arthur was a good soldier but after the war he was admitted to an insane asylum.

- **Alfred Barnes - Private, 13th Illinois, Company H.** Alfred was taken prisoner at Chickasaw Bayou on December 29th, 1862. He either escaped or was paroled and was taken prisoner again at Madison Station, Alabama, on May 17th, 1864. He moved to California after the war.

‣ **Lawrence Whalan/Whalen - Recruit, 13th Illinois, Company H.** Lawrence had Irish roots and was just twenty-one. He died on July 17, 1862, with sickness caused from the hard march to Helena.

‣ **Edwin Sheehe/Sheehey - Private, 13th Illinois, Company H.** Edwin was from Ireland. At the battle of Ringgold, Edwin fired shots through one of the windows in the log house. Others loaded for him so he could use multiple guns. He danced and sang while he waited and swore at the men for not loading faster.

‣ **Eli Bailey - Sergeant, 13th Illinois, Company H.** Promoted to First Lieutenant in December 1863. Eli was born August 18, 1838. He was a brave soldier and volunteered to go in search of more ammunition at Ringgold. He took heavy fire but was successful in supplying more rounds for the Thirteenth. Eli moved to Kansas after the war.

‣ **Patrick Riley - Sergeant, 13th Illinois, Company K.** Patrick did not play a big part in this book but his story should never be forgotten. Patrick was the soldier who was killed at Ringgold and fell, rolling into the Thirteenth's flag. The relic was eventually recovered and is still stained with his blood.

- **Richard Pierce/Big Tennessee - Private.** Big Tennessee (so called, but he was actually from Kentucky) was a giant of a man, nearing seven feet tall. During his time in Cahaba, he single-handedly brought an end to the prison muggers. He was described as a young man with a big heart. Richard survived the Sultana disaster and lived to be seventy-six. He served in the Third Tennessee Calvary. He was born in Knox County, Kentucky, and was buried there upon his death.

- **Jesse D. Pierce - First Sergeant, 13th Illinois, Company H.** Jesse was stunned by a bursting shell and taken prisoner at Chickasaw Bayou on December 29th, 1863. He was born in Pennsylvania, on April 21, 1822. After the war, he moved to Leavenworth, Kansas.

- **Frank G. Whipple - Corporal, 13th Illinois, Company H.** Frank served as an orderly for Colonel Wyman until December 1862. He fought at Chickasaw Bayou, Lookout Mountain, Missionary Ridge, and Ringgold. He was taken prisoner on May 17th, 1864, at Madison Station, Alabama, but escaped and made it back to his regiment. Frank moved to Kansas after the war.

- **Charles Thompson - Assistant Surgeon.** He was present at the battle of Chickasaw and helped with the wounded, including Emil and Colonel Wyman

- **Jack Kenyon.** It's very clear that after the battle of Chickasaw, Jack risked his life to search for some wounded Lieutenants and rescued the wrong flag. What's not clear is while he is described as a member of Company K, Jack is not listed on the roster, but an Israel, John, and William are.

- **Jake Sightsinger/William Coleman Henderson - Quartermaster.** Henderson was born in Pequea, Pennsylvania, June 22nd, 1827. He requested to be called Jake Sightsinger while they were in Arkansas, and the nickname stuck with him. Henderson's dilapidated tent and collection of animals provided great entertainment for the men. He resigned from his position on July 28th, 1863, due to disability, caused by disease.

- **Burley.** Burly is one of the few fictitious characters in this story.

- **Nep.** Newfoundland dog that belonged to Captain Henry Noble of Company A. Nep was in a few skirmishes but was sent home by the Captain to keep him from being killed.

- **Whistling Boy from Batesville.** This boy became part of the quartermaster's side-show tent in Batesville. His name is uncertain. He was either a member of the Burr family or a freed slave who had belonged to a family by that name.

- **John Wyman - Colonel.** Wyman quit school when he was fourteen. He was an avid reader and a self-made man. The men of the Thirteenth loved him and it was said that he would treat a private the same or better than an officer. He died during the battle of Chickasaw on December 28, 1862, after warning Emil to stay down.

- **Osgood Wyman - Corporal, 13th Illinois, Company C.** John Wyman's son. He was brought to the surgeon's tent to be with his father during his last moments.

‣ **Jesse Betts - Private, 13ᵗʰ Illinois, Company I.** He was one of the flag bearers during the charge at Chickasaw. Jesse later deserted and assumed the identity of George Darrow. He then rejoined another regiment.

‣ **Henry Dement - Lieutenant, 13ᵗʰ Illinois, Company A.** He was one of the first men to arrive at Wyman's side when the Colonel was shot.

‣ **Samuel Plummer - Surgeon for the Thirteenth Regiment.** He was a kind and caring man with a stiff backbone. When Wyman was shot at Chickasaw, Plummer left to assist him and refused orders to return, even when a messenger was sent after him. The surgeon lost his hearing in one ear from an exploding cannister.

‣ **Richard Smith - Captain, 13ᵗʰ Illinois, Company F.** Richard was the man who Travis witnessed losing his arm during the charge at Chickasaw.

‣ **Francis Manter - Colonel.** Mantor placed the entire Thirteenth under arrest for one day. They were released when the enemy approached their location. The exact reason for his actions are not clear, but the following quotes were used to make an assumption regarding Salem's involvement – "…through some provocation, real or imaginary… Colonel Manter placed the entire regiment under arrest." "All probably recollect our dog, Salem, for whom the Thirteenth was so willing to stand up for."

‣ **Theodore Reeves - 13ᵗʰ Illinois, Company D.** Historical notes seemed to indicate Theodore was the soldier grazed in the head by a cannonball at Lookout Mountain, then he continued the charge with a piece of his ear missing.

‣ **Benjamin Gifford - Lieutenant, 13ᵗʰ Illinois, Company E.** Gifford was the man who reported John for accidently firing a weapon in camp which resulted in his court-martial.

‣ **John Davis - Private, 13ᵗʰ Illinois, Company B.** Davis was one of the soldiers that Travis witnessed at Ringgold. He was shot in the mouth, went to the back to have it bandaged, and then returned to the front to continue fighting.

‣ **Walter Blanchard - Captain, 13ᵗʰ Illinois, Company K.** Blanchard was the soldier who had been shot in the knee during the battle of

Ringgold. He was placed in an upstairs bed and gave orders while the men fired out the windows. After the battle, Walter was carried sixteen miles by his men, trying to get help for him, but the Captain died from his wounds.

‣ **Charles Peck - Private, 13ᵗʰ Illinois, Company F.** Charles suffered a head wound at Ringgold and died from his wounds.

‣ **William Howe - Recruit, 13ᵗʰ Illinois, Company E.** Howe lost four fingers on one hand and three on the other. He was in the house with Travis at Ringgold.

‣ **Howard Henderson - Cahaba Prison Commander/Prisoner Exchange Agent.** Henderson was a Methodist minister who had a kind heart. Many prisoner diaries speak of his compassion. While he was away, dealing with exchanges and procuring supplies, Samuel Jones was left in charge.

‣ **Samuel Jones- Cahaba Prison Commander.** Jones was the total opposite of Henderson. He was very rough on the prisoners and suspected of being involved in the death of Hanchette.

‣ **Alfred Douglas- 66ᵗʰ Illinois.** Douglas is believed to be the first man to die in Cahaba prison on December 28, 1863.

‣ **C. W. Eddy.** It is very possible that this is the man who was nick-named Teddy (described in the book by fellow prisoner, Jesse Hawes). Eddy was shot by Hankins and died in Cahaba in April, 1864.

‣ **Amanda, Belle, and William Gardner.** Their house was located just outside the stockade walls. Amanda and Belle were of great help to the captive men. Many of them wrote of her kindness and at least one soldier returned after the war, hoping to sweep Belle off her feet. William was captured by the Union and returned to his home because of the actions of his mother toward the prisoners of Cahaba.

‣ **R. H. Whitfield - Confederate Surgeon/Doctor.** It was Whitfield who wrote a report about the poor conditions inside the prison. This led to the transfer of all able-bodied prisoners and the closing of Cahaba for a very short time.

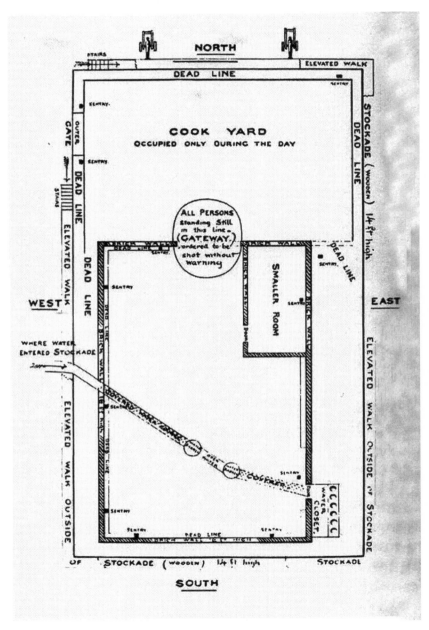

▸ **Guard Hankins.** Prisoner Jesse Hawes's book describes this guard as one of the most heartless and ruthless men watching over them.

- **Lieutenant Crutcher.** A prisoner diary and Jesse Hawes's book explains that a guard named Crutcher stood in front of the cannons and stopped Jones from firing on them during their escape attempt.

- **Muggers.** Thompson, Jack, and Tom. It's not clear who these men were, but they are listed as being the worst muggers of Cahaba.

- **John Nichols - Private, 13th Illinois, Company F.** After John was captured at Madison Station, Alabama, he was taken to Cahaba. He escaped with many others and was recaptured after swimming the river three times, running for miles, and being tracked down by dogs.

- **Frederick Berney.** Diaries describe a prisoner being shot in August, 1864, for crossing the dead line to pick up a piece of wood to cook his food. The only prisoner listed as dying from a gunshot during this month in Cahaba is Frederick.

- **Stephen Caston.** Stephen survived Cahaba prison and the Sultana disaster. He was just fifteen years old. If you want to know more about him, read *Crossing the Dead Line* by Michael Shoulders.

- **Shell and Booze.** These were nicknames of men who helped John Nichols and Travis escape the prison. They are real men, but their real names are not known.

- **Owens - Ohio Regiment.** This man's first name is not given in the diaries. He tried to escape Cahaba many times and was severely punished. He earned the nickname Crazy Owens, from the guards. Owens survived the Sultana disaster by climbing back onto the hull of the boat and waiting for rescue from Mr. Fogleman.

- **Perry Summerville - Indiana 2nd Calvary.** Perry jumped from a wagon, trying to avoid capture, but this resulted in a broken leg. He was taken to Cahaba and spent some time in the hospital. Upon his request, he was removed and placed in prison early. He used bits of his crutches to start fires, until the last section was stolen. He was blown into the water from the Sultana explosion and survived by clinging to debris until rescue.

- **Hiram Hanchette - Illinois 16th Cavalry.** Hiram was an officer and to hide his identity upon being captured, changed his name to Solon. He was the mastermind behind the attempt to overtake the prison. He was later killed under suspicious circumstances while on the way to a prisoner exchange.

- **Mart Becker - Wisconsin regiment.** Just before Mart was captured, he concealed his regiment's flag under his clothing and managed to keep it hidden during his entire stay at Cahaba. He was injured in the hand during the escape attempt but avoided being discovered. When he arrived at camp Fisk, Mart took out his hidden flag and waved it for the Union forces to see, causing a huge outburst of applause and shouts.

- **Jesse Hawes - Illinois 9th Cavalry.** Jesse survived Cahaba and wrote a book about his experiences there. Cahaba: A Story of Captive Boys in Blue.

- **Sultana.** The steamboat explosion is the deadliest maritime disaster in American history but was mostly overlooked in 1865 due to the end of the war, Lincoln's assassination, and the search for and death of his killer. Approximately 1,200 of the dead are known by name but many were placed on the boat without being counted. The death toll could easily be over 1,800 but the true number will never be known.

- **Billy Lockhart, Walter Elliott, Commodore Smith.** These three men gave their accounts of surviving the Sultana disaster. They each describe the terrible choice they were forced to make when begged by gravely injured victims to be thrown overboard.

‣ **Daniel McLoyd/McLeod.** Daniel was one of the victims of the Sultana thrown off the ship by Billy Lockhart and Walter Elliott. Daniel had compound fractures in both ankles and other injuries but survived.

‣ **Samuel Thrasher 6th Kentucky, Joshua Patterson 104th Ohio, Thomas Pancle 3rd Tennessee.** These men gave their accounts of surviving the Sultana by climbing back onto the burning hull, fighting the flames, and being rescued by Fogleman.

‣ **Albert King - 100th Ohio Infantry.** Albert helped to save Anne Annis and said she gave him a gold ring after they were rescued.

‣ **Anne, Isabella, and Harvey Annis.** Anne lost three husbands and a child to shipwrecks. She did not remarry after Harvey and Isabella died in the Sultana disaster. Anne lived to be eighty.

‣ **Frank, Leroy, and Dallas Fogleman.** The Foglemans lived on the Arkansas side of the river. Frank and his sons constructed a crude raft made of logs and saved many lives from the cold water and the burning remains of the Sultana's hull.

‣ **Frederick Hill - Private, 13th Illinois, Company B.** Frederick deserted on March 21st 1862, and was later captured and killed while trying to escape. He was shot by a guard at Helena, Arkansas. The date and location of this event was moved in order to educate Travis about deserters and provide him with even more incentive to stay with the Thirteenth.

‣ **Henry Taylor- Private, 13th Illinois, Company I.** Henry deserted February 16th, 1862. Before deserting, he got into a fist-fight with Colonel Wyman. The date of this fight was moved to allow Travis to witness it. At Batesville, Taylor was sighted and pursued but it is unclear if he was caught.

‣ **Colored Troops.** Twenty-two African Americans soldiers, probably in an Ohio regiment, volunteered to help with the paroled prisoners. None of them are listed as surviving the Sultana disaster. Approximately 186,000 served in the United States **Colored Troops** volunteer cavalry, artillery, and infantry units during the Civil War.

‣ **Carolina Parakeets.** The green birds Travis saw in Alabama were the Carolina Parakeets. The last known specimen died in 1918.

REFERENCES
- Aurora Illinois Historical Society- researchers John Jaros, Michael Fichtel
- Office of the Illinois Sec. of State Civil War muster & rolls c/o Illinois State Archives
- Harper's Weekly February 6, 1864 P.85
- Frank Leslie's Illustrated Newspaper January 23, 1864 P.285
- Bob Taylor's Magazine October 1906, Nickajack Cave by Octavia Bond
- Diary of Lieutenant Samuel Platt 26th Ohio
- The Soldier's Casket No.1 January 1865 P.370
- Diary of Wilson Chapel, Company F, 13th Regiment Illinois Infantry (Phyllis Kelley, Marian Anderson)
- Diary of Charles Wagoner, Company C, 141st New York Infantry
- Loss of the Sultana and Reminiscences of Survivors by Rev. Chester D. Berry
- The Sultana Tragedy by Jerry Potter
- Lincoln's Boys – The Enlisted Men of the Illinois Infantry
- Diary of Franklin Blanchard, Company K, 13th Regiment Illinois Infantry
- Cahaba Prison and the Sultana Disaster by William O. Bryant
- Cahaba: A Story of Captive Boys in Blue by Jesse Hawes
- Sultana by Alan Huffman
- Military History and Reminiscences of the Illinois Volunteer Infantry in the Civil War in the United States, 1861-1865 by S.C. Plummer
- Letters of Ritchie Bushnell, 13th Illinois Infantry. C/O The State Historical Society of Missouri R0675
- At Civil War's end, a steamboat disaster that history forgot, by Claudia Lauer
- Sweet Hour of Prayer- W. Walford 1845
- Story of Annis Family aboard the SS Sultana, by Sylvia Clemons
- National Audubon Society, The Last Carolina Parakeet
- Disaster on the Mississippi, by Gene Salecker
- Journals of A. H. Sibley, 13th Illinois Infantry
- Aurora Illinois GAR Memorial Hall and Museum - Eric Pry
- Wilson's Creek Battlefield Museum – Alan Chilton
- Dr. Louis Intres and the Sultana Disaster Museum

ACKNOWLEDGMENTS

These people helped make this book better.

Special thanks to:

Bill Bullock-Private/cook with Company A (Reenactor) 2nd Colorado Volunteer Infantry, Joe Carlton, Jeannie Wood, Stefani Jones, Destany Lytle, Alexander Michael, Isabella Biggs, Addysun Rodriguez, Hunter Williford, Carlee Duncan, Zaylee Cousins, Joshua Biggs, Cami Carpenter, Logan Hodge, Jim Arnold, Michele Sterrett, Heather Runyan, Tina Hoisington, Guillen Heinzen, and Suzanne Babb.

ABOUT THE AUTHOR

James Babb is an Arkansas author originally from a little town called Pleasant Plains, Arkansas. He moved to Conway to attend college where he met and married the love of his life. During this time, he developed a strange affliction called "Closet Writing," wherein story ideas are born, but shelved in the mental closet. In 2008, a battle with cancer left him with much down time, but no off switch for his imagination, and he began to take story crafting seriously.

As a reluctant reader when in school, James began writing for those same type of young readers, packing his family-friendly stories with adventure and action. THE DEVIL'S BACKBONE became his first historical novel, and two others in the series soon followed.

James travels to schools in Arkansas and surrounding states, speaking to middle grade students. Study guides for teachers and students are also available for several of his books.

JamesBabb.wordpress.com

Made in the
USA
Columbia, SC